FOOTFALLS
TO THE
ALAMO

Shawn M. LaTorre

Copyright © 2023 Shawn LaTorre
All rights reserved.

ISBN: 979-8-9881224-0-1

Portrait of María Andrea Castañon featured on the cover
was created using generative AI software.

Produced by Publish Pros | publishpros.com

PREFACE

History continues to surprise us. We find people on all sides of history trying to get to "the truth." There is no doubt that María Andrea Castañon came into this world in 1803 and, upon disembarking, left a memorable, positive impact on the city of San Antonio, Texas. Her interviews reveal a remarkable journey that started in Guerrero in an area of northern Mexico and found its earthly conclusion in San Antonio.

Her family's spark, however, didn't start in San Antonio; it started in part with ancestors from areas in the mountains and foothills of Guanajuato, a state in central Mexico between the arid north and a lush, tropical southern territory. This was an area that came under the protection and colonization of New Spain in the early 1500s.

As natives of this area, her mother's side moved about the mountains freely — a way of life that continued after her mother Francisca's marriage to a man by the name of José Antonio Castañon. María Andrea, one of the younger daughters in Francisca and Antonio's large family, probably never knew much about her parents' life in Guanajuato. By the time she was born, her family's involvement with the Royal military necessitated multiple family settlements in various territories of New Spain, including the mission and presidio of San Juan Bautista del Río Grande where María Andrea was born. Her father and brothers likely became entrenched in a world dedicated to the defense of New Spain and later Mexico. María Andrea's own life culminated in the vibrant, growing military environment of San Antonio, Texas.

In researching María Andrea's story, I found many gaps. Information on women of the time, especially indigenous or Hispanic women, was often difficult or impossible to find. The beauty of historical fiction lies in its ability to blend documented facts with one's research and imagination to reconstruct plausible circumstances and outcomes of the time.

I've had the pleasure of garnering advice from a few key individuals who guided my version of María Andrea's life. One of these individuals, her great-granddaughter, Maria Olga Gomez, also known as "Vee" Gomez, is living in San Antonio at the time of this writing and serves as an important bearer of the past. She, along with Dr. David C. Carlson, a Spanish archivist at Bexar County Archives in San Antonio, and Liliana Villanueva, his former office assistant, provided countless resources for my research right up to the COVID-19 pandemic. In 2019, Maria Vee Gomez, Rueben Perez, and Robert Thonhoff co-authored the definitive book (a private publication) on María Andrea entitled *María Andrea Castañon Villanueva (Señora Candelaria): Heroine of the Alamo*.

My story is written with love and the hope that María Andrea, or Señora Candelaria, as she came to be known, will be remembered just as much as the defenders of the Alamo, whose names many Texans know by heart. Her story is the story of striving. She and her family persevered through years of violence and invisible elements that threatened their successful futures. In the end, María Andrea became a respected and praiseworthy citizen whose charitable contributions are too numerous to mention.

Ábu (short for Abuela), Izzy (Isabel) Limón, Edgar, Carlos, Shorty, and a few other minor characters are completely my own creation, placed in order to further the historical representations of the story. As I wrote, I kept asking myself, what might María Andrea have known and how would she have known that? These characters provided the answers to this dilemma.

María Andrea's mother, father, brothers, and sisters were, according to my research, authentic individuals. Colonel Cordero, María Gertrudis, and Gertrudis's parents were also real people whose lives I have imagined here based upon stories and research. Some townspeople's names are real, such as John Twohig, James Bowie, Antonio López de Santa Anna Pérez de Lebrón, Colonel Travis, and others, some of whom were involved in several historical battles including the Siege of Bexar, the Battle of the Alamo, and the Battle at San Jacinto.

In short, while the events described, and some of the characters, are based on documented historical events and real people, these are juxtaposed with fictional characters and actions I've created in order to advance a conceivable and indelible story. It is my hope that students of Texas history will better understand the complicated nature of early settlement by examining the life of María Andrea Castañon and her family in Texas.

After the Battle of the Alamo in San Antonio, there were citizens of San Antonio who did not believe María Andrea's story regarding her involvement inside the Alamo during the battle. Although this may have broken her heart, it never broke her spirit. Finally, in the last eight years of her life, citizens such as Dr. Salmon "Rip" Ford took up the torch to insist that this remarkable woman deserved a place in history alongside all the other defenders of the Alamo. I think so too!

I invite you now to judge for yourself whether you personally believe her story.

PROLOGUE: GUANAJUATO, 1780

LAS CHICHIMECAS, PAME, JONAZ, PUREPECHA AND OTHER TRIBES INHABIT THIS AREA

Guanajuato, 1780

April breezes stream steadily through stately pines and junipers along the ridges of Sierra Gorda, the "Fat Mountains," in the Mexican state of Querétaro. Originating down low in el Paso de Hormigas, "the Passage of the Ants," waves of air propel upward as if a mighty invisible beast is foraging its way north towards El Zorillo, "the Skunk," a high point within the Sierra Madre Occidental (Western "Mother") chain of mountains. Life's peaceful setting surrounds the people living in these mountains.

Nine-year-old Francisca, accustomed to these breezes, pauses to marvel at the treetops swaying and bending to the rhythm of nature's forces. She imagines them dancing in waves that seem to ripple up the mountains just to greet her. In this northeast region, several small fields, green and lush with spring's early flourishes, are tended with care by many during the growing season, including her sister and her mother, Ana.

Bordered by terraces, each field is set off by low stone walls meandering along the outer reaches of the mountainside. These boulder ribbons have been carefully placed, stone by stone, by the strong hands of indigenous Chichimecas and others who grow cotton, oregano, corn, melons, and squash. In spite of how much they yield, these fields are not immediately discernible from anywhere except up within the region itself.

Along one of the hillsides, Francisca's mother stops to inhale the fresh, crisp mountain air and turns to locate her two daughters foraging near a small spring that eventually cascades down to feed the lower Lerma River. Careful to avoid pit caves where miners pull cinnabar, the trio instinctively sticks close together.

A green parrot screeches, then flies up from a perch within the greenery somewhere below them. Bromeliads, orchids, and an occasional magnolia surround the area extending fully southward down toward their small settlement at Las Ranas, "the Frogs."

Suddenly, there on the hillside amid thick, verdant growth, Francisca stands with one slender, caramel-colored arm outstretched from beneath her colorful shawl, pointing to a developing settlement along the river below.

"*Mamá!* Look! *Soldados* riding into town! Do you see them? Why are they here?"

Her sister and mother stand and stare in the same direction.

"Francisca, those soldiers come from far away, a place called España, or Spain. They are here to build churches and plazas, and to make more holes in the hills."

"Why will they make holes in the hills, Mamá?"

"They find shiny metals in there. They call the holes the *Real de Minas*, the Royal Mines. Everything they dig out they claim for their leader, a king in Spain. We must be sure to stay out of their way."

"Why must we avoid them, Mamá? Are they bad men?"

"Well, Francisca, anyone can be good or bad, depending on what they're after, but a long time ago, an ambitious one by the name of Beltrán de Guzmán chased and cornered many members of my family — over what? Our gardens maybe? Nobody knows. He and his soldiers rode up into the hillsides on their horses one day and started going after people and destroying many of our villas along the way. Sadly, some people said they even saw a few of our neighbors riding along with his group."

"Are these good people that are riding into town now, Mamá?"

"It's hard to say if these strangers are good or bad, *mí hija*, my daughter. Your Aunt Albina said some holy men in brown robes asked them to come visit the church in La Jaula, San Diego de Unión, tomorrow," Ana sighs, sensing a change on the horizon for her family, their way of life, perhaps even their beliefs. She has been watching these men on horseback for several days now and doesn't have a good feeling about them.

"What are they going to do at the church?"

"I don't know, *mí hija*. I'll check with Papá to see if he thinks we should go with Aunt Albina and Uncle Zenon to find out."

"Hmm. *¡Querida, dear sweet sister Albina!* There you are! You must come with us if we go. If those people are bad, we'll scratch them and kick their horses!"

"Francisca," Ana admonishes. "If we get a bad feeling, we'll simply turn around and run, okay? They may want to tell us that they'd like us to come to their church services, like they told Grandma Petra."

"Okay, *Mamá*. Come on, let's hike down now and look for *cebollas salvajes*, wild onions, and oregano closer to the river. Maybe we can catch some crayfish to take back to *Papá* and *Ábu* before dark."

• • •

The above is a conversation between a character I've named Ana Rivera and one of her very young daughters, Francisca Martínez. Francisca Martínez is the name I've given to the mother of the main character of this story, María Andrea Martínez Castañon. Later during this period of history, a real woman named María Andrea Castañon married Juan Flóres de Abrego, and later still, a man named Candelario Villanueva.

After her second marriage, María Andrea became known as the beloved Señora Candelaria of San Antonio. This is quite possibly her story.

COAHUILA-TE

- El Paso del Norte

SIERRA DE GUADALUPE

Río Grande del Norte

Río Puerco

Rí...

Río San...

Río de San Pedro

- La Junta de los Ríos

SERRANÍAS DEL BURRO

El Ca...

- Presidio de San Carlos
- Presidio de San Vicente
- Presid... Ag...
- Presidio de Monclova Viejo
- La Bavia
- San Fernando de Austria ★ 1

BOLSÓN DE MAPIMÍ

Río de Conchos

- Santa Rosa del Sacramento

Río de Sabinas

- Lampazos de Naranjo
- Monclova
- Can...
- Baján
- San Pedro de Boca de Leones
- Ciudad d...
- Mapimí
- Saltillo

AS FRONTIER

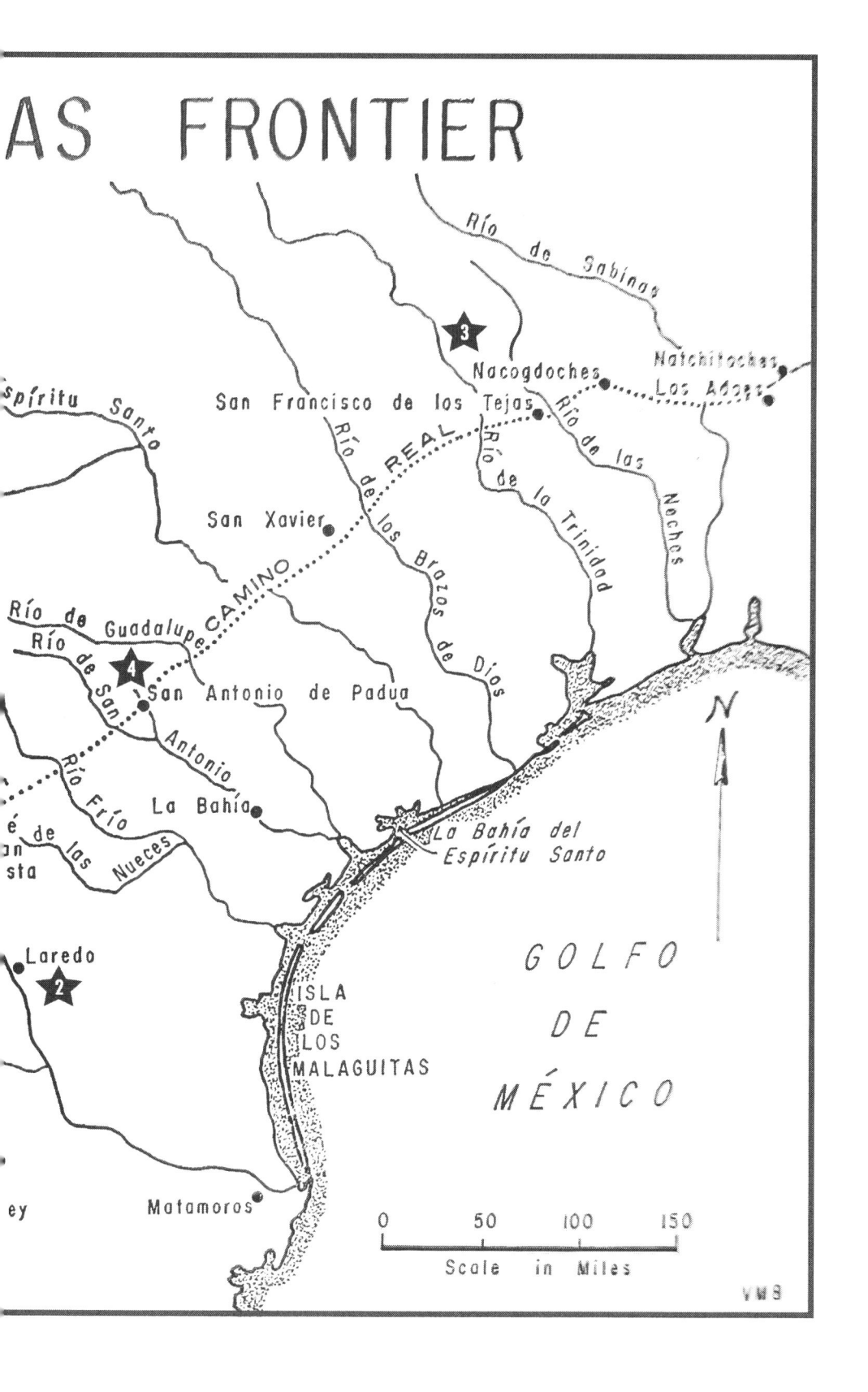

Río de Sabinas

③

Nacogdoches Natchitoches
Los Adaes
Espíritu Santo San Francisco de los Tejas
Río de los Brazos de Dios
Río de la Trinidad
Río de las Neches

San Xavier

CAMINO REAL

Río de Guadalupe
Río de San
④
San Antonio de Padua
Río Frío
Antonio
La Bahía
é de las Nueces
sta
La Bahía del Espíritu Santo

N

Laredo
②

ISLA DE LOS MALAGUITAS

GOLFO

DE

MÉXICO

ey Matamoros

0   50   100   150
Scale in Miles

VWB

PART 1:
IN SEARCH
OF HER STORY

Texas Expo 1936 featured this Alamo image on tiny books given to visitors who signed the Golden Book of Texas, a five by 7 foot wooden book of signatures in Dallas.

CHAPTER 1: REPORTER'S NOTES OF MARCH 1936

JACKI RIZZO, REPORTER FOR TEXAS EXPRESSO, ONE HUNDRED YEARS AFTER THE BATTLE OF THE ALAMO

"In this, the centennial anniversary of the Battle of the Alamo, citizens of San Antonio report seeing a woman draped completely in black making her way to Alamo Plaza at dawn and disappearing around dusk. She is accompanied by a small chihuahua that sometimes stays close to her and other times wanders the streets in town on its own. Many are reminded of Señora Candelaria who lived in this area for years following the historic battle, where she collected donations recounting the tragedy that took the lives of over two hundred defenders inside the Alamo. Many people at the time did not believe Señora Candelaria had been inside the Alamo, though she insisted she was. Some claimed she was overlooked being an indigenous woman who fought in her own way to keep one of the defenders alive within the walls of the Alamo."

(Texas Expresso News, March 1, 1936)

My name is Jacki Rizzo. In the spring of 1936, I'd been sent to San Antonio on assignment as a reporter to cover the city's acknowledgement of the one hundredth year anniversary of the 1836 Battle of the Alamo. However, when I read the newspaper account above, I knew the story I needed to cover would not be that of reenactments accompanied by melancholy music and vendors sharing historical summaries. Instead, I felt compelled to capture the story of this mysterious woman seen wandering about the Alamo Chapel each morning. And so I set out to find her.

I remember her specter perfectly. Cloth fragments were waving behind her as she slowly made her way up Market Street, head down, enveloped in dark bluish-black from head to toe. Ebony translucent scarves flagged wildly behind her, riding the breezes as if they were feathers on some magnificent bird out of place and time. The woman appeared stooped, yet efficient in her movements. I needed to find out if she was the beloved Señora Candelaria, or what might now be her ghost wandering the streets of San Antonio one hundred years later. I felt increasingly desperate to get this woman's story if she'd share it. The story of Señora Candelaria hadn't ever been completely understood in my mind.

I watched this woman appear out of nowhere at dawn near the Alamo for days after reading the Texas Expresso's account. Although her path on the streets never varied, I tried desperately to find, but could never quite discern, its beginning. Each morning, I watched her settle upon a small wooden crate at the corner of Market and Military Plaza, pulling her long dark skirt out in front of her and bundling up against the cool breezes that seemed to propel people toward the Alamo. Next, she'd place a small, blue tattered cloth in front of her and gently set some artifact upon it. Accompanied by a small, chubby chestnut-colored chihuahua, she simply sat and stared unwavering at the limestone walls of the Alamo chapel. Those walls were all that remained of a much larger compound that had included low, flat-roofed limestone homes along one side and military quarters and offices along another. The compound, a former Spanish mission known as Mission San Antonio de Valero, was once surrounded by short stone walls of limestone boulders with iron gates over one hundred years ago.

On the morning of March 6, I gathered the courage to approach the woman and ask if I might speak with her. I waited as she steadied herself upon the crate, arranged the small blue cloth in front of her, and placed something squarely in its center. She sat staring at the cloth for several minutes, finally shooing her dog, encouraging it to run along.

A breeze stirred the avenue's trees, sending runaway leaves cartwheeling through the streets, running pell-mell toward the northeast. This particular morning was startling in its beauty, in spite of the painful memories pressing with unrelenting consistency for so many of the city's descendants.

Sometime during my years studying Texas history at the University of Texas in Austin, I'd picked up a small paperback at a book festival held on the grounds of the Capitol there. Thumbing through the index, I read once again all the familiar names: Austin, Bowie, Crockett, Dickinson, Houston, Travis, Santa Anna, Seguín, and others. In this particular Alamo book, however, one name stood out: Señora Candelaria. I'd studied the names and histories of many San Antonio de Béxar citizens from the early 1800s, including those of the Alamo defenders *not* from the area who had died fighting for Texas's independence. I'd read the names of a few surviving women, children, and slaves of the Battle of the Alamo that had been released once the battle concluded on March 6, 1836. However, this woman's name had never been among any previous records I'd seen.

I felt determined to learn as much as I could about her in my spare time, and what I uncovered, in spite of many unknowns, was an amazing woman with a most interesting and noteworthy history. Now, mysteriously and perhaps portentously, her life and mine were about to intersect.

"Excuse me, ma'am, are you, by any chance, Señora Candelaria, or somehow related to her?" I ventured, eyeing a faded postcard she'd placed on the cloth in front of her feet. The faded grayish picture on the card depicted a low, partly flat, limestone building behind a singular tall tree flanked by a shorter one to its left. The solitary figure of a woman, dressed completely in black, could be seen walking away from the building toward the viewer.

The woman bent forward upon her milk crate perch to straighten the cloth on the ground in front of her, not yet acknowledging my presence.

"*Señora*, hello! My name is Jacki Rizzo. You don't know me, but I'm a history student and contributing writer for the Texas Expresso News. I wonder if I might ask you some questions."

"My heart aches every time I remember this story, I tell you. Look there, right there!" She pointed toward the Alamo, a short distance away. "You cannot imagine the horror of seeing the gruesome losses of so many brave defenders!" She looked up at me, shielding her eyes and squinting. "For so many, many years the townspeople didn't believe I was ever there! So now why should I tell you? What difference does it make anymore?" She shook her head and looked away before continuing.

"My family and I . . . well, it felt as if we'd been set adrift in a river of memories, left in the wake of forgotten and unspeakable horrors. And we weren't the only ones! You know, my story is just a small part of a much greater story that began in Aztlán, a place my ancestors knew. Though I never knew that place or Guanajuato, Mexico, after that, I always felt, no matter where my family settled, that my native culture remained alive within me, here, in the deepest recesses of my heart. For it is in my heart where I received the greatest direction for my life's work. And San Antonio, my final destination, is the place I believe I was given to perform my most critical work."

With that, she looked away and I noticed her eyes tearing up. I realized, as the rising sun revealed squinty eyes milky with cataracts, she could very likely hear me better than see me. I shifted to cast a shadow over her pearly eyes in an effort to protect them from the emerging flare of rising sun rays.

"I was there at the break of day for several of those thirteen days of battle. I ran food, herbs from my sister's garden, and cloth for bandages, and shared news from the outside. My presence had been requested; aye, *qué barbaridad*, such savageness! The terror our town had been living with, you can never imagine. Wartime atrocities haunted me, my family, and many citizens for years afterwards. It's true when they say that one side may call itself the victor, but in truth, there are only losers when it comes to war."

I hunkered slowly down to the curb, waiting for her to regain her composure, as I witnessed a small section of San Antonio slowly waking up. I had come prepared with every reporter's lifelines: Faber Castell pencils, Biro ballpoint pens, Sheaffer fountain pens, and a couple of small glass inkwells. I never traveled without at least five steno pads, and was in this case hoping to capture the story of this engaging woman who spoke with a slight accent and looked like a worn, stately crow in her graceful old age. I glanced over to admire the long black shawl draped over her head and shoulders. It had been delicately crocheted with roses and the fringes adorning its edges shook when she spoke. Suddenly, she exhaled loudly and, while looking straight ahead, began.

"I suppose I can tell this story one final time and let you be the judge," she sighed. "Look closely at this scar that I have worn on my cheek since that time. Do you see it? Only Señora Candelaria would have a scar like this!" Slowly, a brown, bent finger with a claw-like fingernail followed a crease along her bony right cheekbone. "There are still a few descendants alive who know this history! Unfortunately, many neighbors running around here don't seem to give a rooster's comb who their great-grandparents were or what they did to secure this territory! But I swear upon Colonel Bowie's blade in the rectory of San Fernando that what I am about to tell you is the truth, the truth as my spirit knows it."

"I would love to hear your story," I assured her. "If you have the time, might we begin this interview with your earliest recollections and move forward from there? I have as many days to record your story as you can spare."

Settling myself more comfortably on the curb, I inched closer to hear better. From my dark leather satchel, I quickly retrieved my reporting tools. Flipping over the cardboard cover on a new steno pad, I grabbed a fountain pen and signed and dated the first page: *Friday, March 6, 1936.*

Señora Candelaria lowered her head as if to rein in the memories. Meanwhile, I glanced around, catching sight of a small bakery across the street. The aroma of cinnamon and baked goods entered my consciousness, mixed with the clop-clopping of horses pulling a carriage down the street. One horse stopped momentarily to lift its tail and left us in a temporary state of asphyxiation. We both chuckled like hens while madly fanning our faces.

Then, Señora Candelaria began her story. It's an incredible adventure that I will now attempt to capture within these pages.

*Title page and frontispiece of Novena booklet used at Mission Juan Bautista
Image courtesy of Felix Almaraz Jr.*

CHAPTER 2: EARLIEST RECOLLECTIONS

JACKI RIZZO'S NOTES FROM THE INTERVIEW IN 1936

Earliest Recollections

I was born on the first morning of a very chilly December in 1803 at the Presidio of Mission San Juan Bautista del Río Grande. The presidio was part of a larger compound surrounding Mission San Juan Bautista del Río Grande in the province of Coahuila, Mexico. That small area, founded upon the ruins of a Frenchman's fort, eventually became the property of the viceroyalty of New Spain. In reality, you see, I was born a Spanish citizen, for Spain controlled this territory after running the French out. The remains of that mission settlement are today situated in the Mexican state of Guerrero.

From stories I was told, or perhaps I knew this from a dream, I remember friendly faces using hushed voices gathering all around me at my birth: aunts and uncles from Mamá's Martínez side, along with my Papá and Ábu—which is short for abuela, or grandmother—from the Castañon side. A small barn owl winked at me from the rafters, never making a sound, just watching ceremoniously. A small *altár*, meant to bless my arrival, had been set up earlier atop some hay bales. Candles, vegetables, herbs, and a small painting of *la Virgen María* had been carefully arranged. I believe I smelled Ábu before I ever knew whose hands delivered me into the world that evening. She smelled sweet—a wintry fragrance of rosemary, lavender, and sage. Those herbal aromas have stayed with me for many, many years. I often smell Ábu at unexpected moments.

Ábu and my older brothers, Nacho, Carlos, and Justo, later told me stories of their frustrations with trying to plant corn, herbs, chiles, and other vegetables in the mission gardens before I was born. They claimed that the soil, cracked and dry and peppered with large stones needing to be plucked or chiseled out, seemed largely unworkable. Transporting water from the *río*, the river, became a major chore. Since my brothers collected water for the animals from the Río Grande, Ábu insisted they might as well bring extra for her gardens. It was no short walk either! My father warned the boys not to grumble; in fact, all of us were instructed to do as Ábu asked.

I don't remember a time when Ábu was not with our family. Thank goodness she was there, too, for it was she who taught us that we were all a part of a great community bound by the earth below and sky above. She taught us the names of trees, plants, flowers, and animals that lived around us. She considered them neighbors, or *vecinos*. Ábu loved planting and watching things grow. Joyously, she'd prune and tend to her plants each morning as if they were her children being prepared for company. Sometimes I'd catch her sneaking out on nights when the moon was full to forage along the river alone, returning caressed by the scents of chives, oregano, or mint, which soon mingled within the darkness of our small *jacál*, or hut.

It was at Presidio del Río Grande (as everyone called it) that Mamá learned to read as well as work the looms, while the boys learned new ways to hunt and fish by joining the Franciscan fathers. Men and boys were taught to clean and prepare their catches for cooking and storing. My father, a soldier serving the Spanish captains at the presidio, would ride out suddenly on horseback whenever he and other soldiers were summoned.

I have a memory of a small group of raven-haired women gathered around two wooden looms in a small chamber at the mission. These small alcoves blazed with women's talk and laughter as fingers flew, inserting the filling yarn. The completion of a row was followed by a soft clacking as swift, strong arms pulled back on the carrier, setting the yarn into place row by row. Colorful threads radiated out in all directions, magically transforming simple lines into patterns for blankets, shawls, delicate white cotton cloths, and table linens. I remember one time watching as these beautiful creations were folded neatly and loaded onto an oxcart bound for Saltillo to be sold at the fair. Mamá beamed with such pride as she bade a final farewell to those treasures!

Father Conde, the main priest at the mission, allowed Mamá and the other women to select one creation per year to keep. Mamá always selected blankets, but it seemed we waited forever before she'd let us use them. My father made a special wooden box with woven agave fiber handles so we could transport them. I'm thinking now that he must have known we'd be moving around quite a bit.

Some days I ran around with other children near the chapel, trying to catch monarch butterflies in the fall or running through the courtyard just so we could listen to the echo of our voices and laughter. Other days, Ábu took me and my two sisters, Nieves and Josepha, to gather herbs near the river, while my brothers Nacho, Carlos, and Justo tended to the animals or went on expeditions with the Franciscan fathers. As a very young girl, I learned to identify local herbs and plants by sight and smell, including aloe, hawthorn, yarrow, catnip, dill, pine bark, cocoa, vanilla, rosemary, mustard, wild onions, oregano, and garlic. I knew how and when to harvest these plants, and eventually learned what they were used for. Ábu taught me everything about the healing power of these natural finds. We didn't use store-bought remedies at that time. We used Earth's remedies, gathered in nature, to tend to someone who got sick or hurt.

One time, Nacho came down with a fever that I felt sure would kill him. Nieves, Josepha, and I hurried out to the bushes near the river to find elderflowers and hawthorn with Ábu. Desperate to find something to bring comfort to Nacho, my sisters and I bent low, searching carefully between the tall grasses. We followed Ábu from a short distance. Suddenly, the grasses ahead stopped swishing. Our heads popped up to see Ábu, right hand held high, her signal for "quiet, listen."

Breathlessly, we watched as she carefully opened the gray cloth pack she carried over her left shoulder whenever she gathered herbs. She pulled out a couple of wrapped items. Standing still as river rocks, we watched our grandmother mix a paste of what smelled like honey and garlic in a small *molcajete*, or bowl, she carried wherever she went. Setting her pack on the ground, she gently pulled a long, soft gray piece of fabric from inside her pack and draped it over her arm. Holding her concoction with both hands straight out in front of her, she walked slowly toward a mesquite bush.

Nieves, Josepha, and I snuck around behind her skirt, moving in sync as if we were Ábu's shadow. There at the riverbank, a young, shiny-eyed boy, right leg gashed and bleeding mightily near his shin, cowered as he looked up at Ábu. My sisters and I held our breaths, watching as Ábu slowly and patiently applied her homemade paste to his open wound using very gentle strokes of her fingers. After wiping her fingers in the grasses, she wrapped the boy's leg with the narrow strip of cloth, tying it gently and tucking in both ends. Ábu hummed as she worked, something low and guttural that none of us could understand.

Dressed in a loincloth and leather throat band, this long-haired, slender-limbed young boy looked up at Ábu and me and my sisters with watering eyes of immense gratitude. Then, ever so slowly, he crept up from the ground, his eyes never leaving us. He stood facing Ábu, pounded his chest twice, and then turned quickly and limped rapidly away, following a path that led into the brush.

When I asked Ábu if she knew who he was, she replied, "I believe we are all related on this Earth, María Andrea. We must help each other out. Hun Hunahpoo, Mayan god of maize, and other gods have given us all we need to do this, so why wouldn't we? Do you *muchachas*, young girls, know what to use on open wounds like his?"

"No, Ábu, tell us!" My sisters and I gathered around as she searched in her satchel, pulling things out for our lesson.

"We could've used aloe vera squeezed from a plant spike like this or the flower tops of yarrow, like this, if any of us had brought water or oil to make the petals stick. Garlic, always travel with garlic, *muchachas*! It can be mixed with whatever ointment you have with you, like honey or animal fat, to soothe all kinds of bloody wounds.

"Ábu, you used garlic and honey today—I could smell them," Josepha chimed in proudly.

Josepha, my oldest sister, was very observant, and smart, too. She didn't ask many questions because she learned very quickly just by watching, by listening. I could tell she was determined to know what to do the next time she might be faced with a similar situation on her own.

"Yes, I happened to have honey and garlic in my pack today. Honey stops the blood flow on smaller cuts and wounds. Both honey and garlic help prevent infection and take down swelling. Yarrow is one of my favorites; you've seen me use it a thousand times, especially for stopping blood flow on larger injuries, but I didn't happen to have enough of that with me. If we find any flowering, we might cut some to take back.

"On days that I have to give up one of my cloth bandages, I must be sure to make another to replace it before I go out again. These are things you girls must always carry; be ready for anything, my dears. For now, let's find some elderberries to take back for your brother Nacho, *pobrecito*, poor little guy."

I couldn't wait to learn more about the uses of herbs after that. I've thought of her words often, especially since I've had many opportunities to use Ábu's remedies for soldiers and citizens alike in the violent conflicts that surrounded my life.

My father spent his days riding with the Spanish military, often alongside the former governor of Coahuila y Tejas, Colonel Manuel Antonio Cordero. The two tried to keep peace with the indigenous people who weren't thrilled with Spanish incursions and settlements. My father also supported Colonel Cordero in upholding the law in common cases where thieves stole livestock or property.

I don't remember much more of this early time, other than seeing clouds of dust erupt as herds of cattle and horses stampeded through the mission and presidio areas. Ábu, extremely agitated by these animal intrusions, would grab a long stick to ward off the stomping marauders, spinning every which way to keep them from trampling her plantings at the mission. Mamá said she was a sight—short Ábu out there running, hollering, and cursing the animals as well as the horsemen, all the while smacking any horses and cowboys' legs that came within her reach. What came out of her mouth was not the sort of language the mission friars encouraged, Mamá would remind us with a frown.

My brothers said Father Conde often drifted around in his brown robe looking dissatisfied, lonely, or distressed. Mamá insisted it was because of his frustration with the way native families came and went as they wished from the mission. His plan, from Ábu's perspective, was to keep as many laborers as possible working within the mission grounds. Father Conde's directive from the Holy See in Querétaro was to save as many souls as possible, and at times it seemed he was fighting a losing battle. Mission San Juan de Bautista's residents began dwindling in number.

Anyone wishing to enjoy the facilities of Mission San Juan Bautista or the protections provided by the military of the adjoining Presidio del Río Grande had to do three things: help out on a daily basis; become Catholic by learning the new beliefs, prayers, and songs; and agree to leave old beliefs behind. In return, residents would receive shelter, food, protection, and religious instruction just like my family did. Even families living outside the mission or presidio were welcome to come for services and instruction provided by the Franciscan fathers. In fact, if a military man from the presidio married a neighboring resident or *vecino* of the nearby villa, something that was encouraged, the couple was permitted to live outside the presidio to raise a family, while still receiving support from the mission and presidio leaders. In this way, the Spanish empire could continue to grow with many, many Catholic converts. All were instructed to worship their one true God.

"Snakes," Ábu used to say, "love to see other snakes in the same pit."

Señora laughed at this memory.

Ábu called the Spanish *serpientes*, or snakes; Mexicans she referred to as *lobos* or wolves; and light-skinned people she called *gavachos*, or foreigners. All of them were asses in her mind. She didn't have much good to say about any of them. Even the Franciscan fathers she referred to as "sacerelotes." This was a play on words: *sacerdote* is Spanish for priest and *elotes* refer to corn cobs. Ábu, with her quick wit, put the two words together to refer to priests who looked like walking corn cobs. Ábu had something to say about anyone who came into her sights on any given day!

Señora paused to laugh and shake her head at the memory.

Aye, *díos mío*! My god, such memories! Ábu was suspected in more than one catastrophe at Mission San Juan Bautista. Let's just say the Franciscan fathers learned to keep an eye on her.

Señora chuckled and I smiled, hoping I'd hear more about Ábu as Señora continued her story.

CHAPTER 3:
LETTER TO KING CHARLES IV, 1794

LETTER TO CHARLES IV OF SPAIN, OCTOBER 1794, FROM FATHER CONDE

I didn't have the heart to share this with Señora Candelaria, but I'd mimeographed a handwritten letter I'd found in the archives of San Antonio's Historical Museum. This letter, in its original form with no wax seal, appeared as though it must never have been sent.

Your Most Gracious Majesty,

May the grace and peace of Our Lord Jesus Christ be with you and your beloved family as we write to inform you of the progress of Mission San Juan Bautista del Río Grande, situated in the province of Coahuila y Tejas in the year of our Lord 1794. We are just now in receipt of your orders for secularization of our mission, a bittersweet conclusion to nearly one hundred years of efforts.

Father Clem and I wish to respond in a timely fashion to Your Majesty's command to send an official report regarding our work with the native inhabitants as we attempted to guide them into the fold of those who worship the One True God. This process is a complicated one; our progress we will endeavor to relay with respect, though at times you may sense the frustration with which we've had to carry out certain aspects of our duties. We don't mean to diminish the importance of our Mission, Your Royal Majesty, nor the seriousness with which you entreat this inquiry regarding Spain's new territories.

Mission San Juan Bautista del Río Grande has offered both suitable lodging and protection from the incursions of many unwelcome natives on the frontier in which we are situated. We continue to offer a daily routine that includes morning prayer, work, training, meals, relaxation, Sunday services, and, when appropriate, participation in religious holidays and sacraments such as baptism and holy matrimony. We've offered celebrations for citizens in the nearby villa in addition to the many services available to converts who reside within our walls.

Over time, many soldiers from the presidio have married and become citizens of the villa del Río Grande where they are raising families outside of the Mission autonomously, yet they remain in your service, Your Majesty, and share in communal Presidial duties, often returning to us for Sunday worship with their families.

Much food from our gardens is harvested each spring. Fish and game are provided with the help of our mission settlers and we've endeavored to create a very welcoming, self-sustaining atmosphere here at Mission San Juan Bautista del Río Grande.

On a daily basis, however, we've encountered curious native people who wander in to observe for a few days, enjoy our meals, and help out with gardening and cattle duties (perhaps), yet when it comes time for the most holy part of the following day, morning worship, many wander back outside the confines of the Mission to congregate and sit near the river. We've tried many times to round them up, but Father Clem has no patience with their surliness. Often, I find him simply left on the ground at the riverbank, having been pushed, punched, and kicked senseless by them.

Father Clem and I have been of service here for over two years now, currently housing thirty regulars from various tribes staying within the Mission. For census purposes we ask them what tribe they are from, how old they are, and if they are married. Because we cannot understand their answers, we are forced to write down what we think we hear, often writing down a physical description instead of a name that we do not understand. Yesterday, Father Clem wrote "Manos de Cochino" or "Hands of a Pig" as a name for a potential male convert. I found that unacceptable and reminded him of our mission, after which he changed the notation right away to Rigoberto.

In addition to the thirty truly devoted converts willing to join our worship and sing songs with words that are foreign to them, we have about twenty native individuals who come and go seasonally. When they have an urge to hunt or fish, they leave and we don't see them for months. When they are finally hungry and the weather is getting cold, they return and we must act happy to see them. To some extent we feel we are being taken advantage of. But we continue to strive to do the Lord's work in order that we may get these savages to become more civilized, if only for a season or two.

We've instituted a system of punishments for dealing with civil matters, as several fights have broken out over very silly matters. I very nearly got my nose broken by getting in the middle of a dispute over the theft of some bread off one neophyte's plate; such is the disrespect that many of these Indians display toward us. Father Clem suggested assigning a military presence from the nearby presidio, and I thought that was a wonderful idea, especially at meal times. When there is an available soldier, this is easily accomplished.

In addition, we've been forced to require our converts to at least clothe themselves or they will be asked to leave. We can and do provide simple cotton shirts and pants for those who will wear them. Certain levels of nudity interfere with our instruction, we feel, and sometimes lead to uncomfortable interactions between the men and women, who seem not to be bothered by open courtyard displays of love making. We've utilized a military presence to convey the message that that type of heathen behavior is completely unacceptable here.

Yesterday, we counted 56 horses, 250 head of cattle, 47 goats, and 328 chickens. We had over a hundred horses last month, but we were victims of theft for the second time this month by some unknown natives, who apparently rode *through, opened the corral, and sped off with at least fifty of our finest horses. Last month's inventory showed fifty-seven goats, so we are not sure if ten wandered off or were stolen as well. One neophyte by the name of Orzi, or something like that, pointed to another convert inside the mission and then to the corral. He seemed to be suggesting that one of our very own converts was responsible for the theft. It's terribly difficult to communicate under these circumstances.*

Some of these natives, truly most of these natives, cannot be trusted. It appears they don't trust us either. Father Clem and I strive to follow the accord of the mandate of this appointment here in Coahuila y Tejas, but we both have come to the conclusion that these neophytes must be in some ways inferior in intellect and therefore may never learn the Catholic faith that we hope to instill in them. We wonder daily if they are deserving of our tolerance and instruction. Father Don Benedict, one of our Franciscan brothers, in passing through, asked, didn't we know that it's been said that "Heathens learn best through their buttocks"? This is an old adage he shared, but one that suggests these frustrations are not new. The Most Holy See must be aware of the complicated nature of what we have been charged to accomplish here.

So that you may become better acquainted with Mission San Juan Bautista del Río Grande as it is today (since a representative has not yet had the opportunity to visit), we enclose a drawing of the layout of the grounds: the mission, presidio, horse barns and corral, cemetery, kiln, workshop rooms, granary, and cattle and goat grazing areas, along with our many gardens. Also enclosed is a census listing our converts that makes note of their essential information and tribe, as well as an inventory of items used inside our church, kitchen, and around the grounds.

With this, please consider that we have attended to said inquiry by Your Most Holy Majesty with as much care, detail, and heartfelt honesty as possible in this, the year of our Lord, 1794.

We continue to pledge our constancy in your service and the service of One Lord and God for the salvation of all of mankind in order that we may increase the territories of New Spain in your name.

In one God we praise,
Father J. Conde, Apostolic Minister, Father J. Clem, Eucharistic Minister
Mission San Juan Bautista del Río Grande, Coahuila y Tejas

P.S. Please advise regarding a timeline for the secularization of these mission grounds and materials. Until instructed otherwise, we will continue working with our converts.

CHAPTER 4: PALAFOX, 1806-1810

Señora continued her story.

 I'd like to share with you another incident that I just barely recall that took place when I was very young, around seven or eight years old, I believe. My whole family headed out on the Camino Pita, "Pita Road," to help Captain José Diaz establish a brand-new settlement in the villa de Palafox. He'd been put in charge of its development by Colonel Cordero.

 Located on the left bank of the Río Grande, this thick wilderness of spiky vines and sharp cacti awaited just a short distance from Presidio del Río Grande. In spite of my family being promised ownership of some number of acres of land, Ábu and Mamá were not happy. Both sat with long faces, looking utterly distraught at having to leave Presidio del Río Grande. They'd met so many pleasant people at the villa there. Mamá said she'd just been placed in charge of teaching a couple of new residents about the operation of the looms around the time we were called to leave. Ábu thought leaving her gardens to the care of those Spanish *serpientes* would ruin everything. Although packing up and leaving was a small distraction from their disappointment, Mamá recounted that their dreams completely dissolved once they saw their "new" completely untamed settlement area.

 Ábu stomped around complaining to everyone that Palafox was a total embarrassment for a Spanish village—no public buildings, no decent mission space for weaving, no building materials for corrals, and, worst of all, only gravelly, dry desert sand for gardening. There were hardly any buildings; this land seemed feral—still being cleared of cacti, mesquite, and scraggly underbrush. Establishing this as a settlement was supposed to be our job now—ours, the new settlers! I rarely mention this stop to anyone because, strangely, our stay turned out to be very brief.

One morning, I walked outside of our tiny, ramshackle *jacál* just as Ábu was talking to someone half hidden behind a tree. She handed this darker, brown-skinned man something and it seemed to me that the two were friendly. I was very young at the time and I'm not sure if this was a dream or not.

"Who were you talking to?" I asked Ábu as the native man crept off into a nearby grove of mesquite. "I saw that man look down and unwrap something you gave him."

"Hush, child! He's just a new neighbor," she snapped, gathering and folding all of our blankets that she'd washed by hand and set out to dry the day before.

"What did you give him?" I pressed further, in my curious, childlike manner.

"Just a few pieces of flint and a little chocolate for keeping an eye on things!" she assured me, packing the blankets in the wooden box my father had made. Strangely, she proceeded to drag that heavy chest of blankets under a tree and sat down to rest on it.

"What are you supposed to be doing, María Andrea? You, Nieves, and Josepha need to get together and wash clothes as soon as this wind lets up. Have Carlos hike with you to get some water while Justo gathers sticks. It looks to be a perfect day for it." Oh, my grandmother made a great commander!

Three days later, we awoke to the cries of "*Fuego! Fuego*! Fire! Everyone, get out; the place is going up in flames!" Those frantic shouts and cries were accompanied by the sound of feet running away outside our *jacál*. My family and I ran, and Ábu huffed and puffed, trying to drag the wooden blanket box. She hollered for Carlos to come back and help her. The underbrush and dried tree branches made for easy fuel, lighting up the sky and making it feel as if we were all engulfed in some kind of fiery kiln.

Someone reported that a band of native people had been seen rampaging through. They burned the beginnings of Palafox to the ground and stole any horses and livestock they could gather. They exited by tromping through Ábu's rustic but newly tilled community garden.

We'd taken to burying small treasures next to an agave plant at Ábu's instruction, so we unearthed them quickly as we readied to run, watching the tiny *jacáles* of Palafox crackle and pop in flames. Other families ran with whatever few possessions they could grab from their small dwellings. Men hollered, a few women cried, and the children mostly kept out of the way, trying to make sense of what was happening.

To Ábu's absolute delight, our family and several others soon found ourselves gathered on the Camino Real, the "Royal Road," which was the main dirt path. Everyone started walking toward Laredo. Mamá prayed the rosary the whole way, asking for safe passage and protection for us all. Ábu followed her, dragging a stick, singing, twirling, and occasionally muttering something about Spanish snakes. I don't recall where my father was, but I am quite sure he must have been out on assignment with Governor Cordero or other soldiers; he wasn't in sight on this road as far as I recall. Mamá said my father and his soldiers most assuredly went in search of the individuals responsible for the senseless destruction of everyone's newly built *jacáles*.

Our good friend from Mission San Juan Bautista, Edgar, fell in line on his horse with my little cousin, José Paulo, seated in front of him on the saddle. The two of them followed behind my family, providing extra protection. Edgar appeared whenever things got tough for Mamá and Ábu to handle alone. He helped my mother and Ábu with men's duties and directed my brothers to help out. Edgar could be a little rough on the boys, but Mamá insisted his discipline was necessary to teach the boys to listen to orders when their father was gone.

One time, we had all been on horseback along the Camino Real from Laredo to San Antonio for a baptism when, seeing household goods strewn along the side of the road, Mamá stopped and signaled for us to wait while she slid down off her horse to pick them up. These were Mamá's belongings, packed on the cart traveling ahead of everybody for her to give to her sister. Evidently several items had fallen off the *carrito*, or horse cart, and now lay scattered and dusty a short distance ahead along the route.

All of a sudden, Edgar rode up, placed himself and his horse alongside Justo, and, with a swift hit, batted him completely off his horse before pulling it off to the side to watch Justo get up.

"What the hell?" Justo shouted, brushing dust and dirt off his pants and shirt.

"Help your mother," Edgar stated simply using a husky low voice. He held the extra horse steady, waiting for Justo's next move.

"Why can't *you* help her, you lazy dog?" Justo shouted, heading back to mount his horse rather than help Mamá. As soon as the words left his mouth, he knew he was in trouble. The rest of us stepped off the road into the trees to take a break and watch the fallout. Carlos got down off his horse and reached over to hold the reins of both Edgar and Justo's horses. Carlos knew better than to step in.

"What did you call me, son?" Edgar had whipped down off his horse, setting José Paulo on the ground next to Carlos. He approached Justo nose to nose. "You're almost a man, Justo; it's time you act like one. You can see your mother needs help, so get your ass off that horse and help her!"

Seeing Justo's face flash red with anger, Edgar growled, "If you so much as touch me, boy, I'll give you something to remind yourself of the big mistake you made on this day."

Justo stepped back, wiped his nose on his sleeve, and slowly ambled forward to begin picking up some of the towels and wooden bowls scattered about, as Mamá continued picking things up without so much as a backward glance. With each piece, he huffed and gave Edgar the evil eye until all the things were gathered. He then jerkily assisted Mamá in tying them back into a bundle that could be attached more securely to the inside of the cart. Finally, giving Edgar a hateful sneer, Justo mounted his horse and slowly took the lead just behind the carrito.

Edgar, about the same age as Mamá, was born in Guanajuato, Mexico, and was the son of natives of the Otomi group, one of the largest and oldest indigenous tribes of Mexico. He, Mamá, and Ábu could speak Nahuatl, the language many of their tribes had in common and one that few of us kids could understand. His family knew Mamá's grandparents and great-grandparents. Unfortunately, Edgar's family disappeared in Mexico City, leaving Edgar in Guanajuato by himself.

One time, frustrated with Carlos for making a faulty fishing pole, Edgar called my brother a *tuza llanero*. Ábu laughed so hard we thought she was going to fall straight into the river. None of us knew what that meant! She finally confessed it was a type of rodent that burrows into the hillsides of towns. We didn't think it was that funny, but apparently it was a joke from Guanajuato that only the two of them and Mamá understood.

We found out later that Edgar's parents and older brother hadn't left him; they'd been killed in a skirmish with warring tribes of native peoples just outside of Mexico City. Since that time, he'd become like a member of our family, except he wasn't really, and my brothers never let him forget that.

PART II: LAREDO

CHAPTER 5:
LAREDO, OCTOBER 1810-1818

Settling In

Señora Candelaria withdrew a silver-handled hairbrush from her skirt pocket. Stamped and barely visible on the back side, I saw the words "Minas de Guanajuato," the Mines of Guanajuato. She laid it gently upon the blue cloth in front of her next to the postcard.

I leaned over to examine her hairbrush more closely without touching it. "It's exquisite, Señora! I can't wait to hear more about this. Please go on when you're ready."

While I changed pens and flipped pages in my steno pad, Señora straightened her skirt and tightened her head covering to combat the steadily increasing breezes. She then continued.

• • •

Laredo felt like a welcome relief after the trauma of escaping Palafox. Many of us held a simmering fear that fire-bearing hordes might come in the night and burn our *jacáles* to the ground.

A favorite memory from Laredo is of us *muchachos*, kids, standing, arms outstretched wide, spinning and spinning in the plaza of the majestic Cathedral of San Augustín. In bits and spurts, we fell dizzily to the ground, laughing, only to stand up, throw our arms out to our sides, and spin around over and over again.

Our joyful voices echoed throughout the courtyard. Time seemed to stand still. We lived only in those moments, jubilant and cheerful. Oh, how I wish I could have bottled the sights and sounds of us laughing and twirling endlessly like *trompos*, spinning tops. These memories seem magical, ethereal, like hazy smoke, now. We were oblivious to the political changes happening all around us. I'm grateful for that time, actually. Every child needs to experience interludes that take them away from the world's wider business and the troubles that lurk just around the corner, threatening to swallow them whole.

By this time, 1810, I was only six or seven years old. My family, especially my father, had been of service to the Spanish military under Colonel Cordero for several years. My parents listened to this tall, handsome, blue-eyed Spaniard speak optimistically of creating strong, protected Spanish settlements at Mission San Juan Bautista, then Palafox, and now Laredo. His followers were increasing as word of promises for land ownership spread. An entire labor, 177 acres, was offered for farming. A league of 4,428 acres was offered for those who wished to graze livestock. Can you imagine? All this in exchange for just two things at that time: improving one's new property and converting to the Catholic faith, something everyone in my family except Ábu had complied with long ago. My mother converted to Catholicism back at Mission San Juan Bautista. She took quite fervently to carrying around a small, beaded blue rosary and praying daily.

Yes, offering protection inside the missions and promising land ownership were part of the Spanish plan for enticing folks to settle in Texas.

"Please tell me your family was able to secure some of this, Señora." I smiled. I noticed I'd been leaning in, eager to hear more of her history. What she relayed to me included details from a perspective that either my history studies had left out, or I hadn't paid attention to. I wondered how and if land ownership conveyed with each family's movements as they followed the Spanish to develop new settlements.

"Did your father seem to be keeping up with his family as you moved from place to place?"

I can't be sure if he stayed physically close to us or not. He was a bit of a phantom that appeared when we least expected him. I'm sure he wanted us to believe he was never too far in case of an emergency, but I felt more estranged from him as time passed. I quit wondering where he was. We had Mamá, Ábu, and for many years Justo for dealing with emergencies. Edgar too, of course. As for securing our promises of land, well, I'll tell you more about that later.

When my father did come home, he happily accompanied us to mass. It provided him with a chance to catch up with other settlers as well as share military news. After mass, he often made arrangements to swap animals or get help repositioning the scraggly tree limb fences we called the *abatis*. He loyally supported Colonel Cordero's efforts to minimize native peoples' incursions as much as any other type of rebel incursions. There was no shortage of people who felt slighted by the Spanish, or irritated with the native peoples, or frustrated with Mexican laws. Honestly, my father didn't seem particularly interested in what was going on with his own family. I'm sure Mamá filled him in on any news that she thought was important for him to know.

Anytime settlers reported trouble, off my father and Colonel Cordero rode, usually in the company of other soldiers from the nearby presidio. I'm sure you've heard of the sword and the cross. For every mission church, a presidio was built nearby to house soldiers for protection. I think this pairing was one of the reasons my mother stuck so closely to the missions. Over time, she and Ábu no longer felt familiar with the native tribes in the areas we traveled. The missions with their nearby presidios provided a sense of security and familiarity for many converts.

The Colonel seemed very happy to have my father, an excellent horseman, traveling alongside him. Amid the chaos and disorder of things most of my family didn't even understand, we managed to stay together by following in the Colonel's wake.

The sun finally began to warm the concrete around us, and although the two of us were seated in the shade of a large pecan tree, the soft breezes slowed as we sheltered from what had soon become a blistering late morning sun. Señora pushed her head covering off as I pulled two small bottles of water from my satchel, offering her one. She took it gladly and opened it shakily, gulping a couple of sips. She then closed the bottle and set it next to the crate upon which she was seated. She seemed eager to resume her story.

Just then, a small, energetic chihuahua appeared, circling and sniffing me. The tiny fireball moved on and looked up at Señora expectantly.

"Vaya fiera, go on you little beast!" she spat in a low growl, waving both hands as her scarves flailed all about. "Come back at lunchtime!"

I sensed a toughness about this woman, watching as her dog lowered its head and tail and wandered off again. In a matter of seconds, I saw it prancing happily toward the Alamo, the rejection quickly forgotten.

・・・

I remember many hot, sticky mornings in Laredo picking up twigs to start fires for clothes washing day. Nieves, two years older than me, waited patiently for the big boys, Nacho, Carlos, and Justo, along with our cousin, José Paulo, to amble back from the Río Grande with water to fill the large metal washing pot dangling over the fire pit. Our youngest brother, little Esteban, loped a ways behind. Nieves carefully rearranged and stacked firewood tinder. I'd take and arrange her twigs inside the fire pit, readying them for lighting. Monday wash days meant no time for playing with the animals or mixing mud in the barrel to repair the outside walls of our family's *jacál*, activities the younger ones especially enjoyed. Doing laundry was pure labor that lasted nearly the entire day. If bedding was included, we'd need several basins full of water, filling the next one whenever the previous one got too sudsy.

One time, I remember Ábu saying she could feel rain coming in a day or so. My sisters and I felt added pressure to get things washed and dried in a hurry. We might be able to wash and hang them outside, but, if need be, we could always drape them around inside the *jacál* to dry. We didn't prefer to do this because Ábu complained the added moisture made her bones ache.

Finally, Carlos and Justo, panting and looking like a couple of droop-eyed oxen with a long branch resting on their shoulders, appeared carrying two pails of water, one at each end, splish-splashing as they scurried, knees bent, toward us. Behind them, José Paulo, usually dragging a stick, marched along singing some military song in Spanish. At the sight of them, Nieves would stop weaving grasses, stand up from her seat on an overturned bucket, and run to get the washboard and soap kept under our small patio.

Once the boys poured the water in the washing pot, saving some for a small bucket in case of emergency, it was time to start the fire. My oldest brother Nacho loved this job. He'd pull out his tinder box and then carefully remove a knife he kept strapped to his leg. Colonel Cordero and his commanders provided knives to all their soldiers and sons, but Nacho's knife was special: the handle was carved from the bone of deer antlers. Most others we'd seen were made of *fierro*, or ironwood.

Nacho carefully stooped and stood to the leeward side of the fire before striking the knife against the flint from his box. After several attempts, a tiny piece of tinder lit and he slid it under the smallest twigs we girls had balanced at the bottom of the fire pit. Within minutes, a mighty fire warmed the metal pot dangling from the wooden tripod. Oh, Nacho was a fire bug! He felt so proud of his fires.

"Come on Carlos, Justo, let's go check the fences!" Nacho would holler, strapping his knife back onto his leg, then tucking the tinder box in his back pocket. He and my older brothers would run toward the outer boundaries of the property, deliberately leaving José Paulo and little Esteban behind to "help" us with the washing. We knew we might not see those older boys until dinnertime.

With Nieves and Josepha at my side, handing over lye soap wrapped in an old piece of cloth and covered in beef tallow, we began the day-long process of washing everyone's clothes, including Papá and Edgar's. I'd add a few pieces of clothes at a time to the hot water, stir them around, then remove each piece with two long sticks. Nieves would then scrub them on the washboard with the soap while leaning over a large boulder. Once the clothes were cooled, Josepha would carefully return the wet, scrubbed pieces to the water, stirring them around gently to rinse them until it was time to remove them. Once the clothes were put outside on a rock to cool, we'd wring everything out and then would finally lay each piece over nearby mesquite bushes to dry.

"José Paulo, run and get more sticks to add to the fire, *por favor*!' Hearing the request, little José Paulo, I think he was about five at that time, spun off and scampered about the bushes near the *jacál*, gathering pieces of tinder in a basket that we kept just for that purpose. Yes, I can still see him so happy to be of service, running and searching everywhere for sticks or leaves to bring us. Sometimes he'd scurry so fast he'd stumble and fall, and then would have to gather all his sticks up again. He'd call for Esteban to help him, scrambling as if he was in a race.

"You know what those boys do when they're out there, don't you?" Josepha asked me one morning.

"Fix fences, I suppose." I suggested.

"Those boys are marking off their land, partitioning our labor of land for each of them plus Dad."

"What about our portions?" I stirred the pot's contents.

"Sister, if we want land, we'll have to come into it. You know how you come into land?" Josepha prodded.

"No, not exactly," I said, pulling smaller pieces of laundry out with a long stick, acting as if I wasn't listening to every word. I'd never really thought much on this topic, to tell you the truth.

"You marry a man who has land, that's how! If Dad were to be harmed or not come back, you know who would come into this land? The boys! If Mamá took possession, she'd immediately turn it over to them."

"Wait, Josepha. Are you saying I'll never have a league or a labor of land?" I swished the remaining clothes around, brushing hairs away from my face and considering the injustice of this new revelation with furrowed brows.

"Not likely, María Andrea. Land somehow gets assigned to the men. Sure, everyone would like a league or labor of their own, but pay attention. How many women do you see raising cattle or farming on their own? Doña Maria del Carmen Calvillo inherited Rancho de las Cabras from her father, but she's a rare case. She's one of the richest women cattle owners around. Usually, it's only widows with no family, which she became, by the way," Josepha shook her head as she finished that last sentence.

"I thought the promise was for our family to get a league and a labor of land because Papá helps Colonel Cordero and the Royal military. We're the ones left behind to keep up the property while he does that."

"All settlers are promised that, but how many cattle do we actually have here? One cow? As for crops, we can't grow anything in this godforsaken dust bowl except Ábu's herbs! I doubt that any of us will get any part of this land, María Andrea. But let the boys dream away out there!"

By the end of the afternoon, the final laundry pieces came out soapier than they went in, so Josepha began using less and less soap to wash each successive batch. She seemed suddenly very quiet, caught up in thoughts of our recent conversation, perhaps.

We were just finishing up when a sudden gust of cool wind sent flames from the fire pit shooting across the bottom of my skirt, igniting it before I could do anything to prevent it! Josepha heard me cry out and flew around the pit, grabbing the small wooden bucket and throwing water over my skirt to douse the flames. I stood back, dismayed, and immediately began shivering from this sudden drenching.

I must have looked upset because Señora leaned across her cloth. I felt a soft swish as if she touched my hand. "Aye, señorita, many dangers lurked on the open frontier! Fires were but one of them."

I felt relieved at not burning my skin and I thanked Josepha for her quick thinking. But unfortunately my one and only skirt had become charred and unbecoming. As I stood staring down at it, out flew Mamá and Ábu, looking like a pair of wild hyenas!

"*Qué tónta*! What an idiot!" Ábu scowled. "You know better than to stand downwind of a fire. Hasn't your mother taught you anything?"

Mamá squinted at Ábu as if she wanted to say something, but then turned to me and shook her head sadly. "María Andrea, let the boys take care of men's work around the fire! Where are those boys? They should be here to put that fire out in this wind!"

When Mamá and Ábu started on a tirade of insults, there was no stopping them. I suppose it was one way to let loose their frustrations at being stuck out in the middle of nowhere.

Señora exhaled, and shook her head sadly, perhaps envisioning the two elder women that day.

Nieves tried to intervene with the truth, after all, laundry was women's work, but the two wouldn't listen. Because of this, Josepha threw one of Mama's clean blouses into the dirt and stormed inside.

"Go on now, tend to the chickens, *mís hijos*, my children. Josepha, get back out here before this fire dies down and rewash that blouse! María Andrea, take the little ones where they can't get into trouble—maybe over near the chicken coop," Mamá scolded. Shaking her head, she stomped back into the *jacál*, hands on her hips. Josepha flew back out, bumping past her to grab little Esteban's hand and stomping off toward the chickens, stepping on the wet blouse in the ashy dirt as she went. She was a fiery one, that Josepha!

As for me, I felt humiliated and ashamed for something I had had no control over, but I was unable to defend myself. I really think Ábu and Mamá wanted to make sure we girls understood that our fates were only as good as theirs. No better and no worse, regardless of anything else we might imagine, dream, or hope for. Ábu and Mamá sometimes acted this way with Josepha in front of others, though Josepha's anger could boil up like a volcano and backfire on them, causing them a huge embarrassment that reflected more on them than on Josepha. She'd usually find something to throw down before marching off in anger.

As I grew older, I felt a fiery determination to prove to Mamá and Ábu that they were mistaken about us girls. This was not how I planned to live my entire life! Like Josepha, I knew I needed to figure out a way to get my hands on my own piece of property if that's what freedom meant.

Señora exhaled loudly and squinted upward toward the sun for a few minutes, closing her eyes and warming her face. Finally, she lowered her head and resumed.

After having completed the washing, we girls would lean on the wooden support of the front stoop, fingers red and shriveled, carefully picking hairs off of our sweating faces. I sometimes wondered whether we were living the life of Spaniards or Mexicans. It seemed to me that we were all native people trying hard to be something else in new territories we weren't familiar with. I honestly remember wondering to myself, "What exactly are we doing here? Who *are* we? The mountains and mission of my youth dissolved into one meandering Río Grande. But where was this big, beautiful river taking us?"

There seemed to be no relief, whatever the answers to those questions were. But this was in the days before anyone had time to feel bored and no one dared to whine. I simply closed my often-watering eyes and said nothing, hoping the day would come when I might finally be free of such constant drudgery. I begged the great spirits for a day when I could feel passionate about doing something, anything, more meaningful than just surviving.

On the frontier, duties were dictated by sundown, then sunrise. More duties were required every day without end. It was just how people lived and developed settlements. Well, most people.

A sudden downpour, though welcome, could send the walls of our small *jacál* running down into a muddy landslide. Repairs would need to be made, and we girls made sure we were ready with our mud barrel. We'd drop everything else to make repairs as soon as the rain let up. But oh, how my heart longed for a different sort of existence. I watched my family more closely now and tried not to resent them when I saw the boys leave for fishing or hunting while we sisters stayed put doing chores.

Well, I believe *la Virgen María*, or the eternal spirit, or someone from the great beyond eventually heard my desperate pleas!

I watched a gentle smile form on Señora Candelaria's face.

"What are you remembering now?" I asked, reaching for one of her small hands and noticing how cold and frail it felt.

She suddenly looked in my direction and squeezed my hand. "Did you have chores to do when you were younger, Miss Rizzo?"

I gently placed her fragile, bony hand back in her lap so I could flip my steno page. "I did, Señora. My brother took out the trash and I fed the dog. In time, I washed my own laundry and did everyone's dishes, too. I guess the chores weren't exactly equal at my house either, come to think of it. My brother sometimes paid me to take the trash out for him!"

We both chuckled at that.

Being a female Castañon, I was expected to assist with chores every day nonstop. Some days, Josepha and I might be grinding corn, spinning wool outdoors, feeding José Paulo, and later caring for little Esteban. Other days we might be out brushing and watering horses or mules in the corral, riding one of our horses around the corral for exercise, or planting and gathering herbs with Ábu. However, one chore I was never allowed to take part in was fence repair. For this, the boys rode several miles on horseback, never alone, along the perimeter of our property. This was extremely risky on account of the Comanche. My father insisted the boys go together and he sometimes even accompanied them when he was home.

Señora closed her eyes for a few minutes.

Whenever Ábu scolded one of us, my father, if he was home, would approach the offender, smile discreetly, and whisper, "Careful, Ábu is *muy Azteca!*"

This we all understood to mean, be careful or Ábu might decide to sacrifice you! It made us smile and feel like our own separate tribe. In time, we began to raise our eyebrows, point, and whisper, "*Azteca!*" to one another whenever Ábu went off on one of her rants. Her tirades increased over time. With each successive move our family made, it was evident that the years were catching up to her. Her language, *aye de mí*! My goodness!

I smiled and glanced down at my notes, surprised that my fountain pen was about to run out already. Luckily, I'd brought others and I replaced it as fast as possible. I was anxious to hear more, and to document everything Señora said about her family.

"Who in your family did you most look like, Señora?" I asked.

She leaned forward and slowly picked up the silver hairbrush from the cloth. Staring at her reflection on the back of it for a moment before setting it back down, she smiled and continued.

Everyone said I favored my mother, Francisca, and her side of the family more than my father's Castañon side. The people of my father's side were shorter and a few, known to be stubborn, were always arguing. By the time I stopped growing taller, I overshadowed my father and Ábu. The Castañones that I met were generally of medium height and quick, with subtle grins and quiet laughter. (The name Castañones means "chestnut gatherers.") Mamá's side, although more reserved, was always gracious and welcoming to us kids as long as we were behaving.

As for my disposition, I suppose I inherited a bit of my easygoing nature from both sides. I felt like I developed a tough, unique blend of strength and resiliency that was all my own, though. Ábu laughed when she told stories about my birth and said she'd never known a baby to look so much like *un insecto bastón*, a walking stick. By the time I turned thirteen, I was taller than both of my parents and Ábu.

In our final years in Laredo, Ábu and Mamá began to worry about the way men looked at me, while I pretended not to notice their attentions. I had to contend with a serious situation of looking quite a bit older than the young teenager I really was.

Señora closed her eyes. I began to wonder if she was revisiting a jacál, her yard, or a special moment in Laredo. Before I could ask, she opened her eyes, continuing almost as if in a trance.

I still see *los molinos*, three weathered, wooden windmills with thin blades, turning and cutting the air with soft swishing sounds as breezes deliver the crisp scent of rain blended with fresh dirt. For miles, I see nothing but open territory—the Chihuahua Desert, dotted occasionally by small groves of struggling mesquite trees or spindly *sotol*, desert agave, on the horizon. It appeared as if our acres were unbounded, when in fact 177 of the Castañon family's acres remained secured by a border of old stumps of mesquite *abatis*, a kind of fence made with sharpened tree branches. The skeletal line of *abatis* at times revealed gaps caused by wind, storms, or other forces that took hold just as soon as our backs were turned, necessitating constant repairs.

"You can't trust a place unless you can see a hundred miles in any direction," Ábu would say, facing into the wind and staring at the horizon. She liked sharing this wisdom so much that she repeated it often to every one of us. I can still see her standing outside, hands on her hips, bobbing and inhaling and taking in the satisfaction of her son's family settlement. She relished us having such an inventory: a corral with three Spanish goats, three beautiful tall horses—Borrego ("Sheep"), Philemon ("Loving"), and Milagro ("Miracle")—and a young mule, Terco ("Stubborn"); a small barn; five sheep; ten chickens; two turkeys; and two head of cattle that grazed lazily along the banks of the Río Grande. Ábu transformed into the beautiful, content woman of my past whenever I saw her reflecting tranquilly outside. Our move to Laredo proved to be a good one, for her at least.

I noticed Señora's head slowly falling to her chest and felt that this had been enough storytelling for today.

"Señora, would it be alright to continue this interview tomorrow? You seem to be tiring and I should probably refresh my notes."

"Yes, yes. That would be fine, Miss Rizzo. Where is my sweet Caramela . . . ah! Here she is now."

Señora poured a little water into one palm and held it out so Caramela, her small chihuahua, could take a sip. Caramela then waited anxiously for Señora to collect her items and stand up. I hugged Señora gently and waited for the two of them to begin their walk home before setting off in the opposite direction.

• • •

A Wooden Ashtray

Somehow, Señora Candelaria had beaten me to the curb the next morning to continue our interview. There on the blue cloth in front of her she'd placed a small carved, wooden head of what seemed to be a Maya or Aztec native with a bird on its head. In the place of his ear was a large blackened bowl whose charred interior looked as if it had been used many times. Beside that lay a light blue rosary. I was most curious to hear how these two artifacts would enter the day's story.

"Good morning, Señora! I see that you brought some new items to talk about today! The soft blue glass used for the beads on this rosary is beautiful, and I bet I can guess who it belonged to at one time. This other piece I'm not too sure about."

"I always have something new to talk about, Miss Rizzo. My life has been so full, I could bring you stories loaded on the backs of ten pack mules!"

"I'm sure you could!" I laugh. "Alright, let me get my steno pad, and when you feel ready, please, let's begin."

"Let me start by telling you about José Miguel Sanchez Navarro, who we called Don Navarro."

Navarro was a Mexican landholder who sided with the Spanish, since they controlled much Mexican territory at the time. This man owned the most land in all of Latin America, people said. He and Colonel Cordero got together and, as I understood it, Don Navarro was a big reason the Spanish were able to bestow acreage, animals, and supplies to the settlers. After several kidnappings, animal thefts, and *jacál* and corral burnings—all tactics used by the native peoples to discourage settlement in what they felt were their territories to begin with—Don Navarro brokered a peace treaty with some very angry Apache. Thanks to him, raids by the Apache diminished considerably across his properties. Unfortunately, Comanche assaults began to fill the void and continued in a most heinous and severe manner. Even Ábu feared that tribe, such highly experienced horsemen as they were and indiscriminate in exacting revenge on those who were clearing and marking off lands that their people had been traversing and hunting on for decades.

Pulgita, "Little Flea," our family's trusty ranch dog, could spot and announce visitors on our property long before we'd ever see them. The problem was, Don Navarro didn't believe in arming his ranch settlers for fear they might revolt against him or against one another. This made thieving easy; marauding bands of Comanche rode through, taking whatever they wanted, and we women, often left behind on our own, did our best to keep ourselves hidden. Many Comanche traded stolen livestock from the settlers for guns from the French up north in Louisiana.

Once the natives were armed and we settlers weren't, life became a hellish game of survival. Families were scared every single day in many of those settlements.

In spite of Pulgita sounding the alarm, natives still rode off with one or more of our horses, goats, or cows. My family could do nothing but hide, curse, and watch the natives yelping with pride as they hauled off our family's livestock.

In May of 1818, an early morning Comanche raid resulted in the abduction of my brother, three-year-old Esteban. *Pobrecito*, poor little guy, got snatched off a goat he was trying to ride around the corral. He was swiftly carried away and my parents never heard from him again. This was life in a desert wilderness back then. Many families suffered this fate, not just ours.

Mamá never considered for a moment that she or Ábu could have prevented Esteban's abduction. Instead, Mamá hid her pain at first, simply shrugging and saying she hoped none of the rest of us would be so stupid. Of course, she also grabbed her blue rosary, this blue rosary, and fell to her knees, weeping softly and praying. Aye, Mamá!

Señora paused, becoming pensive and putting her head down as she wrung her hands in her lap. Finally, she straightened her skirt, looked up, and continued in a louder voice.

Ábu began hollering, "Aye, *pelotudito*! You stupid little ass, Esteban! *Éstes pinches changos del bosque*, these damned forest monkeys have no idea what they've taken! You're not even potty trained!"

Suddenly I saw Ábu snicker, "Ah ha! Yes! I've got you now!" She plucked a large spider off her arm, threw it down, stomped on it, and then picked it back up and walked inside, holding it between her thumb and pointer finger. She placed the withered spider carefully into this very wooden bowl that she kept by her chair. She'd burn it later as a sacrifice to Hun Hunahpoo in hopes of getting our Esteban back.

Pobrecito Esteban, our little dreamer, covered in scars from working the ranch. He always tried to keep up with his older siblings. A giant half-moon scar marked his forehead from being kicked by one of our horses, yet that didn't stop him; he continued to wander about, slapping and pinching the underbellies of the livestock. One of the horses took a small bite out of his tender head and made it bleed. That boy never cried.

Ábu, who witnessed the whole kidnapping from inside the *jacál*, later shook her head sadly, rocking back and forth as a smoky wreath encircled her head. She got after the rest of us saying, "Look, you kids had better wake up if you want to take a proper journey to *Tamoanchan*! (This was a term from the Aztec language for the paradise from which the human race was conceived.) You see those monkeys on horseback; get yourselves back inside this *jacál*!"

It was her way of adding a frustrated postscript of authority to state the obvious. Rattlesnakes and drought could be tolerated so long as a family stayed together to remedy the effects of such inconveniences. But raids by natives left many families, including ours, with absolutely no favorable options. We felt helpless.

When my father returned and learned what had happened to Esteban, I remember him shaking his head slowly. "Well, that had to have been a very sad day," he said, removing his hat and retreating to the back stoop. He'd often sit outside and consider the landscape when something went wrong. I realize now how utterly vulnerable and helpless we all really were.

"Miss Rizzo, are you crying?" Señora leaned forward and patted my shoulder.

I wiped my eyes quickly with my sleeve and looked up at her. "Sorry, Señora, but this is too much to imagine. Losing a brother and then everyone carrying on, some angrily, and not being able to do anything about it. It's just so . . . terribly . . . unfair. Sorry, I'll compose myself here in a minute."

"Miss Rizzo," she continued tenderly, caressing my arm and closest hand, "It was terribly sad, but the saddest thing about all of it was our vulnerability as settlers out there in the wilderness. That's just the way it was for so many of us trying to make a better life for ourselves. There were risks. These territories, well, they really belonged to others or perhaps they really weren't meant to belong to anyone. You're a sweetheart for caring so deeply about it."

Sniffling, I recovered and managed a faint smile. But I had to sit with this information for a few minutes and Señora sensed that. She rearranged the artifacts on her blue cloth.

"Okay, Señora, I think we can go on now. I'm very sorry."

When I think about our family and how independent we all were, I remember that we had to carry on as if we were our own sort of army. Typically, Nacho, Carlos, Justo, Josepha, Nieves, and I, being the oldest of the Castañon children, took orders from Mamá and Ábu on a daily basis. Often, José Paulo or Esteban became our charges to supervise and direct. Remember that my father stopped at home only intermittently. So many skirmishes in neighboring territories demanded Colonel Cordero and his soldiers' constant attention. Being asked to improve land was no small task without a father around, let me tell you!

My family spent considerable time improving our portion of the Navarro property. Ours was part of a much larger tract of land called a *latifundio*, a large estate. We worked daily to clear out underbrush, build corrals and fences, and turn the soil for gardening—anything to make the place more habitable. The entire *latifundio* operated under Spanish rule on land that was at times considered to be Mexican territory. Originally, it was open range land freely utilized and hunted upon by the natives. Evidently the Spanish, Mexicans, and natives never agreed to any land sharing, so each group continually made life difficult for the others coming in to claim it. We became part of a throng of people claiming and building Spanish ranches and settlements. The native people passing through knew nothing about this, nor did they care to learn the meaning of latifundio.

"I suppose the concept of land ownership could have been new or unacceptable to the original inhabitants," I added to Señora's account.

"Miss Rizzo, do you have any experience living out in the wilderness?"

"I don't know where to find wilderness anymore, Señora!" I laugh. "I imagine living out there must have been incredibly difficult, if not nearly impossible. I wouldn't know how to survive, I'm afraid. I'm a city girl, accustomed to apartments, small patios, and walking around city parks. I've not seen vast undeveloped areas of land other than a few open fields between here and Austin. That's why I'm completely amazed at your life story so far! I'm trying to picture it."

Señora smiled at me, nodded, and seemed inspired to continue. Just then, a trolley full of partygoers rolled by. A young, dark-haired woman hollered "hello!" in our direction as she laughed and pivoted out to the side, hanging on by one hand.

A jacál in northern Mexico
Frederick Starr, In Indian Mexico (1908)

CHAPTER 6:
POLITICAL TENSIONS

MANY SIDES' INTERESTS COME
HEAD-TO-HEAD BEGINNING IN 1810

Shortly after we arrived in Laredo, in late November of 1810, if I recall correctly, my father took Nacho and Carlos aside near *la cocina*, the kitchen, one Sunday and asked what they would think about riding with him and Colonel Cordero. Trouble was brewing, he said, with a gang of rebels organized by a priest by the name of Father Miguel Hidalgo y Costillas, or Father Hidalgo. Colonel Cordero needed more men to help put down a revolt by these rebels in Goliad at Presidio La Bahía, Goliad's presidio. The boys could serve as scouts, away from the action, Papá assured everyone. They needed the boys to help keep an eye on rebel movements and report back to him and Colonel Cordero.

Mamá and Ábu didn't think it was a good idea to get Nacho and Carlos involved. but then again, both were grown ranch hands—Nacho was twenty-two and Carlos seventeen. Other than assisting with cattle drives that took them away for sometimes weeks at a time, they provided the bulk of the outdoor labor and security around our little ranch. But now my father insisted they were old enough, quick enough, and strong enough to help bring in a little more income for the family. Besides, he reminded Mamá, both of these young men needed something else to do now that they'd completed our corral. It was plain to me that their hearts, like mine, had been withering like summer grass in the fields for quite some time. Although they never complained, they'd been waiting patiently for an opportunity like this to come their way.

"Plus," Papá proudly announced, "Justo is fifteen now, a young man experienced enough to handle the livestock and help around the *jacál* by himself." As my eyes shifted to Justo, I saw him fighting back tears. With a long face, he sighed heavily but said nothing. He knew this meant he was being left to watch over the rest of us. Although it wouldn't be that way forever, for now this was quite a big responsibility—a turning point for the future of our family in many ways.

Mamá shook her head, grabbed her blue rosary, and stomped outside, hands on hips as she glared at a sky darkening with large gray thunder clouds overhead. Occasional flashes of lightning cast eerie shadows highlighting her silhouette standing below our spindly pecan. A sudden downpour broke loose but she didn't come back in. She stood out there under that tree, letting rainwater trickle down her face and mingle with her tears as she prayed, one blue bead at a time.

My two oldest brothers, on the other hand, could not contain themselves. They began packing immediately! Each owned a small satchel for their horse and these they loaded with an extra shirt, socks, a comb, and their knives. They didn't concern themselves with the politics of the time and knew little of the trouble that siding with the Spanish, as my father had done, might bring. To them, this was the greatest adventure of all—to ride with Colonel Cordero and maybe even carry a gun for protection. To ride for king and country!

Señora closed her eyes for a moment before continuing.

I am reimagining the sight of my short, feisty father and these two oldest sons of his. Both sons, taller than Papá, mounted their horses and headed off proudly into the crisp morning air, cowboy hats tilted back and boots set firmly in their stirrups. Papá took the lead, his rifle loping at the right side of his horse. The rest of us stood, watching their heads bob up and down with each stride of their horses as they made their way out of town. I can still imagine them and, unlike Mamá, I felt very happy for my brothers to get away with Papá. It was time for them to see what else was out there!

Less than a year later, however, the realities of their work began to hit home. One evening, just after I'd fallen asleep, I woke up to a great shouting match outside the kitchen.

"Who have you been hanging out with, son? The devil himself?" Papá poked a finger up into Carlos's chest, roaring like a dragon. Carlos, momentarily taken aback, then sensing a possible advantage, slapped Papá's hand away, overcome with a newfound force of determination. He stepped forward to shout back into my father's face, standing as tall as possible and looking down with his fierce dark eyes and short black hair.

"Me? I'm telling you that your so-called friends are enemies of the people here, Papá!"

"How dare you say that?" my father countered. "How the hell would you know?" Papá, whose neck veins were beginning to show, bent forward and thumped Carlos again on the chest. This time, Carlos wasted no time shoving my father back with both hands, pushing him back into a wall where he knocked Mamá's small blue crucifix and rosary from its peg near the cabinet to the floor. Surprised by my brother's boldness, my father grabbed Carlos by the hair, crumpled him over, and rammed him into the floor. Carlos scrambled to regain his stance and in an instant the two were locked together, sputtering and thrashing around all four sides of the room. Papá spun Carlos around and threw him into our table, knocking it over and causing Carlos to lose his balance.

I'd already been plastered against the wall in the hallway for a few minutes when Ábu must have finally heard the commotion. Both she and Mamá, dressed in nightgowns, appeared in the doorway to investigate. By then, all anyone could see were two plates broken into pieces on the floor and two bodies punching each other with great vigor, rolling about. My mother started forward, but Ábu pulled her back.

"You think you know better than I do, son? Is that what you think?" Papá sputtered as he bent over and put Carlos's head into a headlock, stepping to his side and twirling him around. In a matter of seconds, the two rolled again to the floor. Carlos lifted his leg to kick one of the overturned table legs hard. It shattered. Papá let him loose for just a few seconds, time enough for Carlos to turn and punch him squarely in the jaw. This set off another round of the two twisting about the floor, thrashing each other, bumping up against chairs, knocking some over, and pushing the now broken, overturned wooden table up against the front door.

"Salcedo, Menchaca, Herrera—all these strong Spanish leaders have been executed, Papá. Why? For having their own ideas, that's why. The Spanish that you've taken up with are obviously not respected here; they will not succeed in the end! Why do you continue to follow that horse's ass of a Cordero around like his little puppet?" Carlos shouted. Mamá gasped and covered her mouth in terror.

Papá tightened his grip until Carlos's face began to turn bright red. He frothed at the mouth and sputtered, "I'm choking!" Ábu crossed her arms and pursed her lips as Mamá closed her eyes and lowered her head, whimpering softly and shaking in shock and grief.

Looking squarely over his son's head, upside down, but directly into his eyes, my father replied, "Son, the measure of a man lies in his deeds. I have spent half a *lifetime* establishing my place in Spanish terrain and I don't intend to become a coward now in the face of flimsy sentiments."

"I'm not a coward, Papá. I just don't want to end up like Antonio Delgado, dead, after fighting against forces as evil as José Arredondo—who is a Spanish Royal, *your* side, by the way, and that of your revered Colonel Cordero! Nor do I wish to prance about like a pompous Cristóbol Domínguez, subjecting anyone who disagrees with me to petty cruelties and abuse." Carlos squirmed out of the chokehold and lay breathing hard, nose bleeding, on the floor, face up and eyes closed. I watched Justo slink past us, seeking refuge outside to sit on the steps.

Papá, kneeling, bent his head, panting to catch his breath as his back heaved up and down. His hands, raw and bleeding, clutched his knees.

I wondered how my father would respond to what Carlos had just said. I felt a tear roll down my face. I'd never witnessed any of my brothers going up against my father in such a way, and it pained me greatly.

"Well Carlos," my father continued, "if you think any son of mine is going to take up with General Toledo or any other ragtag band of green-flag waving, rebel land-grabbing Republicans, you'd better find yourself another place to live. I have pledged to *never* betray the Spanish king and my word is my honor. Colonel Cordero has pledged to protect his king, me, and us—yes, this family—to the best of his ability. So, before you go about biting the hand that feeds us, you'd better hope to live as long as I have to know what's really going on."

I felt more tears falling. It was getting harder to contain my sorrow at hearing what my father was saying. Another place to live? As if Carlos could be given up so easily like a cranky old horse or goat.

Ábu at last stepped swiftly out of the shadows to comfort Carlos, dampening a small towel to wipe his face and righting a chair for him to sit in.

"Listen to me right now, both of you. Please, my sons," she directed firmly, stomping hard on the floor. She let her arms fly wide as she preached side to side. "Fighting is never pretty. I've seen enough of it to last a lifetime! So I know history will favor whichever side wins—but we can *never* know if we are on the winning side while the battle is raging, now can we? We can only hope and strive for our own happiness, good fortune, and survival. Who doesn't want that?

"I don't give a scorpion's ass which side wins these messy battles. As long as I am alive and, more importantly, my family still breathes. One's family represents the most precious undertaking that we commit to on this Earth! This family has supported the Spanish crown since *before* the days of Mission San Juan Bautista, though maybe not before our days roaming the mountains of Guanajuato, which none of you *kids* would know anything about." Ábu made the last part of that statement almost under her breath, but I heard her.

"Listen, José Antonio, my son. Maybe the younger generation wishes to support the Republicans, or the native people, or the Mexican government in these territories instead of the Royalists. At least consider letting your sons make up their own minds. Please, no more fighting. We are family, we are a clan, and we need to stick together, even if our beliefs differ. No one has kicked me out for refusing to honor the Catholic faith—not yet, anyway." Ábu turned and continued gently wiping Carlos's face.

Mamá, Nieves, and I stepped forward out of the shadows. We slowly approached Papá to give him a hug as he wiped off his hands and turned to get himself changed in the back bedroom. His thick shiny dark hair, normally turned back neatly just like Colonel Cordero's thin light hair, now hung in blocky, black clumps near his fiery, bloodshot eyes. The air grew thick with silence and sniffles. Josepha had heard everything from under a blanket in our room but couldn't bring herself to get out of bed to witness any of it in person.

The next morning, Carlos and his horse, Rebel, were gone.

Papá said nothing as just he and Nacho saddled up their horses to meet with the other Royalist soldiers. Ábu silently handed them their lunches, while Mamá and the rest of us turned to go about our daily chores around the *jacál*. We spent that day with no words, mourning the likely loss of Carlos from our family. We were lucky no unfriendly natives came around at that time because we didn't have our usual determination to even watch out for them. They could have taken all of our livestock and burned our corral for all we cared that day.

Near the end of October 1813, Carlos reappeared one morning, looking *muy vaquero*, very much like a cowboy, as he rode up on a tall dark horse that I didn't recognize. I was out front washing and hanging clothes on bushes with Nieves and Josepha. Little José Paulo was running about, picking up pecans and throwing them at squirrels.

"Carlos?" I cried. "It's so good to see you! Where have you been?" Nieves ran up to his horse and I followed suit, while Josepha hung back, stirring the laundry and staring dully into the sudsy water. Once he dismounted, we three hugged for several minutes.

"It's good to see you too, sisters," he said, holding each of our faces in his hands and gazing into our eyes. He went over to hug Josepha, then picked up José Paulo, holding him in a bear hug until he squirmed to be put down.

"Well, I spent some time out riding with the so-called rebels until many got shot at Medina not too long ago. I managed to escape the Royalist forces by jumping off my horse and running straight into the Trinity River. I'm so glad Ábu taught me to swim at Presidio Río Grande—it truly saved my life. I swam downstream with a few others like María Josefa Candida and Antonia Rodriguez."

He removed his soft-brown cowboy hat, wiping his forehead with his sleeve.

"I'm telling you, María Andrea, Nieves, Josepha, you cannot imagine the horrors that men and women, Mexicans and Americans *both*, are experiencing at the hands of the Royalists under the command of the soldiers trained by Colonels Elizondo and Arredondo. I saw it with my own eyes. If you travel the lower Laredo Road for any reason, please, I'm warning you, don't look to either side or you will lose your appetite completely. Heads and body parts of many members of the Republican Army of the North, as we call ourselves, are staked along the route as a warning to others who might wish to conspire against the Spanish Royalists. You see why I had to leave home? Papá apparently supports the violent tactics used by these Royalists. We just never knew it."

"Why would Papá take up with a bunch of evildoers?" I asked, wringing out a long dark skirt of Ábu's and stretching it across a low sage bush to dry. My mind kept trying to make sense of it. "Something doesn't sound right about this, Carlos."

"Well, I'm beginning to wonder if Colonel Cordero, in his Western Provinces, is unaware of what his other hand in the Eastern Provinces is doing. There's an old warehouse called La Quinta where captured women from the Battle of Medina were forced to shuck, scrub, and hull twenty-four bushels of corn a day to feed the Royalist armies as far away as Veracruz! These women have just now been set free. Their men? Dead at the hands of a firing squad. Their children? Set free to roam the streets begging for food. A few men and women—including María Josefa, her niece Antonia, and I—swam the river to get away and then, after walking the rest of the way to San Antonio, these ladies found that the Royalist army had taken possession of their homes. They were left with absolutely nothing.

"San Antonio is not the town I thought it was; people are starving there now and many are running north toward Natchitoches, Louisiana, and further before cold weather will make the trip harder. They're hoping to fare better under the protection of the United States. Most are completely penniless now, without livestock, money, or the homes they once owned. These settlers will have to start all over again. This is what Cordero, Papá, and their men have brought us, sisters."

"Carlos, remember what Ábu said. War is hell. It's rarely a negotiation game. Right now, it sounds like the Royalists are in the lead. For your own welfare, don't you think you should be fighting on Papá's side, at least for the time being? I mean, coming around here as a Republican army representative is dangerous. From the other side of the fire, Nieves snapped, "Edgar says the Republican Army of the North is done for."

This was the most political discussion I'd ever been a part of, but I could tell that Nieves, like me, was truly trying to understand the chaos going on around us. I never could tell what Josepha knew or didn't know; she kept so quiet. But when she popped in with a comment, it seemed she knew quite a bit about what was going on. When Papá was home with the family, he never discussed his work, instead delving into domestic matters and making repairs. We couldn't count on him for information, that was for sure.

"Most of those who didn't flee northward claim to have changed sides, and I, too, may need to consider this if I want to stay around here. I don't know what I'm going to do. I'm not sure if I'll ride with Papá ever again, though. I should say, I'm not sure he'll have me. I can say with certainty that Republican or Royalist, I will never engage in the sort of merciless killing I witnessed at Medina. I can't stop hearing the cries of women and children and screams for mercy in my head. My god, it was awful."

"You know what they say, Carlos, only the dead get to see the end of war," Josepha added sullenly. "I don't think this violence is going to let up anytime soon."

Mamá quickly scampered out with a cup of water for Carlos, who winked at her and thanked her for her thoughtfulness. He drank up quickly and handed the cup back to Mamá, who now stood silently among us. Justo joined the group, backslapping his brother in a giant hug and ruffling his hair.

"Whether Papá'll have me or not, I'm staying out at one of the Pérez's ranches to think things over. When Papá gets back, will you tell him what I've told you? Just see if he is aware of what his sovereign Royalists did at Medina. We'll see how things work out from there. Not that he ever discusses anything with his family."

Carlos hugged all of us again, working his way around the circle to Mamá, who he walked back to the *jacál* as both whispered in low tones. Shortly thereafter, he mounted his horse and was off, leaving nothing but a trail of dust and me and Nieves fanning mightily to keep it off of Ábu's drying skirt. I turned to look at my brother riding off, thinking what a fine young man he looked to be already. I began to wonder how things would work out between him and my father too.

Señora rubbed her knees with both hands and I sensed she'd had enough storytelling for the day. We called it quits and agreed to meet again the following morning.

Ábu's cenizero carved from the wood of a guamuchil tree from Central America.

CHAPTER 7: MOTHER FALLS APART

TEXAS'S WAR FOR INDEPENDENCE FROM SPAIN BEGINS (SEPTEMBER 16, 1810 TO SEPTEMBER 27, 1821)

When we reconvened the next morning, I brought a small cup of coffee for Señora and a doggie treat for little Caramela. Señora snapped the treat in two, saving half in her pocket for later and throwing the other half to Caramela, who quickly devoured every crumb. After taking stock of street people passing by, I settled in comfortably, pulling out my writing tablet. I started off by asking Señora about the effects of having her brother Carlos change sides for a while.

Things seemed very complicated. Carlos deciding not to support the Spanish was only one piece of the confusing puzzle. The very next morning, Josepha hustled outside as Nieves and I were gathering twigs for another fire.

"Sisters," Josepha announced, "Mamá is crying in her bedroom and I can't get her to stop. I don't know what's wrong, so I'm going to send Justo to get Edgar."

"Maybe she's sad about Carlos," Nieves suggested, her innocent nine-year-old voice taking on the tone of someone much older. A look of serious concern wreathed her chubby, round face. "Or do you think Mamá's sick?"

"No, Nieves, waving goodbye to important men in her life is nothing new to her. Now she's learned about the deaths of many of her friends in Guanajuato. We all know she's never been able to truly leave that place behind," Josepha responded in her sarcastic, matter-of-fact way.

When Edgar arrived, he sat on the bed next to Mamá, who sat with her head in her hands facing the wall. "Francisca, I'm here," he murmured, softly stroking her long black hair. He gently rubbed her back as she continued sobbing. Holding his hat in his left hand with his suede jacket remaining on, he considered what to say as he looked down sadly. Apparently, he knew very well what was going on.

The rest of us kids stood quietly in the hallway, listening to their conversation.

Between sobs, Mamá cried out, "Oh Edgar, my friends, my family. What is happening? Carlos told me so many people we know have died at the Alhóndiga de Granaditas, that big grain warehouse in Guanajuato. For what? I don't understand what is happening! Spanish firing squads spilling the lifeblood of Father Hidalgo, Ignacio Allende, Juan Aldama, and José Mariano Jiménez? Their bodies decapitated? Why?" Mamá's voice pleaded for answers as she picked up a pillow and sobbed into it.

"Francisca, I'm so sorry," Edgar replied. He paused for a moment to compose what he would say next. "It's not easy to understand all the chaos, but there's a war for Texas's independence underfoot. Father Hidalgo apparently was stirring up trouble. He and several of his parishioners took control of the prison at Dolores. Because of his political activities, his head was spiked and placed on display at the top of Alhóndiga, near the market in Guanajuato that you and I know very well from years ago."

Mamá wailed loudly upon hearing this and threw her blue rosary at the wall, where it crashed and slithered to the floor next to her bed. Josepha's eyes widened as she looked over at me, stunned that Mamá would ever throw her precious blue rosary. Nieves looked at me with tears in her confused eyes and I put my arm around her as I wiped a tiny tear off her cheek. I, too, struggled to understand what was going on.

Edgar explained, "Though his blood has run cold, the blood of Father Hidalgo's followers still runs hot, so convinced they are that the Spanish must be driven out of Mexico." Nieves let out a whimper and I quickly covered her mouth, shaking my head no.

"Father Hidalgo's dreams for independence continue in many parts of Mexico even without him, Francisca. The rebels, as the Spanish call them, continue to do his work. This was their territory, they claim, and there's some truth to that."

Puzzled, Mamá turned with puffy eyes and questioned, "But why do they want independence for Mexico, Edgar? The Spanish protect us. The money from the silver mines in Guanajuato is used to build churches for the people, is it not? Can't people see this?"

"People talk about the sword and the cross, Francisca," Edgar continued. "The Spanish display crosses to represent the Catholic faith they bring in to these territories. It's their symbol to draw newcomers to the church, where they hope to guide the thinking and beliefs of these new followers. The Spanish teach the new converts to pray and have faith in the one true God, who, according to the Spanish Catholic beliefs, died on a cross to save all of mankind. Besides converting people, the whole Spanish system supports and is supported by a man who lives miles across the ocean in Europe, a royal king that nobody in these parts has ever met!

Edgar paused, set his hat aside and continued.

"However, there are times when soldiers from the presidio, knowing that their first responsibility is to protect the church and its followers, may have to chase down and even kill thieves or others who oppose their new teachings and ideas. Father Hidalgo was a man of the cross, but he was known to spread strong ideas of hatred toward immigrant settlers. His view was always that the Spanish and others, like the French before them, entered Mexico, built their churches, gathered their followers, and then took advantage of them by taking too much silver from Guanajuato to enrich their king. Over time, Father Hidalgo grew bold enough to kill for his beliefs; his message was that these people—these Spanish and French immigrants, European settlers, or 'invaders,' as he called them—needed to leave Mexico and leave its natural resources to the people who settled here originally, the native Mexican people.

"The battle at the Alhóndiga, Francisca . . . It was either kill or be killed. Many of our friends and *vecinos*, or neighbors, died cornered in the plaza of the warehouse at the hands of a very angry Spanish military. I'm so very sorry. Please understand that there are still many who favor the Spanish and see the good that they do."

I looked at Josepha, surprised that Edgar could explain all of this so well. Even I could understand it now. Josepha looked back at me with pride in her eyes as she pursed her lips and shook her head slowly and silently. I had the feeling she had already come to understand some of these things better than the rest of us.

Edgar continued, "Think about it, Francisca. The presidios built alongside every mission are filled with soldiers for protection. Their job is to protect the settlers and their territories along with their assigned mission church. The Spanish are not all-loving people; they will kill in order to gather and protect their followers, so strongly they're attached to their missions. This is not new behavior—it's been like this since the beginning, Francisca. You've got to know we're starting to see sentiments changing here toward the Spanish."

My mother exhaled loudly, wiped her eyes, and, while still talking to the wall, made her feelings clear.

"Then Carlos was right. I just want to take my family and go back to the hills of Guanajuato, that beautiful area near the mountains of Mexico where my family's history began. Edgar, life was so much simpler then." Mamá sniffled, then straightened, exhaled loudly, and began to compose herself. "Here I am with a family whose loyalties are split. I have terrible dreams that someone I love is about to die as a result of all of this. I know I'm supposed to be strong, as Ábu constantly reminds me. . . Speaking of whom . . ." she turned quickly toward the doorway. "María Andrea! Josepha! Nieves! Where is Ábu?"

I chimed in from the hallway, "I'll go find out, Mamá." As soon as I'd backed out of the room, I smelled it. Smoke. Josepha and I ran around the back of the *jacál* to find Ábu kneeling and rocking before her wooden *cenicero*. The wooden ashtray of hers, set between uneven patio walls made of large rocks, held a burning effigy—a medium-sized lizard that smoldered slowly as smoke curled skyward in slow-moving, languid gray veins. I started toward her but Josepha held me back. She put a finger to her lips to hush me so we could hear Ábu's low throaty rumble of a prayer. It turned out, we couldn't understand a word of what she was chanting. Sensing that we needed to let her be, and seeing that her fire was small and contained, we drifted slowly back to the front of the *jacál* just as Edgar was leaving.

"Justo, keep an eye on your mother, *amigo*," Edgar commanded. "I'll be back later to check on her. In the meantime, make sure these animals are fed and watered.

Josepha, you, Nieves, and María Andrea take over the meals for a while, okay? Your mother needs to take a break. Make a little extra for me tonight, if you don't mind."

As soon as he rode off, Justo groaned, "Does he really think we need him to tell us what to do? *Pendejo*, bastard, stupid ass!"

Josepha and I giggled guiltily, mostly at Justo's newly acquired use of profanities. I thought to myself, no one knows what needs to be done around our *ranchito*, our little ranch, better than we do. You know, at times Edgar did act a bit like a *pendejo*.

We got busy with our usual chores and left Mamá and Ábu alone. Emerging from her room, moody and quiet, Mamá shuffled outside, as if in a trace, to sit on an overturned wooden bucket next to Ábu for the rest of the day. The two of them sat, staring at the smoldering *cenicero* for hours. Nieves dutifully brought them a few twig batches to refresh their tiny fire. There they sat, side by side in complete silence, staring into tiny dancing flames that soon turned to white ash. Later, we called them in for dinner. I'd forgotten that many of the families Mamá had heard about were most likely families Ábu knew as well. It must have been terribly sad for both of them. Their grief drew their minds miles away and even when we spoke to them, it was as if they didn't hear.

While cooking up our usual tortillas, nopales, beans, and rice for dinner, Josepha, Nieves, and I decided that our family needed a happy diversion, perhaps a trip to the fair in Saltillo! We thought we might propose the idea in a couple of days. Just talking about the attractions we'd heard about at that fair perked Nieves up enough to set the table with no more tears.

Unfortunately, what came next would take Mamá and the rest of us even further away from her mountains in Guanajuato, as well as any hopes of the family visiting the fair in Saltillo anytime soon.

"If it seems like our lives were one big roller coaster without the fun of a fair, that's exactly how it felt!"

"Yes, well, sometimes that's life's reality, it seems. Here's to the roller coaster of life!" I chuckled, raising my coffee cup up to meet hers.

We both nodded, sighing faintly as we toasted one another, then took a few breaths and a couple more swigs of coffee before continuing.

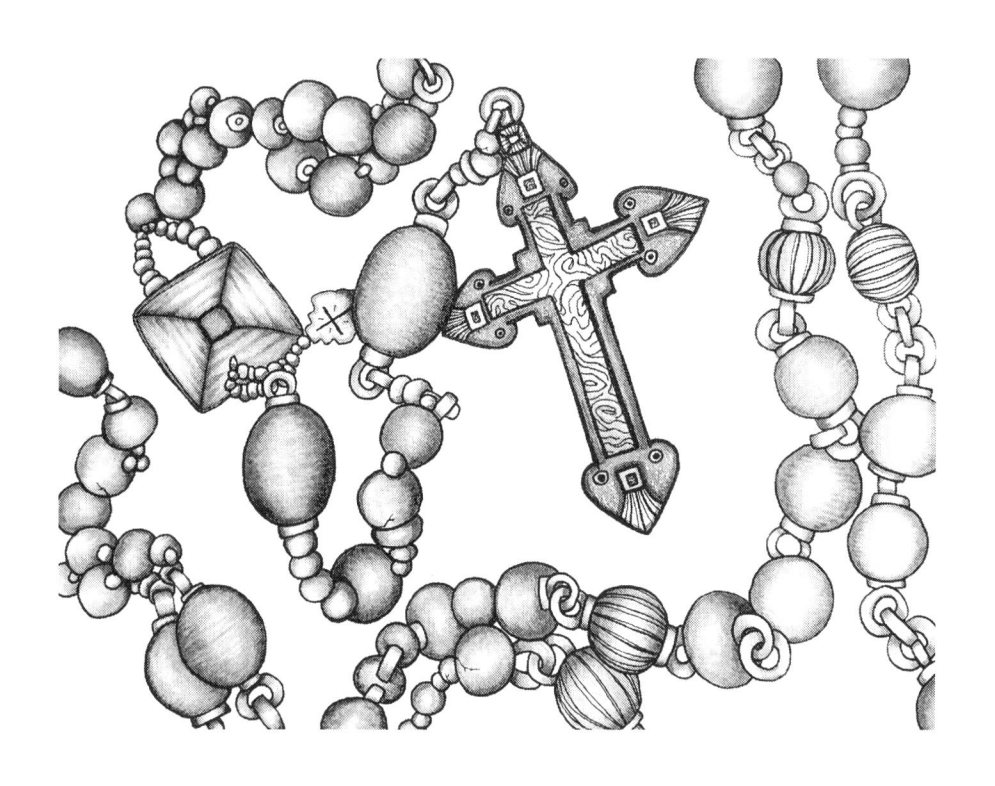

Rosary image courtesy of OliveOriginalStudio on Etsy

CHAPTER 8:
A KINDLY COURIER, 1818

A MESSAGE ARRIVES IN LAREDO REQUESTING ANOTHER MOVE

I could see that Señora was tiring, her voice becoming fainter, until she touched upon a special memory that brought her back to life.

"Now, Miss Rizzo, I must share a final story about Laredo before we stop for the day. Someone special presented himself there, though I didn't know anything would come of it at the time."

"Alright, Señora, if you're sure you feel up to it, let's continue!"

One morning in Laredo, Justo was just finishing up with the animals when our dog, Pulgita, started barking. Spying a dead bird floating in the stock tank, Justo cut a nearby tree branch to fish it out, all the while scanning the area and admonishing Pulgita to quiet down. Those of us inside the *jacál* gathered near the doorway to see what the excitement was all about. Was it a native? Mamá grabbed a hoe that we kept inside next to the door.

Upon hearing the sound of a cowboy's creaky saddle approaching from behind, Justo put himself on guard. Slowly lifting his hat, he wiped his sweaty brow using the dark, musty bandana he always kept in his back pocket and he whirled around quickly, one hand at the ready near his lower leg. He squinted upward to see a scraggly, dark-haired, dirt-covered cowboy pulling in the reins of a spotted, healthy-looking brown mustang.

"Whoa, hold on there, *amigo*. I'm a courier with a letter for someone in your family," he said, reaching back to rummage in his *mochila*, a well-worn leather saddlebag. He pulled out a small folded envelope and, reading aloud, asked for Señor José Antonio Castañon.

My brother stood up, slowly taking his hand off the knife he kept strapped to his calf. Standing as tall as he possibly could, he responded, "This is his property, señor, but he's got business with soldiers nearby."

The stranger held out the envelope. "Well, then, I'll thank you to be sure he gets this message when he returns. It's from Colonel Cordero himself, intended for the whole family, most likely." Before handing it over, he asked, "Please, might my horse and I have some water?"

Justo, my sisters, and I could hardly contain our giggles watching this dusty courier attempt to dismount. Unable or forgetting to put his left foot into the stirrup, he fell with a heavy thud onto his back, knocking dust and dirt up into a giant cloud that hung suspended in the air for quite a few seconds. He immediately rolled to one side and stood, brushing himself off as he hopped up on his right foot. Nieves moved to assist if needed.

As he stepped forward to take the tin cup I brought out, it became apparent that this handsome, dark-haired messenger was partially lame in one leg. His left boot angled out oddly as he kept righting his stance. But so determined and businesslike was he that he once again held the message out with pride until Justo stepped forward to retrieve it. I remained to place a bucket of water under the horse's muzzle, where he began smoothly inhaling it. The courier winked at me and said, "Thank you kindly, señorita!"

"Have you seen any natives out there today?" Justo asked.

"Naw, not today. Started out a bit later than I'd planned, so most have probably done their fishing by now. I do worry about that though, from time to time. The only difference between me, a scout, and a spy is which side wants to know what I'm doin'!"

I looked over, puzzled, at Josepha. She pursed her lips, raised her eyebrows, and nodded in agreement.

After a couple of minutes, he lifted the horse's head from the bucket. Pulling the reins back over its head, he said, "Come on, Relámpago." (The horse's name meant "Lightning.") "We'd better get on our way." When the stranger lifted his hat to thank us, Justo assisted the man by cupping his hands at the left side of the horse, thereby allowing this dusty traveler to mount with dignity using a knee up. With one hearty thrust over the horse with his good leg, the courier mounted successfully, lifted his hat once again in gratitude, and turned to ride swiftly off toward the river.

Justo, Josepha, Nieves, and I figured what his visit implied. Just as soon as the courier rode off, Mamá and Ábu flew out of the *jacál*. Mamá wasted no time opening the handmade envelope encasing a message written on the inside of the same tiny piece of paper.

"I have that message right here in my pocket, Miss Rizzo. The same message my mother read in 1813!"

Señora pulled a tiny withered packet from her pocket, opened it, held it between her hands in prayer for a few moments with her eyes closed, and then continued.

My mother read this very message in Spanish aloud to us:

From: The Honorable Colonel Manuel Antonio Cordero
To: Señor José Antonio Castañon and Family
I hope this letter finds you all well and in good health. . . .

Right away, Ábu interjected, "No, señor, *estámos enfermo*, we're sick!" Ábu spat in front of her, shooting a piece of wood she'd been chewing to the ground. " I have a feeling I should have remained wandering the hillsides of Guanajuato. He's going to ask us to move again," she shouted.

Mamá read further.

> *This notice is to inform that you and other military families of the former Navarro Latifundio in Laredo are being asked to resettle immediately in the northern territory of Nacogdoches. Please gather necessities, including food and water, and head to the spot where the Laredo Road meets El Camino Real within two days. From there, our group will travel north to a new settlement in Nacogdoches.*

When Mamá read that part, Ábu turned into a tiger!

"Aye, *culeros españoles*, Spanish asses!" Ábu stomped and growled using her deep voice. "I'll drown myself first!" She pulled her skirt up like this to wipe her nose.

Señora picked up the hem of her skirt and wiped her own nose to demonstrate.

"No, no, NO!" Ábu cried, stomping her foot loudly upon the ground, like this!

Señora stomped each of her feet on the street from her seated position. A couple of people passing by paused to see what was happening and then, heads still turned, they continued slowly on their way.

My sister Nieves gathered closer to her, putting an arm around Ábu's shoulder. We'd never seen Ábu act this wild before.

Mamá continued reading:

> *Four soldiers will arrive to accompany families on the third of September. All livestock are to be taken to the same vicinity of the Camino Real, where additional soldiers will be sent to gather them. These will be reallocated as your new settlement areas are determined.*

"Those *ladrones*! THIEVES! Are you crazy, Co-lo-nel?" Ábu pleaded dramatically, punctuating each syllable with arms extending up into the air to no one in particular, like this.

Señora raised her arms to the sky, repeating "Co-lo-nel" a couple of times as she shook them. I watched her, completely spellbound, hoping my notes could somehow catch her inflections.

But there was more to the message. Señora continued, settling back down on her crate.
My mother read further.

I personally plan to meet families being resettled by the end of September. Our stay there will be brief, with an end target resettlement in San Antonio de Bexar sometime the following year.

I watched as my mother closed her eyes, paused, and inhaled loudly for a moment before continuing. This allowed Ábu time for another interruption. Her rage was truly animal-like. My whole family remembered it very clearly.

"*Véte a la verga*! Go to hell or piss off, Colonel!" Ábu shouted, stomping in circles, arms reaching for the sky. "We barely got our new corral completed. You want us to move to Nacogdoches now and then again to San Antonio? Aye, *qué tristeza*! How sad! This is a sad, sad thing, Colonel. I will journey to Xibalba, the Mayan underworld, before I even reach the river!"

Ábu covered her face with her skirt and shook her head no, over and over, like this.

Señora again picked up the hem of her skirt, pulled the fabric up to cover her face, and shook her head no, over and over. I could imagine Ábu's fury and sense of helplessness.

I remember sweet Nieves moving to comfort her, putting one hand on Ábu's slowly rocking back, hugging her tightly from the side, and assuring her everything would be okay.

Mamá concluded the letter shakily by quickly reading the closing.

Your cooperation in this matter is greatly appreciated as always, Colonel Manuel Antonio Cordero

Ábu, rocking, whispered softly, "Aye no. No, we stay here, Co-lo-nel. I'm sorry, we're gonna stay right here." Mamá hugged Ábu and turned her to begin walking her slowly up the steps to our *jacál*, the rest of us following in a solemn procession.

Mamá set the letter on the table slowly, then briskly grabbed her blue rosary hanging near the window, where she'd moved it for protection. She began praying the Hail Mary. *"Díos te salve, María, llena eres de grácia, el Señor es contígo."* (This meant "Hail Mary, full of grace, the lord is with you.") Then, motioning to the rest of us, Mamá sighed, "Get over here, all of you. On your knees, we need to pray!"

"We need to tell Papá," Justo mumbled in frustration, thumping down to the ground on both knees at the same time. His voice had changed lately, taking on lower tones. I'd noticed a thin gathering of black wispy hairs appearing on his upper lip about the same time. He'd sulked about in those days, having had to turn down two opportunities to join fellow ranchers with cattle drives, and with this latest news, I imagine he knew there'd be little chance of getting away for quite some time.

"Oh, he knows, *hijito*, my little son, believe me. I'm very sure he already knows," my mother said with an air of something—was it resignation or pride? "And when he gets here," Mamá said, straightening, "we need to let him see that this family already knows what we need to do. Remember, we are a military family and we will do this once again proudly, not only for your father and Colonel Cordero, but in the name of God, Spain, and all that is holy and protects this family."

"Yeah, Spain," Justo grumbled.

As all of us prayed, kneeling on the pounded dirt floor, Ábu rocked wildly in her chair, forcing it to convey back and forth across the floor of the tiny room. Each of us sighed, prayed more loudly, and moved out of her way with great frustration whenever she and her chariot approached. As she rocked, she spit pieces of a twig she'd been chewing to her sides here and there. Once she got to the end of the room, she stood fiercely, grabbed both arms of the rocker while balancing the twig in her mouth, and promptly turned the chair around to start another journey. The whole scene even irritated my ever-pious mother, I could tell.

"Quite honestly, I was surprised at Ábu's childish behavior. But then again, I told you how much she loved our land in Laredo."

"Yes, you did tell me, and you mentioned how each move was taking more and more of a toll on your dear grandmother. She must have been a very strong woman, maybe even strong willed, in her time," I added.

"Oh, yes. She may have been short in stature, but Ábu told me she could outrun nearly anyone back in her day, all while climbing mountains with a baby on her back! I remember seeing her run outside, grab Nieves in one arm and a barking Pulgita—who was half Ábu's size—in another, and run all the way back to the *jacál* from the chicken pen upon seeing natives approaching in the distance. Unfamiliar natives frightened Ábu greatly," Señora said, smiling and straightening her skirt. She paused before continuing.

I had to wonder where this fierce woman was, though, as I watched a sniffling, angry, and spiteful old woman, wrapped in her mission blue shawl with her gray hair tied up in a bun, spitting wooden splinters down on the ground and sputtering a fury of curse words when something displeased her.

A few years before, right there in Laredo, Ábu had been abducted by a Comanche when she stepped outside to see what Pulgita was barking about. As she stood, admonishing the dog and looking around, a Comanche rode up quietly from behind the *jacál* and grabbed and lifted the kicking, growling old woman!

I heard her hollering and looked out the window just in time to see the native set her in front of him crosswise, still kicking, and off they sped. A few yards into the woods, according to Ábu, he stopped and tied her hands and feet with a rope and a soft-gray cloth as she spit, kicked, and continued cursing him. He managed to roll her to the back of his horse and tie her face down before mounting and galloping a short way off. At some point, he stopped and lifted Ábu back down off the horse and rolled her into the brush. He then untied her hands and kept the rope. Apparently, Ábu managed to untie the cloth around her feet and run back home. When she got back, I noticed her staring long and hard at that piece of gray cloth she had carried back with her. I asked her where that came from, but she had just shaken her head, folded it, and tucked it in her herb satchel.

My father teased her and said that the Comanche probably didn't like the way Ábu smelled. Ábu responded by saying she smelled better than the butt end of that Native! Oh, Ábu threw her head back and laughed and laughed at that. The rest of us tried to imagine her sniffing around in the middle of a frightening abduction. Surely she didn't!

We both smiled, giggled, and shook our heads as we imagined the sight of those two.

I do know that Ábu bragged often of the fact that she herself came from indios feroces, fierce Indians, of the Yucatán, a state in Mexico located on the Gulf of Mexico. Her sacrificial altares, she claimed, could bring about changes in the weather, a better harvest, and perhaps even the protection and return of loved ones. My father warned Ábu that if she wasn't careful, an out-of-control fire from her offerings would notify all the Comanche to head over for a family barbecue!

Señora and I laughed again at this thought.

"Did Ábu continue making offerings later, regardless of where you settled?" I wondered.

"Oh yes. After church our small jacáles always smelled of charred remains, indicating to my family that Sunday was Ábu›s day of worship as well. Mamá swept any runaway ashes out the door when we got home so we wouldn't track them into our bedding at night."

Señora closed her eyes just as her tiny dog reappeared, circled on her blue cloth, and sat down atop a silver hairbrush, panting and squinting up at her.

"Señorita, Caramela and I must rest now. Please, let's meet again tomorrow. I need to tell you about what happened next in Nacogdoches."

"Of course, Señora. You've shared much today and I'm very grateful! I can't get over how full and exciting your life has been. May I walk you home?"

"Oh, no, Caramela and I will be fine on our own, but thank you, Miss Rizzo," she stated, slowly stretching her legs out in front of her, preparing to rise from the milk crate. "And thank you for the coffee and the treat for my friend here, who anxiously awaits the other half!"

"You're most welcome! I can't wait to hear about Nacogdoches," I said, extending a hand to help her stand up. "After a couple of years in Nacogdoches, you spent the rest of your life right here in this town, San Antonio, right? I'm curious now just how and when you ended up in this beautiful city."

"My blessed San Antonio, city of a thousand angels. I don't regret a minute of it," she smiled, grabbing her crate with one hand and hugging me gently with the other. "But first, Nacogdoches, Miss Rizzo!"

"Certainly, Señora. I'll bring some hot cocoa for us tomorrow. These morning breezes can be quite chilling!"

"Oh, yes! Anything hot and sweet, Miss Rizzo!"

"*Alright then. If you'll excuse me, let's plan to continue tomorrow!*" I dropped my steno pad and pen inside the leather satchel, rubbed my two aching legs, and stood, reaching for the sky before beginning the familiar short walk back to my hotel.

When I turned around after just two blocks, Señora Candelaria and Caramela were nowhere to be seen.

PART III: NACOGDOCHES

CHAPTER 9:
LAREDO TO NACOGDOCHES, 1819

That same morning, I glanced down at Señora's blue cloth and noticed it now displayed a faded postcard depicting a two-story limestone building with the words "Old Stone Fort" printed below. I carefully handed her the small hot chocolate I'd brought. She thanked me and shooed Caramela off her cloth as she arranged her long, dark skirt with one hand.

"Well then, Señora! You look well rested this morning! Are you?"

"These days, I'm always well rested, my dear," she laughed. "What are we talking about today?"

"I reviewed your story so far and have a couple of questions. First, I got to wondering if every member of your family traveled together each time you moved. Who accompanied you from Laredo north to Nacogdoches, for example? That was a trip of over four hundred miles!" I quickly turned to a new page and pulled out a ballpoint pen.

We always did what Colonel Cordero or his representative asked. My father respected that man greatly and would have had it no other way. We all got pretty good at moving too. Everyone in the family gathered their few belongings and folded their own personal mission blanket and placed it inside Papá's wooden box with the others. It was such a struggle to keep possessions, but we had a few loose items that we set in a small pile on an old sheet stretched on the ground outside. The boys moved what little furniture we had to a small wooden cart, or carrito, that would be pulled by Terco, our sturdy but stubborn mule. Usually my father, Carlos, Nacho, and Justo prepared the horses and strung the other animals together for walking.

Edgar almost always accompanied us, providing an extra set of hands to help load things on the cart and mule.

Terco carried our small, sheet-wrapped pack containing everyone's clothing, a couple of cooking pans, and a few keepsakes. That pack was secured with a rope made by Ábu from agave fibers. Two small stools dangled on either side of Terco as he walked. Of course, Ábu's small rocker would be lashed to the cart somewhere. Once we saw Edgar and Papá tying everything securely, we knew it was time for our departure. Papá sometimes joined us and other times went on ahead, scouting the *camino*, the road, for danger.

We ladies mostly rode horseback with my brothers. Sometimes we'd take turns sitting on the seat of our small cart. Other times we walked alongside the horses for a change of pace. Justo alternated riding with Ábu and Mamá. As I said, my mother's "trusty neighbor" Edgar always moved with us, irritating the boys and barking orders every so often. Edgar served as a very important assistant for our family, Mamá reminded us. She scolded us to mind what he asked and help him out. Edgar rode in the back so he could watch everything as we moved through these often-unfamiliar areas. That way he could put in his two cents to point out things that might need correcting.

Edgar was the one person who checked on us frequently no matter where we lived while Papá was off riding with the soldiers. My father was quite grateful for him, most of the time. Sometimes Edgar would show up after a rain to help us make repairs around the *jacál*. He could outride my brothers when they raced and could outshoot Carlos when aiming at targets while riding bareback. Stocky and muscular, with a slow, easygoing gait, he always managed a wide smile under that mustache of his for my mother or Ábu when they asked for assistance with something. We kids never asked him for anything, with the exception of Josepha, who requested his assistance getting on and off a horse. He was one of those men who always had an intuitive understanding of people and situations around him. He was a watchman. He made it his business to know everything about everybody, and this came in handy during times of war. If we wanted to know anything about the goings on around these towns, we just had to ask Edgar.

As we ambled north toward Nacogdoches, kicking up dust and swatting flies, Ábu muttered and scowled, cursing Colonel Cordero under her breath and making her horse walk, with great agitation, around occasional puddles, small pits, or medium-sized branches that had fallen in the road. Even in her old age, my grandmother could command a horse better than most of us. Her zigzagging, however, was just another irritation that slowed us down as flies and mosquitos nearly ate us alive. Ábu carried a salve made with white yarrow that she slathered all over her face, making her look like a terrifying phantom. None of us wanted to ask to use some of it for fear that her moaning theatrics might slow the whole train down.

Nacogdoches, in some ways like Laredo, turned out to be a risky place to raise a family, as my mother would admit later. There were too many thieves and bootleggers anxious to trade weapons for horses—horses that supposedly had been previously stolen by the natives.

It was in this town that Ábu leaned over to snatch a small, green lizard and took a bad tumble off our tiny porch. She'd been seated outside on an overturned bucket braiding garlic when we heard her screaming in pain. Ever since that accident, her tongue ran unabated and she began talking to Javier, her dead husband, in her sleep. She hollered out commands, telling him to wash his face or take off his moccasins before getting into bed. She was getting to be quite difficult to manage. Mamá hushed us anytime we giggled about her ramblings or the boisterous effects of flatulence caused by our bumpy travels.

Once we settled in, Justo finally cut loose a bit from the ranch but unfortunately got involved running stolen horses up to Natchitoches, Louisiana, with some local men. He said the money was too good to pass up and the mustangs didn't belong to anyone as far as he could tell. When my father found out about it, it was another sleepless night for the family after the two rode up and walked inside. My father, frustrated after dragging his son home and bailing him out of jail, threw his gloves down on the table and pressed down forcefully on his mustache with his thumb and pointer finger.

No sooner had both of them stepped inside our *jacál* than my father turned around and roared, "Son, what the hell do you think you were doing?"

All of us took to our doorways to listen in the shadows.

"I was making money—just what the judge said, well, that's about the truth of it," Justo moaned, hanging his shaved head, arms crossed, as he leaned against the doorway.

"Did it ever occur to you that stealing horses and cattle and running 'em up north is a crime, a *big* one? THEFT, son!"

"In case you haven't noticed, Papá, there's nothing to do in this town except shovel shit at old man Craig's ranch or pick cotton at old man Kirkham's. I'm tired of doing that kind of work! I've done enough of it! There's guys making good money runnin' horses and cattle. Why can't I get a piece of it? I've been hanging around here taking care of everybody else for long enough."

My father's eyes narrowed; he looked like he wanted to punch Justo, but he kept control this time and continued, almost growling.

"If you don't have enough to do, then assign yourself to the military, son! Do something that won't get you locked up for ten years behind bars!"

"You mean do something around here that will get me an arrow in the back from angry natives? No thanks. I'd rather help dock the slave ships in La Bahía."

"You'd better think more wisely and plan more carefully, son!" my father warned, picking up and slapping his gloves back down on the table. "But first, you owe this family eight reales for the bail I just paid to free you from that jail. There's going to be a hearing, and you'd better stick around here long enough to try to defend yourself. If the judge doesn't like your story, prepare to sleep with thieves, gamblers, and murderers, because that's exactly what you'll be doing. A man is judged by the company he keeps, Justo, just remember that."

Justo, thickset and sturdy, seemed a better match for a physical fight with my father than either Nacho or Carlos, but he was not a fighter in that way. He fought with words and ideas. This seemed to be a favorite pastime of his whenever he got around Edgar or my father.

"Papá, if a man is judged by the company he keeps, why do you continue to side with the Spanish, who kill anyone who gets in their way? They killed a lot of people at Alhóndiga, at Medina five years ago, and in San Antonio too. Will you shoot me if I disagree with your ideas?"

I watched my father move closer to Justo, squint his eyes, and point a finger toward his son's chest.

"Justo, sometimes a man has to choose sides, and I've chosen the side that I believe is doing the right things for our people."

My brother crossed his arms, unafraid. "Edgar said in war, there's no discussion—it's either you fuck them or they'll fuck you, is that the way it is?"

Excuse my profanity, Miss Rizzo. Somewhere my brother had picked up that awful word and we were shocked to hear it, but that's what he said to my father.

By this time, my father's face had turned a crimson red. Veins stuck out in thick, blue rivers coursing up and down his neck. Still, he held himself in check, though he stood as tall as he possibly could and positioned himself even closer to Justo's face.

"Son," he growled, "do not use such language around this *jacál*, you hear me? I need to speak to Edgar about the vulgarities he is teaching my sons. I don't care if you are twenty-five years old, you need to watch your mouth around here. That's *enough* out of you!"

As calmly as ever, Justo looked at him and repeated his question. Josepha, Nieves, and I creeped closer but ducked low behind the wooden half-wall to our dining area. It wasn't like Justo to fold; my father had to know that.

"I'm asking you, Papá, is this the way it is, honestly, when it comes to war or living around people whose ideas are not the same as yours? I'm not seeing a lot of negotiations going on, are you?"

"We don't negotiate with rebels, Justo. I'm fighting for what I feel in my heart to be right, not because I intend to hurt or kill someone. True justice and fairness are always a matter of opinion. Once I give my word, I'm an honorable man, and I carry out orders. Let there be no question in my commander's mind whether or not I will be there to support him and the Crown."

Justo never could leave well enough alone.

"But in the end, it's the same, isn't it? If, by fighting for what you believe or think to be right, you have to knock off a few natives, Americanos, Mexicans, or Tejanos, then what Edgar said is true, isn't it?"

"I can't talk sense into you, Justo. Stop listening to Edgar. I mean it. And that's an order!" Papá stomped off through the *jacál* toward the back door, opened it, and sat himself down to cool off outside.

"Señora! I'm trying to absorb your father's words. What does a father do in times like that? What argument can he make? How does he justify his position in the face of sons who don't believe as he does? I feel like these must have been timeless trials. I completely

understand how these kinds of family conflicts must have developed, Señora, I truly do. How did Nacogdoches compare to Laredo as far as the land, the people? You'd gone so much further north; I imagine the environment seemed different in some ways."

"I can't say what all the heads of households did in times such as this, but I can tell you that many had to contend with differing opinions within their families. Our father stated his viewpoint, made clear his thoughts regarding loyalty, and most likely expected his sons to believe as he did. Ábu was the force of reason when tempers flared in our family."

When we first arrived in Nacogdoches, the town looked tired, withered, beat up, and war torn, with very few settlers. Many of the small *jacál*es were mere rubble piles with pitted limestone rocks strewn here and there. Broken tree limbs with dark, moldy hay could be seen scattered in different directions. Something had gone on there, we could feel it. We'd just missed something big, it seemed. I wondered why Colonel Cordero or his superiors would send us to a place like this.

"We're gonna live *here*?" Nieves asked with disappointment as soon as she saw our tiny *jacál*, its entry askew with an uneven door jamb and raggedy deer skins flagging in the breeze inside two small window frames.

"Just for a little while, sister," I assured her, putting my arm around her shoulder. "Then we get to move on to a much better place called San Antonio, where Josepha and I are hoping to work in Military Plaza. You'll get to help Mamá with Ábu and all of us will dance to the *guitarreros*, those talented guitar musicians, in the Plaza on the weekends!"

I even performed a little dance as if I had a long skirt on to cheer her up.

"Wait, you and Josepha are gonna work with the Chili Queens, right María Andrea?" Nieves asked me.

"That's what Edgar suggested. He said we're going to *love* San Antonio even better than Laredo! Well, I've never been there, but that's what all of our neighbors say about that town these days."

José Paulo, my cousin who'd joined us for this last settlement before departing for Cuba with my father, studied the details of the many rocks and long grasses used for our *jacál*. The mud and vertical beams fascinated him as well as the thatching used in between to keep the rain and critters out. Because he remained ever alert and keenly observant, we soon came to count on sweet José Paulo to be the first to tell us of any situations needing attention such as leaks, scorpions, snakes, or unannounced visitors. One of the younger newcomers to our family clan, José Paulo, at the age of fifteen, exhibited the same quick movements of Ábu and my father, with the quiet, serious nature of me and my mother. He was an easy, helpful, and welcome addition.

We finally got some history on the place. Some neighbors told of a time in 1813—a mere five years earlier—when Spanish Colonel Arredondo, feeling that certain people in Nacogdoches had conspired with rebels based in the Old Stone Fort, ordered all citizens arrested if they were suspected of taking part in any rebellious behavior.

Our friend Edgar said he'd passed through there at about that time to visit a friend whose mother was dying. When he heard about Colonel Arredondo's plan to round up rebels, he quietly spread the news, as Edgar was known to do, warning all neighbors, all *vecinos*, to stay put. Fearing they'd be picked up and thrown in jail, even those who'd never heard of the main rebels, Bernardo Gutiérrez or Augustus Magee, the neighbors mostly hid in their *jacál*es or fled town into the wilderness for a while. Edgar managed to convince the Spanish soldiers to leave him and his friend's family alone; they had more pressing concerns than aiding rebels. Besides, he assured them, they hadn't left their tiny *jacál* for days on account of helping to care for his friend's sick mother.

Edgar said he watched as Spanish soldiers, prancing into town on horseback, took great pleasure in tearing the town to pieces, battering stone walls, and burning trees, clothing, blankets, and the belongings of any suspected rebels. Afterward, a smoldering ghost town was all that remained. Evidently it was just beginning to normalize when we arrived.

Mamá, who didn't like what she was hearing from Edgar, sighed heavily, shook her head, and walked silently outside with her rosary.

Unfortunately, more trouble would find us.

My father, Nacho, and once again Carlos surprised us in September when, along with Colonel Cordero, they rode up for a visit one afternoon. They wanted to see how we were settling into our new place.

Dismounting and removing their hats, my father hugged Mamá, who then motioned for all of them to come congregate in the shade of the one barely surviving pecan tree in the yard. Nacho, tall and muscular, Carlos, tall and lean and with a leathered look from riding the ranges, and Justo, short-legged and stocky, gathered to hear each other's news. Papá and my two brothers told us they were involved in some military business keeping an eye on things near the Old Stone Fort. That fort, located at the intersection of the Old San Antonio Road and la Calle del Norte, the north street, was the very first two-story building we'd ever seen. It was not far from our latest *jacál*. I've placed a postcard showing it, right here on the cloth.

Colonel Arredondo, a man named Ignacio Pérez, and a group of soldiers had been sent to drive out a group of people they called "filibusters" who were somehow printing messages for newspapers and preparing flyers to hand out saying that Spain should get its soldiers out of Mexican territory. Evidently someone named James Long, frustrated with how boundaries between the United States and this Texas territory were being drawn, began meeting with citizens at Camp Freeman right there in Nacogdoches. He hoped to set up his own government. My family most assuredly didn't get involved with any part of it, but a lot of folks around us did. Papá told us to go about our business and never *ever* to speak so much as a word about our brothers or our father to strangers. People were taking sides and it was impossible to tell who supported what.

One day, José Paulo found a folded flyer stuck underneath the wood of the windowsill. I have it here in my pocket somewhere. Ah, yes, here it is!

Señora shakily handed over a folded, cracked, and faded piece of paper for me to see.

"I'll read it aloud, Señora. I think I can make out what it says."

Soldiers and citizens:

It is more than a year since I left my country, during which time I have labored indefatigably for our good. I have overcome many difficulties, made friends and obtained means to aid us in throwing off the insulting yoke of the insolent despotism. Rise en masse, soldiers and citizens; unite in the holy cause of our country! I am now marching to your succor with a respectable force of American volunteers who have left their homes and families to take up our cause, to fight for our liberty. They are the free descendants of the men who fought for independence in the

> *United States . . . and as brothers and inhabitants of the same continent they have drawn their swords with a hearty good will in the defense of the cause of humanity; and in order to drive the tyrannous Europeans beyond the Atlantic.*
>
> Bernardo Gutiérrez, Sept. 1, 1812

Gutiérrez was trying to mount an army against the Spanish. I didn't understand the language until Edgar translated its meaning for me. Gutiérrez and an Irish American named Colonel Magee had been meeting with officials in the Republican army. Edgar told us this military leader, Colonel Magee, rode about carrying a plain green flag. He had backing from the United States and began offering forty dollars a month and a league of Spanish land, which was 4, 428 acres, to any volunteer who'd join their Republican Army of the North to help drive the Spanish out.

I remembered that Colonel Cordero, ever the gracious gentleman, said he believed the trouble started over the boundary between Louisiana, an American territory, and Texas, a Spanish territory. James Long decided the Sabine River was not a fair boundary to divide American territory from Spanish territory. He went so far as to get himself declared chief of a new provisional government, the Long Republic! He also claimed he had backing from the United States, which he did not.

"Can you imagine, Miss Rizzo?" Señora shook her head and giggled. "*Qué cajones! What boldness!*"

I shook my head and puffed, feeling incredulous. "Well, I guess anyone can declare himself or herself chief of a new government. The question is, who will honor their new title, right, Señora? But the offer of money and land must have provided quite an incentive to join him!"

"That's exactly right. It seemed like much ado about nothing to my family at the *jacál* though. We already had our promise for a league and labor of land. As you can imagine, James Long promising this as a self-proclaimed leader of a new government became a very big concern to the Spanish military and Colonel Cordero. So, Colonel Cordero gathered his soldiers, including my father and brothers, and chased those guys right on through town all the way to the coast at La Bahía, where they met up with Spanish Governor Salcedo's fighters.

"However, before departing from our family gathering under the pecan tree, Colonel Cordero took this opportunity to throw another zinger in."

"Oh, Señora. What would that be?"

Colonel Cordero mentioned that soldiers were doing important work for the King in a place called Cuba. The King wished to train not only more soldiers there, but tailors! I saw Mamá glance at Ábu, who just rolled her eyes and sighed, "Aye, *díos mío*," right in front of Colonel Cordero!

Colonel Cordero glanced at her, then tipped his hat and closed by saying that he looked forward to seeing us all in San Antonio soon. My heart skipped a beat, and I smiled at him, just imagining the next stop in our journey. I wanted to jump and cry out, "Yes, yes! We'll be there! Maybe just take me on your horse right now!" but I kept myself in check and merely nodded politely, hands folded in front of me, before he rode off."

Señora chuckled at the memory.

Justo, who had grown a thin, dark mustache, walked in to close the remaining circle under the tree. In a quiet tone, he told us that as early as last June, James Long had taken it upon himself to declare Texas independent from Spain and, by July, he had sailed to Galveston and ordered a fort to be built at Point Bolivar to keep out any more incoming Spanish ships, called gallons or galleons. He even declared a pirate by the name of Lafitte to be governor of the island! Nieves and I could hardly believe these stories and didn't know whether to be excited or frightened. It was as if we were mere lily pads in a pond of activity—anchored to the soil and swaying at times on the surface, but never quite able to see what was really going on just below.

Spanish Colonel Pérez and his soldiers ran James Long and his new rebel friend, José Félix Trespalacios, all the way back to Louisiana. Nieves and I exhaled with relief at this conclusion. Maybe now we could dry our clothes in peace! Josepha stood, arms crossed and unimpressed, as Edgar rode up on horseback, dismounted, and joined the family circle next to her. Justo continued sharing the news.

"I'm telling you, Mamá, those Americanos have a lot of coins behind them. That's the only way James Long has been able to attract the troops that he has so far. But we've come here to put a stop to him right now," Nacho declared firmly with a nod and a smile.

"I'm very proud of these boys, Francisca," my father added. "Colonel Cordero and these boys serve King Ferdinand the Seventh by doing his good works. We try to make peace with the natives as we attempt to keep guys like James Long in check. It's a never-ending job, but it's also our duty to provide security for the new settlers of these Spanish territories." This he proclaimed proudly, glancing momentarily at each one of his sons, who'd all decided to join him--at least for now. I'd never seen him look so full of loving pride. Oh, that he could have expressed the same for those of us moving about like chess pieces for this King Ferdinand the Seventh of Spain!

It would not be the last time Colonels Pérez or Cordero would have to contend with James Long, but driving him and his followers out of Nacogdoches appeared to be successful for the time being.

That day, I felt a new energy after catching up with the latest news. I was able to put a few more pieces of the Nacogdoches puzzle together. Plus, my heart overflowed with joy at getting to see my father and brothers together again! We talked for a long time and my sisters and I fetched water and some corn tortillas filled with beans for our "guests."

After listening to all these bits and pieces about the comings and goings in Nacogdoches, most of which I'm sure Ábu didn't understand or perhaps even care about, she wandered into the circle and asked loudly, "Well, who's winning?"

My brothers laughed, looked at one another, and smiled. Justo replied, "We are, Ábu, whether we are or not, we're going to say, *we* are!"

"*Entooonces* . . . well then!" she laughed, rolling her right arm around in front of her in a motion for them to be on their way. We all laughed and hugged one another while Mamá ran off to the kitchen to gather more wrapped tortillas and cheese to send with these handsome soldiers as they took their leave.

Finally, just my mother and Ábu walked around the circle, hugging our visitors long and tightly and wiping away tiny tears; these were probably welling up on account of not knowing when or if such a reunion would ever occur again.

I fought back my own tears, watching my father and his sons mount and ride off down the dusty road, joking and laughing together. I'll never forget the serenity I felt at the sight of them riding off that day. Serenity and a desperate longing to go with them.

Señora rolled her right arm out in a gesture of displaying something and mimicked in a low voice, "Entooonces, well then. . ."

We both laughed until I caught sight of Señora's laughter turning to sniffles. I watched as a tear fell, which she quickly wiped away with a scarf. We sat silently for a few minutes. She swallowed, looked up toward the sky, and paused. I imagined the memory was a sweet one that she'd never forgotten. After some number of minutes, I slapped my steno pad closed and reached out for her hand.

"Señora, I suppose that was the end of the excitement with James Long, as far as your family was concerned."

"Oh, no!" she said, suddenly revived. I quickly reopened my pad of paper and continued to document her story.

By October, Ábu and I noticed a man riding around Nacogdoches on a tall, caramel-colored mare followed by a small band of Americanos in military formation. Our neighbors identified him as James Long. He wasn't hard to spot with his small black tie, white shirt, and soft-beige hat. Not exactly a cowboy hat, but a short-brimmed, squarish hat somewhat in the shape of a flat-roofed *jacál*. Apparently, he was back claiming the town in the name of his green flag!

Not too long after Long's show of occupying Nacogdoches, which is what Edgar said that was, Colonels Pérez and Cordero returned with their own company of Royalist soldiers to sneak up and charge right behind those rebel soldiers. The group, including my brothers and father, ran the Americanos back out of east Texas. Any men caught would be jailed as rebels to the King. Of course, these insurgents, or rebels, as everyone called them, ran their horses like the wind to escape capture. But we felt sure Colonel Cordero, with the help of my father and brothers, must have captured a few!

My family watched horses flying back and forth once again, dust hanging forever above our rubbly street. Washing laundry was fools' work. Somehow, we never got caught in the middle of this conflict, but there remained an ever-present feeling, just like that dust suspended in the air, that trouble lurked just around the corner. We didn't always know exactly what it was or who was causing it. Plus, we'd been advised to keep to ourselves, so that's mostly what we did. We sure couldn't keep our clothes clean in that town!

My father stopped in at least once a year, but he never spoke of his work, asking instead to hear what we'd been doing, as if that ever changed. He had all kinds of ideas for improving the place, but, honestly, our hearts weren't in it; our minds were already dancing toward the southern sky in colorful swirls of turquoise, yellow, and red toward San Antonio.

"Señora, if you're not too tired, could you tell me more about this Old Stone Fort shown on the postcard you brought?"

"Oh, yes! The Old Stone Fort. That was about our only diversion in Nacogdoches. We loved walking through there!"

Old Stone Fort Nacogdoches in 1885

My sisters, Edgar, and I took Ábu and Mamá to this trading post on the last Saturday of each month. A cross between a farmer's market, an import house, and the natives' swap meet, the Old Stone Fort transferred more goods, horses, and people between the United States and Texas than any place we'd seen yet. I was beginning to understand the flow of commerce from the north to the south and vice versa a little bit more.

Mamá swapped one of the boys' mission blankets for a new skirt for me and sweaters for her and Ábu. Ábu picked up small cloth bags filled with slippery elm bark, as well as clusters of dried lavender and yarrow for her medicine bag.

Edgar showed us Señor Cadieux's guns neatly lined up along a narrow wooden table. These were from folks who wanted to swap their guns for horses and cattle. Mostly natives gathered excitedly around that table, which, Edgar grumbled under his breath, explained where so many settlers' livestock ended up as well as why fighting hostile natives was getting harder and harder. Edgar said cows, calves, and horses were valued at ten dollars each, so someone could get rich selling them.

"Señora, I suppose Edgar may have accompanied you there more as a bodyguard than anything else," I smiled.

"I suppose so. Whenever young men looked sideways at any of us, Edgar would stop, put his thumbs near his belt where his pistol showed, and present a certain look of challenge. That'd be the end of it!"

Señora chuckled at the thought, adding that she and her sisters didn't stand a chance of meeting anyone new with him along.

"How did you know when it was time to leave Nacogdoches to head to San Antonio?" I asked.

"Oh! Let me explain! Ohhh . . . like the golondrinas, or swallows, catching a favorable draft, we were about to be lifted into the air to fly from our monotonous routines at last!"

Señora stood up shakily, lifted her arms out like a bird, and then slowly settled herself back down on her crate, rearranging her skirt and brushing flyaway hair from her face.

I paused writing. Picking up her hot chocolate and taking a couple of sips, she gulped, made a toast in the air toward me, and set it back down, excited to share the next part of her journey.

CHAPTER 10:
NACOGDOCHES COURIER MESSAGE

FROM NACOGDOCHES TO SAN ANTONIO

Señora Candelaria inhaled and, with a smile on her sweet, leathery face, continued. I stood up to stretch and sat back down to open my steno pad and dig out a fresh ballpoint pen.

I must tell you, I'd already learned that Colonel Cordero served as acting Spanish governor of Texas from 1805 to 1808 after serving as governor of Coahuila y Tejas, Mexico, for several years. So, even though we called him "Colonel," or "Governor," he had actively earned his titles in those capacities much earlier. Other Spanish governors such as Manuel María de Salcedo, Cristobal Dominguez, Ignacio Pérez, and Antonio María Martínez also served. But Colonel Cordero seemed like family to me.

I turned seventeen in Nacogdoches about a month before a piece of special correspondence arrived in January. Ábu spit and began issuing her usual litany of curses upon the governor, Colonel Cordero. After Nieves finished handing the courier a small cup of water to drink and offered his horse a few sips from our bucket, my mother bid goodbye to the courier as she turned toward the nearest shade with this new piece of mail.

Almost theatrically, Mamá unfolded the envelope, sighed, and snapped it high out in front of her. I saw a strange and startled look come over her face as she paused, drawing the correspondence down closer to read. The handwriting on this correspondence looked quite unusual—curvy and artistic. Mamá and I were astonished to see the signature: Colonel Cordero's wife, Gertrudis, had written it!

"That must have been unusual to receive correspondence from the wife of the former governor," I added.

"It was unheard of for us! Few women had time to learn to read and write back in those days. My mother could make out some Spanish and a little English she'd picked up from the mission fathers, but I didn't know of others. Look, I have it right here, Miss Rizzo, in my pocket. Look at this exquisite penmanship."

> *From: Honorable Doña María Gertrudis Pérez Cordero*
> *To: Esteemed Family of José Antonio Castañon*
>
> *My husband and I hope this letter finds your family well there in Nacogdoches, despite the latest filibusters and native incursions.*

"Aye, díos mío." Ábu swooned and slumped against a tree, slowly sliding down to the ground. Josepha ran over to lift her back up.

> *I am writing at the request of the Colonel, who wishes to invite one of your daughters to work with me at the Governor's Palace in San Antonio. We are hoping your youngest daughter, María Andrea, might enjoy working in the employ of the Spanish crown on matters related to the Colonel's health as well as matters relating to the upkeep of the Palace. The matters would include assisting with preparations for events and visits by foreign dignitaries.*

"Qué? Qué dice, what is she saying?" Ábu suddenly stood at attention, furrowing her brow, squinting and blinking at the tiny message.

> *If you are in agreement with this request, please report to the Governor's Palace once you get suitably settled and I will happily meet with María Andrea to review the grounds, show her to her room, and discuss official duties.*

> *You may choose to travel to San Antonio with my father, Colonel Ignacio Pérez and a company of his soldiers for increased safety if you'd like. He plans to complete his work there in Nacogdoches and return to his home here on February 2.*
>
> *We thank you for your kind attention as well as your family's ever-loyal service to his majesty, King Ferdinand VII.*
>
> *Fondly,*
> *Doña María Gertrudis Pérez Cordero, in the year of our Lord, 1820*

I sat smiling, waiting for Señora's response. She smiled back and clapped both hands on her thighs.

"Well, Miss Rizzo, there you have it! My family looked at each other and burst out laughing, hugging one another, and dancing around. Oh, such relief at last!"

Ábu turned in circles, muttering something and raising a fist to the light-blue, cloudless sky.

My heart felt full to think that Doña Cordero knew my name *and* that my assistance was being requested at the former Spanish governor's home, the Governor's Palace, in San Antonio! Colonel Cordero, according to Edgar, was increasingly fragile and in need of constant attention. This left his wife having to manage the business of their many ranches and soldiers on her own. Imagine! A woman in charge of all that!

Although this request meant another move, I remember my mother throwing her head back and smiling to the heavens. She hugged me while holding this little, withered envelope to her chest, so ecstatic was she about my new job prospect.

By this time, Ábu quietly shook her head up and down, gently took my face in her hands, and whispered, "Finally *mí nieta*, my granddaughter! At last! Someone gets to see how the other half lives!"

Honestly, it didn't take long for my elation to be overcome by doubts. I didn't know anything about Doña Cordero or any other member of the Spanish aristocracy. How do those people live? How will I be treated? I even wondered if my mother could get along without me when I took on these new duties, as all of us had shared the duties of running our many households. We women took care of our many *ranchitos* without the help of my father and most of my brothers. These were tough jobs, especially since we were feeling somewhat abandoned after my father and cousin José Paulo took the King's assignment and sailed off to Cuba.

Could Ábu endure another move? Intermittently, I brushed aside these fears and began to dream of a whole new future for myself. I simply knew I had to do this. Here was an opportunity I couldn't walk away from. I'd been waiting for my life to begin somehow, some way, and here it was, right in front of me. I had to cling tightly, come what may.

What I was about to learn and witness at the Governor's Palace would change the course of my life forever in ways I couldn't have imagined.

Señora paused and put her hands together in prayer. She lowered her head for a few minutes as I waited silently, wondering if this was too much for her already today. When she resumed, she spoke haltingly.

Let me back up a minute. In Laredo, just before leaving for Nacogdoches, I ran into the young courier . . . the same one who delivered the message to my family about moving from Laredo to Nacogdoches. He was a sweet and good man whose name I found out to be Juan Silverio Flóres de Abrego. My mother and Ábu said they knew and respected his family, also from Mission San Juan Bautista del Río Grande. Now his family-owned ranches around the San Antonio area, they said. Well, I saw him first in Laredo, then again in the Nacogdoches farmer's market, where he spoke to me and bought me flowers. I never told Mamá.

He turned up again in San Antonio a few years later, looking for me. He was such a good and loving man. Silverio would eventually become my first husband.

Señora looked toward the sky and began speaking to her former husband.

"Aye, Juanito, may God bless you wherever your spirit lies. Francisca, your beautiful daughter, and I prayed for your return every night; we missed you so. We didn't know for sure whose cavalry you'd taken up with nor which side you were fighting for. We never heard a word for such a long, long time."

"That must have been very hard, Señora. He just disappeared?" I asked.

"Yes, dear. That was quite common in those days of constant skirmishes. Many women lost family members, often never knowing where or how they died. But eventually, after many *attempts to find out what happened to him, I got the news that he had been killed, most likely in the fall of 1831.*

Look here; look what I found of his!"

CHAPTER 11: SILVERIO'S JOURNAL, 1818

NACOGDOCHES

Señora pulled out a small, yellowed sheet of folded paper. She shakily handed it over to me, and I read it aloud after she explained what it was.

"Miss Rizzo, that is a page from Silverio's travel book that I found later. As a courier, he was accustomed to keeping careful notes of his whereabouts. This entry is from Nacogdoches in 1818. I would have been about fifteen years old at the time."

Juan Silverio Flóres de Abrego's Day Book
Saturday, November 21, 1818 (translated from Spanish)

I saw a lovely young lady smelling cantaloupes at the mercado in Nacogdoches this morning. I completed a small purchase of

strawberries for me and my horse and stepped over next to her. She stared down at my boots for quite some time, and when she finally looked up, I felt sure that I had seen her somewhere before. She smiled shyly and stepped hurriedly around me to leave. I watched her go, a long, shiny, black braid flapping down her back as she slipped down an alleyway. I managed to get back on my horse to follow without her knowing. Around San Augustín Plaza, she disappeared. I tried to find her but wasn't successful today. My only hope will be returning to the market on Saturdays. I am determined to go every week for a month in hopes of seeing her there.

But no luck . . . no luck the next day . . . I couldn't find her.

Ah, finally, I found her! Unfortunately, she had to see me fall off my horse upon arrival at the market, but I bounced right back up, brushed myself off, and said hello as she passed by. Her lively, dark eyes seemed somewhat interested, but I could hardly catch up to her. When I finally did, I found out her name: María Andrea. Last name? Unknown. She wouldn't tell me.

I introduced myself, Silverio, but when I asked to accompany her in the market, she didn't reply. I respectfully took the liberty to walk with her very slowly, holding and turning my hat nervously as we wove our way through elevated crates of vegetables, stacked fruit, dead partridges, and pralines.

I only stopped to buy her some flowers. Mrs. Piñeda, the seller, said I didn't have any credit with her, but upon looking over and seeing María Andrea, our eyes met for one brief instant. She understood my predicament and agreed, eyeing me warily as she tied the small bundle of daisies. She wrote my name down for next time.

So, I must remember: I owe Mrs. Piñeda two small coins. María Andrea laughed when I said with a bow, "For you. Flores, flowers, from Señor Flóres!" Mrs. Piñeda, on the other hand, did not look amused.

María Andrea blushed, then thanked me and quickly ran off to buy some vegetables. She stopped back by my side briefly to tell me that her family is moving to San Antonio soon. My heart is broken. I sadly watched her flit off down the center aisle of the outdoor mercado, long dress and apron held to the left with one hand and her flowers and small paper sack in the other. One long, dark braid bounced one way then the other as if she were skipping. Mrs. Piñeda's eyes narrowed, and she twisted her mouth murmuring, "No cuentes con ella" (meaning: "don't count on it").

"Isn't this the sweetest notation ever, Miss Rizzo? I cried when I found his travel notebook. It contained this and other affectionate thoughts and plans penciled in his unmistakably neat printing. There it was, slipped between other pages, the small notebook placed with another in his small bag of holey socks."

The two of us sat quietly, feeling for breezes, welcoming a warming sun, and sipping the last of our coffee as we watched passersby taking pictures of themselves in front of the Alamo. Caramela appeared and we took this as our cue to wrap things up for the day. We agreed to reconvene the next day, and Señora offered to bring marranitos from the bakery across the street. These pig-shaped gingerbread cookies were a favorite of hers, she said, so I bade her goodbye and agreed to try one tomorrow. She felt like family to me already.

PART IV:
SAN ANTONIO

CHAPTER 12:
A MOSAIC OF EARLY SAN ANTONIO

San Antonio

Because I knew Señora Candelaria would be talking about San Antonio today, I brought a small copy of a painting of Colonel Cordero I found at the library. In it, he is pictured with one knee on the ground, drawing with a stick what may have been military plans to a group of mounted soldiers. His white horse stands obediently nearby, reins cascading from its muzzle to the dry earth. I awaited Señora's arrival, bundling up against those familiar early-morning breezes hustling down Market Street, as I seated myself on the familiar curb once again.

At last, I saw her figure moving, almost flying toward me, it seemed. As she approached, I hugged her gently and moved so she could get settled. After carefully placing her crate down and seating herself, she took a moment to arrange the same blue cloth on the ground in front of her. Today, she placed a picture of the Governor's Palace upon it. Off to the side, she promptly set down a small paper bag of what I imagined were pastries.

"Buenas días, Señora! Today I've brought something for you to look at."

I leaned in and set my picture on the cloth next to hers. Without a word, she slowly reached down, picked it up, and moved it vertically and then horizontally in front of her eyes, squinting, for nearly a minute.

"Ah, yes, that's him! Colonel Manuel Antonio Cordero!" She smiled. "My father adored him, Miss Rizzo. Mamá didn›t know whether to trust him or not; he certainly took her husband off on military campaigns too often. Ábu, well she cursed the very air we shared *with him, for her own reasons. I came to form certain opinions of him, which I'll tell you about shortly."*

Before Señora launched into her story, I quickly prepared, dating the next few pages of my notebook and readying to take notes. I felt certain this narrative could be broken down and written up to share in one of the Historical Texas columns. Caramela approached and sat next to me for just a moment, staring into my eyes, then at the pastry bag, as I petted her soft coat. Suddenly, distracted by the smell of something else, or sensing that I would not indulge her, she stood and strutted off down the street, heading directly toward the Alamo once again.

• • •

I hardly know where to begin. San Antonio of the early 1820s seemed so very exciting to seventeen-year-old me, my sister Nieves at nineteen, and Josepha at twenty-one. Josepha promptly became engaged to a man she met who worked at a small stable near the newly opened Cassiano's Mercantile. She soon married and moved in with him to help with his mother. She was so proud to let us know that his mother was teaching her to read and write Spanish, a language our family spoke but had only learned to decipher crudely, mostly out of necessity when messages arrived via courier.

"I'm learning to read and write, sisters! It's all part of my plan for the day that I come into some acreage in the future. I hope you'll both remember what I told you!" Josepha winked and whispered, "Don't forget, property ownership is the first step," in my ear one evening, smiling deviously, before departing Mamá's *jacál*. Honestly, I felt a pang of jealousy.

Nieves and I had helped Mamá and Ábu settle into a small *jacál* on Calle Dolorosa, "Sorrowful Street," near Arroyo San Pedro, "Saint Peter Gully or Creek." Her *jacál* was situated near the northern corner of a Delgado family property. I'd been given two weeks before having to report to the Governor's Palace, so I spent that time exploring town with my sisters. The weather, sunny and breezy with cool mornings, caressed us like old friends.

The weight of my past, dusty and bleak, lifted, and somehow I could look around and consider things through new lenses of possibilities. There we were, surrounded by all kinds of things on the move: busy people in the marketplace, the San

Antonio River, horses clop-clopping down the streets, and colorful bougainvilleas swaying along with Indian paintbrushes, roses, and fragrant herbs. Even Ábu, in her weakened state from traveling, seemed content for a change, staking off ground to cultivate a backyard herb garden once again.

Nieves, even while helping Mamá, met and courted a handsome, feisty young soldier from Nacogdoches named Guillermo. He made Ábu laugh with his fast-talking tales of skirmishes in the woods, sideswiping trees while dodging arrows, bees, and bullets. Mamá often sat listening to him with an uneasy look, most likely worrying that her sons might be fighting alongside such carefree and seemingly nonchalant soldiers. Guillermo unfortunately got shot in a siege not too long after his proposal to Nieves. Someone reported that he'd quickly scrambled up a tree to escape capture, but since the tree had had no leaves at the time, he had instead become an easy target. Nieves' face lost its glow, and she swore she'd never love again. Josepha and I doubted that.

As for me, I felt sure I'd find a husband in this town when I wanted to. But I didn't want to have to depend on that. I needed to accomplish something by myself. San Antonio sparkled with the lives of all kinds of people. We found ourselves among pleasant Canary Islanders and Tejanos who'd settled this area long before the rest of us arrived. The last current of incoming settlers seemed to be from foreign countries across the ocean or from the United States to the north. Some settlers even brought slaves with them. I suppose they hadn't heard that the Mexican government didn't allow slaves, and San Antonio seemed like mostly Mexican territory at this time.

One day, the three of us sisters wandered into Cassiano's Mercantile to look around and see what merchandise lined the shelves. Mr. Cassiano, a tall, friendly *güero*, a fair-skinned and light-haired man, seemed very kind. He asked us who we were and where we'd come from. He and his two older sons had just arrived in San Antonio themselves, he said. The whole family was as anxious to learn more about the place as we were!

While we were talking with him, a lady with pinned-up hair entered, wearing a fancy, long, light-green cotton skirt with a white cotton blouse half covered with a light-gray decorative shawl. Completely ignoring the three of us, she stepped around us, interrupted our conversation, and greeted Mr. Cassiano. She then engaged him in conversation, so we politely stepped back.

"Do you sell rods for curtains, Mr. Cassiano?" She crossed her arms and pivoted, looking askance at the three of us. Eyeing us up and down, her face exhibited a strange look of disregard, as if we were some kind of unwelcome intrusion.

"We do, Mrs. Dickinson, how many would you like?"

"Just two will do. Twenty-four inches is what I need to hold the fabric I bought to cover each window." Her reply and demeanor suggested that she came from royalty. While Mr. Cassiano showed her the rods, we took our leave, but not without chirping cheerful goodbyes.

"Thank you, Mr. Cassiano!" Nieves sang out loudly.

"We'll stop back soon to see what else is new," Josepha chimed in happily, looking back at Mrs. Dickinson.

"Great, ladies! Welcome to San Antonio. I hope to see you again!"

At Mr. Cassiano's reply, Mrs. Dickinson turned with that same disgruntled look upon her face, eyeing us up and down unfavorably. Once we got outside, I asked my sisters what that was all about.

"She looked at us as if we were *piojosas*, lice ridden," I whispered.

"She did! Acted as if we'd stolen something from her," Josepha puffed.

"Yeah, she definitely had some kind of problem with us," Nieves added. "Maybe she thought we were flirting with one of her newly arrived love interests!" We all burst out laughing at the thought and began skipping down the street, forgetting for the moment all about it.

Arm in arm, the three of us happily continued our investigation of a few shops along the way home. Josepha bought us each a coconut cookie from a nearby *panadería*, a bakery, which made our hands quite sticky. She bought one for Mamá and Ábu as well, though she asked to have theirs wrapped.

Once we were home, we told Ábu and Mamá about our excursion and strange encounter at Cassiano's. Ábu pursed her lips and raised her eyebrows a couple of times but remained completely silent. Mamá, on the other hand, said she'd noticed something similar while walking with our mule for water and food staples across town. Mamá brushed it off, saying that we were new to San Antonio and that "people just didn't know us yet." Ábu, on the other hand, again scrunched up her face and rolled her eyes when Mamá offered that explanation.

"That reminds me, Miss Rizzo! I have something here for you to try—a marranito. It's a pig-shaped gingerbread cookie!" Señora pulled two gingerbread cookies from the small bag on her cloth and handed me one.

"This is delicious!" I cried, after sampling a bite. "It reminds me of Christmas for some reason. Oh, I know—gingerbread houses, of course! Mmm. Thank you for introducing me to sowbelly cookies, Señora. I never thought I'd be eating such a spicy delicacy on the streets of San Antonio!"

"You mentioned that San Antonio felt like a welcome change for all of you, away from ranching and the rough, unsettled territories of Nacogdoches and Laredo. Did you feel somewhat safer from attacks by native people who traversed the area, and perhaps less focused on military maneuvers?"

"Señorita Rizzo, San Antonio has always been a military town, as far as I know. In the early 1800s, the Alamo was originally a presidio, a fortified military settlement, reinforced to serve as such on account of several attempts to take over San Antonio. Soon it included a mission church, and several other missions were built nearby: Mission Concepción, Mission San José, Mission San Juan, and Mission Espada. All of the missions needed defending, for the cattle and horses each owned in addition to the holy golden relics protected inside. As more and more settlers arrived, unhappy natives attempted to raid peoples' horses and livestock in retaliation for their intrusions upon territories that had long been traversed by their tribespeople. Presidio soldiers got involved in tracking down many thieves. The military presence here has been unmistakable and quite necessary. In some ways we felt safer here, but we became aware of more acts of thievery and therefore aware of increasing consequences for those breaking the law."

"I know you mentioned this, but can you describe the people who lived in San Antonio when your family arrived in 1820?" I asked.

There were other indigenous people whose families first settled in and around the area many, many years before we arrived. A few of these indigenous folks took refuge in the mission system here and remained as citizens by the time we arrived. Some helped translate between soldiers and native tribesmen or between native tribesmen and priests. Before Spanish colonization, we must remember this area along the river had been occupied for thousands of years by various cultures of indigenous people who were incredibly self-sufficient and treated the land with great reverence and respect. The Payaya or Yanaguana Indians were part of one tribe that called San Antonio home for centuries before we ever got here.

Another group, the Canary Islanders, or Isleños, were also here before my family arrived. Sixteen families had been sent to San Antonio by Spain in the early 1700s as part of a plan to add jovial, easygoing settlers to a relatively barren San Antonio. The Spanish king figured the Isleños would mix and create families easily with all groups, and they did. I learned that some of the Canary Islanders volunteered to relocate to San Antonio, while others said their family had been forced to settle here. I personally never met a Canary Islander I didn't like. These families seem to have been chosen deliberately and with great care.

Then there were the local Tejanos, Texans of Mexican heritage whose forefathers had worked the ranches and land for years and years before northern settlers ever set foot here. Many Tejanos settled further north in Texas territory as conflicts arose in some of the southern Mexican states. San Antonio was Mexican territory when we arrived, but we'd just come from areas controlled by the Spanish. Some referred to the incoming *norteamericanos*, or North Americans, as Texians. But a Texian might be a person from France, Italy, Germany, or some other place as well. It was just a term we used to distinguish them from the Tejanos of Mexican heritage who had established themselves in these areas many, many years ago. Some of the indigenous folks preferred to be called Indios, rather than Tejanos. San Antonio was and still is a rich tapestry, a colorful mosaic of people! The Spanish king encouraged intermarrying, so the amazing possibilities in people you see today are the result of King Ferdinand the Seventh's vision for peaceful settlements.

In April of 1836, after the Battle of the Alamo and the subsequent battle at San Jacinto, Texas became an independent republic. It remained so for almost ten years. After that, it became part of the United States. So much volatility! You can see how a child born in San Antonio might be considered Spanish, Tejano (a Mexican Texan), Texian (an Anglo settler of Mexican Texas), Mexican, and later, a United States citizen. So much depended on what year a person was born, where the family had come from in the first place, or how long their family had been settled here.

Spanish-controlled areas of Texas, however, followed the dictates of the Spanish king. Mexican Texas was controlled by the Emperor of Mexico City, who was also quite far away, and of course later, the Republic of Texas was self-governed for over nine years by its own leaders. Today we know Texas as a part of the United States of America, like all the other states that follow federal and state mandates and make their own local laws.

In 1819, one year before my family arrived, San Antonio had been devastated by terrible flooding. The water rushed so fast and so high, it combined San Pedro Springs with the San Antonio River! It picked up *jacál*es and carried them miles downstream. Many animals and people drowned; others were led by Governor Antonio María Martínez to higher ground on homemade rafts. People still talked about the damage by the time we arrived, and many homes and government buildings, including the Governor's Palace where I stayed, showed water marks over a foot high on the walls! I'd never seen anything quite like that.

Our new *vecinos*, or neighbors, warned us of speaking out against the government, whichever one that might be. They told of a time in 1813 when Colonel José Juaquín de Arredondo, a Spanish military official intent on reminding everyone of royal authority, began seeking out rebels of the King among the villagers here in San Antonio. He chose three villagers a day for two weeks and shot them in front of the others right over there in Military Plaza. He then imprisoned women and children thought to be disloyal at La Quinta, a hastily built building that used to be right over there on the main square. They were forced to grind corn and make thousands of tortillas to feed Spanish troops. Arredondo confiscated every gun in town and took possession of homes and property belonging to anyone he suspected of challenging the authority of the Spanish crown. This seemed to be a familiar story, one that my brother Carlos had shared with us at an earlier time.

Between Arredondo and his henchman, Ignacio Elizondo, who ran down and killed even more suspected rebels fleeing San Antonio, it probably explained why, even seven years later, there were very few people living in San Antonio when we first got there. Those that remained seemed understandably quiet around strangers and suspicious of new settlers, not knowing which way their loyalties were leaning.

As soon as Mamá and Ábu heard this kind of talk, they were terrified and quickly set about arranging a dinner for our entire family. That evening, they warned *all* of us, my brothers as well, never to speak of our father's work. We were instructed to say only that he went away on a military campaign and, so far, had not returned. This was the truth, and that's what we told anyone who asked.

"But your family supported the Spanish king, so why would you need to worry?" I asked, confused now.

"Yes, Miss Rizzo, San Antonio clearly retained Spanish supporters when we arrived, but so much anti-Loyalist sentiment was stirring, not only among the residents, but within the Mexican military patrolling from time to time as well. Remember, San Antonio was one of the last Spanish strongholds in Texas. It was the capital of Texas at one time when much of Texas was Mexican territory. Many Mexicans from the interior didn't like what they saw going on at the hands of the Spanish military here. Soon, people started despising American settlers coming in as well."

"Was there anything else going on at this time to cause friction between the Spanish and the Mexican governments?"

"Oh, yes! This had to do with the native people and trading, something Edgar reminded us about."

When San Antonio began losing out on materials to trade on account of its dwindling population, Louisiana became a commerce hot spot. Natives and Americans from the north swapped horses, slaves, guns, and other goods there. Edgar told us that certain Natives were stealing from settlers' ranches and even some of the missions around San Antonio. They'd run stolen livestock up to Natchitoches, Louisiana, to trade for guns. The North Americans who began flowing in befriended some of the native people and freely gave them arms to keep the peace, not understanding that the consequences of their actions only meant more armed conflicts. In some ways, this sort of trade leveled the playing fields of war, as they say.

Also, the Mexican government didn't allow slave holding, so landholders in Mexican territory—north of San Antonio but south of the United States—who used slaves to grow and pick cotton classified them as "servants." Sometimes they got away with it, sometimes they didn't. As more and more *norteamericanos* received leagues and labors of land, some of them hung their hopes on raising cotton and getting rich doing it. They felt they needed slaves to help with that, since that's the way they'd raised cotton in the United States. Mexican President José López de Santa Anna, however, didn't agree and wanted *norteamericano* immigration stopped.

While we were living in Nacogdoches, that trading post that we'd enjoyed so much in the Old Stone Fort was also a hot spot where unhappy farmers, ranchers, and disgruntled Americans could meet and talk. James Long, the leader of the Republic Army of the North, began using that trading post to incite rebellion. Governor Martínez sent Colonel Ignacio Pérez with over five hundred men to destroy the army that Long had created. While they were at it, Colonel Pérez's men investigated several ranches and farms on the Mexican side where Americans had set up cotton farms. They burned their cabins, confiscated their food, and ran their horses and mules off. They warned the natives in the area not to trade with any Americans. This trading post was a place my family was very familiar with back when all this was going on. We didn't know it then, but we'd been right in the thick of this risky business.

Shortly after we'd settled in San Antonio, Edgar told us about some runaway slaves who'd surrendered to Colonel Pérez in Nacogdoches recently. They'd run away from their master, a cotton planter in Western Louisiana. They were forced to join a march of rebel prisoners back to San Antonio. Governor Martínez, having no safe place to house these incoming prisoners nor food to feed them, sent them all off to Monterrey, Mexico, for interrogation under the watchful eye of a small group of soldiers. Governor Martínez solved that dilemma for the time being by sending those poor slaves into southern Mexican territory.

As winter approached, however, poor Governor Martínez was at his wit's end. He apparently sent the Spanish viceroy a message saying that he would no longer be responsible for defending and controlling our province here. People were starving, soldiers were defecting, and there were little to no resources for anyone.

"How was your family getting this information, Señora? That seems fairly sensitive, militarily." I wondered aloud.

"Edgar. Edgar knew all the couriers. He made it his business to know everything about everyone! People liked him, so they'd tell him things. Yes, he surprised us with some of the things he knew. Our family could trust him; he was like an uncle or a big brother to me."

"So, was that the end of Governor Martínez's term then? It sounds like he felt completely abandoned and ignored by the Spanish king at this point."

Governor Martínez turned out to be the last Spanish governor of Texas. His outcry actually sparked a turning point, but nobody knew it at the time. As the governor lamented in despair over the deteriorating condition of San Antonio, several Americans rode into town. One, a wealthy landowner named James Kirkham, was looking for his runaway slaves. Another, James Forsythe, was searching for somebody no one had ever heard of, and a man by the name of Moses Austin arrived, seeking permission to start a colony of settlers two hundred families strong. Leaving off any mention of slaves for his proposed colony, Austin merely said that families would be encouraged to grow cotton to compete in the world's latest craze for things made from soft, fluffy fibers. Austin's proposal would offer a feasible solution to San Antonio's struggling growth and development: enticing more settlements by attaching offers for land to those who settled. Tejanos and *norteamericanos* agreed on one thing: Texas needed more settlers. If those settlers were intent on growing cotton, a very valuable commodity for San Antonio, then so be it.

A plan was devised where *empresarios*, or contractors, who introduced new settlers would receive 66,774 acres for each two hundred families. That seemed very inviting to these healthy entrepreneurs with money on their minds. It would have been inviting to us too, but of course we didn't qualify without a male head of household.

"*So, your family arrived a year after a torrent of rain and flooding, at a time of rising tensions between the Mexican and Spanish governments, and when more settlers and entrepreneurs—mostly from the United States and Europe, I presume—were being allowed to cross the border into Texas like ants heading for sugar! Gaining that much land as an incentive would be very inviting.*"

We laughed, Señora pointing as she spied a couple of ants carrying a dead grasshopper down the street at that exact moment. Señora sighed and shook her head.

"*Aye, yes, the times were so chaotic! But I had a job to do at the Governor's Palace. Mamá and Ábu settled in doing other peoples' laundry, while Nieves took a job assisting a sickly neighbor. We were so busy, we just didn't preoccupy ourselves with political things too much.*"

"Did you even notice more settlers coming into San Antonio?" I asked with skepticism.

"*Well, yes, that we noticed. Because with all these norteamericanos and Europeans coming in, new businesses started popping up and Military Plaza practically turned into a nightclub. But with the increase in immigrants, more Mexican military personnel arrived to oversee the situation because Mexican President Santa Anna, as I mentioned, was not happy about the influx."*

"Were there clashes in town between the *norteamericanos* and the citizens of Béxar in San Antonio?"

The tension really lay between the Mexican government, Spanish occupation, and worries of which of the two governments the *norteamericanos* would respect and support. In 1821, Agustín de Iturbide, a Royal military officer, defected to the side of the Mexican rebels and declared Mexico free from Spanish control after decades of turmoil. Before he did, he drafted the Plan of Iguala, a call for independence from Mexico which firmly established the Catholic religion to the exclusion of all others in Mexican territory. It also established a rule for complete social equality among the rich and poor alike, to include all ethnic groups.

New settlers accepted the terms quite readily in exchange for so much acreage, but, make no mistake about it, many secretly resented it. They'd come from areas where families had the freedom to choose their faith and only certain people were entitled to privileges.

Father Refugio de la Garza, parish priest of San Antonio de Béxar, kept very busy meeting and bestowing blessings upon the newly converted settlers and their families. Each family received an official certificate as proof of their compliance. Aye, we'd see Father de la Garza bumping up and down the streets all day in his oxcart, heading this way and that, mopping his forehead in the heat and meeting with people who had to sign their agreements before he'd hand out certificates stating that they now belonged to the Catholic faith.

The Spanish eventually took their leave after 1821, but soon Texas's Mexican officials in the capital , Mexico City, had to decide what to do about all these *norteamericanos* who continued flowing into Texas, buying up land, being deeded land as promised, and bringing slaves to work cotton plantations. As I mentioned, Mexico had outlawed slaves. Less than a decade later, a new law prohibited *norteamericanos* from entering Texas at all—with or without slaves.

But before this later conflict with the *norteamericanos*, and going back to our early time in San Antonio, Stephen F. Austin and his party, the first and largest group of Anglo-American settlers, arrived in San Antonio in August of 1821. Stephen F. Austin was the son of Moses Austin, the man who'd earlier proposed starting a colony of settlers in San Antonio. Authorized by the Mexican government to introduce three hundred families, Stephen Austin entered with the guidance of Juan Seguín, a longtime resident and well-respected rancher from the area. Stephen's father, Moses, had developed solid, approved plans for this colony of nearly three hundred land recipients before he died of pneumonia, leaving his son to carry out his dream. Interestingly, the "Old Three Hundred" group of settlers arrived in Mexican Texas with over four hundred slaves, who would become part of the colony as well.

• • •

"Oh dear, it's getting late and we haven't even gotten to the part about your work at the Governor's Palace yet, Señora! I'm very sorry if my questions took you off topic; it's all so very interesting. I'm grateful that you can remember so many details and I'm fortunate to get these memories down on paper. However, I don't want to tire you out too much, so what do you say if we call it a day for now? I can't thank you enough, really, for agreeing to share all of this. It's a gold mine of information for those of us who've been quite confused by so much of Texas's history!"

I tucked my pad and pens away and held her tiny, fragile hands for a moment, smiling and admiring her sweet face. I then gently helped her to her feet.

"Yes, good idea. I'll need to find Caramela before I start heading back. But shall we meet here again tomorrow, dear? This next part of my life is very lively! And just to be clear, leaving all those ranches behind meant, well, truly leaving behind all of our ranches, leagues, and labors forever, though I didn't give it a thought at the time. Somewhere in that time before we'd left for San Antonio, I'd patched my last jacál, hung my last bit of laundry across bushes to dry, and just didn't know it. Somewhere in there, I'd traveled the Laredo Road for the last time and crossed rivers atop horses, never to travel that way again. Life is a journey, Miss Rizzo, and we never really know where or when our last stop will be!"

"Hmm, well this isn't ours, I hope! I'm looking forward to hearing more, Señora. Yes, let's meet again tomorrow morning right here."

Once again I hoisted the bulky leather satchel over one shoulder. As soon as Caramela appeared to accompany Señora, I turned to begin the short walk back to my hotel. I pondered *the truth of her final statement as I wandered west toward my hotel and into the warmth of a colorful setting sun.*

Hair comb image courtesy of OliveOriginalStudio on Etsy

CHAPTER 13:
SAN ANTONIO, 1820

For our meeting today, I arrived to find that Señora Candelaria was already seated and had placed a decorative black lacquer Spanish hair comb and an ornately embellished Spanish fan on the small blue cloth in front of her.

"Good morning, Señora!" I began. "I'm excited to hear more about your time in San Antonio. I see that you've brought a couple of very beautiful artifacts today."

"Yes, I have. These will remind you as I speak that, upon arriving in San Antonio in 1820, I was entering a world where Spanish aristocracy ruled. On this cloth, I've placed treasures given to me by my friend Doña Gertrudis Cordero, who said they'd been sent from the Colonel's family in Spain. She used them and later gifted them to me!"

"They're exquisite, Señora! I can tell by the scrolling of golden embellishments that these look more Spanish than Mexican," I added. "May I pick them up to look more closely?"

"Of course, my friend! They've been through floods, fights, family relocations, fandangos, and more, so being examined now would be their pleasure!" she cackled.

At this time, the year is 1820. The women of the Castañon family, including our increasingly brittle and verbally obstreperous Ábu, have just resettled in San Antonio de Béxar. We traveled there at the request, once again, of Señor Cordero, who by then had reached the age of sixty-seven. To show his gratitude to my father and my family for years of sacrifice and support, the governor's wife, Doña Gertrudis, requested my service at the Governor's Palace! You remember her request arrived by means of her personal written correspondence sent by courier.

Once we got settled in town, Ábu began shouting out, "Well it's about time someone in this family gets to live like a Spaniard!" to passersby in the alleyway as she worked in her small herb garden out back. Mamá spent more and more time trying to quiet her and keep her busy. She was like a small child that we had to keep our eyes on all the time.

The Governor's Palace—aye, *díos mío*! I saw living quarters that I could never have imagined! There were wooden carved benches with red velvet seat coverings and bedroom furniture with ornate, leafy artistry and delicate gold paint, all having been sent from Spain. Window coverings cascaded to the floor with so much textured fabric, I could've made long skirts for every woman and child in Laredo from them! Room followed room with Saltillo tiles spilling out, creating narrow walkways running down the length of either side of the inner courtyard. Stone arches crowned each doorway along the walkway and each door opened to view a luscious interior courtyard adorned with roses, hibiscus, and carefully manicured lemon and lime trees. This beautiful greenery surrounded a central fountain depicting an angel with a bird held high in one hand and another hand reaching down for a small dog running beside. My senses floated to the heavens every time I passed through this courtyard!

Immediately to the left of the entry to the comandancia, the military headquarters, as the Palace was called, a long stuccoed dining room provided ample space for a long, dark, carved wooden table with sturdy benches on each side. This dining room showcased a simple fireplace with logs stacked against one wall, while a few ornately carved high-back chairs lined another.

Passing through the dining hall to the right, a semicircular staircase wound up to the rooftop, where assistants washed laundry and hung things to dry. Below the stairwell, three small, colorfully painted terracotta pots waited patiently atop a carved wooden chest for an opportunity to impress guests. These pots, often carried to the dining table filled with fragrant blossoms from the courtyard, were for special dinners, adding a simple but elegant touch to the table.

The Palace rooms had been laid out in a familiar Spanish-style quadrangle, with the governor's residence at the back left making up one large room; a chapel for private prayers; a small room that served as a beauty parlor for Doña Gertrudis and her visitors; and a room for selling commissary goods: military guns, bridles, saddles, saddle blankets, and religious icons. Along one wall in the commissary, burlap sacks of dried goods, such as rice and corn, were stacked atop a table.

Two groundskeepers lived in a small outbuilding to the south. Two assistants and two cooks stayed together in a small inside room with bunks off to the left of the courtyard. Along the right walkway, Doña Gertrudis reserved larger rooms for the Spanish captains of the military garrisons when they visited. This residence area, a base for Governor Cordero, also served as a working office for Doña Gertrudis and the military captains. For this reason, all of us hired assistants were asked to respect the space of others working or retiring there, however temporary any of their stays might be.

Doña Gertrudis clearly stated, "Be sure to keep a distance from the military captains within this residence, María Andrea. Some of these captains will be riding off to battles and may never return. We want them to enjoy San Antonio to the fullest extent while they're here, so we invite them outside to attend the fandangos in and around Military Plaza. Once there, they may dance, drink, sing, or eat as they wish until they retire back here by eleven p.m. You should plan to make any final rounds and preparations for bedtime with the Colonel at nine and then retreat to your own quarters before the captains' curfew."

Doña Gertrudis clarified all of this a couple of times. My job was to be as businesslike as possible at all times and not speak to the captains unless spoken to by them. When I happened to see the condition in which some of them returned each evening, I understood even more—staggering, with bloodshot eyes and shirts half tucked, sometimes singing while stumbling upon their own boots. Oh, if courtyards could talk!

Señora chuckled at the thought and continued.

When Doña Gertrudis escorted me to my room for the first time, I couldn't believe my eyes! My room, neatly tucked next to the corner of the inner courtyard to the left, was situated next to the governor's main residence and the commissary. I had my own small sitting room off to the side of my sleeping quarters. Doña Gertrudis provided me with two long faintly flowered house dresses, one with soft-pink roses and one with light-blue violets. I received two white aprons to wear over these for my work each day. In addition, she provided me with two long light-brown skirts with white blouses to wear when asked to do other chores around the palace or in Military Plaza. I soon found out what those other chores entailed.

With authority, Doña Gertrudis continued my introduction to the Palace.

"Beginning tomorrow, I'd like you to meet with Governor Cordero and me to talk about what you will be doing here each day. I will show you around the kitchen and the roof of the *comandancia*, and show you how the rooms are laid out. Do you have any questions for me at this time, María Andrea?"

I could hardly contain my utter happiness, but all I could think of was, "No, no questions except, what do you want me to do right now?"

"Whatever you'd like, María Andrea," she replied kindly. "Bathe, prepare your bedroom, try on your clothes, relax, explore the commissary, or walk about the courtyard. I'll meet you in the governor's main residence tomorrow morning at eight. Remember, you are to serve as his personal assistant."

"Yes, ma'am," I replied, turning and scampering off to my room.

When I met with the Corderos on my first day, I stood proudly, wearing the blue flowered dress and crisp white apron. Using the silver horsehair brush I'd managed to keep with me through all of our moves, I braided and rounded my hair back in a bun. I caught myself standing even more proudly, smoothing and smoothing the cool whiteness of my apron. over and over, as I remembered Ábu's send-off: "You were born a Spanish citizen, María Andrea, don't ever forget that."

I must admit I was shocked to see Governor Cordero lying on his bed with soft-yellow cotton blankets tucked all around him. His handsome and familiar tanned face and shiny, black eyes turned to look at me, and he extended a long, pale, and shaky hand. I gathered it into my own as I curtseyed and then released it. I realized later that the last time I had seen him vigorous and healthy was years ago in Laredo and then Nacogdoches. It had been quite a few years.

He spoke softly. "I'm so glad that you have come to help Gertrudis and me, María Andrea. I think you'll find the accommodations of the Palace quite satisfactory. As for me, well, I seem to have good days and bad days lately," he said, leaning up on his right elbow. "On my bad days, I am unable to do more than command from my pillows, as you can see. On my good days, I may be able to ride off to Monclova, though I haven't gone to visit there in quite some time. I had an office there when it was the capital of Coahuila y Tejas. I'm hoping you will help me regain some strength to get back there to gather some things. "

"Your father was one of my most trusted and loyal supporters throughout so many of our Spanish campaigns, first in Coahuila, then Laredo, into Nacogdoches, and even, in a way, here in San Antonio. He allows me the honor of having his daughter help nurse me back to health. I cannot thank him or your family enough."

I saw his eyes begin to water and he turned away. I had never been this close to Colonel Cordero or his wife, Gertrudis, before. I felt saddened to see him in this condition, instead of the tall, stately, golden-haired, commanding presence I'd remembered from years ago.

I didn't know what to say, so I simply replied, "Governor, the pleasure to serve has been ours. I, too, wish to be at your service, sir."

Doña Gertrudis entered the room and ushered me over to an area with a small table covered with several medicine bottles, a ceramic bowl, and a stack of small white towels. She explained the nursing duties that her husband would require on his "bad" days: helping him get out of bed to go relieve himself; reading any incoming letters; responding to certain mail and ensuring all mail got sent by courier; making sure the cooks delivered his meals on time; assisting with heating water for bathing; heating milk to make hot chocolate; allocating his daily medicines; and any other duties that might arise in the course of his day.

Suddenly, I couldn't hear anything else Doña Gertrudis said as I panicked. Reading and writing? I didn't know how to read and write. I'd never had the opportunity or time for school! Should I admit this on my first day? I decided to wait until I could speak with Doña Gertrudis alone. Then I would explain and hope that she wouldn't send me home in favor of getting someone more educated.

"You need not do any cleaning other than here in the governor's room; I have assistants for the other areas of the *comandancia*. Please take any of his or your sheets, pillowcases, and clothing to the laundry area on the roof in this cloth sack," she continued. "My assistants will return the items in a day or so. A clean set of sheets and towels are kept in a drawer near the Colonel's bed. Wood for making fires to heat water or milk is stacked in the dining room opposite the stairwell. Saturdays and Sundays you will have to yourself because I have contracted with one of the other assistants to take over on those days."

"Days off?" I realized at that moment that I'd never in my life had something called "a day off!"

Señora chuckled.

"However," Doña Gertrudis continued, "if you are interested in assisting on certain evenings during your free weekends, I can pay you to help with fandangos and meals in Military Plaza for our residents, former captains, and soldiers. I'm sure we'd all enjoy having your company."

My ears perked up at the sound of this offer because it sounded like fun rather than work! But my obligation to speak with Doña Gertrudis about my reading and writing skills hung heavily on my mind for the entire rest of the day. I'd never been in the company of a woman as self-assured and confident as Doña Gertrudis before. I simply had to determine a way to get her to keep me on as help.

That evening, I found Doña Gertrudis sitting on a bench in the courtyard writing a letter. She looked beautifully serene with her hair pulled up in a Spanish comb, wearing a white-collared blouse with long puffy sleeves and a long tan-colored skirt with delicately embroidered green stems and violet flowers dancing along the hemline. She wore a pair of ladies' tan-colored cowboy boots with swirls tooled into the leather. Her posture seemed so regal, confident, and sweet; she seemed very approachable in this moment. I watched as she pondered, then wrote something on a small piece of paper. She then paused to ponder further, smiling.

I decided this must be the time to admit my lack of education to her, before the issue became a problem. My fear was tearing my stomach apart.

"Señora Cordero," I cooed, hoping not to cause too much of a disruption.

"Yes, María Andrea! What is it, my dear?" she turned and sat upright, seeming sincere in wanting to know. Standing with my head lowered, wringing my hands, I admitted, all the while trembling, the truth of my situation. Her eyes looked confused.

"María Andrea, why have you never been to school, dear?" she asked.

"I . . . I . . . I never had time for school, Señora. My sisters and I worked around the many *jacále*s we settled while my brothers took part in cattle drives, joined the military, or ran errands for people. No one ever mentioned the importance of learning to read or write, Señora. I don't think I knew where the schools were. I'm very sorry."

Doña Gertrudis seemed honestly surprised to hear that I'd never been to school, probably wondering what I'd been up to all those years. However, being the gracious Doña that she was, she finally smiled, sighed, and stood up to walk me back toward my room, patting me on the back. She didn't say anything for a few moments. I fully expected her to ask me to just pack my things and get out. I figured she'd find someone more suited for the job. But instead, this is what she said: "I will teach you then, María Andrea! We can't have men being in charge of all the important matters, now can we?"

I looked at her as a tear rolled down my cheek, and a gasp of breath caught in my throat. I couldn't believe my ears! I smiled, and we laughed together for just an instant. She hugged me and told me not to worry! I'll never forget that moment of kindness. It was one of the sweetest of my entire life.

"I would love that," I sighed, wiping my tears as my spirits lifted. "I promise to be an excellent student!" I bounded over to my room, feeling as if I had expelled every worry I ever carried. With the winds of fear having been banished, I suddenly felt very tired and fell onto the bed into a deep and splendid sleep.

Later, while lying on my bed, I got to wondering just when the governor's wife would have time to teach me to read and write. I didn't have to wonder long, however, for the very next morning and many mornings after that, once the Colonel had been tended to with his morning activities and had eaten and swallowed the last swig of his hot chocolate, he napped. This is when Doña Gertrudis slipped into his room, motioning for me to join her in the courtyard. There we sat, side by side on that same bench, as she patiently and happily started teaching me letters and sounds. Her lessons were short, but I was an eager student so I listened and learned quickly. I studied further on my own as time permitted. Doña Gertrudis instilled in me a great desire to learn.

Soon, I conquered small words like *gato* for cat and *perro* for dog, then short love poems. Soon, short stories became a part of my world. I was in absolute heaven because of this woman. She had such patience and belief in me that I began to believe in myself. In time, she taught me numbers and addition, subtraction, and multiplication. Mathematics, she said, revealed a magic every woman needed to know, especially one working the fandangos like me. I would later come to understand the importance of this education even more clearly.

I still remember the words of one of my favorite poems by Juan Meléndez Valdés, a Spanish poet:
Tódo es páz, silencio tódo, tódo en éstas soledades me conmueve,
y hace dulce la memoría de mís males.
In English, it translates to:
All is peace, all is silence, everything in these solitudes moves me
and sweetens the memory of my sorrows.

Doña Gertrudis copied it for me on a small piece of paper in Spanish on one side and English on the other. In time, I could read both. I kept that paper, folded like many of the correspondences we'd received from the governor, for a long time. It was a great comfort in the years to come. I took it to Mamá's house one weekend, where I shared it with her and Ábu. They danced about with delight—for both hearing the poem and seeing me read it in Spanish and English! Ábu wiped away a tear when she heard me read it the first time.

Before long, Doña Gertrudis and I became great confidants. I found out that she was thirty-three years old when I started there; her husband, the Colonel, was sixty-seven. Doña Gertrudis turned out to be a descendent of the Canary Islanders who'd arrived in San Antonio long before the founding of San Fernando Cathedral. Her story was a familiar one; she certainly fit the description of being friendly and confident.

Canary Islanders had begun a settlement immediately near the spot where they would later build the beautiful San Fernando Cathedral. Doña Gertrudis's grandparents were among these early settlers. There were many unfulfilled promises upon their arrival, a story she'd heard a thousand times from her grandmother, but Doña Gertrudis simply stated that discontent is often the travel companion of new settlers, and she'd entertained none of it.

"You don't have to tell *me*," I thought to myself.

In the community, Doña Gertrudis became known as La Brigaviella—the Brigadier General—because of her confidence and apparent ease in handling Governor Cordero's duties. She would often command the review of troops from atop her white horse in front of the palace. I watched her ride before the full length of soldiers gathered there, looking for perfect lines and unflinching attention. Standing three deep in formation for her inspection, they'd wait as she cantered back and forth and then back again to conduct a second review. In the end, she saluted and nodded her approval to the soldiers as their sergeants marched to the front to salute her. The sergeants then turned and marched their men off the grounds.

I was awestruck watching Doña Gertrudis dismount and immediately set about arranging a gathering, sometimes for over fifty people, complete with dignitaries and musicians. She ordered fresh *cabrito*, goat meat, and delicious foods to be set out in her own dining room for later that evening. She told me that Canary Island women are highly respected, unlike the women of certain other groups that she didn't clarify. Canary Island women were often afforded great responsibilities such as managing ranches, money, and the collection of debts.

I had never imagined a woman being able to do all those things! My mother, though she managed quite a bit, certainly couldn't manage business affairs, nor would my father ever ask her to. Although Ábu often acted as though she was in charge of everything, she had never been formally educated nor been given the official position to be the one in charge. There was a delicate dance between her and my mother when it came to making decisions for the family.

Although thirteen years separated Doña Gertrudis and me, we shared stories of our diverse pasts while the Colonel slept.

"Who cleaned your houses? Did you have an assistant or slaves traveling with you?" Doña Gertrudis asked me.

"My parents had seven slaves, Doña Gertrudis—me, my brothers, and my sisters!" I laughed. "We cleaned every one of our *jacál*es, washed laundry, made meals, watched the little ones, and kept up with the garden."

"The animals—horses, cattle, pigs, goats, whatever you had—who tended to them, María Andrea?"

"Well, we only owned a few animals, and their care mostly fell to my brothers. Sometimes native people rode through and stole things from us, like one of our animals and my brother."

"I'm so sorry. Did you notify the authorities?"

"The only authority we knew was your husband, Doña. So we'd wait weeks sometimes before seeing him or my father to let anybody know. My little brother Esteban was taken by a band of Comanche and we've not seen him since."

"Oh, no, María Andrea, I'm so sorry. I've heard such stories but never met someone personally so affected by the ways of the Comanche."

I completely understood the life of living in the wilderness, maintaining ranches, coping with native incursions, establishing homesteads, concocting home remedies, and keeping a family fed. Doña Gertrudis enjoyed hearing my side of this. My stories were foreign to her experience growing up in San Antonio and eventually taking over her parents' former living space, the Governor's Palace.

Doña Gertrudis understood the importance of living, giving, laughing, dancing, and leisure; making land contracts with a skillful eye; and running a military with captains and leaders who mostly could be trusted. I couldn't hear enough of her history; I found it so intriguing that, as crazy as it sounds, I began to dream of a future like hers for myself.

In time, I found out that Doña Gertrudis's parents, Juan Ignacio Pérez and Clemencia Hernández, paid eight hundred pesos in 1804 for the Spanish Governor's Palace and made it their home. Doña Gertrudis, as a teenager, grew up in that large place. The palace served as a center of military and social activity when she was just a young lady. No wonder she seemed so confident. I realized that her parents bought the palace when I was two years old, sleeping on a pallet in a small room off the courtyard of Mission San Juan Bautista del Río Grande! We'd truly grown up worlds apart.

Many people continued to call Señor Cordero "governor," even after his terms had ended. It seems like there were a hundred governors in Texas at one point, all military or former military men, and I couldn't keep them straight.

A few years after Gertrudis and the Colonel moved in, some of the larger palace festivities moved to nearby Military Plaza, requiring more hands, musicians, and much more food and drink. Doña Gertrudis's father, a lieutenant colonel in the Spanish army, drew many leaders to the area, especially during the time he served as interim governor of Texas.

When Doña Gertrudis married Colonel Cordero, they moved into a residence in Durango for a while, but, years later upon their return to San Antonio, the palace became the property of Doña Gertrudis. Her parents moved back to their small, yellow house on Dolorosa Street, very close to where my mother was living when I was working at the palace.

I found life under the tutelage of Doña Gertrudis very exciting! Each week, I tended carefully to the needs and correspondence of the Colonel, while at the same time, the excitement of plans and upcoming events kept running through my head. I especially longed to spend time under the stars, swaying to the music of Military Plaza on weekends.

Señora paused from her recollections and looked toward the Alamo. I took that opportunity to ask her what she thought of Colonel Cordero.

You must understand that this man, Colonel Manuel Antonio Cordero y Bustamante, a lieutenant colonel in the Spanish army, was a very well-respected man who served for a time as governor of Coahuila y Tejas. He had been placed in charge of vast territories that included the Mission and Presidio San Juan Bautista, where my parents lived when I was born. He had been born in Cádiz, Spain, and spent nearly his entire life dedicated to the protection of the territories of New Spain.

Ábu met him at the *comandancia* one time before she died and embarrassed me by pointing at him and whispering loudly, "Now there is a man of great flatulence and wealth! Make sure he shares some of that silver with you!" I apologized sincerely and quickly walked her out.

I gasped upon hearing this. "Oh, Señora, I cannot imagine how you felt!" Señora cackled quietly, shaking her head.

Aye, Ábu! That woman was a force! How was I to know Colonel Cordero would only last another three years? Year after year of making peace treaties with the Apache, paired with having to run down Comanche and Mescalero who continued to threaten the ranches of his Spanish settlers, took a great toll on him. In the Colonel's final days, I heard him having conversations with Chief Red Cloud in his fever dreams.

"Chief," he would say, "I give you lands next to the river, good, fertile lands to graze and water your animals, but you *may not* attack my settlers growing cotton nearby. Promise me this, so that your people and my people can live in peace. If you attack my people again, I will track down each and every one of your people and have them all killed. Do you hear me, Chief?"

Over and over, he negotiated peace treaties in his sleep. Doña Gertrudis stepped in and out of the room where I tended to him, a sadness wreathed about her face.

I wondered if she ever imagined his condition as penance for marrying a man over thirty years older than herself. But this age difference wasn't unusual for the times.

"Miss Rizzo, maybe we should rest for today. How about that? Tomorrow I'll tell you about my very first fandango. Now that was something you'll want to write down."

"That sounds fine, Señora Candelaria. I'll just gather my things and be on my way. I want to walk over to the Governor's Palace today and take a quick look around."

"Oh, yes! Well then, Caramela and I'll walk that way with you. In fact, tomorrow, let's sit outside the palace and I'll tell you about my work there. Would that be alright with you?"

"That's a great plan!"

The three of us wandered over to the Governor's Palace, where I bid goodbye to the pair.

I walked inside the building once the two had continued on their way and found it much smaller than I'd imagined. It was laid out pretty much as she'd described. In the courtyard, a friendly docent found me and ushered me back to the front to sign in.

CHAPTER 14:
TRANSLATION OF ÁBU'S INTERVIEW, 1821

CAMPO SANTO VOICES

The following is an interview between Josepha and Ábu. It was written and translated by Josepha on Ábu's eighty-fifth birthday. Ábu requested this gift of writing for her family on her birthday.

Josepha, let me ask you something. I want you to write this down. What if a descendant of a native princess lived in your midst and no one, not even she, ever knew or cared? What does it mean or matter today? What if incoming Spaniards years ago invaded and killed many of your ancestors? You know this from the stories, so you despise those Spanish snakes for it. Then suddenly, a day comes when one of your own children chooses to take up with this same Spanish army occupying lands in all directions. What's a mother to do?

My husband Javier and two of our two sons, Xenon and Jesús, worked the silver mines of Guanajuato until a cave in at the mine of Las Rayas killed all three, along with many others. Having had no daughters, I was left to wander nearby streams and hillsides with my youngest son, José Antonio, and his wife, María Francisca, and their family. As a group, we roamed about, settling briefly in San Diego de la Unión, Márfil, San Luis de la Paz, and San Juan Bautista del Río Grande with other families we knew. Anguish settled in my bones and I struggled with it at every stop.

Then, of all the uncertainties I could possibly encounter, my youngest son decides to join the Spanish military! Not wishing to die in the mines like his father and brothers, he makes this decision at a very young age after years as a successful street vendor selling chestnuts. He consults his wife, seeking no input or advice from me. Who am I? I am only his mother, who understands the history of our people. I spent two days gathering lavender and hawthorn along the hillsides by myself just to calm down when he told me this news. How could he ever understand my peoples' pain and my peoples' history with those Spanish gold diggers? How many times had I said to him, "Antonio, the past might surprise you! No story lives unless someone wants to listen, and son, you're not listening!"

And he would say, "That was then, Mamá. This is now."

I decided at that time to stop retelling the story of Princess Eréndira that generations of grandmothers had passed down to me, a story that clearly illustrated that my people were revered fighters against injustice, people of the sun and moon.

According to the story, my ancestor, Princess Eréndira of Guanajuato, no friend to the Spaniards, set herself and some native fighters up on a hill where she could get a bird's eye view of incoming Spanish. When the time was right, she and her group attacked a band of arriving Spaniards. She personally killed a Spaniard and stole his horse, later using it to train others in horsemanship. This is why the Castañones, or "chestnut gatherers," became excellent equestrians to honor our ancestors. But which of my grandchildren even understands this today?

During a follow-up battle for revenge, some Spanish warriors found and murdered Eréndira's father in his sleep. Eréndira heard of his death and went to see if it was true. According to the old stories, this was when our Purépecha people began to lose hope that they could ever live peacefully with Spaniards.

Nobody really knows what happened to Princess Eréndira after that. Some say she drowned in the Pastita River, never having learned how to swim. Others reported that she left the area to train nearby tribes for continued war against the Spaniards. One story suggested she killed herself for falling in love with a Spanish monk, something one must never do.

Another legend claimed that she was kidnapped by her own people and hidden in a cave way up high on La Bufa so the Spaniards would never be able to find and kill her. But, as much as my grandmother insisted that Eréndira was related to us and we must pass her story down, I must confess, the retelling pretty much died out with me. Possessing a warrior spirit seemed of no interest to my granddaughters.

As much as I despised those Spanish snakes, I began to suspect that my family might eventually live a more secure life by taking up with them. After all, the Spanish held all the privileges. Their generosity allowed many to enter the missions, where priests taught new things, including a new language and songs and a new system of beliefs. Sadly, stories of the sacred mothers or warrior women like Eréndira were forgotten or left out.

My son, Antonio, his wife, and his family—your family, Josepha—agreed to leave the native ways behind. I alone secretly refused to convert to the required Catholic faith of the Spaniards. My faith in many gods and goddesses was too strong to simply discard for a new belief in just one god. No, that wasn't the truth for me, but I couldn't let anybody in the missions know of my refusal. I had to play along as best I could. This was a requirement of settling within the missions.

After leaving the Mission and Presidio San Juan Bautista del Río Grande, we improved several territories that the Spanish officials said became "ours." I found this idea that people could own land quite interesting. These Spaniards might have said they'd loan us the land because, long after we're all gone, Josepha, that land will still be there under the care of someone else. But Antonio seemed hungry for land to call his own when he saw others marking off their portions. I saw the same longing in you and your brothers.

Your father took up with a Spanish leader by the name of Cordero, who took him under his wing, kept him alive, and took him on many, many expeditions on horseback across dangerous terrains. Of course, in the end, the snake sent my only surviving son, along with your young cousin, off to Cuba. Your father was a man with a wife and large family. *Imagínate*, imagine! Never to be seen again. Aye, *díos mío, éste culero de Cordero*—this ass of a Cordero. He had no idea what the concept of family was all about.

Way before my Antonio and your cousin José Paulo left, I smelled a rat with that handsome, blue-eyed Royal Cordero. But I kept my comments out of earshot of my son, who by that time was happily married with many children, earning a military wage, content to receive the promise of many acres, and very proud of his work.

After each relocation, I *thought* we might actually try claiming some land that had been promised and be done moving around. I felt like our family had become respected members of the Spanish military tribe. And we were, but that military tribe moved around as much as my native tribe back in Guanajuato! That's just the way it was at that time. Luckily, Antonio and all of you had been well trained for this way of life. I, however, got very tired of it as I grew older.

María Andrea, your sister, was born in New Spain. She came into this world under the winter moon of gratitude in Mission San Juan Bautista del Río Grande. I can still see the magical light of a waning gibbous moon streaming rays of good fortune into the room right across her tiny face at the mission. The whole family gathered to watch her drop gently into the hay from your mother's loins. You were there! I don't remember hearing María Andrea cry. I only remember seeing her look around with wonder that she made it out alive, surprised to greet all of us in such a place.

I love all my grandchildren, and of all my granddaughters, you, Josepha, have such wisdom. Nieves is the faithful one. María Andrea's shiny eyes cannot disguise her longings. Although all of our natures could not be more different, our strength of commitment to family propels us forward. We are truth seekers, striving to understand the things and people around us, all the while being grateful for life and the many opportunities it presents. Like me, I'm sure all of my grandchildren will be grateful for any chance to make contributions for a better life wherever their roads may lead them.

I believe my Castañon descendants are destined for prosperity and happiness. You will all create your own stories, but I hope there'll always be somebody who listens and those who will not forget. As each of you travel the river of time, I ask that you remember the people of your past. Honor them. Speak their names. Never forget. When you hear the gentle coo of an owl, that will be me staying near to you forever.

Thank you, Josepha, for listening and writing this down as my gift to the family on this glorious morning of my eighty-fifth year.

CHAPTER 15:
A FIRST FANDANGO

Señora Candelaria and I met on the curb outside the Governor's Palace as planned the following morning. Caramela sniffed the plants along the walkway before bounding off once again in the direction of Alamo Plaza. On the cloth that morning, I saw the Spanish comb and fan again.

Let me tell you first off that I'd never heard of a fandango before I arrived in San Antonio. The very first fandango I ever assisted with took place shortly after my arrival at the Governor's Palace to celebrate Doña Gertrudis's birthday on February 6, a Sunday. She'd turned thirty-three years old in January of 1820 just after I'd turned sixteen in December.

Being the new assistant to the palace, Doña Gertrudis asked for my help with preparations for a small dinner and dance to be held in her honor. We attended mass that morning, she with her family and me with mine, at the nearby San Fernando Cathedral. Usually I had the day off, so I would normally go and spend time with my mother or sisters, or I might wander the *mercado*, the market, picking out fruit and candies to keep in my room at the palace. But this Sunday was special, so I quickly returned to the *comandancia* with Doña Gertrudis to begin preparations.

My first fandango would take place that very evening. I learned many things by the time the evening ended, not just about fandangos but about a couple of people in whom Colonel Cordero had placed his trust, as well.

Since Doña Gertrudis's favorite color was green, her mother and I made dark and light-green tissue flowers to hang. We painted colorful leaves with roses along the center of the dining table that we could wash off afterward. I braided some Mexican feather grass to drape across doorways and, after her mother contributed several candles in jars with sand at the bottom, we placed them throughout the walkways in the courtyard to light later on in the evening. Aye! The ambience looked so incredibly colorful and magical at the palace that evening!

I filled the three earthen jars below the small stairway with water and inserted small sprigs of greenery and holly berries from the courtyard. These delicate bouquets we used as festive red and green centerpieces along the dining table.

Doña Gertrudis surprised me with my very own fandango dress and shawl! Made of a soft-green brocade, the dress fit my waist perfectly. She gifted me a special slip to wear underneath the dress that made it flare out slightly at the bottom. She then asked Graciela, one of her assistants, to pull my hair up using hair pins from the small salon. As a final touch, Graciela placed a black, shiny Spanish comb at the top of my head in the back.

"There you go, Miss, you look like a Spanish princess now!" Graciela smiled admiringly, holding her arms wide as if to take in the sight of me.

Even Doña Gertrudis, being a governor's wife, marveled at my new look. She loaned me a simple gold necklace with an emerald to wear that evening. I did feel like Spanish royalty! I reminded myself that I was born a Spaniard, so this was my chance to act and dress like one, at least for tonight.

Oh, I'll never forget that evening!

Around the dinner table, I still remember the exact seating order. Colonel Cordero was at the head of the table and Doña Gertrudis was to his right along the side. To the right of Doña Gertrudis sat Adela de Veramendi, a friend of hers. To Adela's right sat a man by the name of José Vermin Cassiano, the son of the wealthy merchant that my sisters and I had met earlier in town. At the end of the table sat the aged Baron de Bastop. To his right sat Father José Antonio Díaz de León, a Franciscan minister of Texas missions. Then Doña Gertrudis's mother, Clemencia Hernández, and father, Juan Ignacio Pérez, completed the table group.

Graciela and her assistant Sophía waited on the six table guests while I tended mostly to the governor and Doña Gertrudis as instructed. The two young assistants, tall and graceful Graciela and short and quick Sophía, had also been provided with beautiful floor-length dresses: a red one and a forest green one, with satin of the same color tied below each bodice. Their raven-black hair, meticulously braided, had been carefully coiled and pinned in the back. They, like me, shuffled around wearing soft black slippers. Father Díaz de León began with a prayer at Doña Gertrudis's signal, and everyone bowed their heads as he spoke:

"Heavenly father, we ask that you bless these gifts of family, friends, and sustenance to commemorate the celebration of María Gertrudis Cordero's thirty-third birthday. May you also bestow blessings upon the city of San Antonio, its missions, the parishioners of San Fernando, and all the world as we witness changes in the wind far greater than we can imagine for our future, a future we pray will be filled with peace and prosperity. Please look upon the safe return of Father de la Garza as he completes his service as provincial delegate in Mexico City. These things we pray, oh Lord, amen."

Everyone chimed in, "Amen."

As soon as the prayer ended, Graciela, Sophía, and I filled the guests' glasses with wine, offering white or red, for a toast to be offered by Colonel Cordero.

Colonel Cordero slowly stood up from his chair as soon as all the guests had been served. With blue eyes shining, he held his glass high, smiling and nodding at each guest around the table as each raised a glass to acknowledge their host. The Colonel looked regal in his blue and red military jacket topped with a white embroidered collar, and with his dusty-golden hair, graying noticeably on the sides, combed back, shiny and fragrant with hair tonic. Looking down at Doña Gertrudis, seated to his right, he began.

'Thank you all for gathering to celebrate with us tonight. I'd like to propose a toast to my beautiful and capable wife, María Gertrudis. This captivating woman has skillfully managed this *comandancia* many times in my absence. In the six years we've been together, I've never known her to complain about anything besides scorpions, floods, flies, and mosquitoes! Let's all toast to a happy and healthy future for dear Gertrudis."

Each of the guests smiled, turning to clink their glasses with those seated nearby. Doña Gertrudis blushed and smiled, spilling white wine on her hand and wrist as she toasted her friend, Adela. I quickly fetched a small towel, to which

Doña Gertrudis shook her head, giggling and said, "No need, but thank you, María Andrea."

As we three brought out the main dishes of chicken, rosemary potatoes, and fruit compote, accompanied by bread and butter, I heard interesting bits and pieces of conversations around the table.

"Spain doesn't really give a pigeon's shit about Florida; the United States can have her and all of her alligators besides," Baron de Bastrop railed. "What we need now while Spain still retains title to Texas is settlers!"

"I've heard that a man by the name of Moses Austin has applied for an empresario grant to bring three hundred Anglo families from the United States to Texas," Mr. Cassiano replied.

"Yes, he's here in town already! Hell, I'm trying to convince Governor Martínez to let Mr. Austin bring these solid, hard-working, Catholic families in from Louisiana. We could begin to establish a real town with these kinds of citizens!" Baron de Bastrop flopped back in his chair, snatched his glass, and took a long swig.

"I'm not sure Governor Martínez will allow it, Baron. Austin wants to charge fees of each family—twelve-and-a-half cents per acre in his assigned area! Sounds pretty steep for folks who'll need to build homes and corrals and accumulate livestock. I just heard Moses talking about it at Shorty's Cantina the other night. He's anxious to bring folks in, but I don't know how well those taxes will go over, and I told him so. Remember, he's looking at 200,000 acres!"

Mr. Cassiano shook his head, sighed, and ran a hand through his hair. "I think the governor's reluctance may have something to do with more than just taxing. There's the issue of cotton farming with slaves. Mexico will not allow slaves, so what will Austin's settlers do with all that land to turn a profit without slaves if they plan to grow cotton? People say owning other people is wrong, but these folks comin' in are accustomed to it. Up in Louisiana, slave trading is big business."

Colonel Cordero and Doña Gertrudis's father had their heads together. These two were intent on the topic of filibusters, people engaged in unlawful activities coming in from a foreign place.

"Remember, we had sixty-men—sixty-men, Colonel—runnin' James Long and his men out of Nacogdoches, but the damned group was like cockroaches. Soon as we'd run 'em out one end of town, we'd get word they was meetin' at the Stone Fort at the other end of town. Long was even invitin' citizens to come hear his sob story about how the Sabine River was no fair boundary between Louisiana and Texas," Señor Pérez relayed. "Seems like public sentiment is turning against us in some parts, Colonel."

"Well, Zambrano was supposed to be in on that mission, remember?" Colonel Cordero countered. "But he got sidetracked battling some deserters who'd run off with several of their best horses. That's what he claimed, anyway. He and three of his men tracked the thieves down and managed to get the horses back. A man can only handle so many complications at one time. He should've had some of his men patrolling the other end of town one way or another. It could've prevented some of Long's monkey business 'til my men and I got there."

"I'll be glad when things settle down, won't you Colonel? John Twohig tells me that Moses Austin ran an advertisement in Louisiana recently looking for colonists to populate 'the *Republic* of Texas.' That's quite a presumption—a republic—isn't it?" Mr. Pérez took a giant sip of wine, almost choking on it, his eyes never leaving Colonel Cordero.

Colonel Cordero, the educated man that he was, courteously replied, "Heraclitus once said, 'No man ever steps in the same river twice, for it's not the same river and he's not the same man.' Texas is changing, Juan, and I'm not the same soldier I was when I arrived, fresh and green from Cádiz. I cannot foresee the future, but at times I glimpse a territory very unlike what we thought we'd have here by now. I'm tired, to tell you the truth. I'm not a young man anymore and I'm not sure how much impact all my work has even had on this place."

The Colonel raised his glass as if to toast Señor Pérez and took a big sip.

I happened to notice Mr. Cassiano speaking to Adela, Doña Gertrudis's friend, who was blushing and drinking as Señora Pérez eyed her warily from across the table. He appeared to be very interested in her, so I walked that way, offering wine to the baron. He declined, but Father Díaz de León consented, smiling much too much in my face as I poured.

Shortly thereafter, music jolted everyone at the table to attention. The dance was about to begin in the next room!

A trio of musicians arrived on cue for the first dance: two violinists and one trumpet player. I should tell you that one of the violinists turned out to be my dear cousin, José Paulo, returned from Cuba without my father. He looked incredibly handsome in his dark jacket with red piping. He wore a white dress shirt topped with a small red tie around the collar. He wore his dark hair slicked back, just like the Colonel's. I couldn't believe he hadn't let us know of his return.

The musicians set themselves up in the far-right rear corner of the long room. Earlier, we'd placed a small table along the back left wall, which had been borrowed from Doña Gertrudis's parents for platters of colorful iced cookies: coconut banderas—cookies colored like Spanish and Mexican flags, and marranitos—gingerbread pig cookies, along with sweet syrupy pecan pralines. How festive these platters looked, set upon a white linen cloth embroidered with colorful flowers! To the side, we placed a small vase of delicate winter berries with evergreen leaf branches and added a small amber pitcher alongside small wooden cups for water. These would come in handy for the guests to use when they took their leave of dancing.

All of this had been carefully planned in advance. Doña Gertrudis's plan, shared with me in great detail beforehand, was that the Colonel and she would dance her birthday waltz alone after dinner around dusk in the center of the dance room floor while others gathered around to watch. At some point, she would hug and kiss the Colonel goodnight and signal to me. I was then to accompany the Colonel from the large room back to his private residence near my room at the far end of the north walkway. Meanwhile, the music and dancing would continue.

When the time came, the Colonel and I walked arm in arm, cutting through the center of the guests with him joking all the way. He said he was utterly shocked at the Baron de Bastrop's giant belch at the end of dinner. I had heard it, but felt compelled to keep clearing the table. It was so loud that Doña Gertrudis's mother covered her mouth and practically swooned at the side of the room to catch her breath!

I could tell the Colonel was worn out, but he looked happy to see Doña Gertrudis glowing with delight, so pleased with everyone's efforts for her thirty-third birthday. I prepared the Colonel's warm wash basin, hung up his beautiful blue military jacket, and draped his pants over the chair.

Stepping up into bed, he then bade me goodnight, saying, "Get out there and try one of those dances, María Andrea! It will do your heart good! Did you know that fandangos are Spanish courtship dances?" My stomach seized at the mention of courtship.

I smiled as I left him and thought for a moment that I just might try one of the dances. But once in the dance area, I froze, completely terrified. More people had arrived; the room was suddenly filled with strangers who seemed to be staring at me with inquiring eyes. I felt as if they demanded to know, "Who are you?" For some reason, I felt very out of place at this first fandango!

I decided to post myself behind the table with cookies and drinks. Spanish dances at a fandango are very formal, with the gentleman's left arm, bent at the elbow, held out for the woman. The woman's arm and hand then cover the stiff bent arm of her partner for a few steps in one direction. Then the direction changes for a half circle and soon the couples split and line up to face a second line of dancers. Each dancer steps forward to move around their previous partner and then each begins again with a new partner. So much formality in a quadrille! Occasionally, the musicians would insert a sudden pause and the dancers had to stand still as statues until the music started up again.

Socially, a fandango gave young ladies and gentlemen a chance to meet and dance with a lot of different partners. If a particular pair liked each other, they'd leave to huddle at the cookie table to talk further. As I glanced around, I suddenly noticed something peculiar.

Doña Gertrudis spent a fair amount of time greeting guests as she moved about the room, but she always returned to an area near Mr. Cassiano. He showed signs of attraction, it seemed to me, toward the governor's wife now, rather than Adela. Adela was off talking to a handsome young man at the snack table. I had a strange inkling that Doña Gertrudis felt something special for Mr. Cassiano too.

Just then, a stranger approached my table and asked if I would like to dance the next song. I could hardly breathe! I quickly shrugged him off, saying that I was only there to assist Doña Gertrudis, not to dance. He looked completely dejected, but only for a second. Pivoting on one foot, he quickly approached another young lady and the two began their formal prancing. I exhaled with relief, carefully arranging and rearranging cookies and combining platters. I made a point to approach my cousin José Paulo to ask about my father during an intermission. José Paulo just shook his head no and stood to stretch.

At the end of the evening, the guests hugged Doña Gertrudis, thanking her for a wonderful time as they headed for the door. Her parents approached me on their way out, thanking me for all the help I had provided and saying how lovely the evening had been from dinner to dance. I was feeling rather proud of it all!

One young lady suddenly approached the snack table for one last serving of cookies at the end of the evening. She looked me up and down, clicked her tongue, and scrunched up her face in a manner that seemed to suggest I looked silly in my fandango dress. I thought I recognized her from somewhere, but I couldn't quite place her.

After the guests left, I began clearing the dining and snack tables with Graciela and Sophía, removing our festive garlands and returning the pitcher and cups to the kitchen area.

"Did you see María Gallardo? She must have been drinking before she even got here . . . falling down two times . . . that wasn't her dress causing it, either," Sophía whispered.

Graciela and I shook our heads quietly, washing off the painted roses on the dining table. "María Andrea, who was that man who asked you to dance? Why didn't you dance with him?" Sophia smiled.

"I have no idea who he was," I responded, "but his pants were so tight, they must have belonged to his younger brother. And his *bigotes*, that bristly mustache, stuck out like a tarantula! No... he wasn't bad. The truth is, I really don't know how to dance," I sighed. Sophía and Graciela joined together with quiet laughter, holding their arms out and swaying from one side to another, arms bent at the elbows and heads held erect. I laughed until my stomach hurt at their exaggerated demonstration.

"It's way more fun singing and dancing in Military Plaza with the *guitarreros* and mariachis, don't you think, Graciela?" Sophía asked.

"Oh, yes, the guitar music, trumpets, and violins are so much easier to dance and sing to!" Graciela seconded. "Just wait and see, María Andrea!"

"Who was the lady in the purple dress with white lace around the neckline?" I asked them. "She sneered at me at the end tonight in a very odd way."

"*That* was María Gallardo! Don't pay her any mind; her husband ran off with a lady from Louisiana who had *lots* of horses and she's been mean as a viper ever since." Sophía clarified.

"She's taken up drinking and thinks no one notices," Graciela added.

As I was folding some linens from the table, I thought I heard the scuffle of feet and sound of laughter along the walkway in the courtyard, so I shuffled quietly over and peered out just in time to see Doña Gertrudis being chased around the fountain by Mr. Cassiano. I couldn't believe my eyes! The Colonel's wife being playful with the son of a local merchant? At this hour? I looked over at Sophía and Graciela, who only returned my glance, raised their eyebrows, and quickly scampered away to the kitchen.

Doña Gertrudis stopped at the door to her quarters, turning around to hug and send Mr. Cassiano off, at the same moment I returned to peek at her. Before opening her door, she held her closed fan to her lips as if to say, "Let's keep this between us." Disappointed, I put my head down and retreated to the kitchen. I said nothing to the two assistants, who kept looking at me in total silence as they washed, dried, and put away dishes.

I wasn't sure how I felt about all this the next day. I heard someone leave in the early morning hours. I caught a glimpse of tousled hair and rumpled clothes as I was preparing hot water for Governor Cordero to wash up with. I expected it to be Mr. Cassiano, but it turned out to be one of the old captains, who must've fallen asleep in the courtyard. He stumbled and smiled as he passed me near the fireplace. Doña Gertrudis didn't stop in for our daily reading or math lessons that day; perhaps she felt too exhausted.

I began to consider the longings of a young woman's heart that night as I reflected upon the situation of a handsome elderly man married to someone of such capability, beauty, and vitality. Those old military captains who had tried to speak with me at the fandango that evening had been swiftly handed a napkin with cookies as I made myself look busy, even scurrying to the other end of the table in one case. I had wanted no part of their attention. Some, older than my father, had thought it wouldn't hurt to try, I guess. I couldn't imagine being betrothed to one of those old codgers, Miss Rizzo.

My biggest regret though, is that I never took the opportunity to dance with the one young man who asked me politely. It turns out, that was the only chance I'd ever get, all dressed in my Spanish finery, to dance at a formal fandango. Yet, there I remained, a frightened spectator feeling out of place, disconnected. I suppose I felt insecure, perhaps sensing a current of ridicule from a couple of female guests.

"Well, we live and we learn, don't we?"

I nodded my head and looked tenderly at Señora as she sat here sharing her most intimate fears and feelings with me. As a woman, I understood what she was saying completely.

People, tables, and items for sale at an outdoor market at Military Plaza in San Antonio. Photo: Sturdevant, E. K.(1887)

CHAPTER 16: MILITARY PLAZA

Señora closed her eyes and sat quietly for a few moments. When she opened them, I continued with a question.

"How did the gatherings in Military Plaza compare to the more formal fandangos?" I asked, imagining an outdoor venue with less formality in terms of the dress, behavior, and even age of those in attendance. Señora pulled out four brightly colored ribbons and set them atop the hair comb and fan on the cloth.

Military Plaza . . . how shall I describe Military Plaza in those days? It was as if the town took immense pleasure congregating in one simple, large, dusty, and indelible arena. Here, aromas and music mingled in what we thought was something that would endure forever. In the mornings, market sellers brought fresh produce, eggs, chickens, clay cups, bowls, and caged birds. I didn't frequent the morning markets, but Josepha did. She joined maids and cooks from the nearby hotels who arrived to select fresh produce and eggs before anyone else arrived. Usually, her friend accompanied her. Women didn't wander unaccompanied; this just wasn't considered safe or proper in those days. After the domestic workers, other local citizens arrived to socialize, purchase a few things, and scrutinize whatever was left. By midday, the plaza was usually cleared out.

Around dusk, the plaza once again came to life, slowly transforming into a giant throng of cowboys, business gentlemen, musicians, women, and soldiers. At its heart were the Chili Queens. These community cooks got quite competitive about wanting to be known for serving up the tastiest food for the cowboys and soldiers who wandered in hungry. It wasn't long before smoky air burst with music and exciting aromas drifted up from small brick ovens and grills. One could smell *cabrito*, or goat, and *pollo*, chicken, on the grill and hear muffled murmurs of men and women talking and laughing more and more loudly as soon as the moon made its way to the party.

I worked there on occasion for Doña Gertrudis and visited whenever I got the chance with my sisters. I can never forget the sights, sounds, and smells of that time and that place, or the fun we had there. It's been said that the more men sweat in peace, the less they bleed in war. If that were true, we wouldn't have lost all the men we did. All this gathering didn't seem to stop the battles going on all around us. Some people were starving, and not just for food. They needed one another's company. In their hearts, I have to believe what they really craved was seeing some amazing dream of living together in peace come true.

Señora smiled and arose from her crate. She gestured for me to take her arm.

"Come this way, Miss Rizzo, I want you to see the area I am talking about."

I stood and gently took her arm, which felt fragile as a whisper. Slowly, the two of us walked a few blocks to a simple open field between dusty brick buildings.

Yes, here. This plaza was used by the military for formal soldier reviews when my family arrived. It hosted large farmer's markets and social gatherings, as I said. It was bound on one end by long wooden tables flanked with benches belonging to the Chili Queens. Hay and wood wagons parked along the sides by that building; their anxious and accommodating vendors came prepared to keep the food fires burning.

Water carts and wood carts began rolling slowly around the plaza, especially at the start of each evening. Drivers offered assistance to each Chili Queen as she was getting set up. Using wood bundles from her pick of the cart men, each Chili Queen started her fires and began warming specialties over simple stone ovens, while pots of water, filled by short barrels brought over by the water men, were heated for making coffee and hot chocolate. In spite of the dust, many interesting alliances were formed in Military Plaza, I can tell you that!

One morning a few years later, my sisters and I went to see all three of my brothers: Nacho, Carlos, and Justo, proudly mounted on horses, this time wearing, not the Spanish uniforms, but the complete Mexican military uniforms. They moved about in various formations to please their captains. Oh, they looked so regal!

Evenings and weekends, however, this entire space became a social outlet for all kinds of people: young and old, Spanish, Irish, German, Mexican, Native, Italian, Tejano, Anglo, Black, and Canary Islander—it teemed with an amalgam of the most beautiful people from all walks of life. It was incredible to see and such a relief to feel like I belonged to it. I truly felt a closeness and a familiarity to these people.

Oh yes, Military Plaza at night . . . just imagine this wide-open space here filled with dark silhouettes moving this way and that. The sounds of muffled voices, laughter erupting at one table and then another, and the music of *guitarreros* and sometimes a violin striking up familiar songs enveloped us. This music would later be accompanied by impassioned voices, which would become even more emotional as the evenings wore on. Sometimes fights broke out and men would gather around to watch or pull the warriors apart, lest a city official should see them and begin discussions of shutting the plaza down.

Women arrived, never alone, usually wearing colorful long skirts with embroidered blouses, their long hair braided and wound with ribbons in circles at the backs of their heads. Some men wore their military uniforms to impress the ladies, leaving their puffy, white-sleeved shirts visible; others wore gently worn ranch clothing with straw hats. It wasn't long before tables glowed with the impassioned faces of gamblers, lovers, friends and storytellers.

"Mmm . . . *I can practically feel the dirt and dust flying everywhere as carts ramble about and people begin dancing to the sound of 'La Golondrina.' Are you familiar with that song, Miss Rizzo?*"

"No, Señora, I've not heard of it. What's it about?"

"*It's about a bird, a swallow, the golondrina.*"

Señora began to sing in a faint, sweet voice in Spanish.

"*A dónde irá, velóz y fatigada, la golondrina que de aquí se va por sí en el viento? Se hallará extraviada, buscando abrigo y no lo encontrará. . . .*"

"You have a lovely voice, Señora!" I noted.

"*Thank you, Miss Rizzo. It's a bit of a sad song, really. It starts off asking, 'Where will you go, oh tired little swallow, tossed about in such wind with nowhere to go?' It ends with words saying that the singer is also a wanderer like the tender swallow, someone who'll remember the patria, or homeland, and cry with its memories."*

I thought I saw tears forming while Señora quietly hummed more of the song. She then turned to amble slowly toward another part of the plaza, so I followed.

"I can see that you treasure these memories, Señora, but where would you say your own homeland was? It must have been very hard for your family to wander about as it had."

"The truth is, the sadness I feel when I hear 'La Golondrina' is for Mamá and Ábu, the ones who so strongly longed to return to the old ways of life they'd known in Guanajuato. All their lives, their hearts seemed to remain in the mountains there. As for me, my dreams looked only forward. San Antonio is where I was destined to be. My sisters and I didn't long for those other places. I felt like my history, my life really started here, Miss Rizzo. Even as I felt tossed about in the tempests of strange times and violent battles, this city became a part of me. San Antonio is my home."

"Military Plaza served an important role, then. It really became a central meeting place for many settlers in the community who might not see others on a day-to-day basis," I added, hoping to get her mind back on something cheerful.

Oh heavens, yes! Roosters crowed morning and night in all the excitement. Dogs, sometimes mangy with ribs showing, roamed freely. A sudden GA GAWK! would go up whenever dogs and hens got too close. Dogs would be chased off by angry roosters, who'd lower their wings to the ground while dancing the intruders right back out of their territories.

Right over there, I can just imagine Señora Mora filling a table with row upon row of the tastiest empanadas of pumpkin and pineapple. To her right, over there, I remember a grill with chicken and dove pieces roasting in endless supply. To her left, a giant iron fry pan of yellow corn sizzled and popped. "Will the *caballeros*, our favorite cowboys and soldiers, stop at her table or ours tonight?" we'd wonder, adjusting our braids and then wiping our tables clean.

Before nightfall on weekends, this plaza exploded even more with the incredible aromas of chili pots being prepared. Chili Queens would usually cut onions, garlic, and jalapeños and often cook their ground beef at home. Then they would bring these dishes to the plaza to reheat along with beans and rice. On special occasions, if Micaela, Señora Mora's daughter, had time, corn bread might appear, having been baked and removed from a stone oven in a flat metal pan, maybe even accompanied by a brick of fresh butter for the table. Those Moras were hard to keep up with! We tried offering special goat cheese and cornbread made with jalapeños to go with our chili to entice visitors away from their tables. Sometimes I suppose it worked!

"When you worked at Military Plaza with Doña Gertrudis, what did your duties entail?"

On weekends, Doña Gertrudis asked me to cover two long sections of her wooden table with red tablecloths to make our seating area more attractive. I set out forks and metal or wooden cups and checked to make sure we had sturdy benches set up along each section of table. Sometimes, my mother and sisters would join me. Much effort went into creating a delicious, hearty meal and a clean, comfortable seating area outside for those who came by. Visitors often included friends or family of the Corderos. Doña Gertrudis didn't care about the income, she just truly enjoyed showing her hospitality to visitors and military personnel.

After setting up, my job was to take orders and serve what customers requested. Doña Gertrudis oversaw the food supplies and chatted happily with our customers, stepping from one end of the long table to the other to engage in conversation. Some patrons preferred to stand and eat. Others chose to sit and stare at the cooks or listen and sing along with the musicians. Some regulars seated themselves, ordered food. and started right in on some good story between bites with whoever else sat down alongside. We kept a large barrel, half filled with sudsy water, to hold the dirty eating utensils, plates, and cups. Underneath the table, we kept jugs of clean water for washing and rinsing.

Someone in the shadows would usually be selling tequila or some other alcohol. Drinking alcohol and gambling almost always resulted in loud encounters, maybe even a fight, by late evening. Card playing, dice, and betting led to many frustrated competitions out here. San Antonio's city officials debated the issue of gambling and whether or not to allow it in Military Plaza many times.

Juan Silverio Flóres de Abrego showed up while I was working a weekend in Military Plaza. He told me that Colonel Cordero had arranged his meeting with Doña Gertrudis in this very same place, at the very same table, supervised at that time by Doña Gertrudis's mother, Clemencia! The governor spotted Doña Gertrudis assisting her mother and the other Chili Queens and made his move.

I tried hard not to spend too much time talking to Silverio, and eventually I felt I should let Doña Gertrudis in on who kept sidelining me at work. She smiled and raised her eyebrows in a suggestive way, which made me blush and avoid him for a while. Mamá saw Silverio and me talking and reminded me that she and my father had known his parents since their time at Mission San Juan Bautista. Sensing her approval, I felt more inclined to talk with him.

Looking that way, toward San Fernando Cathedral, you could see young couples in silhouette veering this way and that. Men held the waistlines of young ladies as they walked, talked, laughed, and blended into shadows. Soon I would take breaks to walk the same way with Silverio as the *guitarreros* played and cried into the night, roaming the unsettled vastness of the plaza. One night. Silverio asked me if I ever thought of settling down.

"María Andrea," he said, "I don't have much to offer, other than a few acres of ranch land, but I wonder if you would ever consider marrying a man like me. I can read and write, I receive monthly wages from the military, and I do think about having a family one day."

I blushed and looked up at him. "Silverio, my days and nights are spent with the Corderos. I only get away on weekends here. Maybe when I complete my work at the governor's *comandancia*, we can discuss this further." I smiled, thinking to myself how immediate and strong my response sounded. Doña Gertrudis must surely have been wearing off on me!

"I'll wait then, *muñequita*." He always called me his little doll. "Who knows! You may complete your job sooner than you think!" I looked at him, confused by that remark. He laughed, took me in his strong arms, and hugged me tight to him, swaying to the music of some sad song playing on a violin across the plaza. I melted into his leathery tobacco smell before coming to my senses and gently pushing myself away.

Returning to work the tables with the Chili Queens on weekends, Nieves pointed out how much time she thought Silverio spent gambling. I paid no attention to her warning, since so many of the men, military and civilian, played cards and gambled in the plaza on weekends. They needed that outlet in those days. It only bothered me when fights broke out, especially if no one intervened.

Mmm, yes, I can see it, hear it, and practically smell it all again . . . I felt completely caught up in the pulse of Military Plaza.

Señora closed her eyes and began quietly humming that same golondrina song as we turned and walked back to our usual meeting spot.

CHAPTER 17: GOVERNOR CORDERO TAKES A TRIP

GOVERNOR CORDERO LEAVES FOR MONCLOVA, 1823

Back to Governor Cordero. In the spring of 1823, Governor Cordero felt stronger after battling a tough winter of coughs, body aches, and general malaise. Some thought he still suffered from a bit of depression since Mexico had gained its independence from Spain shortly after my family arrived. That governmental change usurped any military and political power the Spanish held there. San Antonio became unmistakably Mexican territory as of 1821, which brought a whole new host of problems that I'll talk about later.

When the Governor suggested taking a trip to Monclova, Doña Gertrudis thought it would do him good to get back on his horse and ride out to visit friends there, and clear any military papers out of his office once and for all. I wasn't so sure, but she insisted and began to make a list of necessary travel particulars.

Things still felt slightly strained between me and Doña Gertrudis, though our math and reading lessons did pick back up eventually. I found myself feeling deeply saddened for Colonel Cordero, knowing that his wife seemed to be somewhat attracted to someone else. I felt disappointed in Doña Gertrudis, too, for appearing to soak up another's attentions under her husband's nose.

The night before he left, the Governor and I sat together at the small table in his room, where he reviewed and organized correspondences while I folded his white cotton kerchiefs.

"What do you think of my trip to Monclova, María Andrea? Have you ever been there?" he asked me.

"No sir, I have not, at least not that I can remember. I'm very happy that you feel strong enough to make the trip. How long will you be gone?"

"Oh, about a month or so. My office used to be there when it was the capital, so it's time I go clear things out. The Spanish are truly done here, as you've probably been aware. I cannot thank you enough for bringing me back to life with your magical herbal teas and tonics. The vanilla and cinnamon you add to my hot chocolate make me crave it all the more! I swear it revives me each morning!"

He was being so kind, and yet I detected a touch of melancholy resignation in his voice. He continued, "I want you to know that, whatever happens, things are fine with me. Even when things haven't been okay, I know that they will be soon enough. You've taken great care of me and I appreciate it. Were it not for you and your concoctions, I doubt very much that I would be able to make this trip."

"Do you mean you feel fine as far as your health?" I wondered aloud.

"Yes, I feel fine with that and with Gertrudis. She's always respected, valued, and appreciated me. She's made me smile, laugh, and feel loved. It's been hard for me to reciprocate; I'm an old man, María Andrea. You may be too young to understand. But I really do understand the longings of a young woman's heart."

I watched carefully as the Colonel began stacking old communications and then tied and threw them to the windowsill, as if tossing any mistaken assumptions he'd made about his future. He shakily grabbed his saddle bag and inserted a few darkened glass bottles of medicinals that I'd prepared for his trip, wrapping each in a kerchief.

"She once told me that happiness is the meaning of all existence and that she's enjoyed nothing but happiness living here with you," I shared, trying to ease the melancholy enveloping him.

"Well, it has made me very content to see her so fulfilled," he replied, looking up from his packing. "It's all any honest man wants, really. Did you know I decided I should marry shortly after my friend and fellow governor, Colonel Manuel Salcedo, was assassinated by a rebel captain named Antonio Flaco? He'd served as governor for about five years and got shot down on the very day of his thirty-seventh birthday. His sudden death cut my heart to the core. Suddenly the military work I'd been doing took a back seat to the sort of life I really wanted to live. But I suppose I was an old man by the time this dawned on me."

"Yes, well, Gertrudis said there's no man who will be in her heart forever the way that you'll always be." I stood and set the remaining kerchiefs on his bedside.

He took a step toward me, then said tentatively, "María Andrea, when my time comes, I'm sure you are aware that your services will no longer be needed here at the palace."

This sounded rather abrupt. I stopped straightening his bedspread and stood to face him with a kind but saddened face. "Sí Señor, though I hate to think about that time coming."

He continued, "I want you to know that I have opened an account at my Irish friend John Twohig and his partner Nathaniel Lewis's bank in your name. In that account, I've placed some funds for you to purchase a small business or *jacál* of your own. The truth is, I'm sorry that your father never returned from Cuba; he was one of my best friends and the finest soldier I've ever worked with. Those years we spent riding for king and country hold some of my fondest memories. He'd be very proud to see what a smart and beautiful young lady you've become."

I gasped and inhaled, suddenly shaking, tears forming at the mention of my father. I'd thought of him on rare occasions since my family's arrival in San Antonio. The last time was when I saw José Paulo playing his violin in Military Plaza.

"Gov-Governor Cordero," I stammered, "I, I don't know what to say! You are most generous, sir!" I managed to step forward stiffly and embrace him very quickly, something I'd never done in all the time I'd worked there.

"My father always spoke so highly of you. I don't know why he left your services. I don't, quite honestly."

"He left for Cuba, another Spanish territory, to please the Spanish crown. I never should have agreed to send him, María Andrea. At the time, the king issued a request for assistance. Your father had been suffering from a serious infection caused by a wound he received from a native's arrow. Hobbling about, he felt rather incapable of resuming any equestrian work, so he volunteered to go for training as a tailor in Cuba. Unfortunately, he proved so talented, his Majesty requested he remain in Cuba to serve the Spanish military."

He looked at me sadly. "It was my fault, I'm afraid. I had no idea the position would lead him away from his family forever. At least your cousin, José Paulo, came to his senses and made the trip back from Cuba to be with all of you."

"Well, I have no doubt my father meant to continue working for good causes. You'd have thought he was born in Cádiz with you! He called you his brother, Colonel."

Trying to change the subject, I added, "I wish you safe travels on your trip to Monclova, Colonel Cordero, and I'll look forward to seeing you upon your return. If you need anything more before you go, please let me know. I'll have some hot chocolate with cinnamon and vanilla ready for you in the morning before you depart. If there's nothing more, I'll retire to my room, sir."

I curtsied, turned, and bounded down the courtyard, wiping away tears while pondering all that the Colonel had just shared with me. Until that moment, I hadn't been convinced that my father left Mexico for Cuba to please the Spanish crown. So, it was true and Colonel Cordero had something to do with it. Why had that realization escaped me all this time? Money in a bank account? I couldn't grasp it all, honestly.

Lost in a whirlwind of emotions, my heart recognized one thing as inevitable, while my mind desperately clung to the joy that this brief chapter at the Governor's Palace brought me. A joy that would soon be gone forever.

I quickly forgot about any bank account. I began to wonder if my father was all alone in Cuba or if he had forgotten about his family here and started a new life. Whatever he was doing, he was losing precious time with his family here. Why didn't he come back when José Paulo did? We'd never know because José Paulo only shook his head sadly and became mute when we grilled him about Papá's whereabouts. I imagine the truth was too painful for José Paulo to relay.

That night I dreamed I was riding a fast mustang horse, zig-zagging through dense, unfamiliar territory as mesquite trees brushed and cut my face and arms. Wind whipped my hair from one side to the other, but I kept riding down a winding path in front of me as fast as I could. When the horse finally and quite suddenly stopped, we stood on the high bank of a giant river trying to figure out how to get across. I couldn't find the right time or the right place to cross, so I impatiently paced back and forth along the riverbank, slowly being hypnotized by the colorful, swirling, flowing water.

Suddenly, out of nowhere, a woman with long dark hair, wearing only animal skins, galloped alongside me on a white horse screaming and pointing a spear across the river, "There they are, kill them all!" I glanced across the river in the distance and saw Colonel Cordero with Spanish soldiers riding fast in our direction. But try as I might, I couldn't turn or get my horse to move. I woke up drenched in sweat and terrified.

CHAPTER 18:
GENERATIONS CRUMBLE

GENERATIONS CRUMBLE
AS NEW ONES TAKE HOLD

News of the Colonel's death in Monclova quickly reached San Antonio. Doña Gertrudis insisted on going with her father to retrieve his body and bring it back for a proper military burial. Her mother begged Doña Gertrudis to wait with her in San Antonio, but Doña Gertrudis, being the strong-willed, confident woman she was, would not have it.

The next time I saw Governor Cordero, four sturdy men were pulling his stiff, pallid body from the back of a small wooden two-wheeled wagon pulled by Doña Gertrudis's father, Señor Pérez. Señor Pérez appeared sullen and pale. Without a word, he slapped the reins of his horse to return home once the wagon had been emptied. The four groundskeepers placed Colonel Cordero's covered body atop a long table that the assistants and I had prepared in the foyer of the Governor's Palace.

When Doña Gertrudis disembarked from the wagon, she appeared a slight, crumpled figure, heaving and unable to catch her breath as she was helped down. Overcome with grief, she kept her head low, turned, and ran into the palace alone. Those of us gathered stood at attention and listened to her wail as she moved through the courtyard to her bedroom. I thought about how quickly life is created and how quickly it can depart. The air around me seemed brackish, and everything I looked at took on a strange, muted hue with the governor's passing.

Doña Gertrudis's mother arrived to provide support and comfort to her daughter but left soon after to make arrangements with the undertaker and with Father de la Garza at San Fernando for the Colonel's mass and burial. Her own husband would require attention as well, from what I saw upon his return.

The Colonel's words, "Whatever happens, things will be fine with me," circulated over and over in my mind. Was he aware of Mr. Cassiano's apparent friendship with Doña Gertrudis before the fandango? If I had noticed their amicable gazes, perhaps he'd noticed them before he retired that night. Could he have possibly meant he was fine with that? So many uncertainties swirled through my mind when the Colonel died, never to be fully resolved.

During the Colonel's absence, I'd spent much time visiting with Mamá and Ábu at the *jacál* on Dolorosa Street.

"*Quién es ésta mujer*, Francisca? Who is this woman?" Ábu asked my mother over and over, referring to me.

Sadly, Ábu didn't recognize me at times. Mamá said she caught her trying to light the back shed on fire several times. She advised me to be on the lookout for Ábu gathering twigs so I could ferret them away when she wasn't looking. I hid her piece of flint in the crock of a tree, too high for her to see or reach. I felt guilty watching her shuffle in circles, confused, trying to figure out where she'd left it.

Mamá, who stood about five feet tall, slightly shorter than I was, often wore the same faded pink house dress with a tattered beige sweater, an outfit that made her look much thinner to me, suddenly. Her long graying hair, always pulled back, released several strands to fly freely about her face. This also made her seem weary lately. I realized one evening that Mamá hadn't really had anyone helping her with Ábu. Nieves had moved in with a fatherless family, providing assistance for the children during the day and helping with a very elderly neighbor of theirs at night. She shared her earnings with Mamá for food and rent as I did.

Josepha, now seeing someone new—she wouldn't tell us who—continued working for Cassiano's Mercantile and, on most weekends, also helped a widow with children in town. Although Josepha lived elsewhere, she did remember to visit and bring money to Mamá when she could. My brothers were off doing whatever men did: taking care of their own families, serving in the military, drinking, gambling, or working on somebody's ranch in their spare time. Though they did stop in to check on Mamá, I rarely saw them, except in passing from time to time in Military Plaza.

One Saturday, I remember it being a cool spring morning, I took Ábu out for a walk. Breathing in the fragrances of oleander and phlox bushes along the walkway in San Antonio felt intoxicating! I found myself gazing at the sparkling San Antonio River and then the majesty of San Fernando Cathedral and realizing just how much I truly loved this city! All roads brought me here, to this beautiful and colorful place, and I felt so grateful for that.

All of a sudden, Ábu crumpled and drew away from my arm. She started pointing at people, calling them *"indios looocos"* or "crazy Indians" in a high-pitched voice, creating such a scene! When I tried to calm her, she turned suddenly, gasped, and screamed, "AYE?! Who are you? HELP! *Ayúdame*! Somebody help me! I'm being stolen by a Spanish snake!" She threw my arm off of hers and turned to shuffle away in the opposite direction. I quickly retrieved her, shushing her with "Ábu, it's ok; it's me, María Andrea. Let's go see Francisca. Come on now, let's go see your daughter Francisca." From then on, I decided that sitting quietly with her under the tree in my mother's front or back yard would be all the recreation I could manage with her any more.

I moved back in with Mamá the following spring after the Colonel's death to provide some sort of assistance for Ábu.

One evening, I took a break to wander Military Plaza with Nieves. A dreamy full moon seemed to be blinking on and off between swiftly drifting clouds. These clouds created the effect of intermittent flashes of moonlight throughout the plaza, casting shadows and creating eerie, subtle movements. The environment seemed strange. Something was off.

The smells of corn tortillas mixed with chicken and goat charring on grills added alluring aromas throughout the darkness. Couples and small groups, like cicadas in far off mesquite trees, created a buzz of friendly conversations. Nieves and I jumped into the shadows with our friends to lend our happy voices to the songs of the *guitarreros* mingling within. We were quite young and carefree, willing to get swept up in whatever the evening held for us.

Suddenly, out of nowhere, someone grabbed my arm, "María Andrea, it's Ábu. She's gone. She burned herself up in the fire pit out back of your mom's. You and Nieves had better get over there right away." Edgar took and held both our arms, rushing us all the way to Mamá's *jacál*. Familiar memories flooded my mind of so many years spent with Ábu. In the clouds crossing the moon above, I swear I saw my silver hairbrush float by that night, followed by a wild woman on a horse.

I recalled with great fondness many evenings sitting at the fireside, when my sisters and I took turns brushing each other's long, dark, shiny hair with the brush Ábu had given me to see who could fashion the neatest, tightest, and most even braids. There is such calmness in having one's hair brushed! We wore these same braids for four or five days before washing and starting another competition. Mamá and Ábu served as the judges and, though we couldn't know for sure, it seemed each of us secured victories in equal numbers.

When I'd had some time, I'd enjoyed gathering Ábu's arm in mine, stepping outside, and slowly promenading around her herb garden out back. We'd stop to survey and pluck a bit of basil, thyme, yarrow, rosemary, chives, and parsley, smelling each one to Ábu's great pleasure. We'd then shuffle slowly to the front yard, where she'd take stock of her wild roses, aloe, and bougainvilleas before motioning that she wished to sit in her favorite cedar chair under the large pecan tree.

She often asked me, "Which one are you, now?" and I'd laugh and reply, "Ábu, you know who I am! I'm your granddaughter—the one with the hairbrush who braids hair better than my sisters!"

"Oh, yes, María Andrea, it's you," she'd say contentedly. "Will you brush my hair and braid it today?"

To which, I'd reply, "Yes, *abuelita*, of course."

Under that pecan tree, with soft breezes caressing us, we spent much precious time together, sometimes in loving silence. Though I doubted she could hear it, a mockingbird somewhere above often ran through a splendid medley of songs. It imitated melodies from all kinds of birds in the area—cardinals, sparrows, blue jays, and whip-poor-wills—as I gently stroked and brushed Ábu's long white hair. Sometimes she fell into a sweet slumber and I'd have to gently pull her back into the chair. Once I finished her braid, I wound it gently into a tiny soft mound at the back of her head and tucked and pulled the ends to keep it in place. I'd always end by looking into her eyes and exclaiming, "*hermosísima*! So beautiful!" This made her open her eyes and smile, pulling me in for a kiss on the cheek.

So, that evening when we rushed back to Mamá's house to find a conflagration raging in the backyard, my eyes did not want to comprehend the gruesome visage of the flesh and bones of dear Ábu lying there amid the ashes and burning embers of her collapsed chair.

I wondered how she'd even managed to drag that chair to the back. Left alone for a bit that night, she must have decided it was time to take her sacred journey to Xibalba—that place in the Mayan underworld, something she'd talked about more lately—while gathering sticks to throw into the fire pit. Ábu threw in stalks of rosemary too, and that is what we smelled on the night of her departure. Rosemary, the herb of memory, circulation, and upset stomachs. That's what she taught us. I took this to be her sign that we must never forget her, or the origin of the blood that runs through our veins. I knew, too, that she wished for us to carry on without sadness and upset. Her time on this Earth had finally drawn to a close. A new journey awaited. This she strongly believed.

In time, I felt a genuine connection to the past each time I brushed my hair with that silver brush or, years later, brushed the hair of my daughter Francisca. When I was brushing, I recalled the treasure that was our dear, sweet Ábu. I knew I'd never forget her. I understood that the people we love become a loving lifeline built into our hearts forever.

Nieves, Josepha, Mamá, Edgar, a neighbor, and I wept as we gathered in a circle around the fire pit and said a prayer. Mamá had stopped to visit a friend after church that evening when news of the fire reached her. By the time she got home, burning embers and a charred batch of bones remained; this time it was too late.

Losing the feisty, strong Ábu that I had known had occurred years before, but losing her in the flesh affected me in so many ways. I continued to look for her at every full moon, when I heard the hoot of owls, in the pink flowers of the bougainvillea bushes she planted, in her beloved herbs, and within the ashes of every fire we gazed upon. We still place rosemary in a *cenicero*, or ashtray, to remember her on All Souls' Day on November 2.

I miss her more than I can even express. I felt like my father's world was one of adventure and dominating fresh frontiers. That had to be such a disappointment for Ábu, that he and many of his children showed so little interest or concern with her past, a life beyond our current locations. Ábu's was a past she could have told us much more about had we taken the time to ask her. But we were too caught up in the middle of a blossoming, intrusive, and turbulent Texas, I suppose.

"I'm so sorry, Señora. So sudden and unexpected. It sounds like she was such an important figure all throughout your life. This is quite evident in the stories you've shared with me so far. I feel deep sorrow just hearing about your loss."

Señora hung her head for quite some time, silent in the torrent of memories, perhaps. She eventually looked up, wiped her nose, and continued.

That trip to retrieve Colonel Cordero from Durango proved too much for Doña Gertrudis's father. He fell quite ill upon his return to San Antonio and succumbed to a fever a couple of months later. His wife, Clemencia, followed him to the grave two short years after that. When Colonel Cordero died, followed so suddenly by her father, Doña Gertrudis asked her mother to move back into the palace with her.

Doña Gertrudis quickly set about finding someone to rent her parents' former residence, just a stone's throw from the palace. A young blond man, willing to seize the opportunity, stepped right up. Now who do you suppose that might have been?

"Mr. José Cassiano?" I guessed.

"You're a bright one, Miss Rizzo! That's exactly right."

Doña Gertrudis's mother Clemencia was laid to rest in 1825 in San Fernando Cemetery next to her beloved husband. Ábu's ashes were scattered in the Campo Santo nearby.

In the spring of 1826, a year later, Doña Gertrudis married José Cassiano. She invited me to her wedding, so I put on the only fancy dress I owned: the beautiful light-green brocade fandango dress that she'd given me to wear for her birthday party! I asked Mamá to put my hair up, but instead of using the shiny black Spanish comb, I asked her to insert a small spray of bright pink silk bougainvilleas that I'd purchased from the *mercado* for Ábu a few years earlier. These were tied together with bright ribbons that hung down in back.

As I walked over to the cathedral by myself, I thought back to six years earlier when I'd first worn that dress. At the time, I truly believed Spain would somehow seep into my bones and transform me from a simple native girl to royalty just by rubbing shoulders with the Corderos. But the allure of Spanish royalty faded quickly. My soul radiated pure indigenous Tejana; of this I felt more and more certain.

Doña Gertrudis's wedding ceremony took place quickly, with the few of us attendants being invited back to the palace for lunch. Mr. Cassiano proved a kind and gracious man, but there remained something between us that I cannot explain. He exuded an aspect that made me uncomfortable. He was the first *norteamericano* I'd actually spoken to, so perhaps that's all it was. But Colonel Cordero was correct. The longings of that young lady and the passion between the two was undeniable. Those two souls needed to dance together. So, I resolved to be happy for both of them.

CHAPTER 19: A TALK WITH MAMÁ, 1826

Once Colonel Cordero had been laid to rest and Ábu's ashes scattered in Campo Santo, Mamá had more time to sit with me and share stories. Intrigued with stories of my time at *la comandancia*, she questioned me repeatedly for details. What was the relationship between young Doña Gertrudis and Colonel Cordero like? How often did Doña Gertrudis's parents visit? How did her parents treat one another? What were my duties for the Colonel? How often did Doña Gertrudis hold fandangos at the palace? Who attended and what gossip entailed? She wanted "all the dirt," as they say! She'd never had much excitement in her own life now that I think about it.

I looked up at Señora and nodded, feeling as if she'd just made another discovery during this interview.

One morning, we were sitting out back having coffee. Mamá told me Carlos had stopped by earlier in the week. He told her that the soldiers hadn't received payment for their services for a very long time. Governor José Félix Trespalacios, fuming at the lack of response from the government officials in Mexico City, convinced the *ayuntamiento*, the town council, to establish something called "a bank of issue" in our town to help cover salaries until the Mexican government found it in their hearts to pay their soldiers' wages. Carlos felt hopeful that a bank of issue would bring back some of the soldiers who'd just left Béxar's military to try their hands at farming and ranching. (Béxar, pronounced "bear," became the county seat of San

Antonio.) Some of these former soldiers resorted to running stolen cattle up north since so much livestock roamed around unbranded, he reported.

Mamá told me she was worried Carlos might be thinking of resorting to illegal behavior so he too could better support his growing family. She reminded him what it would look like to his boys if he got caught and put in jail.

Mamá spoke highly of Governor Trespalacios. Edgar told her the governor recently bought a printing press so the town could put together its own newspaper. Trespalacios wanted to title our paper E*l Correo de Texas*, or *The Mail Correspondence of Texas*. Everyone was talking excitedly about it at church, according to Mamá. Soon, the officials in Monterrey caught wind of it and "offered" to buy the printing press from the governor. Edgar reported that the printing press disappeared within two weeks. So much for a local newspaper. This was Mexican territory, and the citizens were once again being reminded who was making the rules.

For some reason, mention of the "bank of issue" suddenly reminded me of Colonel Cordero's offer of my bank account. It'd completely slipped my mind until this conversation.

"WHAT?" My mother choked on her coffee, spilling it on her sweater. "Oh, María Andrea, that's, well that is . . . *Aye*, heavens! How much did he leave for you? Have you thought about what you will do with that money? Is it still there?" she inquired breathlessly.

"I don't know, Mamá. I completely forgot about it with all the changes lately. I don't know how much he left for me, where this bank is, or even if the Colonel's money is still there. He mentioned John Twohig, that I remember. Maybe we should keep our ears open for opportunities around here, in case there *is* money. *Please* Mamá," I begged, "do not tell anyone of the bank account. I want to pretend it isn't even there for now, because it probably isn't."

I glanced over at the pink bougainvilleas blooming near the alleyway. I remembered how carefully Ábu had planted and cared for them, leaving us to enjoy their brilliant blooms as we conversed in the shade of the one willow tree out back. Ábu's herb garden off to the side at the back of the *jacál* now offered stars of white garlic flowers dancing among tiny yellow yarrow spikes with sage-green jagged leaves. Onion greens reached upward next to generously blooming and fragrant oregano, Creeping Mother of Thyme, and basil. I basked in the nostalgia of it all.

"Oh, *mí hijita*, my daughter!" Mamá cried out. "Perhaps Ábu was right. Maybe one of us will live a privileged life after all!" Mamá smiled sweetly and scooted her small wooden chair closer to mine. She leaned in and whispered something incredibly important. She'd heard Shorty García was looking for a buyer for his cantina on Market Street now that his wife had passed. Monica García had recently died of cholera, and Shorty claimed he no longer had the desire to keep up with late nights anymore. Besides, he said, his legs were just too tired, and his back was beginning to give out.

"But María Andrea, what do you know of running a business, *mí hija?*" Mamá asked, leaning back in her chair and brushing her hair out of her face with the back of her hand while glancing over at Ábu's herbs. A dreadful realization clouded her face. She didn't think her daughter could ever do it.

"Mamá, look at me!" I cried out. Francisca Castañon turned a weary face with tears in her eyes toward me. "I can do anything I want to! Doña Gertrudis taught me mathematics and how to read. Maybe my writing is not so strong, but really, Mamá, I feel like I could manage a party house, an inn, or even Shorty's Cantina as long as I have some help. I really can do anything I put my mind to, Mamá! Doña Gertrudis certainly didn't let anything or anybody hold *her* back!"

My mother looked at me with a doleful sadness that I found irritating. She dabbed at her eyes with the bottom of her sweater. "Who would you get to help you? I'm too old and your friend María DeLeon would never even step foot in a party house or cantina for fear she might get tequila on her satin slippers!" We both laughed at that thought, then sat silent.

"Do you know Shorty, Mamá?" My doubting mother, nodded slowly, realizing she was about to step into the middle of something potentially life changing.

"Could you find out, without raising suspicions, what he is asking for his business? His place is still right over on Market Street, right? Not far from here at all."

This time, opportunity was knocking and I had to figure this out fast. I realized I didn't even know how much money the Colonel left for me, but whatever was there, *if* any was there, I figured it might be enough to at least make some sort of down payment. Then I'd just have to earn the rest by running the business. Mamá assured me she could find out the asking price of Shorty's, and she did—in true Francisca form—the very next day!

By 1826, Shorty and I turned a deal after a visit with Mr. Nathaniel Lewis, Shorty's banker. In a small office off the main plaza of downtown San Antonio, Shorty and Mr. Lewis worked out a deal where I would hand over a portion of Shorty's five thousand dollar asking price up front. I could give him one thousand dollars, the amount deposited by Colonel Cordero directly to Shorty. The rest would be due, plus interest, every month to Mr. Lewis. Mr. Lewis immediately paid off the balance of the business himself to Shorty. Mr. Lewis, in charge of my account at the bank, made sure I understood that if I missed any payments, ownership of the establishment would go to him because, after all, he'd already paid Shorty the total asking price. I realized that, in a way, I was really buying the business from Mr. Lewis. Shorty got the money he wanted for his business, and now it would be up to me to keep things moving in the right direction by making each monthly payment to Mr. Lewis. Once I did that, I would truly own my own business!

I was on top of the world! Who could imagine a woman-owned cantina in the heart of San Antonio? A darker-skinned, female proprietor at that. That would be my establishment, with me being the proud owner of Shorty's Cantina in 1826! I couldn't have felt more confident and secure in making this move. Mamá was ecstatic and wished Ábu could've been there to see me running the place. I told Mamá that if Ábu were here, *she'd* be running the place, not me!

Señora Candelaria and I both laughed at this.

If it hadn't been for working with Doña Gertrudis, I never would have considered going into business for myself. I wouldn't have thought women could do such things. I would have known nothing of mathematics, and perhaps only a little English. I surely wouldn't know how to read a business invoice. Had it not been for my daily lessons at *la comandancia*, and my work in Military Plaza with the Chili Queens, none of this would have been conceivable. I'm forever grateful to Doña Gertrudis for that, and to Mamá for eventually coming around to believing that I could do such a thing!

I thought, too, of Josepha's advice that I'd need to figure out a way to "come into" some money or property if I ever wanted to be prosperous. To be prosperous, one needed to own something. Typically, women didn't purchase such things on their own. Well, I'd show the family that I could have a piece of prosperity—my own labor of land, in a way!

I thought about how unusual it would have been for a young woman like Señora to take such responsibility back in the early 1800s. She seemed like a true pioneer in many ways.

CHAPTER 20: SHORTY'S CANTINA

SHORTY'S CANTINA GETS A NEW OWNER 1826

"My goodness, Señora! You must tell me about Shorty's. This is a surprise in your story. I didn't know any of this about you!"

I threw myself into this new business in early 1826, learning as much as I could from Shorty himself. He spent many afternoons sitting with me and discussing trusted suppliers for wine, tequila, beer, and other mercantile goods. He warned me about certain locals to watch out for—men I had never met, but whose names I committed to memory. Best of all, he continued working at Shorty's in the evenings for quite some time to help keep an eye on things. Some customers probably never realized that I was the new owner.

"You need to keep Izzy Limón," Shorty insisted. "She knows these guys like the back of her hands! She can outfight most of 'em and has been known to throw a few into the streets on their ears. She's a trustworthy one, she is. Tough too. And Mario, my bartender, is pure muscle. He's a little slow on the draw, but once he smells trouble, he knows how to put out fires once and for all. You just gotta give him some sort of signal."

Shorty recommended that I outlaw gambling inside my establishment, something easier said than done since he had allowed customers to roll dice and play cards as long as they didn't get out of control and bother other customers. He said our city officials would look more highly upon me as a female business owner if I could accomplish the banning of card playing and gambling, at least for a while. It took a good amount of time to get customers on our side for this one. Izzy turned out to be just the kind of waitress I needed to get the job done.

Running that cantina amounted to a trial by fire, Shorty said. One evening, I walked out from the back room just in time to duck a body flying by. It hit the far side wall, slid down, and remained slumped there, motionless, like a potato sack. A fight had erupted over cards before I even knew it was happening! I looked over to see Izzy grabbing Pasquale Buquet by the lapel with her left hand and smashing and holding her classic broken bottle to his throat with the other. She stood him up and led him briskly to the door, where she threw him out.

Standing in the doorway, she warned him, "There'll be no more gambling in here, Pasquale. If you can't abide by Señora's rules, you can gather your cards and play monte in the streets with those other *diablos*, devils, outside." Just like that, she'd thrown this giant man out. She then sauntered over to the card table where his two *amigo*s sat, wide-eyed and fearful. She picked up the table on one side, letting the cards and bottles fall off into their laps and then to the floor. Using a low, guttural, threatening voice, she told them to get out, bowing with the broken bottle she'd smashed to look into their faces.

"*Váyanse*! Get out of here, all of ya's!" she yelled, grabbing the tabletop and bumping the legs of the table up and down. "You know the rules. If you come in here again to gamble, I will shoot your knees out. Now GIT!" She stated this with such authority that the two at the table rose, grabbed their dripping hats from the floor, and set out as fast as their wobbly legs would take them.

"*Espérense*! Wait! *Bufetes*. You clowns get on over there and carry your *amigo* Miguel out too. He's as bad as the rest of ya's."

Inhaling and shaking her head, Izzy finally exhaled then winked at me as I stood, wide-eyed, across the barroom. Here I stood, the new cantina owner, looking on in shock as Izzy began calmly wiping off the table, setting chairs back in place, and sweeping up broken glass and cards as the two gamblers grabbed the arms of their friend and dragged him across the dirt floor, to the door, and out into the street.

"It's very typical, Señora," Izzy chuckled. "I've seen these guys come in here before. I'm not opposed to gambling actually, but these guys are always trouble. Maybe if we take away their toys, they'll come in and act in a civil manner. Until then, I'm just gonna keep throwing them out!"

I thanked Izzy and knew that I had much to learn. A cantina's clientele was very different from a fandango's! Over time, I got to know many of the *gavachos*, or foreigners, in San Antonio. They'd stop in for a drink or, in some cases, a few—guys like James Bowie, John Twohig, Deaf Smith, Colonel Travis, John Hays, Davy Crockett, José Cassiano—yes, him! A favorite regular of mine was Lieutenant Francisco de Castañeda, who'd been stationed at Béxar for over a dozen years. He owned two small houses on the northwest corner near the Alamo and would come in accompanied by certain Mexican commanders and soldiers. So many military men, and even a few fugitives, drifted in and out of San Antonio back then. Shorty's was a great, dark refuge to grab a quick bite, make plans, have a good laugh, and enjoy a drink or two. Within two short years, more and more of my customers were men who'd just come in from the United States. Soon, this city became home to folks from all over the world coming in to mix and do business with the local Tejanos.

I recognized one señor who started coming in by himself from time to time: Juan Silverio Flóres de Abrego. Apparently, this courier from Laredo hadn't forgotten me! He lived just outside San Antonio. Sometimes he rode out with a military unit and would be gone for days at a time. His job as courier frequently took him out of town on short trips. We'd sort of lost track of one another.

An arrow to his left foot as a young boy had caused that slight limp; as a result he'd also lost a couple of toes. I could perceive his gait even in the dark of the cantina whenever he entered. Silverio frequently bragged that he could do just about anything in spite of that old injury. It sure didn't affect his jovial personality one bit.

"*¿Qué cuentas*, María Andrea? What do you have to say? What's new around here?" he'd ask, smiling as he watched me serve him a tequila shot along with his favorite taco.

"Not much, Silverio. You know Doña Gertrudis married José Cassiano last April, right?"

"Aye!" he growled. "I'll never know what a lady like that sees in *un zurullón*, a turd, like him," Silverio took a swig, raising his eyebrows to watch my reaction.

"Why would you call José *un zurullo*, Silverio?" I stood across from him with my arms crossed to signal my disapproval.

"He and his family come in here and act like they own the place, that's why. He spent time running slaves in Louisiana, María Andrea. Then he comes to Béxar, becomes Catholic, hangs out with the *ricos*, the rich people, and helps his dad open a store, all the while scheming to accumulate more."

"Accumulate what, Silverio? As for slaves, this town hasn't allowed slaves as long as I've been in San Antonio." I began wiping down the counter, listening and waiting for his reply.

"Wealth, land, women, whatever he can get his hands on. I've run messages from him to lots of places I can't even mention. Ach . . . *eses norteamericanos y sus ideas*. These North Americans and their ideas, María Andrea. And don't think if they had their run of the place we wouldn't have slavery here. 'Cause I know we would!"

"What do you mean, *sus ideas*?" I pressed him.

"Their ideas, María Andrea! They have money and land, not always gotten by fair means either." Silverio took another swig. "I'm pretty sure some of the cattle being run up north by Cassiano's associates right now come from your good friend, Mr. Pérez's herd."

"Now, that can't be true, Silverio. Señor Pérez applied for a cattle brand long ago that his family continues to use, even after his death. They mark all their cattle," I countered, setting bottles in a box under the counter.

"Don't mean nothin,' sweetheart. I've run up alongside many cattle drives and the original marks on them beeves are still visible in spite of alterations made by rustlers. If you ever plan to have cattle, you'd be wise to get a cattle brand, María Andrea, but just know that don't stop natives and thieves from runnin' 'em up north to sell in Natchitoches. Only helps if you have honest neighbors and a good gun."

I left the bar area to tend to a couple of customers while Silverio finished off his tequila. Soon, he left some money on the counter, waved his hat high in the air toward me, and headed for the door. I knew he'd be waiting for me outside once we closed up for the night. He always waited for me when he was in town, and I looked forward to our late-night walks together.

One night he asked me, "Where is your father, María Andrea? There's something I want to ask him."

"None of us knows where he is, Silverio. He didn't come to San Antonio with the rest of us. He remained loyal to the Spanish to the end, you know. Josepha guessed that once he felt like the tide was shifting toward Mexican rule, he sailed for Cuba, too ashamed to face his sons and family."

"What did he have to be ashamed of, María Andrea? Was he not a good provider for your family?" Silverio probed.

"We all looked up to him, but the truth is, we didn't really know him. Once my father made up his mind, he was loyal to a fault: he fought ferociously as a Royalist, and he expected his sons to do the same. In his mind, the Spanish king with his missions and presidios offered the best options for people. It had to be a terrible blow to him when Mexico gained independence and sent the Spanish home."

"So, María Andrea, have you noticed a bit of conflict between the Mexican officials and these new incoming settlers? That Law of April 6th forbids further immigration from the north. No more *norteamericanos*. What do you think about that?"

"I'm not happy about it, to tell you the truth, Silverio. This town had less than a thousand settlers when my family arrived; you know how it was. The indigenous people, the local Tejanos, and the Canary Islanders didn't always see eye to eye, but they got along fairly well. For some reason, folks didn't want to settle in this wilderness. Once offers of land for cattle and farming went out in exchange for settling here, San Antonio began looking like a small and prosperous town. Stores. Banks. Cantinas. 'Course, I'm speaking as a woman in business now, but I don't see the Mexican government supporting either its soldiers or its citizens the way I wish it would. These settlers coming in with their coins, Silverio, are helping to set up a real prosperous town. I'm getting tired of feeling ignored when it comes to the services we need. Mexican taxes keep rising every year. Where exactly is all the money going that I'm paying, Silverio? What does it provide?"

Silverio just smiled when the questions got too hard and swept me into his arms. He seemed so satisfied with his life and full of some magical elation just to be alive and breathing. I loved talking to him, even when we disagreed. I felt such energy and protection with every hug he wrapped me in!

CHAPTER 21: A MARRIAGE, A BABY, AND A DISAPPEARING HUSBAND

MARRIAGE TO SILVERIO, 1827

As time went on, I got to know Silverio as quite an industrious, honest soldier and thought to myself that he might be "the marrying kind," as my mother used to say. He was so unlike many gambling scoundrels I'd met after leaving the Governor's Palace. One of the many evenings he walked me home after my bartender Mario and I'd locked up, we walked but a short way when he stopped suddenly, turned, got down on his good knee, and shakily opened a small fuzzy-brown box.

"We've talked about this before, María Andrea, and now that you're out of the Governor's Palace and making a living for yourself, I'm asking you: will you marry me? I don't have much, but you know I'm a good, honest man and I plan to provide a place to stay near town. I've loved you since I first saw you in the market in Nacogdoches as a young girl. I came to live in San Antonio hoping to find you again and make you my wife. I intended to ask your father, but, well, that didn't quite work out."

After attending Doña Gertrudis's second wedding to José Cassiano and later the wedding of a friend from Mamá's church, I felt ready at twenty-four to be married myself. Here was another opportunity I'd often dreamed of. I stood there, holding my hands over my mouth, looking this imperfect, trembling man in the eyes and feeling the energy and promise of another full moon that night. I finally bent down, kissed him, and said, "Yes, Silverio, I will marry you!"

My heart filled with sheer happiness. I helped him up and without another word, the two of us held hands as we continued the short walk to Mamá's *jacál*. Her *jacál* suddenly seemed so small and unkept. Smiling, Silverio pulled me close and kissed me goodnight. I loved the feel and smell of him even more from that moment on: a musky mix of tobacco, his swig of tequila, and his soft leather jacket. I used to catch that scent of his at unexpected moments every once in a while after he disappeared. It brought back sweet memories of a dear, loving man.

"So you did marry this Silverio? I remember hearing his journal entry about seeing you for the first time in the marketplace in Nacogdoches. He had been following you, Señora!"

Yes, he had. We were married in a simple ceremony in May 1827 with my sisters Josepha and Nieves and my friend Doña Gertrudis standing in attendance at Mission San José. My cousin José Paulo and his wife and four children were living within the mission at the time, so they celebrated with us as well. I didn't feel as fancy as I had when I was dressed for my first fandango, but Nieves pulled the hair up on both sides of my head to meet in the back with a small pink rose. I felt calmer, more myself, more mature, and confident. Everyone said I looked simply radiant on my wedding day.

My mother borrowed the white, lacy, straight-line, calf length gown that I wore from our neighbor, Gloria Quiñones, whose daughter Belén had worn it a year earlier. Her husband Gilberto, a kindly water bearer, had unfortunately been killed by Comanche while trying to bypass a skirmish near Coleto Creek. His water barrels, filled to the brim, did not allow his mule to travel quickly enough to escape the attack. Although Mrs. Quiñones happily lent me her daughter's dress, it was the saddest thing to watch tears fall unrelentingly from her shiny, dark, grieving eyes during my ceremony.

Cool breezes soothed us at last. Trees leafed out, offering tender new green shoots reaching for the sun's caress. Fragrant pink bougainvilleas and early white rose blooms around the churchyard blessed us all on my wedding day that Saturday, May 5. Mamá brought over our wedding cake—decorated with white frosting and lavender violets and yellow daisies she'd made herself— ferrying the cake, along with several candles, in a cart driven by Father Jiménez, who would be officiating.

That afternoon, Doña Gertrudis arrived on the back of her white horse with José Cassiano at the reins. She looked as beautiful as ever in a soft-yellow sleeveless dress that covered her knees and fell in folds at her shins. She carried a cream-colored shawl to cover her shoulders for the service. Mr. Cassiano looked handsome in his suit and astonished as always. His blond hair stuck out every which way while his big blue eyes darted here and there in his signature nervous manner. I told Mamá he looked surprised, astonished, or anxious most of the time. When we were alone, Mamá would widen her eyes, mess up her hair, and raise her eyebrows til we both laughed at her private imitation of José.

Izzy walked over to the mission church wearing a straight-line Mexican jumper made of cream-colored muslin, with embroidered flowers dancing along the hem. Pink and purple satiny peacocks on the front set off her lovely caramel-colored skin. She covered her arms with a navy shawl. My sister Nieves, dressed in a pale blue jumper, helped serve cake and lemonade with Izzy at her side on the walkway near the entry to the church after the service. A small group gathered to wish Silverio and me well as a small carriage awaited in the street. Everything about that fresh and lovely morning is indelibly etched in my mind.

I smiled up at Señora and nodded. I could totally imagine it.

Once all the guests had been greeted, Silverio and I took a short ride in the small white *carrito* decorated with garlands of spring flowers. We headed to Military Plaza where we joined a multitude of Saturday revelers for an afternoon and evening of music, food, and fun. José Paulo provided fiddle music for us, along with several other musicians.

I was surprised to see so many people out celebrating the weekend, but Silverio laughed, put his arm around me, and joked, "Come on, María Andrea, people will celebrate a dead skunk if it means music, drinks, and dancing!" He threw his head back and laughed like a cowboy, his mustache twitching at every breath above sparkling white teeth. Today he wore his signature brown suede jacket with fringes and dressy black pants with brown leather cowboy boots. Added to that was a new white shirt and tie bought especially for our ceremony. Aye, he looked *muy guapo*, so very handsome! Quite a few of the Chili Queens recognized him and made a fuss whenever he went over to order something from their tables. I saw several whispering while looking over at me, smiling and waving.

I joined the crowd, this time as a customer not a waitress, singing and dancing 'til midnight. I glanced over at the table where, only a few short years before, Doña Gertrudis and I had served up food for the military captains. Now young Chili Queens carried on the important jobs of joking and laughing with customers and cooking and clearing tables, just as we had done. Every book has pages that must be turned, and I'd already lived that beautiful chapter.

Silverio saved the best surprise for the end of the evening. Unbeknownst to me, he'd arranged for us to move into what used to be Ramón Musquiz's house on the northeast corner of Military Plaza. The year before, the house had been awarded to Deaf Smith as a reward for his military activities, but when Mr. Smith didn't return from Colombia to claim it, Silverio stepped in with the help of his "gamblers," he said (to irritate me, I suppose), to lease the property. I couldn't have been closer to all the things I loved about San Antonio: Military Plaza, the Chili Queens, Shorty's, the Governor's Palace, San Fernando Cathedral, and my sisters. Nieves had taken over renting Mamá's *jacál* after Mamá passed in 1831. Bordering Military Plaza at this time, merchants, including José Cassiano and his family, had set up shops along with men like Juan Barrerra (San Antonio's city clerk), Nathaniel Lewis, John Twohig, and others.

Silverio never cared much about my bank account; he only knew that I was making payments to Nathaniel Lewis because I told him before we were married about the loan I was responsible for repaying. At first he thought I just worked at Shorty's, then later understood I had business payments and bills that had to be paid as the owner of the establishment. Earlier, I'd always paid a small amount to help Mamá with her rent for what turned out to be the final four years of her life. In addition to helping with that, we newlyweds now had our own rent, bills, and taxes to pay, something I kept reminding Silverio about. He responded by laughing and suggesting that I would be less stressed about those kinds of things just as soon as we started a family. I told him I'd be less stressed if he could contribute more money! That only made him mad. The Mexican military paid what they paid, so I never made that kind of comment again. If all went according to plan, I'd have Shorty's paid for over the span of the next nine years, by 1836.

It took us a while to deliver a live baby, but a few short years later in 1831, our beautiful Francisca was born, healthy as could be! I marveled at her spindly, long-legged body and friendly face as we sat outside in the afternoons. The two of us sprawled across my mission blanket, listening to the sounds of mockingbirds, horses, cicadas, and crickets as breezes brought us scents reminiscent of Ábu's flowers, rosemary, and basil. Sometimes we'd catch drifting aromas of cinnamon from a nearby bakery, taking me back to the kitchen at the Governor's Palace.

Those days filled me with a contentment that is hard to express. Life felt simple and fulfilling then and I couldn't wait to introduce Francisca, named after my dear Mamá, to her aunts and uncles and to this beautiful city of San Antonio with its rivers, cathedral, missions, *mercados*, and Chili Queens. I wanted to tell her stories about her great-grandmother, Ábu. I wanted her to know the stories about my family's early years together traveling and establishing settlements in Spanish territories. I wanted her to feel a part of this giant historical river that carried us from the hills of Guanajuato all the way to colorful San Antonio in this big, wonderful place called Texas.

Sometimes I took baby Francisca to a neighbor's house with me, something I know now was a great risk. I'd taken a short day job of caring for Juan Barrerra when he fell ill. He brightened and revived so much upon seeing my baby! Francisca never came down with so much as a sniffle as a result of our visits. Maybe she flourished as a result of Nieves's tender, loving care during the afternoons combined with my herbal remedies, I'm not sure. Warm, wonderful sunshine in the backyard made her very happy.

Silverio held Francisca for long periods whenever he was home. He'd gently sing her Spanish love songs like the ones the *guitarreros* sang in Military Plaza. He was a very affectionate father, as much as we saw him. But San Antonio didn't feel completely settled yet; I wished he would've been able to stay home with us more. Unfortunately, he was called upon frequently to run messages here and there.

When he left, baby Francisca, Nieves, and I would go visit Josepha on Sundays. Having had children of her own by then, Josepha taught me how to burp the baby by sitting her upright on my bouncing knee and how to bathe her so she wouldn't cry or feel frightened in the water. I knew my baby was in safe hands when I left her with Nieves in the late afternoons. At that time, I went to work at Shorty's immediately after our early dinners. Josepha said she and her kids looked forward to visiting with baby Francisca, too, so they'd walk over to visit Nieves some days.

"Fresh air, María Andrea. A healthy baby needs lots of fresh air!" Josepha would say, grabbing her Mission San Juan Bautista blanket and flying outside, baby in arms. I miss those days. My daughter Francisca grew up to be an intelligent and beautiful young lady. She inherited a jovial, carefree disposition just like her father's. When she married years later at what seemed to me to be a very young age, all the memories of my own wedding at Mission San José and our unofficial reception at Military Plaza came flooding back to me.

Later in that same fall of 1831, the last I knew, Silverio'd been carrying military correspondence for Colonel Castañeda. When Silverio didn't return home after two weeks' time and no one had seen him around town, I tracked Colonel Francisco de Castañeda down to ask if he knew where my husband was. The colonel said twenty-seven men were recently lost at the Battle of Gonzales, but he couldn't recall if Silverio was one of them or not. He said those men died doing what brave men do in times of war—fighting—carrying out their mission 'til the end. He sounded so patronizing.

I could feel anger welling up inside me. I dared to ask him how a military leader could not know who or where the men under his command were. How could he not know if he'd lost his courier? He paused, lowered his eyes to meet mine and said, glaring through narrowed eyes, "Sometimes we don't take names until the battle's over, madam." I wadded up my kerchief and threw it to the ground. I then turned and stomped away in disgust. To think I'd admired this man!

Colonel Castañeda stopped by Shorty's two days later with some flowers to express his heartfelt sympathy for how he'd acted. He said he wanted to thank me and my family for being a part of the fight for Texas liberty. In fact, Silverio had been one of the men who died by joining the fight with the Mexican army, which had been attempting to take that old cannon from the folks in Gonzales. My heart felt ripped in half. Why hadn't anyone come to tell me this before? *Flores* for the death of Señor Flóres de Abrego? Hmm. Did he really consider that to be compensation?

I fully realized only then that I'd never see Silverio again. Feeling completely numb, I stormed over to my sister's to pick up baby Francisca around ten that night, leaving Mario to lock up. When I told Nieves what the Colonel said, she grabbed the flowers I'd brought and threw them outside in the street. The two of us hugged and cried ourselves to sleep. I felt saddest about the fact that I couldn't even remember what the three of us had done the last time Silverio stopped home to hold his daughter and me.

I stood up and moved over to squat and hug Señora for a few moments as she paused for this painful memory. Caramela suddenly appeared and settled on across her feet.

"Maybe we should quit for today, Señora. What do you think?"

"I suppose we should, dear. What followed Silverio's disappearance and death would only lead to more heartbreak, Miss Rizzo. But I must share it tomorrow after I settle my mind."

"Of course. Let's get some rest then and meet back tomorrow. I think Caramela is ready to accompany you home a bit earlier today!"

CHAPTER 22: MORE LOVED ONES DEPART, 1831-1833

Gazing over at the blue cloth on the ground in front of Señora Candelaria, I searched for clues of what information this new day would bring. The cloth was folded, empty.

"I hope you slept well, my dear. Are you ready, Miss Rizzo?"

"Yes, I am. I brought two new pens and steno pads, so I'm ready to write!"

Cholera. Smallpox. Influenza. You name it, these diseases snuck into our city and claimed the lives of hundreds all around town. We knew some sickness or another always lurked in our midst, so we prepared as best we could with what little supplies we could find. Soldiers kept getting killed in any one of a multitude of mounting battles, some never knowing what the conflict in which they were fighting was even about! Some of the hardest losses for me turned out to occur in the years 1831 through 1833.

I've already told you about the disappearance and death of my dear Silverio. That was certainly one of the most painful losses, plunging me into single parenthood and leaving baby Francisca fatherless.

Mamá died in the fall of 1831, the same year Francisca was born. I truly wished my mother could have met this precious namesake of hers. If Ábu would've met her, I'm very sure she'd have made some remark about her mother, me, having given birth to another *insecto bastón*!

Yes, it was October 23, 1831, that my dear mother Francisca died unexpectedly of "a pain." She'd been complaining about intestinal pains, but most of us thought she was eating too much salsa, something she made fresh almost daily. She and Edgar could eat an entire batch in one evening, rolling it in tortillas and spooning it over goat cheese. Edgar would arrive with varieties of the hottest little peppers we'd ever tasted. The two of them sat outside during many evenings on the small patio Edgar had cleared and leveled outside her *jacál*. They'd simply pass the time eating, talking, and laughing. Sometimes they spoke in that language I didn't understand.

Using Ábu's guidance in a dream, I concocted a few remedies for Mamá, but these soothed her only for short periods. Soon the pains reared up uncontrollably, and I felt completely helpless.

In the end, Josepha, Nieves, and I tearfully packed our mother's few possessions from the Calle Dolorosa house and took what none of us could use to San Fernando church for those in need. Mamá didn't have much, but each of her daughters selected one of her precious mission blankets to keep. We swept and cleaned the premises.

Nieves remained there for a short while, renting the house before turning the place back to the Delgados. My mother was buried in the Campo Santo, a well-maintained cemetery near San Fernando Cathedral. My brothers Nacho, Carlos, and Justo and my cousin José Paulo made it for her service, but all of them disappeared too soon afterward to discuss any business. They seemed increasingly like strangers to me and my sisters.

After the burial, Edgar, who loved our mother greatly, and whose company she had craved for the laughter and news of Laredo and Guanajuato he'd bring, stood below a lone scrub oak at Campo Santo with his hat in his hands, head bowed low, wiping his eyes throughout the service. He never approached our family, but instead turned slowly to mount his horse after the service. From a distance, I was surprised to see Josepha run over, reach up, and ride off with him along the river.

My good friend and mentor, Doña María Gertrudis Cassiano, the former María Gertrudis Cordero, died of dropsy and was laid to rest in the cemetery of San Fernando on September 29, 1832, nine years after her first husband, Colonel Cordero. Her second husband, José, would go on to marry another and another and then another, accumulating things, mostly property, at every step just as Edgar had predicted. In the end, he shared his accumulations generously I heard.

In early September 1833, James Bowie's wife Ursula Marie de Veramendi, her parents, and her stepbrother all died of cholera in Monclova. James took it incredibly hard, drinking himself into what I figured would lead to his own premature burial. I cut him off early during the evenings at Shorty's, but he had other sources for drinks. I loved Ursula, his wife. She knew no strangers and made it her business to extend kindness to everyone she met. She had made my family feel welcome by inviting us to lunch at her parents' house after church on Sundays when we'd just arrived in San Antonio. A more kind and welcoming family I'd never met. When Ursula died, I felt like I'd lost one of my best friends.

In 1833, my cousin Encarnación, who married a volatile scoundrel of a soldier from Laredo by the name of Ylario, ran away after being compromised or forcibly raped by the man. We were frantic. No one was able to find Encarnación, so my aunt Petra wrote a letter to the then Mayor Antonio de la Garza asking for his assistance in finding her. She begged him to find and apprehend Ylario. Meanwhile, many neighbors took time off to search for our dear cousin, with no luck.

Nine months later, we were notified that Encarnación died during childbirth on July 8, 1833, at the age of twenty-six. Her tiny baby, delivered with great difficulty and possibly in unfavorable and unclean surroundings, died just three days after her mother. Rumor had it that Ylario sneered, rubbed his hands together, and walked out after taking one look at his dead baby daughter. There never was a sadder funeral than this one, first on account of losing such a beautiful young mother and then for the loss of her baby child. It took months before any of us could even talk about it without breaking down.

My brother Justo swore he'd track Ylario down and make him pay for what he'd done. Well, Ylario was found dead in a creek about a month later. Cause of death: unclear. No one was charged. Because of mounting tensions between Mexicans and Texans, compounded by certain native tribes, it was impossible to know how he'd been killed or by whom. It could have been anyone unsympathetic to his military leanings, or even someone he owed money to. We never knew for sure.

CHAPTER 23:
PRESAGE TO THE SIEGE

OCTOBER 1835

In early October of 1835, I began imagining how we might celebrate another anniversary of my running the cantina. Soon, I would take total possession of the business. Shorty stopped in one evening, stooped and ornery-looking and walking like a very old man now. But age couldn't dim the twinkle in his dark eyes, framed by a head of very thick salt and pepper hair. He slumped down at the bar, so I grabbed a cup, into which I poured his favorite tequila with a tiny shot of orange juice. I stood opposite him with my arms spread wide on the bar.

"Shorty, it's good to see you! How've you been, Señor? I've missed you!" Without waiting for his reply, I cheerfully lowered myself onto my elbows and continued, "I'm thinking it's not too early to plan a fiesta to celebrate the cantina operating under my ownership when I hit the final year. It's already been nine years! Can you believe it? I'll have Señor Lewis paid in full very soon! I have to thank you for giving me this opportunity, Shorty. Without your support, this—"

"María Andrea," Shorty growled. "Don't you see what's happening here? Have you noticed all the Mexican soldiers flowing into town? There's going to be big trouble in San Antonio . . . and *soon*. I have a feeling you'll be lucky to keep this place running after the end of this year. What will you do if this business is confiscated like so many others have been?"

"Confiscated? Shorty, yes, I've seen the Mexican soldiers rolling into town, wave after wave. They stop in here all the time. Martín Perfecto de Cós and his men sit and order food and drinks at a table right next to a table where James Bowie and Ben McCulloch might be seated. Or they'll straddle the bar next to Juan Seguín and his friends Gregorio Esparza, Salvador Flores, and Antonio Cruz de Arocha. They're all fine men keeping me in business. What's so bad about that?"

Head tucked close to his chest, Shorty swiveled discreetly to look around in the darkness at the clientele. The candles and kerosene lanterns shed only enough light to let folks see dimly lit faces and tabletops. He then leaned forward across the bar to make sure no one further down was listening and whispered, "Those damned *norteamericanos*, María Andrea, that's what the problem is."

Whispering back, I replied respectfully, "Shorty, those 'damned *norteamericanos*' are bringing people here, families, and starting businesses! San Antonio's finally starting to look like a real town with churches, businesses, roads. Some of my best customers are *norteamericanos*! As far as I can see, the folks whose families have been here for hundreds of years, like Mr. Seguín's, don't have any quarrel with the newcomers from the north. They conduct themselves like friends and neighbors."

"Be careful what you wish for, María Andrea. Edgar tells me that Mexican General Cós is preparing his army for a fight over this town as we speak. Cós is General Santa Anna's brother-in-law, if that gives you any idea what to expect. He hates Americanos; he wants them out of here! He's fortified the town plazas west of the river, just itching for a fight. He's preparing the Alamo right now! You won't be seeing Ben Milam and his boys in here for a while. You know why? Because they're out gathering Texan forces along Salado Creek. Something's about to burst wide open here."

"What in heaven's name does everybody want, Shorty?" I pleaded, beginning to wonder for the first time if I truly *would* be able to hold on to the business long enough to truly own it. Just a few more payments . . .

"Each side wants the same thing: to be in control of San Antonio and all of Texas," Shorty snorted, shaking his head. "But each side wants to do things their way, and . . ."

Just then Edgar walked in, ducking his head under the doorway, boots clicking on the hard dirt floor. As he walked toward us, he carried his cowboy hat, and

I noticed his boots seemed to be covered in more mud and dust than usual. He sat down next to Shorty. He, too, swung around to eyeball the customers before swinging back around and saying anything.

"Hey, Edgar. How're things with you?" Shorty moaned with a sidelong glance.

"They've been better, I guess you could say," Edgar said, knocking his knuckles on the bar. "Looks like trouble is on the horizon, and it's a little too close to home," he sighed, lifting his cowboy hat and plunking it on the bar to his right. Mario approached to serve him a shot of tequila.

"We were just talking about that," Shorty sighed. "Seguín, Bowie, and Fannin plan to lead an advance toward the missions later this month where the Mexicans are shoring up for a fight. I saw Captain James Neill ride back into town and we all know what that means. He's the Texans' man for artillery preparations. What have you heard, Edgar?"

"I saw Mexican soldiers wheel a couple of cannons up close to the Alamo. One of Colonel Castañeda's men says that Mexican General Ugartechea has promised to bring in reinforcements. There's no doubt a big battle's about to bust out. I came to suggest that you, María Andrea, might want to lock and board this place up for a while. Go stay with your sister Nieves and your daughter; stay off the streets. If it were me, I'd send Izzy and Mario home until further notice too."

"Now why would I do that, Edgar? This cantina's a refuge for folks from all sides, all positions in life. I have a few final payments to make to Mr. Lewis, money owed to my sister Nieves for taking care of Francisca, and I owe several vendors for goods purchased. I can't just close up and walk off. I pray daily that I'll be able to make my payments at the end of each month as it is, and sometimes it's pretty close!"

"She might be right about that, Edgar," Shorty conceded. "Maybe if you stayed in town, you could stop in and check on things, hang around, and just 'listen' for news," Shorty suggested, head still hanging low as he spoke in soft tones, checking out two new Mexican soldiers in uniform who had walked in and were heading toward the side wall.

"I could probably do that. Hell, who knows what's going to happen here? How about another tequila, María Andrea?"

I realized then the importance of keeping my ears open for news. It wasn't enough to pray for peace so I could make my payments; I needed to contribute in some way. Ever since Silverio died, Edgar waited outside to walk me back to my sister's like he used to before I was married. From this point forward, I decided I needed to use that opportunity to share whatever I'd heard and ask him questions about what he knew in return. I couldn't tell for sure which side he supported in this latest atmosphere, the Mexicans or the Texans, but, either way, he knew a whole lot about what was going on and who was in town.

My cantina truly was the calm in the middle of this incredibly complicated storm. I even convinced Shorty, before he passed, that we needed to allow card playing and gambling again. It seemed like the men needed an outlet, something to look forward to besides being marched off for battles or skirmishes, followed by hearing news of more deaths. I must have been convincing because he gave me his blessing.

It dawned on me that, as proprietor, I probably should also pay more attention to what was happening politically in San Antonio as well as in the whole territory of Texas. Decisions and laws affected me and my business, so I should make it my business to pay more attention to who was doing what.

One evening in late October, Colonel Travis himself and Stephen Austin stopped in with San Antonio's mayor José Angel Navarro for dinner and drinks. They kept their heads so close together, I couldn't really tell what they were talking about. When I came to clear their plates, I heard something about Juan Seguín and his men advancing on the missions. Then they stopped talking until I left. Later, I heard Colonel Travis mention the name Edward Burleson as a possible replacement, but I didn't know for what or for whom.

Shortly afterward on the same night, Mexican General Ugartechea walked in with his Lieutenant Castañeda. Spying the Texans in the dimly lit cantina, they politely nodded their heads to signal hello and walked to the other side of the barroom for a table. Izzy identified the Mexican military men for me. Both just wanted something to eat and drink, so we served them with smiles and ears wide open while we joked about borrowing their shiny medallions to help us light up the place a bit. They treated me and Izzy with great respect as they ordered tamales, rice, and tequila. The two of them also spoke in such hushed tones that I couldn't hear a word of their conversation.

Later that evening, a drunken John Twohig got up and stumbled over to the Mexican military men's table to ask if they needed any more cannons. "I heard that you missed out on that one in Gonzales," he slurred, "but I know where you can get one real cheap if you need one! It won't fire worth a damn, but it's a cannon!" His body swerved back and forth at the edge of their table as the two distinguished Mexican officers sat back and waited for him to finish. Izzy hurried over, apologized, and led John carefully back to his table near Mario and the bar.

Izzy later told me that John was referring to that fight over an old six-pound cannon that took place in Gonzales last month. The two military officers showed great restraint by simply sitting back in their chairs, ignoring Mr. Twohig and letting him blabber on. They chuckled and quietly resumed their conversation as soon as Izzy escorted John away.

At the end of the evening, I asked Edgar about the cannon. As usual, he knew all about it.

"Well, los Americanos in Green DeWitt's settlement in Gonzales were given a cannon by the Mexican government back in 1831 to help fend off native attacks. Hell, that old cannon, repaired, broken, and repaired again, pretty much only belched smoke every time it sent off a shot, according to Señor McCoy. Once ol' Green DeWitt died of cholera, the Mexican military officers wanted their cannon back, especially since trouble seemed to be smoldering over that way.

San Antonio's mayor, José Antonio Navarro, sent a letter to the mayor of Gonzales, stating that the cannon had been a loan and it was time to give it back. The people of DeWitt's colony refused to comply. Mexican General Ugartechea, commander of Mexican forces at Béxar, then ordered his Lieutenant, Francisco de Castañeda, and one hundred mounted dragoons to drag that dinky good-for-nothing excuse for artillery back to San Antonio de Béxar!"

Edgar threw his head back and laughed at the thought of it. "Aye, María Andrea, I couldn't even make this stuff up!" He kicked a rock down the street for emphasis.

"The damned Americanos, they . . ." he snorted, ". . . they made a . . . a . . . aye *díos mío*! My god, they made a *bandera*!" his voice rose with derision. He could hardly catch his breath for laughing so hard. "They made a . . . a damned flag . . . with the message, 'Come and Take It' painted with a picture of a cannon on it! They were *not* going to give up that lousy, good-for-nothing cannon, come hell or high water. *Imagínate*, María Andrea! *Están locos*! They're crazy! *La hija*, the daughter, of Green DeWitt, newly married Naomi, cut the *bandera* from the material of her wedding dress!" At this, Edgar started coughing and laughing so hard, he had to double over to catch his breath. "Mario, your bartender, said . . . she probably had that made special for her wedding night!" Again, he doubled over, saliva dripping from his mouth. I stood quietly by, speechless, shaking my head until he laughed himself calm, wiped his eyes and mouth on his sleeves, and continued. I failed to see the humor in any of this.

"Soon, like ants gathering on sugar, there were so many Americanos gathered there on the bank of the river to defend their cannon that Mexican General Ugartechea, hearing of the situation, sent word to Castañeda to retreat. He was told to retreat if he knew for sure that his Mexican soldiers were outnumbered. Well, hell yes they were outnumbered, according to one of the native scouts for Castañeda! Old Señor Pontín and those *gabachos*, stinkin' settlers from Gonzales, got to keep their damned wretched cannon after all!" Edgar laughed once again so hard he resumed coughing.

"Good for them, for standing up for themselves, Edgar. But aye *díos mío*, knowing this, I can't believe that Mr. Twohig approached those Mexican officers in Shorty's like that! Those two men handled his intrusion with such grace and decorum. At the time, I motioned for Izzy to lead Mr. Twohig back to his table. Izzy knew enough to step in the back and bring out a quesadilla and a cup of *menudo* to help sober him up. Those soldiers could have killed him right then and there. Mr. Twohig was so feeble, he could hardly stand up straight."

Since Edgar had not witnessed this encounter within the cantina, he delighted in my retelling as I described the Mexican generals waiting patiently for John to finish getting his words out. After hearing everything again, he threw himself down on the road in the dark of the night, laughing wildly. "*Esos pinches gabachos*, those stinkin' foreigners!"

His language could curl your hair. I had to pick him up, lest someone think he was terribly drunk. Maybe he was, I really couldn't tell. It seemed to me he was just poking fun at the Americans that night.

CHAPTER 24:
THE "SEIZE" OF BÉXAR, 1835

OCTOBER AND EARLY NOVEMBER 1835

"So, this cannon created quite a standoff, Señora. But the refusal of those citizens in Gonzales to yield the weapon contributed to even more hostile sentiment toward Texans on the part of Mexican military officials based in San Antonio. I imagine that generated more noticeable tensions in town."

"Oh yes. Mexican Lieutenant Castañeda had left the town of Gonzales with no cannon and his tail between his legs, so to speak."

I heard Juan Seguín telling men at Shorty's that, because of this refusal by mostly American settlers in Gonzales, he predicted it would be just a matter of time before there'd be retaliation by the Mexican army. The Texan army's numbers in town kept increasing just as the Mexican army's did. Texan citizens camped along the river and around the missions while Mexican soldiers took possession of the Alamo and surrounded the town plaza along the San Antonio River. James Bowie told us he'd been stationed at Salado Creek, just outside of San Antonio, to watch for incoming Mexican reinforcements.

The biggest surprise I witnessed came one evening when Colonel Sam Houston and Colonel William Travis entered for dinner and drinks. The more Sam drank, the easier it was for everybody in Shorty's to tune in to their conversation. The dirt floor in there absorbed most conversation, but these two men were hot in discussion!

"What the hell are we waiting for, Colonel? We have an easy advantage now, just like we did after our battle at Mission Concepción," Travis bellowed.

"Keep your voice down, Travis," Houston growled.

"Oh, what for? These folks don't speak English and the ones who do are on our side, Colonel. I don't know what you're waiting for!" Travis spat, leaning closer. "Please, enlighten me!"

"We need to train these soldiers, Travis. Many of these young men have never killed a man in their entire lives. They don't know how to cover or follow orders, nor what our signals are. Plus, we need more cannons. If we sit tight, the artillery will arrive and then we can proceed. Let's not be impulsive; we need to act strategically so we can win this one, Travis." Colonel Houston sat back in his chair, exhaling loudly and continuing to puff on a cigar as his ruddy cheeks billowed in and back out, smoke rings encircling the anxious face of a much younger, pleading William Travis.

"Look, we've got Thomas Rusk, who's just pulled into town with six hundred men from East Texas—*six hundred*—and three companies of over one hundred men are due here mid-November. Why are we standing around, Colonel?" Travis fidgeted with his fork and plate, leaning in. "Let's get in there and get this job done! My men are impatient."

"Well, it's your job, Colonel, to make them WAIT!" Houston roared, leaning in.

Houston then sat back, smoking calmly, squinting and staring hard at Travis all the while and flicking cigar ashes to the floor. Soon, his giant frame stood to leave. Travis quickly evacuated his chair and trailed close behind.

In late November of that same year, Colonel Houston came charging into the cantina, squinting frantically around the room at each person in there, yelling, "Where is he? Where the hell is he, Señora? Mario?" The fringes on his suede jacket shook as he spoke.

"Pardon, sir, but where is who, Colonel?" I set my bar towel down and approached him as all the other patrons stopped talking and looked to see what was happening.

"Bowie! Commander Burleson needs him right *now*! Oh god, he's *always* in here, but not when we need him to be. Just where the hell is that no good son of a drunken bitch?" He started walking toward the bar.

I tried to calm him down. "He'll most certainly be here later tonight, Señor Houston. When he shows up, I'll send him to find you, unless you'd rather stop back."

"Hell, the Mexican cavalry'll be at my throat before I make it back this way, Señora. As soon as he decides to grace you with his presence, tell him to hurry over and talk to Deaf Smith. And don't send him chock full of tequila, either. This is serious business," he growled, turning and stomping out.

I told Edgar about this encounter two nights later when he met up with me outside at closing time.

"Jesús, María Andrea, you get all the intelligence at Shorty's, it seems!" Edgar looked tired, yet relayed information that he already knew somehow.

"West of town near Alazán Creek, Deaf Smith spotted a train of pack animals headed our way from the south. He raced back to let Colonel Burleson know. Burleson ordered Bowie, who he finally found asleep under some bushes near the river, to take forty cavalry and cause a delay of that mule train. Colonels Houston and Burleson were convinced the mules were carrying pay for the Mexican soldiers."

"Well, was there any fighting, or just a commanding turnover of mules from the Mexicans to the Texans?" I asked Edgar.

"There's always a fight, María Andrea. Nobody goes down without a fight these days. Funny thing was, those forty pack animals were loaded! But not with soldier pay. What do you think they were carrying?"

I'd noticed that many of the newly arriving Mexican soldiers were not dressed as soldiers; they looked lean, mean, hungry, and hardly equipped for the recent frigid temperatures. San Antonio was experiencing a fiercely cool autumn, causing many incoming soldiers from Mexico to struggle just to keep warm. Unbeknownst to many, I'd begun leaving small bundles of extra shoes and clothing outside along the wall for them. These were people!

"I'd say the mules were carrying food and uniforms," I suggested to him.

"Nope, grass. *Grass* to feed the Mexican army's animals!" Edgar laughed, throwing his head back and closing his eyes as his whole body shook. *"Esos pinches gabachos*! They confiscated the Mexican army's GRASS!"

"Why are they bringing in supplies like that?" I mumbled, more to myself, but Edgar heard me as we approached my sister's house. "They should be shipping in food and clothing for their soldiers, since so many of the Mexican soldiers are dying of cold and hunger."

"I'm telling you, María Andrea, there's going to be big trouble here. When I see Colonel Jaime Neill, Ben Milam, and Francis Johnson riding into town from the north at the same time I see Mexican Colonels Cós and Ugartechea riding in from the south, each placing reinforcements all around the Alamo, I know we're going to see some action!"

Edgar continued sharing news. "I heard Stephen Austin complaining on the street to a mister Taylor Creed that T. J. Rusk brought all these volunteers in from East Texas itching for some action, yet Austin couldn't get even one of his own officers to agree to start fighting! He's convinced he has enough men to occupy the Alamo, boot the Mexicans out, and take control of San Antonio. Austin seemed half crazed to get to the fighting, but his men chose to listen to Colonel Houston, who advised patience."

I informed Edgar that I'd heard Colonel Houston insisting that Travis's men wait for more artillery and training too.

Then Edgar told me, "The next thing I heard, Austin left town for San Felipe, relieved of his duty per his own request. His order for attacking the Alamo on the 22nd of this month, not surprisingly, went over very poorly. What could he expect among men who once were eager, but now too cold and wet to shoulder their arms? His men are not convinced they have enough supplies to carry them through even one month of a siege now. Even Austin himself started feeling weak and couldn't stop coughing at this point. Food's getting harder to come by to feed the soldiers of either side, María Andrea."

"Yes, I've noticed it with some of my suppliers at Shorty's. Sometimes I lament why this chaos has to happen at the same time I'm committed to making my business successful . . . and trying to, well, keep it mine, Edgar."

"I'm getting too old for all of this, María Andrea," Edgar told me. "On your birthday, I want to introduce you to a friend of mine. You take the night off, and let's celebrate in Military Plaza. How about that?" Edgar didn't usually include me in his social plans, so I knew this was something important.

"Okay, but who is this friend? I don't have a lot of time for playing around, Edgar." I reminded him, yawning, as we approached my sister's house.

"You'll see, but I think you'll like him. He's got a good heart and I've known him forever. We don't always agree on politics, but he's an honest man." Edgar hugged me goodnight, smiling, with his usual, "Take care *amiga*, and may you sleep with the angels."

Edgar left me at my sister's and, as soon as I entered the side door, I saw him turn to walk toward Military Plaza instead of his *jacál*. It was pretty late for gathering, gambling, or whatever else he had in mind. But this was Edgar; always in the shadows, always watching. This was how he gathered so much information.

"Did you take Edgar up on that birthday offer?" I wondered aloud.

When my thirty-second birthday came around on December 1, 1835, I did take the evening off and walked with Edgar over to Military Plaza. I left little Francisca with my sister, Nieves, while Izzy and Mario took charge at Shorty's. I had total confidence everything would be fine without me, especially since it was a Tuesday night. Shorty's wouldn't be too busy.

Military Plaza seemed subdued that evening, though drinking, gambling, and cock fighting were still taking place in the shadows. Soldiers, huddled in groups, stood around nervously glancing at passersby while talking in hushed tones. A dusty restlessness mingled with the smell of cooked goat in the plaza, which cut through the smell of kerosene lamps. We could hear familiar music from a lone violin player playing a slow, melancholy tune over to the side near Cassiano's Mercantile. I looked more closely and realized it was my cousin José Paulo playing. Only a few Chili Queens had set up, their fires blazing low along the periphery on this cool evening. Shadowy figures moved slowly back and forth behind tables. Not as lively as it usually is, I thought. Must be the weather.

Mexican soldiers had begun roaming the streets in the area this very weekend, picking fights with Texan army volunteers along the river and in the plaza. Just a couple of months before, a Mexican general by the name of Santa Anna had overthrown the government in Mexico City and declared himself dictator. In addition to repealing the constitution, partly on account of the American settlers refusing to pay their taxes or tariffs, he vowed to stop the immigrant influx to San Antonio. Some American settlers countered by saying that, without receiving any support or services from the Mexican government, they had no reason to pay taxes. We could just feel the increased strains in relations.

That evening, I thought I saw my brother Justo pass by on a horse wearing a backpack and holding a rifle, but I figured it couldn't be him wearing a plain blue shirt with red criss-crossed suspenders and a tall white hat slumped low on his forehead. This was Mexican military attire. Then I remembered who was supposed to be paying his salary. In my heart, I'd hoped he'd be supporting the Texans, but my brothers had minds of their own. My heart swelled with sadness that he didn't acknowledge me. His eyes stared straight ahead as if in a trance. Maybe he didn't want to see me. I finally shook it off, realizing Edgar was checking my face with a look I couldn't comprehend as we continued walking along.

Once in the plaza, Edgar walked me over to a table and introduced me to a medium, solidly built man by the name of Candelario Villanueva. Candelario had been waiting for us, with a beer on the table next to an empty plate with tiny remnants of beans and corn on it.

Candelario made room for me next to him on the bench. He was *muy vaquero*, very cowboy, in appearance. Candelario sported an easy smile and a bit of a belly. His black shiny eyes and friendly way with conversation made him interesting and familiar to talk with. I liked him immediately because he seemed genuinely interested in what I had to say.

"Edgar tells me your mother and father came from Guanajuato," he said. "I've known Edgar since childhood, before his parents and family were killed outside Mexico City."

"Well, I was born in the Presidio connected to Mission San Juan Bautista, so I never got to spend any time in Guanajuato, but my mother and grandmother, Ábu, told me a lot about the mountains and rivers there. Did your family know my parents?"

"No, my family moved with another group when yours chose to join the mission at San Juan Bautista del Río Grande. Edgar stayed back with us until he got to be old enough to follow after your family. Being that he was the only one left in his family, folks did not encourage him to join the military as so many other sons were encouraged to do. As a teenage orphan, he was free to do whatever he wanted, and he wanted to help out your family. But the two of us never lost touch; he's like my brother. The ugly brother, if you know what I mean!" Candelario laughed with a twinkle in his eye as Edgar punched him lightly in the arm, with his usual, "Aye, *buey*! Hey, you ox."

Candelario complimented my conversational ease, something I picked up from my years at Shorty's. I felt completely comfortable talking and joking with him, and he had no problem keeping up conversation with the confident woman I'd become. We joked around, and yet I noticed he listened and cared about interesting topics such as the incoming *norteamericanos* and the Mexican government's lack of support. He seemed to care about what I thought about the various groups coming in to San Antonio. I must admit, I was instantly attracted to him.

"Have I seen you in Shorty's?" I asked, beginning to think maybe I'd seen him somewhere before.

"I've seen you there many, many times. I see how you treat your customers. I know how well you cook, and how easily you tease and make people laugh. I've been very impressed with you, even if you are an honest woman!" Again, he laughed as Edgar shot him the evil eye.

"Well next time you come in, be sure to tug on my sleeve and say hello! I like to get to know my customers—especially the regulars. And don't go digging in the bags outside. Those things are for the poor soldiers."

"Hell, everybody's poor these days, María Andrea. Does it matter which side they're fightin' for?" he grinned, raising his eyebrows up and down.

I smiled politely. "No, it doesn't—not to me. I've been serving all sides since I started at Shorty's and I don't plan to change that. Shorty's is like neutral territory, as far as I'm concerned."

Candelario laughed, raised his bottle of beer, and winked at Edgar. He sputtered in a guttural tone, *"Bueno! Entooonces!"* It reminded me of something Ábu used to say. He talked to me more about his memories of Guanajuato and about relatives of his who owned small ranches outside Mexico City and San Antonio.

Eventually, the three of us got up and spent a couple of hours walking and talking as we circled the plaza. I stopped to talk to José Paulo and introduced him to Candelario. I invited him to come play at Shorty's sometime. Edgar went around talking to so many people I didn't recognize. When we all stopped to sit back down again, I heard more history from Candelario.

"Everybody knew Edgar, the *muchacho* with no family. But your parents, María Andrea, treated him as one of their own when he came around. He was sweet on your mother, I guess you know that. He took her death pretty hard."

"Now that I think of it, yes, I remember he did hang around quite a bit. Mamá counted on him to help out with my brothers since my father had to be in so many different places working with the military. I had no idea Edgar had no family left during those days."

Edgar approached and mentioned that, with my permission, Candelario would like to begin escorting me home in the evenings. Edgar said his back and legs were beginning to bother him from all those years on horseback. I looked at Candelario, surprised that the two had apparently discussed this, and Candelario looked back at me, removing his hat and bowing low.

"At your service, María Andrea!" he smiled, scooping his hat in a wide half circle.

I shook my head and laughed at that moment, remembering a similar flourish by a different gentleman I'd met in a market years ago. Over time, Candelario turned out to be one of the best friends I ever had. Solidly built, quick, and witty like Edgar, Candelario seemed to appreciate me for just being me. Once the paperwork regarding Silverio's death was finalized, Candelario and I married in a quiet civil ceremony. He knew I'd been married before and adored my little Francisca. Unfortunately, Candelario and I didn't have a lot of time to ourselves in those days as tensions between the Mexican military and the Texans in San Antonio were escalating. Many of our friends in San Antonio left town, but my friend, Ana Esparza, stopped in to let me know she and her family were trying to decide whether to stay or go. I let her know our decision too; we had nowhere to go. We agreed to check in on each other, and we did for quite some time.

Shorty's usually buzzed with activity during these uncertain days. Izzy hustled around serving. She looked like a beautiful bumblebee, moving from table to table.

Mario, more easily stressed by deepening tensions among the clientele, kept drinks flowing from the bar, while Candelario took orders, joking with folks at their tables to lighten the atmosphere. The group of us never stopped moving until, suddenly, the four of us looked around and noticed the place was nearly empty! I can't forget this, it was the Friday after my birthday, December 4.

Thinking it odd, Candelario and I sent Izzy and Mario home from Shorty's to get some rest. It'd been an incredibly busy start to the weekend, much busier than normal, and both of them looked exhausted by ten o'clock. I'd spent most of that evening in the kitchen at Shorty's cooking rice, beans, and *pollo* for our many customers. I felt lucky that a friend of Edgar's from south of San Antonio kept food supplies coming in for us. But now, I wondered where everybody had gone!

At last, we locked the door. Candelario and I plunked ourselves down for a few minutes to catch our breath. I got up to prepare plates with leftovers for us to eat, while Candelario went over to make us each a cup of hot cocoa. Together, we closed out the account book for November, counted the cash, and took inventory of all alcohol, prepared food, and produce. I smiled, believing I wouldn't have trouble making the business payment for last month.

We decided to tackle the painstaking tasks of scrubbing floors and thoroughly cleaning tables, chairs, and the bar area. This was something we did to some extent every evening on account of all the sickness spreading around town. In every settlement we came to back when I was young, Ábu insisted on airing out the *jacáles* every morning and wiping down tables and chairs daily. She believed that miasmas and bad humors hung in rheumy and unpurged air just waiting to settle and make people sick.

It must have been two or three in the morning when, all of a sudden, we heard the rat-tat-tat of loud artillery fire coming from the direction of the Alamo.

"Jesú Chrísto, María Andrea, what the hell is that?" Candelario asked, stopping in mid-swipe at the bar.

"I have no idea, but . . ." Suddenly we heard a loud BOOM. "That was cannon fire, Candelario! It's the Alamo. Let's get out of here! I need to get Francisca," I panted, untying my apron and tossing it toward a hook in the kitchen but missing as I flew toward the door.

"Hold on, wait a minute . . . let's think about this, María Andrea!" Candelario panted, turning me around. "We're better off staying right here. Your sister has Francisca, so those two should be sheltered and safe," Candelario insisted, holding both of my arms as he stared into my eyes. "We need to stay right here tonight, *mi amor*, my love, and walk out of here during daylight hours tomorrow. It'll be much safer. We cannot walk out there right now in this darkness. We could be mistaken for rebel soldiers."

That night we propped ourselves against each other in the aisle of the kitchen near the fireplace, wearing jackets to stave off the frigid air. Covering our legs and feet with clean aprons and towels for warmth, we sat in half stupors, falling in and out of sleep. Artillery fire prevented us from getting any restful sleep, so there we sat, drowsily waiting and hoping for the calm of Saturday morning.

In the early morning hours of sunrise, we must have finally fallen asleep. All of a sudden, a frantic rapping at the door startled us both. Candelario bounded up, grabbed his rifle, and thundered, "*Quién es?* Who's there?" from behind the door.

"María Andrea? It's James, James Bowie. Your sister asked me to check on you. Are you there? María?"

"Yes, James. Just a minute and I'll get the door," I assured him. Once opened, James and a burst of brisk air rushed inside. I quickly closed and bolted the door. He looked like a wild animal, hair flying every which way, with an aspect of concern enveloping his solid, pink patchy face. He put his hands back in his pockets and shivered, pulling his shoulders up to his ears.

"Thank god you're alright! Who is this guy?" James demanded, pointing with his chin. "Is this the guy you were telling me about?"

"James, I'd like you to meet Candelario, my husband. He's been helping me run Shorty's. You've seen him here, I'm sure. We got spooked with all the artillery fire and cannon shots as we were cleaning up last night, so we decided we'd best stay inside 'til morning."

James extended a hand toward Candelario but greeted him with suspicion. "Pleased to meet you Mr. Candelario. How long have you been in town?"

"I was born in Mexico and grew up near here, Mr. Bowie. My uncle works on a local ranch, just a short distance outside San Antonio. What's going on out there?"

Candelario motioned with his head as he leaned his rifle against the wall and pulled his jacket tighter around him, crossing his arms to keep it closed.

"There's a lot of excitement right now. Colonel Neill distracted the Mexican forces with artillery fire at the Alamo while Ben Milam and Francis Johnson led a surprise attack on some of the nearby houses occupied by Mexican soldiers. That's the commotion you heard early this morning. Now we're trying to take possession of the Garza and Veramendi houses north of the plaza. I've got to slip back there to help dig some trenches so we can connect some of these other houses. It's not easy to do while dodging musket fire and cannon shots from the Mexican army, but we can't let up. We'll probably have to burn down a few dwellings in order to get a clearer shot at those guys inside the Alamo."

"Thanks for checking on us, James," I hugged his cold, pale, shivering body and then, holding his elbows at arm's length, thought to ask, "Can we get you something to eat?"

"Oh, Lord above, thank you, María Andrea. I could use a cup of coffee and anything you've got to eat. Is that asking too much?"

"Not at all, James. Candelario, help me make enough so Mr. Bowie can take some back to his men. No charge, Señor Bowie."

Bowie sat down at a table near the bar, removed his jacket, and placed it over his legs. He ran his red, raw hands through his wild, unruly hair. I quickly warmed water over a fire and made enough coffee for the three of us. Candelario cooked up a fast batch of two dozen tortillas to make tacos and filled them with black beans and Spanish rice. We wished we could've included a hearty portion of chicken for each of them, but supplies would be scarce until sometime next week, so I went very light on shredded meat. Mr. Bowie didn't seem to mind or notice.

He drank his coffee, joking as he described for us the head of the Mexican military. "Yeah, that army general of theirs, Martín Perfecto de Cós. They say he's the son of a doctor. He looks like a fancy *waddie* for all I can tell." ("Waddie" was a term for a temporary cattle rustler.) "He's a short fellow who issues orders with two gold earrings flashing in the sun. Travis tells me he travels with gold candlesticks stuck in his saddlebags too. I have no idea what that's all about or where he might have stolen those!"

"Does he have a large army with him?" Candelario asked.

"Oh, he's got men with him, but they look defeated already. They look underfed, without supplies, and underpaid, if ever paid! His men do not look motivated to fight a war they probably don't understand. Some aren't even wearing shoes, for Christ's sake. Several turned around and started walking back southward, they were so cold and hungry."

"I don't understand this, honestly." I puffed angrily. "This is Mexican territory, so why must these Mexican soldiers come in here and start pushing people around, stealing things and occupying the Alamo? This is their territory!"

"Well, María Andrea, let's just say I'm not the only settler despised by Santa Anna. If a settler comes from the north, he's despised and becomes a target of the Mexican military. If a settler comes from France, England, Scotland, or anywhere overseas, he's not welcome here either in the eyes of Santa Anna. Slaves are not allowed, per Mexican law, something that ruffles the feathers of a few of us who have plans to grow cotton. We've also got many local ranchers and farmers joining us in this rebellion who don't need slaves and are not as despised as us newcomers. It's very apparent that I'm not the only person here willing to run those mealy Mexican soldiers of Santa Anna's out of here. Speaking of which, I'd better get back out there so I can help with them trenches!"

Colonel Bowie finished his breakfast, stood up, took a final swig of his coffee, and thanked us both kindly, tucking the newly acquired provisions inside his coat pocket as he turned to go.

"Oh, let your sister know that you're still alive, will ya? And if I were you, I'd board this place up and stay out of the streets, the plaza, and anywhere near the Alamo for a while. Things are heatin' up, and I'd sure hate to see you get hurt. Don't forget about that gift I promised ya." He shook Candelario's hand and headed for the door. Before he left, he turned and said, "Oh, and Candelario, Juan Seguín's looking to pay for more good soldiers if you're interested or know somebody." With that, he turned and walked out into the street.

Candelario looked at me with expectant eyes and shrugged his shoulders. "Well, if we close Shorty's I might think about joining the fight, María Andrea. Let's get these dogs of Santa Anna's out of here so we can get back to business!" My heart sank. I just couldn't lose another.

Then he asked, "By the way, what gift was he talking about?"

I told Candelario we'd talk about it when we got home, but not to worry, it wasn't a diamond! He chuckled at that.

I couldn't even respond to Candelario's earlier statement. My mind swirled with familiar worries. But join up Candelario did, the very next day. Staying with my sister, I continued to get news from him whenever he stopped back in town. On Monday, December 7, just one day after the Texan army added Candelario, dear Ben Milam got shot down outside one of the houses. Candelario and some other soldiers managed to retake possession of the Navarro house as the Texans continued their strategy of inching their way toward the Alamo. They wanted to be in favorable positions for the bigger fight. I couldn't let my mind think about Candelario's fate every waking second. I hugged my sweet sister Nieves and little daughter Francisca daily for long periods of time, praying desperately for an end to this violence. I despaired for even an ounce of elusive peace to surround us as it had once upon a time.

When that particular battle was over, Edgar told me that this incident became known as the Siege of Béxar. Bexar spelled with an "x" and Bejar spelled with a "j" were early names given to San Antonio. The Villa de Bejar was the first Spanish settlement of San Antonio. It originally consisted mainly of the families of the presidio soldiers in San Antonio. At the time of this battle, Mexicans, under the orders of Santa Anna, occupied the Alamo, transformed it from a mission to a fort, and fought for control of the city of San Antonio.

Unlike Colonel Bowie's impression, Edgar described Colonel Cós as a very impressive military man, considering his small stature and undying loyalty to his purported brother-in-law, Santa Anna, earrings or no earrings. If I didn't know better, I'd have thought Edgar seemed quite sympathetic with the Mexican Centralists.

On December 9, Cós was forced to surrender. Edgar said Commander Burleson accepted and immediately sent his men, including Candelario, inside the Alamo compound to grab up all the Mexican weapons, equipment, and supplies. Burleson's men then ran Cós and his remaining soldiers out of town. They wouldn't be taken as prisoners because, as Edgar put it, San Antonio didn't have beans enough for its own Texan army, let alone enough to feed any rival Mexican soldiers.

Edgar warned, "Wait 'til Cós shows up back in Mexico City to inform on his surrender. His commander, Santa Anna, will vow to return and finish the job of retaking San Antonio. Mark my words, María Andrea, the Mexican military will be back shortly!"

Every time I asked him to remind me what the "Seize" was all about, Edgar threw his head back and laughed out loud at my ignorance. I did remember it was called the Siege, but I loved watching Edgar laugh, if only to remind him it wasn't such a critical moment to those of us who just wanted to get back to living our lives and running our businesses.

CHAPTER 25:
BOWIE'S WARNING,
DECEMBER 1835

COLONEL BOWIE PAYS ANOTHER VISIT

"Señora, can we go back to talk about Shorty's for a bit? What was going on in there on a typical evening around this time before you closed up?"

When I took over in December 1826, a customer walking into Shorty's off Market Street might hear the gentle strumming of a solo *guitarrero* singing in somber tones in the corner as patrons—men, mostly—huddled around tables telling stories. Sudden eruptions of guttural laughter might break out here and there as patrons listened to some *ranchero's* funny story. Yes, the stories and conversations flowed like the San Antonio River, some of them believable, others pure nonsense, but all meant to feed the minds and imaginations of these citizens during such turbulent times.

Occasionally, a patron might motion for Izzy Limón, my waitress, to stop at his table. Izzy typically wore a frilly, colorful Mexican blouse tucked into a long black skirt. Her beautiful, shining, jet-black hair would be pulled up and pinned back. She could weave between tables and patrons with efficient skill, stopping to tease here and there, drumming up business just by being there and joking with customers. But men knew not to mistake her beauty with license to cross a line with her.

She wasn't one to fool with. She drew the lines, and men soon learned to let her take the lead.

Izzy possessed a strength of character that might allow certain liberties, but if taken too far, she could turn and smash a bottle at someone's throat in an instant. I felt lucky to have her assistance because Izzy was tough. She grew up in Laredo, where her father, a supporter of the Mexican Revolution, got shot down in a gunfight. With four surviving brothers and a mother who died of heartbreak, Izzy was no stranger to fighting, whether with knives, fists, rifles, or pistols. She once said violence was her nanny; the two grew up together.

One evening about a month after the Siege, Izzy stopped to joke around with one of the patrons at the bar. A large, handsome, angular man sat staring into his drink, waiting patiently for what, she didn't know. Mario, the bartender—known to sometimes join in a conversation at the bar if things were slow, as they were this particular evening—told me later that he was completely confused by this customer's behavior. The man was coughing so much, Mario decided to step away from the bar and join in on table talk that night. Meanwhile, the guy at the bar sat silently, eyeing the wall for quite some time and never interacting with or motioning for Mario at all.

"What's the good word, James?" Izzy asked, bounding up from behind and sidling up next to Colonel James Bowie. I saw her take a sidelong glance at him, perhaps noticing how sickly he seemed. She then stepped back a few steps.

"Oh, hi, Izzy. I was hoping to talk to María Andrea. Is she here tonight?" He leaned to the side to cough down toward his boots. We heard a lot of coughing that December.

"She's in the back, scraping and washing plates. I'll let her know you're here, darlin'."

When I stepped up from the back, wiping my hands on a small cotton towel I kept tucked in my apron, I recognized Colonel James Bowie, one of our regulars. He was a man suffering from circumstances he could not control, just like dozens of others I saw each evening. I watched many good men slide slowly into ruin. Some abandoned their families or lost loved ones to cholera, smallpox, influenza, pneumonia, dysentery, or any of a multitude of diseases overtaking our town. I saw good, strong men, confused by the battles being waged all around them, deciding to work solely for the pleasures of the moment—drinking, gambling, or laying up with ladies of the night at the other end of town. Locked in traumas, they felt as if they had no future. James had surely lost his spark from just a month before when he'd come looking for me after the Siege.

As soon as James spotted me on this particular evening, he quickly turned on his stool to face me, his raggedy blond hair uncombed as usual and spiked in all directions.

"Good evening, María Andrea. How are you doing? Did you manage to get those rabble-rousers out of here last night? I'm sorry I didn't stay, but I wouldn't have been any good in a fight considering the state I was in."

"Oh yes, Izzy had to shoot a hole in the wall over there before they figured we were serious about closing time, but they all eventually left. Mario came in early to patch it up for us. What's on your mind tonight?"

"Well, María, I have something for you that belonged to Ursula, my wife. When I saw the red flag of no quarter hoisted above the cathedral of San Fernando yesterday, I felt like I should give you this in preparation for the big battle that's coming."

"What does the red flag mean? I hadn't even noticed it, James." I whispered.

"It's a sign that Mexican General Santa Anna and his army that've returned and been polluting San Antonio with their presence for weeks now will take no prisoners when we fight at the Alamo. He intends to kill any and all soldiers that his men come up against, *everyone*, including yours truly. I'm sure he'll allow women and children safe passage, but, then again, maybe not. He's a crazy, unpredictable, vicious demon, María Andrea. We plan to defeat him with everything we've got—but unfortunately that's not much right now!" Colonel Bowie leaned low to his right and coughed several more times.

Regaining his posture, he lifted his left pant leg and removed a steel knife about eight inches long. Unsheathed, its blade flashed brightly and was topped with a shiny brown ironwood handle.

I gasped in horror, "Colonel Bowie, why would you flash that in here? Put it back out of sight now! Please, sir!"

With eyes like a hawk, Izzy flew back to the bar, carefully removing Colonel Bowie's cup and pausing at the bar to listen. She flicked her head as a signal for Mario to pay attention.

"It's not for here, María Andrea. Take it home for your family. Let your sister know where you hide it. The way things look right now, you'll be needing it before Easter. That husband of yours, Silverio, isn't here to protect you. Does anybody yet know where he's at? Good *god*, María, where is that man? You need some protection."

James's drinks were beginning to take hold, and he had forgotten that I'd remarried.

"Jim, this knife is a most beautiful creation," I told him, holding it low behind the bar and turning it over carefully in my hands. I promptly returned it to its sheath. "I suppose you designed it yourself."

"I did," he mumbled.

"But you must know that I cannot leave things like this lying around here nor at the house. No, no, no, señor! That would bring very bad luck."

"María Andrea, take it, please. You would honor the memory of my sweet Ursula. She loved you like a sister. . . please, take it . . . just in case."

I let out a sigh. "Oh, James . . . aye, señor. . . . I suppose if I must, okay. Here, let me give you a coin for it. I must pay you. It's just my superstition. Thank you, Señor Bowie. I don't know what to say. How can I thank you for thinking of me and my sister?"

"No need, María, no need. I'm much obliged. But, seriously, just whatever happened to that husband of yours?"

His hazel eyes flashed painfully at me and, for just a moment, I thought in another time and place James and I might have been closer friends. But I quickly put that thought out of my mind, setting a cup of water in front of him and hastily wrapping the knife in a towel so I could stash it.

I reminded him what I'd found out, mostly to get it off my chest once again. I was, like many others, informed of my first husband's whereabouts too long after a battle that left him dead outside Gonzales, probably left to rot alongside other bloody soldiers.

"Last year in early November, Silverio said there was a ship called the *Mary Jane* leaving for Galveston that would sail on to Matagorda. Francisco de Castañeda needed two male cooks. Well, he and Silverio sat right over there discussing this. Silverio thought he could work in the galley of that ship. The next thing I heard, my husband changed his mind. He'd been asked to scout around Gonzales instead because it was closer to home. I had a hard time keeping up with his movements, honestly, but I felt happy with his decision to stay off that ship and be closer to home.

But I reminded him at the time, "Silverio, in case you haven't noticed, we're having a baby very soon!"

"It's only a quick assignment, María Andrea," he pleaded. "I'll earn extra and we can put the savings toward getting a bigger place to live that'll have more room for the baby."

In the end I gave him my blessing because few opportunities came up for Silverio, his left foot having been injured the way it was. Other than the courier job, the military could use strong men like him as scouts. He was such a good man, Mr. Bowie, I couldn't argue with him over taking this other opportunity."

"Well, wwwhere is he, María Andrea?" Bowie slurred, hanging his head as his eyes slid closed.

I continued my story, more for myself to heal than for Mr. Bowie, who'd already forgotten several times that I'd ever told him this story.

"I hadn't heard from him or anyone else for weeks. I was afraid my dear Silverio was just gone. He stopped back shortly after the baby was born, and a time or two after that, but he never got to see his beautiful daughter, Francisca, take her first steps or grow beyond her first couple of years. I tried to get in touch with this Francisco de Castañeda. I finally tracked him down to ask about Silverio's assignment. He said several men were killed in the Gonzales skirmish way back on October 2. He stood right there and told me he had no way of knowing if Silverio was one of them or not! Can you believe that?"

"Yeah, I can believe that, alright. That sounds like our military: If you're not here, please raise your hand! I'm sorry, María," Colonel Bowie replied in a low voice, realizing he shouldn't be making a joke.

"This officer finally reappeared one evening, issuing me an apology and a death notice while handing me a batch of flowers. Nieves promptly threw those flowers out into the street when I told her where I'd gotten them."

I picked up a cloth and began wiping the counter vigorously as unexpected tears welled up in my eyes from reliving the injustice of it all.

"These are very unsettling times. I'm truly sorry to hear you lost your husband in all of this chaos. I lost my whole family, María Andrea. Ursula and I was just startin' out when we lost two sons. They'd barely taken a breath of life and poof! Gone to heaven with the other angels. Oh, how Ursula cried and cried. Next the reaper took both elder Veramendis, their stepson, and my dear Ursula too. My god! I know how hard it is when folks expect you to just move on. You can't do one thing about it or in your case, you didn't even know for quite some time what really happened. How're we supposed to just move on?"

"That was the hardest of all. Then finding out the truth so late. I did move on James, just like you have. We have to. Silverio was never coming back and I had to face that reality. I later married Candelario, remember? He's been such a blessing to me and Francisca. My customers like him so much they've taken to calling me Señora Candelaria!"

"Then there's the guilt, María Andrea. Was this the Lord punishing me for things I'd done in Louisiana? Why was I off doing whatever in hell it was I was doing with my brother Rezin? I should've been with 'em, María." With his eyes glazing over, Colonel Bowie hung his head for a moment and closed his eyes. I watched a tear fall and splatter on the wooden bar.

After a minute or so, he sat up, downed the rest of his drink, slammed the glass down on the counter, and shakily stood up. He fished a few coins and a bill out of his pocket to leave on the counter, then shuffled slowly toward the door, staggering this way and that. He bumped a table and cursed it on his way out. Then he turned in the doorway, lifted his hat, and bid us goodnight. That's when I was left with the gift he'd promised me.

I had no idea that the next time I'd see him, I'd be responsible for keeping that man alive.

CHAPTER 26: SANTA ANNA ENTERS SHORTY'S

FEBRUARY 23, 1836

Candelario and I reopened Shorty's when we heard the news of the surrender of Cós during the Siege. But Edgar knew what he was talking about. Colonel Cós's defeat at the Siege of the Alamo was not the end of things. Hundreds more Mexican *soldados* marched into San Antonio to make it perfectly clear that, regardless of Cós's surrender, this was still very much Mexican territory.

Around February 13, Edgar and Colonel Bowie both reported seeing a bedraggled Mexican infantry brigade marching into town under the command of a man named Gaona. A member of their group reported to Edgar that they'd lost fifty oxen and plenty of provisions making the trip from south-central Mexico. Many soldiers, along with their women and children, died along the way. They'd started off in cold weather that turned rainy, then icy, with freezing rain followed by falling snow. These conditions were quite unusual and put a huge dent in the group's morale, as you can imagine, not to mention the toll it took on their health. Desertions were high and water scarce, according to Gaona. I continued to wonder how Edgar secured such information without getting shot. It's likely the people who'd survived the long trip were in such bad shape they were willing to talk just as much as they were looking for help.

Those of us along Market Street and elsewhere around town kept our eyes down and stepped briskly to our destinations starting on a chilly, wet Tuesday, February 23. That was the day General Santa Anna himself showed up seated atop a magnificent-looking black stallion. Townspeople reported that he looked regal but arrogant, quite unconcerned as to the condition of those troops trailing behind him. If he'd have turned around, he would've seen a trail of hundreds of disheveled, starving soldiers who were cold and wet and barely able to stagger behind their general on frozen feet. Some were barefoot, others in *huaraches*, or sandals, typical of southern Mexico. Ana Esparza reported seeing the general prance up and down each street on his horse with such an air of superiority, all the while sneering with disrespect at our citizens and our villa. Mostly everyone stayed inside, praying he and his soldiers would just pass through and leave us alone. His soldiers, on the other hand, creeped about town at night with lean and hungry looks, ill prepared for the cold, untrained for battle, and once again, many without so much as proper clothing. These men, much bolder or perhaps desperate, began helping themselves to whatever they could find in people's houses. I purposely set out a few clothes and shoes at the corner of the street for them to take.

Most of our friends with ranches left San Antonio to seek refuge in other areas. Too soon, San Antonio began to feel unsafe and unsettled. Our *vecinos*, or neighbors, reported theft of livestock and home furnishings as soldiers began entering properties, making themselves at home, and ordering women to cook something for them to eat. They demanded that our San Antonio women prepare them a place to rest at night too. With so many local men gone, there were stories that some soldiers helped themselves to even more than that.

"They look deflated," I told Nieves. "These soldiers coming in to fight with the Centralist Mexican army have no energy. They're starving! Any sentiments of anger or defiance have now melted away with their fat, leaving them with only protruding bones. They look like the walking dead—*esqueletos*, pure skeletons!"

Nieves and I kept the door locked and hid, bundled up, inside our *jacál* with young Francisca during the day. Just before dark, I'd make my way quickly over to Shorty's. Although I'd opened back up after the Siege, I had to shut Shorty's down again, something I dreaded on account of the bills I owed. I'd hoped to stay open through the end of February so I could make my payments, but it was looking doubtful that I should even attempt that.

I remember looking around inside Shorty's many evenings before Santa Anna arrived. I noticed sturdy-looking people from all walks of life dropping in for a bite to eat, taking a break, and enjoying a few laughs and a drink or two. Some were clearly wealthy *soldados*, military men from Mexico's Army of Operations, and others were wealthy settlers fresh from the north planning to join the fight for Texas's independence from Mexico. They were aware they'd be fighting against many of the men seated along the other wall, but until the call to battle came, they were simply living life. We fed them all and, while I kept my ears open, I asked no questions. I just basked in the joy of seeing people have a good time while telling their stories. Don't think I wasn't fully aware that the situation outside my cantina was calling for more bloodshed and that those evenings would soon become just ethereal memories.

The following Friday, February 26, just after closing time, I stood at the bar, nervously tallying up income and expenses in the account book for the evening while Candelario wiped down tables. Would I have enough to pay the bills? Soon, we'd be closing the place down, so either I was going to make it this month or I wasn't. Suddenly, Candelario and I heard a loud crash. Looking up toward the door, we watched a very cocky Mexican officer and two young *soldados* come sauntering in. The trio had kicked open my locked door! Here they were, swaggering, knocking stools down, and kicking tables over with their fine black-heeled boots until they came to the bar where Candelario and I were standing, incredulous, unable to believe what we'd just seen!

One of the *soldados*, hardly more than a teenager with curly black hair, looked around the place, shifting his lanky legs with an uneasy sense of urgency. The other, much shorter and ruddy skinned with pock marks dotting his complexion, sniffed, then scrunched his face up in disgust at our cantina and spit on the dirt floor.

"*Tienen tequila?*" the leader sneered, adding more spit to the floor. "Do you have tequila, madam?" he repeated even louder. "Madam? We'll take three glasses!"

"Sí, Señor," Candelario answered firmly, grabbing a bottle and pouring three small cups with a quickness that made his shaking hands quite obvious, at least to me.

"Where is the owner of this cantina?" the officer belched after downing his shot.

"She's right here," Candelario replied, and then thinking better of it, added, "Er, we're both the proprietors, Señor."

"What is your name, Señora?" The dark-haired officer turned to me, lowered himself to my level, and, with a hostile air, stared directly into my eyes with his black, beady ones. His breath, a smelly mixture of spoiled milk, mesquite, and tequila, demanded again, "I asked your nombre, Señora!"

"My friends call me Señora Candelaria," I replied, meeting his eyes while slowly closing my account ledger and placing it on a low shelf just below the counter in case there would be trouble.

"Do you have a future here, Señora Candelaria?" he sneered as his two side soldiers let out bawdy laughs and giggles and slammed their cups back on the bar.

"Yes, I believe I do, Señor," I answered firmly, noticing the strings on the golden epaulets adorning the shoulders of his red jacket shaking. He seemed to be trembling in spite of his bravado. I thought to myself, who is this unremarkable man who carries himself with such an air of bold superiority? Where's Izzy when I need her? She'd know how to handle these outlaws. Candelario looked over at me. I sensed in his eyes a look of sad humiliation, perhaps on account of his inability to do anything about this confrontation.

"Well, madam, maybe you do and maybe you don't!" he continued, taking off his wide red hat and throwing it on the bar. Shiny black hair, swept back along the sides of his head, gave him a more polished look, yet the elegance of his red standing collar with golden embroidery seemed out of place for such a cold, ill-mannered personality.

"What will happen when the Mexican government confiscates *all* the businesses of San Antonio? Hmm?" He drew closer to my face and continued staring at me, raising his eyebrows at the question.

"Sir, this is Mexican territory right now. I don't understand why the Mexican government would confiscate something already registered to me under its authority," I calmly replied, indignantly grabbing a cloth to wipe down the counter. I could see Candelario eyeing me nervously, perspiration beads forming on his forehead.

This impertinent invader then slammed his hand down on the bar where I was wiping and shouted, "Madam! If you think these damned foreigners, these *gabachos*, streaming into San Antonio will let you keep your business, you're sadly mistaken. You should be kissing the boots of the Mexican army right now, not supporting the slimy Spanish, French, Native, Anglo, mestizo, or *quién sabe qué* that make up the Tejano and Texan army. You think you'll have a future with those guys in charge?"

With that, he belched loudly and let out a shrill, high-pitched laugh, prompting his two sidekicks to join him with their belches. He leaned to the right, swiping the cups off the bar and sending them tumbling to the ground. He suddenly stopped and turned to Candelario and then toward me for a final word as he pitched forward to grab his hat.

"Remember, madam, the Mexican government allowed you to establish this business; I guarantee no other government will stand for a woman owning a business like this filled with the lazy, no-good, land-grabbing *gentuza*, the riff raff, that you serve. Think about that should your Americano friends take control. You'll be washing dishes in their back rooms while they reap the profits, not you."

Candelario and I held our breaths as the three turned and wandered toward the door, stepping around overturned furniture and once again kicking the door open so hard it smacked the outside wall as they exited into the darkness. Inside, a small patch of plaster fell to the floor at the same time a candle extinguished itself.

Candelario and I stood in silence until we heard their horses gallop off. He then hugged me tightly in silence for a few seconds, and I could feel him shaking as he ran his hands over my head.

"Don't listen to him, María Andrea. He is, without a doubt, one of the worst vipers known to man. I don't believe his insinuations at all. I hope to hell the army here can defeat him and send his men limping right back to Mexico City where they belong. For god's sake, let's pray for a Texas free of the tentacles of that dictator."

"Who was that high-collared monster, acting like an emperor instead of a general? Was that . . . ?"

Candelario looked at me wearily, wringing his hands. He hung his head momentarily, then inhaled.

"That, María Andrea, was the unmistakable Generalísimo Antonio López de Santa Anna himself. *El pinche presidente*, or should I say, dictator!"

Candelario slapped both hands down gently on the bar, shaking his head and sighing. "The very stinkin' monster in the flesh. What he doesn't know, or maybe he does by now, is that men are arriving here daily from all over the United States and even Europe to take his army down. That's how important and big this next battle's gonna be, María Andrea. Aye, *díos mío*, Texas has got to win this one."

"*Qué coraje tienen de venir aquí en tal manera*! Such boldness for them to come busting in here in that way!" I shook my head while numbly walking off, heading over to see if I could still lock the door.

I needed a few moments to sort through my confusion, so I started righting toppled stools and tables. Walking slowly, as if in a trance, I stayed even with Candelario as he extinguished each of the lanterns and candles along the stone walls. I was trying to make sense of the issues. But my mind kept coming up confused.

"Tomorrow let's talk to Edgar and see if he can help us board the door and windows, María Andrea. I'm afraid you'll have to close this place down again for a bit. When you do, let's take the painted sign down outside too, so the starving Mexican army won't kick down the door thinking they can get free food or drinks here."

I didn't close her down that exact night. I kept thinking about my loan payment and bills. Everyone knew a big battle was getting close, but I wanted to wait until we had no choice. The next day when we told Edgar, he suggested I give it no more than a week before shutting Shorty's down for the second time.

• • •

"Miss Rizzo, let's stop for today, alright? I'm going to need some energy to tell you about what came next. I'm sure you know, but it was all so much more than I ever would have imagined."

"Yes, Señora, I was afraid you might need extra time to prepare for the final parts of your story. San Antonio now found itself turned upside down, carved up with sentiments on both sides of this independence issue. Let's talk more tomorrow!"

I helped Señora stand and then packed my pen and steno pads back into the leather satchel as I had on all the previous days. I hugged Señora good evening just as Caramela bounded over to meet her. As usual, the two shuffled away even more slowly toward the Alamo.

CHAPTER 27:
BATTLE OF THE ALAMO, PART I

FEBRUARY 23 TO MARCH 4, 1836

I arrived the next morning to find a small muslin bag with lavender and cinnamon sticking out of the top. Inside, other fragrant herbs had been carefully stuffed. Next to the bag, Señora had placed the same postcard of the Alamo that she'd shown me on the first day of our interviews.

"I know today's session will be difficult for you, Señora. Do you feel strong enough to tell this story right now, or shall we postpone it?" I asked.

"Oh Miss Rizzo, I definitely feel strong enough. This is a story that must be told. It's a story of courage and sacrifice. Some called it altruistic foolishness. No matter how you see it, it's an important part of Texas history. It's about people fighting to their deaths for independence from a government that they felt no longer served them. Their personal motives and visions for the future may not ever be fully understood, but there is no doubt these defenders were true Texas patriots."

The citizens and settlers didn't feel as though they were trespassing on somebody else's territory. The locals felt deeply tied to Texas whether they were descended from ancestors, Native, or Tejano. Some claimed to have been here forever while others were settlers who'd left everything behind in faraway places to start over here with dreams for a better, more prosperous future. As long as they didn't step on one another, this kind of energy could provide a boost to any town. Who wouldn't want that?

But I must remind you that while all of this was going on, there were many citizens—good people like my sisters, friends, and neighbors—who simply wanted to go on about their lives, living, working, and raising their children. Life as many of us knew it had been completely disrupted for a long, long time. Many children had been traumatized or left orphaned on account of all the violence. It's hard to muffle cannon fire from outside jacales. Many citizens didn't quite understand why all of this fighting was happening. We'd lived quite peaceably for years under Spanish, then Mexican rule. But for some reason, things began to feel very unstable. More and more people, women included, decided they would not just sit around wishing for a better tomorrow. Instead, they decided to support one side or the other."

"*Señora, at what point do you remember finally accepting the reality that San Antonio was changing to such an extent that, depending upon the outcome, the town might never be the same? People like Edgar had been suggesting this to you for quite some time, but the signs must have been getting clearer. Here you were, in the middle of a battleground, watching both sides prepare! You could feel it was about to erupt practically at your doorstep, and all of this was only three short months after many hoped the Siege had been the end of it.*"

Señora paused and inhaled slowly. She shook her head yes, looked me in the eyes, exhaled again, and began.

Sometime toward the end of February of that year, 1836, Nieves and I took young Francisca for a morning walk to deliver some laundry. We noticed Mexican *soldados* out in the streets building ladders from wood they'd removed from housing structures and torn apart from furniture taken from nearby homes. Nieves asked me if I'd noticed how many more Mexican *soldados* were now congregating around the Alamo and Military Plaza. I looked up for just an instant on our way home and realized there could be no doubt—we were in for some very big trouble. That was the moment when Nieves and I knew something was not just brewing, but about to come to a roiling boil. I picked up Francisca and we quickened our pace to get back home. Like it or not, San Antonio de Béxar was about to be engaged in another ugly battle very soon.

On the last day of February—that year it was on the 29th, I'll never forget that—Mexican General Castrillón and Colonel Almonte stopped in to Shorty's for dinner and a drink. They were soon joined by other members of the Mexican military, including the unmistakable General Santa Anna himself. Izzy, Mario, Candelario, and I kept very busy serving soldiers during these final days of that month. I'd already decided that this would be Shorty's last night to remain open. That night, Izzy took me aside, whispering that a *soldado* near the door was pushing anyone away who wasn't Mexican military.

"Let it be, Izzy. We can't do anything about it now. We'll tell Edgar later," I assured her. "I'll need Edgar and Mario to help me board this place back up tomorrow anyway."

"Seems like we just received a bit of inventory, put things back together to open up after the Siege, and now here we go again," Izzy added sadly, tossing her cleaning cloth on the counter with a flourish. "Seems like children slapping one another, doesn't it? I'd smack 'em all and send 'em flyin' if they were mine!"

"Yes, Izzy," I responded. "I'm not any happier about this than I was the first time. I've been holding off as long as possible, but I promised Edgar that after tonight we'd shut the place down."

That night, the conversation at one table was worth a front row seat at a theater drama! I grabbed my broom and a wet towel as Mexican General Manuel Fernández Castrillón addressed Santa Anna very passionately, saying something like, "Our Catholic faith prohibits it, your Excellency. Basic rights of all men include the right to live one's life! Ours is not to determine their fate; that is for God on high. Our military ought to consider other means." He sat up straight, swiping his white hair back and pulling up his red collar, awaiting a response.

Then that handsome Colonel Almonte, graying hair parted neatly to the side, chimed in, "It's true your Excellency, certain humane principles of war do not call for such bloodshed. Some of the rebels are there by chance, not by choice. With all due respect, we can win this without a massacre, and perhaps win *soldados* over to our side."

I began sweeping the soft dirt more frantically around their tables, as close as I dared to get.

Santa Anna sighed heavily then sat back, slugging down a shot of tequila before slamming his cup on the table. Izzy and Mario stopped in their tracks to look over at me to see if everything was okay. I quickly nodded, set the broom against the side wall, and got busy wiping down an empty table and chairs next to them.

"Perhaps, gentlemen, you have forgotten Secretary of War Tornel's decree of this past December," Santa Anna began, leaning into the conversation now and almost growling.

"Captured *rebels*, which is who we are dealing with here, are considered pirates. *Pirates* are to be executed. Those men inside that fort are pirates, every last one of them. We will carry out our orders accordingly. Gentlemen, tomorrow at one o'clock, meet at my quarters on Main Plaza to review the plans. Inform the rest of our staff, as I expect everyone to be there."

He then stood to leave, his men rising to follow him out in single file. The last man, the tall and handsome Colonel Almonte, put down coins for all of them as he winked at me, tipped his hat at Izzy, and stepped outside to join the others in the cold. I peeked out the doorway and watched as General Castrillón slowed down to meet Colonel Almonte, and the two shook their heads slowly as they exchanged quiet words.

Edgar didn't show up that evening to walk me and Izzy home, so Mario, Izzy, and I made preparations to board the place up the next day. I felt quite sure that we couldn't delay any longer.

"*Señora, what did you plan to do at this point? Leave San Antonio? Where did you go?*" I asked.

Nieves and I talked about this very dilemma. Some of our neighbors and friends were leaving. Some headed to Casa Blanca, one of Juan Seguín's ranches outside of San Antonio. My first husband's family still owned property—there were several Flóres de Abrego ranches—and I knew they'd welcome us if we traveled there. We knew of other small ranches just outside San Antonio where we'd be welcomed, if only we could get there safely.

Candelario had enlisted with the military again, so Nieves and I didn't see him as much, and I really didn't want to leave without telling him where Francisca and I were going. Whatever plans we were imagining came to a sudden halt with the arrival of a message from one of Colonel Travis's couriers. The message, dated Saturday, February 20, was received five days later by me and Nieves on Thursday morning, the 25th.

It'd been sent first to Colonel Travis and then forwarded to me. Apparently, one of the Alamo's couriers, a Mr. John W. Smith, had carried the correspondence from Colonel Houston by horseback to Colonel Travis at the Alamo.

Oh, that Mr. Houston was a hurricane of a man! Whenever he stepped foot inside Shorty's, the air seemed to shift and people shifted right along as if caught in a torrent of his very presence. I knew a few things about him; he'd been a lawyer and politician from Tennessee. He'd lived among the Cherokee for a while and was very opposed to slavery, having been married to a Black teacher many years before coming to San Antonio. Some years later than this time period I am talking about now, after the Battle of San Jacinto—in which he took part—he was elected the first president of the Republic of Texas. People loved him and his wife, Margaret. Although we were acquaintances, I couldn't imagine what in the world Colonel Houston might want to say to me.

As soon as Mr. Smith rode off, Nieves delicately unfolded the crinkly, square piece of paper and slowly, ever so carefully, struggled to read the message printed within. I can still picture her holding that brief message, desperately trying to sound out the words in her unmistakably sweet, soft voice—a voice that will forever live on in my memory. The reality was, she couldn't decipher the message clearly, so, with exasperation, she handed it over to me to read.

After I'd read it aloud, just as sweetly, Nieves groaned, grabbed the correspondence out of my hands, and proceeded to tear it into a thousand tiny pieces, promptly throwing them into the fire. She then suggested we pretend the message had never arrived!

"Oh heavens! What did the message say?" I gasped.

In the message, Colonel Houston said that he and John Forbes were in East Texas laying out treaty terms with the Cherokee, otherwise he'd have delivered the message to me in person. He wondered if I would please consider assisting with the restoration of Colonel Bowie's health inside the Alamo. Colonel Travis needed someone to revive his second-in-command as soon as possible. Well, you know me. I took his request as a call to duty.

I shook my head and smiled. Yes, I was beginning to understand Señora very well!

It took me until dark to convince Nieves to care for Francisca so I could carry out this request just as soon as I shut Shorty's down again.

"How do you plan to get in there, *hermana*, my sister? Mexican soldiers remain mounted all around the Alamo day and night. You've seen them!" she pleaded.

"I'll figure it out, Nieves!" I assured her. "I know of a small trapdoor to the right of the main entry where bodies used to be sent outside after a mass for burial. I'll try there first."

"You'll return home each evening, then?" Nieves begged.

"Yes, Nieves," I assured her. "I'll leave here just before sunrise and return just after nightfall. I'll be less noticeable in the semidarkness. Tonight I'll gather a few herbs, towels, and water and be on my way tomorrow morning. I have no idea what shape Colonel Bowie is in. I suppose I'll soon find out."

I want this to be understood. I truly believed that my young daughter Francisca, my sisters, my brothers, and I stood a chance to live in a San Antonio free from the yoke of oppression steadily strangling us by an increasingly bloodthirsty Mexican dictator. I'd come face-to-face with him and there was no mistaking his destructive nature. He imposed tax increases that affected everyone, especially those of us in business. He made no secret of his hatred for white people, something that my faith and family did not subscribe to. In my mind, I began to fear that many of us would no longer be able to enjoy the multi-cultural beauty of our San Antonio unless we engaged in some way—big or small—to preserve and protect it.

"María Andrea, no. This just isn't right. It's not right of Colonel Houston to ask you and it's not right for you to leave your baby. What if you are killed there?"

"Nieves, I won't be killed there. Colonel Houston would not have asked me, *me*, of all people, if he had anyone else he could call upon. It has to be me, Nieves."

One thing I knew for sure after listening to Edgar inside Shorty's: I had many friends and acquaintances on the inside of Mission San Antonio de Valero, as some referred to the Alamo. These people, from many walks of life, had supported my business and I felt like I should return some token of that favor. I couldn't turn my back on them at this critical time. I felt a very strong obligation to do my part in this fight for Texas's independence from Mexico, come what may. I began to understand the meaning of loyalty, of choosing a side and sticking with it, something my father had argued about passionately with his sons.

I plunked myself down on Nieves's bed to think. For months, Nieves, my four-year-old daughter Francisca, and I'd kept very quiet, tucked inside this small *jacál* at 716 Dolorosa, peeking out only occasionally during the daytime. I alone had been slipping out around dinnertime to open up Shorty's and then scurrying back after dark. I did all this until I felt it was time to shut things down.

I'm certain young Francisca felt traumatized by the loud booms of cannon shot and pistol fire. These loud noises caused soldiers' horses to whinny, rise up, and stomp in panic. Mud packing between long branches of our *jacál* fell to the floor from all the rumbling, causing Francisca to suffer frequent bouts of inconsolable crying, *pobrecita*, poor thing. Her aunt and I swaddled her in several layers of blankets, rocking her in Ábu's tiny rocker while singing *canciónes de cuña*, lullabies, trying our best to calm her.

Señora began rocking and singing in a low, soft voice, "Duérmete mi niña, que tengo quehaceres, lavar los pañales, sentarme a coser . . ." *This meant,* "Go to sleep, my baby, I have much to do: wash diapers and sit to do some sewing."

She closed her eyes and began swaying side to side slowly. Suddenly, remembering she was in the middle of an important retelling, she sat up, pushed back her head covering, and continued.

"Though artillery fire mostly stopped at night, it was often replaced with loud singing, yelling, unpredictable outsiders, and that awful, whiny Mexican band. The noise was enough to make anyone crazy. Fear controlled our every movement. We knew that unkind soldiers might be roaming around less than a block away, so we took no chances at this time after dark. Now our security tactics were about to change, at least for me.

Long before the courier's message, Nieves and I had considered our options. We had no ranch of our own to escape to as some of our neighbors did; many had already fled. The numbers of *vecinos* heading out of San Antonio seemed to balance the number of Mexican soldiers filtering in. We considered Señor Seguín's ranch again and thought about visiting extended family in Victoria. Unfortunately, getting either place would've been nearly impossible with a young child; horses and carts were extremely scarce. We stopped discussing escape plans once the request from Colonel Houston arrived. We were staying put. The decision had been made for us.

Although I didn't understand all of it, I'd seen enough ugliness to make me want to do something to improve the situation in San Antonio. Nieves cried and shook her head, telling me I was talking like Papá now. Our father, Mr. Patriot, the man who'd never returned from Cuba, she reminded me. I just hugged her until she got tired of arguing with me. I couldn't back down.

The next morning, I awoke to the surprising sound of roosters crowing. I say surprising, because war has a way of quieting even the crickets and nighthawks. Cannons and gunshots quieted these lanky roosters too, but only briefly. Soon enough they scurried about cock-a-doodle-doing and reminding everyone that a new day was dawning.

Mornings did provide a few moments of peace, even in those days. A soft darkness lingered within our tiny *jacál*. The streets outside harbored a few slumbering, frozen, hungover soldiers, figures under blankets barely moving, propped up against the outside of buildings. I occasionally spotted a nervous dog flitting from one side of the street to the other, desperate to find crumbs left from the evening before.

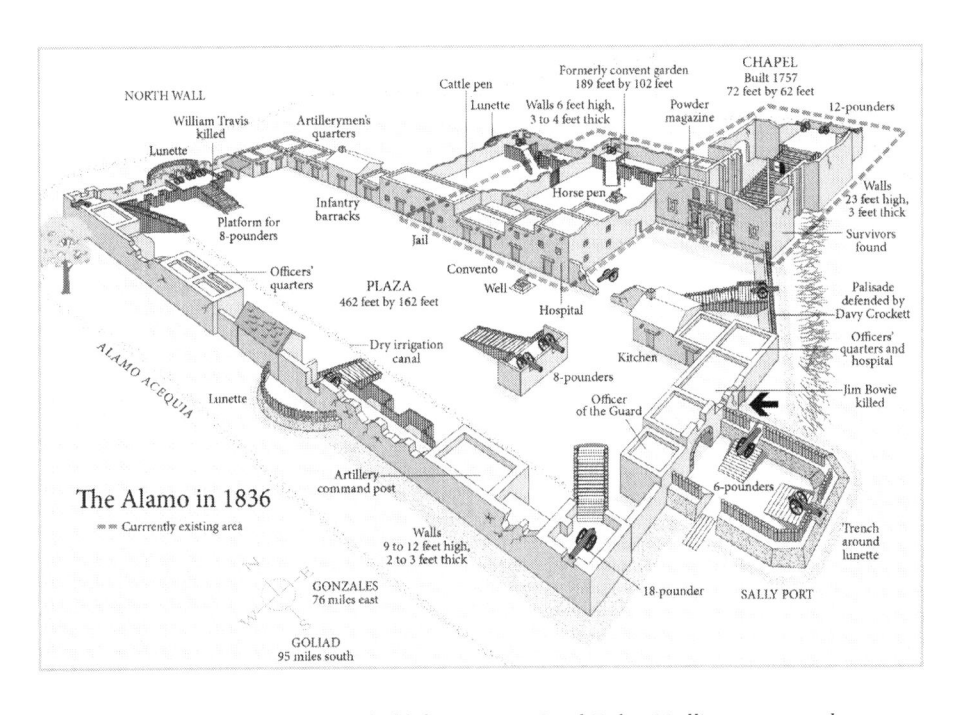

Image courtesy of University of Oklahoma Press. Carol Zuber-Mallison, cartographer.

"Señora, I'm curious, how did you get in and out of the mission undetected, if I may ask? Yesterday, I poked around the building after looking at old sketches of the Alamo. Honestly, I had trouble finding even the front doors into the mission itself. I'm trying to imagine how you entered and exited safely each day."

Oh, I knew that building like the back of my hand. Within minutes, my dark cloak rendered me invisible as I snuck out of our *jacál* before the break of day to do my work. I zig-zagged quickly between staggering, freezing soldiers and brushed one or two off of me. Reaching the white limestone Alamo compound surrounded by mounted soldiers in the morning haze, I quickly climbed down at an angle into the deep trench at the southwest corner. From there, I made my way a little further south and then turned eastward toward the rising sun. I crept along the trench, following a high-walled area crowned with two cannons. This trench extended beyond a small doorway located just slightly above it. That funeral chute became my entry and exit door.

Shielded in the dark by spindly branches of cut mesquite forming an *abatis*—a fence made of spiked tree branches—behind me, I knocked quietly three times and waited for someone to open the tiny door. Mr. Reyes, the guard, soon came to expect me and, after I climbed in, he'd secure the tiny door and escort me to a small room located just to the right of my entry point. My patient's room was situated next to the guard's office.

I spent much of those mornings and afternoons seated on a wooden ammunition box just a short walk from the mission's kitchen, where several local Tejanas—local ladies originally from Texas—kept busy each day making tortillas and singing softly as they cooked beans, rice, and meat for the soldiers. One of the ladies, Mercedes, often ran a bean and rice enchilada over to me, for which I was most grateful. A couple of times she asked if I might be able to bring more flour, sugar, or coffee from outside. If Nieves could spare it, I brought it.

Outside of the Alamo, starting around noon, Mexican bands played on and on. Occasional cannon fire rocked some parts of the compound below, but I couldn't tell where it came from exactly, just that it was one of the cannons above us firing.

My patient lay upon a single dark-wooden bed that'd been covered in a white cotton sheet. They'd brought him down from the hospital area on the second floor near the *convento*, the former convent, to separate him from the others on account of his hacking coughs. Just a shadow of the burly, handsome man I'd known at Shorty's, I saw before me a withered soul in dusty-colored pants and a dirty white shirt covered with his signature gray over-jacket. The man was suffering deafening bouts of coughing, fever, and often delirium.

James Bowie had arrived in San Antonio eight years after I did, leaving a most colorful past in Louisiana, if his stories were to be believed. While in San Antonio, he suffered incredible pain, sadness, and loneliness. A shroud of pure melancholy and grief enveloped his whole being. He'd lost his wife, two children, and both in-laws to sickness and disease. Now, something had a merciless hold on him, too.

My first morning, James opened his eyes a bit. "Ah, María Andrea, it's you, finally!" he croaked. He got caught up with a coughing fit when he saw me. "Can you help . . . cough . . . get me back . . . cough . . . to my fighting weight? Travis don't know what the hell he's supposed to be doing . . . cough . . . without me ordering him around! I need . . . cough . . . to be out there with my volunteers." His coughing wracked his body so, I winced every time his chest and stomach puffed, caved, and then rattled.

His cook, Bettie, began bringing us hot water two or three times a day so I could brew tea using specific healing herbs I'd brought from my stash at home.

"What kind of remedies did you use on Colonel Bowie to help revive him, Señora?" I asked, wondering if she could remember.

Oh, Ábu taught me so many! First, I tried simple honey and warm chamomile tea to calm his coughing fits and soothe his esophagus. These worked quite well to lengthen the intervals between coughs. Another day, I brought ginger root, cut up, and added pieces of it to hot water. This is another strong remedy for coughs, and he seemed to like the flavor better than chamomile.

One day, I asked Bettie for some warm milk so I might add some turmeric I had brought. This concoction was James's least favorite, but it helped the most to quell his coughing, so he drank a bit of it. To bring his fever down, I had to keep swabbing his forehead with a damp cloth. Afterward, he'd shakily fold it, place the cloth across his eyes, and fall fast asleep.

Another day, I made a fresh paste of yarrow, water, and oats to apply to his chest. This brought his fever down almost immediately. Then, of course, I had to swab his arms and chest to remove the sticky paste at the end of the day.

"Señora, I think you're enjoying this," he whispered to me with a sly smile.

"James, *quita su mente de lo sucio*. Keep your mind out of the gutter," I cackled back.

James sipped soup from the kitchen occasionally, but otherwise he didn't eat much. I felt sure his days were numbered and, sadly, he seemed to know it too. Just when I'd start to feel sorry for him, Davey Crockett would prance in with his rifle.

"How's my boss doin'?" he'd ask, standing at the foot of James's bed.

"How many are out there, Crockett?" James would ask, sometimes followed by a coughing fit.

"Too numerous to count, my friend, too numerous to count."

With a sparkle in his eyes, James would respond, "Well, aim carefully 'til you get every last one of 'em, will ya, *amigo*?"

"I intend to, Colonel! We'll pick 'em off one by one if it takes us a month to do it! My boys and I ain't called sharpshooters for nothin'! And if any of them Mexican *soldados* make their way in here, you know what to do, right?"

"Yes, Crockett, I do. I know just what to do. Hey, any word from Fannin yet?"

"Hell, word is that Fannin is lettin' his men decide whether to comply or not on their marchin' orders. What would you vote if you were out lazin' along the creeks in the woods, eatin' fresh fish and deer meat every day while cannon fire and gunshots ring in the distance?"

"He's a scoundrel, ain't he, Crockett?"

"Well, he's either smarter than the rest of us, or someone we can't count on when we need him, James. Not cut from the same cloth as you or me, that's for sure!"

"That's for damned sure, or so it seems, Crockett!" And this is how their conversations went.

At the end of each of my "duty days," as I called them, just after darkness settled in the courtyard, I gathered my cups and towels, leaving any unused herbs packed inside the tiny burlap bag on the table, and set things I needed to wash into my embroidered satchel. I'd cover my head and say goodbye to my patient by holding his hand for moment or two while looking into his eyes. I'd smile while secretly trying to figure out if he'd be there when I returned in the morning.

Davey Crockett

Miss Bettie, Colonel Bowie's cook, returned to his room each evening after I left. She slept on a pallet pulled out from under his bed. I loved that Miss Bettie! She had such a gentle, kind presence and a no-nonsense way about her. She'd start right in chatting with Colonel Bowie about how many tortillas they'd made that day, what mishaps occurred in the sacristy with the children, and which soldiers were arguing, all the while laughing and looking lovingly toward James as she removed her apron, laying it over the post at the end of his bed. Sometimes he was fast asleep and heard little of what she had to say, but she kept right on chittering.

If he did hear, James would reply, "Sounds like you've had quite a day, Miss Bettie, quite a day."

Once she arrived, I stepped outside the door to signal Señor Reyes. He'd accompany me as I turned left to stoop back out the tiny door. From there, I'd dip down into the trench and scurry around to the west corner of the Alamo. Often, when ascending the trench on the other end at nightfall, I'd find myself in the midst of Santa Anna's mounted soldiers or dragoons. They mostly just looked the other way or stared as I scurried past. I honestly got to where I didn't fear them. When at last I reached familiar streets, I looked neither left nor right, but scurried directly back to our tiny *jacál* in the shadows.

One morning as I blanketed little Francisca, Nieves whispered, "How many are there inside the Alamo?"

"*Pués*, well, Colonel Travis says over two hundred," I relayed, arranging my precious bundle between pillows and getting up to heat water for tea over a small fire that Nieves had started earlier. "He's sent for reinforcements, but other than the thirty-two men from Gonzales, no one else has come to assist. Colonel Travis sent couriers out with messages urging Señor Fannin to get his men to the Alamo as soon as possible, but Fannin's either dead, busy with another assignment, or not responding to the dispatches. No one knows what's going on with him."

"What are the chances, *hermana*?" Nieves pleaded quietly in the darkness, folding a washcloth, filling a small earthen *jarro* with water, and finally wrapping dried violets, slippery elm twigs, and yarrow in paper to place in my satchel.

"I know you see the Mexican soldiers milling about the streets all day. There must be thousands of them! So many seem drunk half the time and they're scary in their boldness," she pleaded. "No one, not even you, should walk out there among them."

"Nieves," I countered. "Many of the men inside that Alamo are friends of ours! You've met several at Cassiano's Market, Military Plaza, and places around town—men with families who've come to support San Antonio and all of Texas in being free from Mexican rule. They have dreams of building a better San Antonio and we're included in that dream! Please try to understand, Nieves. I would forever judge myself a coward if I refused to do my part."

Nieves persisted each morning as I rushed to fulfill my assignment.

"María Andrea, do you really need to get mixed up in this? Think about what you've accomplished here in San Antonio since we arrived. You assisted Spanish Governor Cordero. You're the proprietor of your own business. You married a good man, may God rest his soul, and together, God gave you this beautiful daughter. You've just now remarried a second, god-fearing, loving husband, Candelario. Now he, too, is off fighting who knows where. What makes you think *you* must do more for *the people?*"

I didn't want to argue, so I replied softly, "Nieves, yes, I've made use of one hand becoming a respected member of this community, yet there are times when I must use the other for helping those in need. Trust me, sister, this is one of those times. I just feel it."

"Edgar suspects many of these incoming settlers oppose Mexico's anti-slavery laws. He says they really just want to turn our ranches into cotton fields so they can own slaves and get rich using slave labor. What if Edgar's right?"

My mind returned to the note Colonel Houston sent asking me to honor his trust and help out his second-in-command, Colonel Bowie. Somewhere in there I'd read: "You're the only one that I'm sure will make a good effort to save my officer." Colonel Houston had written this! His personal message motivated me greatly to get in there and see what I could do.

"Edgar may not clearly understand the motives of both sides, Nieves. Many of the men I know inside the Alamo wouldn't know the first thing about cotton bolls and fallout. They're ranchers and farmers with little interest in producing cotton. I think they care more about cattle, sheep, and goat farming than raising cotton. At least right now they do."

• • •

March blew in mighty cold, as I mentioned. A feathery, light dusting of snow surprised everyone that spring. I still remember the feel of my feet hitting a shockingly hard, frozen dirt floor just before daybreak each morning.

Frosty, moist air filled my nostrils and exited as soft plumes dancing about my face while I dressed in the same dark clothing each morning. Yes, I had seen certain soldiers of Santa Anna drinking, hollering, helping themselves to food and cattle, and disrespectfully occupying people's homes and businesses. It wasn't hard to spot them, many in blue uniforms with red accents and white suspenders, flowing about our streets. Some wore tall black hats rimmed in a gold color with little fuzzy balls attached to the front.

"Nieves," I whispered one morning. "I love you. Thank you for all you're doing. It's time for Santa Anna and his soldiers to get the hell out of San Antonio." This I said, pausing, as I brushed my hair. My hair used to be down to my waist! I had to tilt my head to one side and then the other just to reach it all.

"Nieves," I continued, "I feel proud to be part of this resistance." But Nieves, aware of the situation with our side's lack of soldiers, only stared at me sadly as she jerkily, with increasing frustration each morning, stuffed my satchel, punching herbs and food items down inside more briskly now.

"María Andrea, maybe it's time for *us* to get the hell out of San Antonio," Nieves uttered. "Those men inside the Alamo are sitting ducks for the Mexican army." Tossing my satchel on the table, she turned and began stiffly chopping *nopal* she'd cook for dinner later. "Juan Seguín has offered us refuge at any one of his various ranches several times now. Ana Esparza told me many of his properties are vacant because the *rancheros* are leaving to support him here in this fight. With Edgar's help, all four of us could leave San Antonio tonight and find a safe place to hide. Edgar would know how to get us safely out. I can't stand the sound of you calling yourself a rebel, sister. Please, let's get *out* of this town!"

"Just listen to me, Nieves!" I begged, approaching her. "We can't leave! Do you think running away will change anything? Santa Anna and his men know no boundaries! Our men want to face him here. Here, where we have so much at stake. Colonel Travis and Señor Bowie truly believe we can take these drunken soldiers and claim San Antonio free from their stinking taxes that provide us absolutely nothing in return. We need to make it clear that we will not tolerate their bloody, violent injustices. We can end Santa Anna's bloody Mexican rule this time. I have total confidence we can find freedom, Nieves. At least, please, let's stay here and pray as our soldiers try! As for Edgar, we can't count on him. No one has seen him around recently. I don't even know whether to worry or not. Knowing Edgar, it's not time to worry, but he's of no use to us at the moment." I turned and continued getting ready.

I pulled my hair to one side and began braiding it, eyeing my dear Francisca asleep again, lying unaware and wrapped in my slightly worn, black and red mission blanket. The silhouette of la Virgin de Guadalupe in the center hadn't faded yet, in spite of over thirty years of use. I looked at my baby girl and glanced around the whole room, wondering what the future would hold for any of us.

Nieves's bed, a rustic cedar construction previously belonging to my mother, seemed to make itself each morning. Situated along the opposite wall near a small table with a lit candlestick and rosary, Nieves always laid her red, white, and black striped mission blanket on top with another soft-green and beige one folded at the foot. Mamá's silver crucifix with light-blue beads hung slightly askew on the wall above the head of her bed. Francisca and I slept on a straw-filled, soft raised pallet on the ground against the wall opposite Nieves.

Each evening provided such a sweet reunion. When faced with the prospect of death, for some reason I felt rejuvenated just to make it home. My life had a purpose and I knew if I should die, I would die with dignity trying to do something for the community's greater good. Going inside our *jacál* each evening felt like climbing into my own cocoon, my own sanctuary of contentment and joy. Did Papá ever experience this?

I washed myself thoroughly, then hugged Nieves and finally checked to be sure sweet Francisca was warmly tucked in before falling exhausted upon the pallet. Nieves and I whispered back and forth about the content of our days until one of us fell asleep first; that would usually be Nieves.

I did suffer momentary doubts that I shared with no one. Oh, I sounded quite sure about my mission when I spoke with Nieves, but in my heart I started wondering if I should be staying back with my family. I realize now that I made a decision that put my sister and daughter at great risk, not to mention myself. Why could I not stop thinking about those men in the Alamo compound? They seemed so determined to fight and win this battle. James Bowie himself had said that if a person sees something wrong, that person should not stand idly by. We must be compelled as citizens to act. And yet . . . there was Francisca.

All these years later, the new threat was not Spanish occupation, nor the kind of Mexican authority we'd lived with peacefully for years, but instead what some people said was a mentally ill Mexican dictator suddenly enforcing tight control over Texas territories. He despised *norteamericanos* and anyone European as well, who made plans to come in to set up businesses and homesteads. But remember, many of these people had been promised leagues and labors of land specifically to come to Texas or to settle in certain areas, just like my family had been. Suddenly folks realized that they would now have to fight for what had been promised.

Señora paused, took a sip of water, and waited for my next question. I looked over my list and selected one.

"Señora, what surprises or realizations set in after a few days of your entry to the Alamo?"

I was surprised to see so many medical doctors hastening about inside the Alamo courtyard. They included Dr. Pollard, Dr. John Sutherland, and Dr. Alsbury and his wife, Juana, to name a few. They wore serious looks on their faces, complaining about the lack of regular medicines and tools on hand needed to do their work. Hearing their complaints, I realized fully why I had been called upon: these doctors found it challenging to perform medical work without their customary medical effects.

It became clear that Colonel Houston sent for me because he knew that, thanks to my grandmother, Ábu, I was knowledgeable in the ways of the *curandera*, the herbal healer, and could, using herbs, heal almost any affliction. I'd done it many times with various citizens and soldiers, including Colonel Houston himself one time. He figured I could do it again with one of his colonels.

This confirmed my beliefs that Colonel Travis acted in the best interest of James, as much as those two bickered. Perhaps Houston forced his hand; I'm not sure. I also noticed that Colonel Travis sent communications out frequently, in all directions and at all times of the day and night, frantic for reinforcements.

Colonel James Bowie was someone I knew quite well from my work at Shorty's. He was well past saving, though, and had been sick for a very long time. But only the Lord can decide when a person's time has come, so I committed in my mind to do what I could and told no one, not even Nieves, that he was likely a lost cause. He seemed comforted just by my presence and maintained his sense of humor, joking with both me and Davy Crockett whenever energy and opportunity came together for him.

"Where the hell is Candelario, María Andrea? You must like those magician types that know how to disappear."

"James, Candelario Villanueva is fighting with a Texan volunteer unit, so although I don't know exactly where he is, I know what he's doing. I gave him my blessing, and I think you should too."

"María Andrea, if you'd a married me, I wouldn't a left a pretty, young wife like you home alone for so long."

"James? That's *una gran mentira*, a big lie, and you know it!" James got a sheepish grin on his face.

"Well, he's a lucky man if his wife takes his first name too!"

"I don't mind, as long as they call me Señora instead of Madame. We all know what the Madames do!"

"Yes, well, there are those needs too, Señora," he chuckled, with that same sheepish grin.

As I mentioned, Crockett stopped in daily, and sometimes twice a day, to check on James. He even handed him a pistol to keep just in case he might need it for defense, saying, "James, it's not my trusty Betsy, but it'll shoot the horns off a devil! Don't be afraid to use it if you have to."

Now, I admit I took the pistol away, as James's delirious states often included fighting Natives and someone named "La Feet." I planned to give the pistol back if things got dire. Most of the time, though, he held it, never knowing it was empty. The truth is, he was too weak to do anything with it anyway. As soon as he fell asleep, I took it from his hands and stuffed it under his mattress for another day.

CHAPTER 28:
BATTLE OF THE ALAMO, PART II

MARCH 4 TO MARCH 5, 1836

"Señora, perhaps that's enough for one day. You're probably getting tired by now," I suggested, noting the tone of her voice falling.

She looked up, half startled, and said, "Oh, no, Miss Rizzo, I can't stop the story here!"

I smiled and sighed, gazing upon her excited, watery eyes. I retrieved an embroidered kerchief and a small bottle of water that I'd brought especially for her on this day.

"Miss Rizzo," she began, *"I never thought I'd be telling this story again, and now that I've met you, it seems like the first time anyone besides family has really listened! Imagine! It's taken a century, my friend."*

"It's a fascinating story, Señora, and I know it must have an ending, but in some ways, I'm not ready to hear it. It feels like I just arrived and met you, and here we are, about to part after hearing the worst."

Now my eyes were beginning to water as I gently took her ethereal hand in mine. She reached over to squeeze mine with both of hers, and it just felt as if she'd gently brushed the top of one with her cheek. She slowly retrieved her hands and shifted upward momentarily to stretch, then settled back down, arranged her skirt, wiped her eyes with her kerchief, and continued.

On the evening of Friday, March 4, I waited for a second bombardment to subside, draped myself, and was just about to locate Señor Reyes to let me out to go home when Colonel Travis approached. He politely asked if I'd be willing to take a proposal to General Santa Anna, who was mounted outside. He said I was not obliged to do this, but he felt fearful of being ambushed by Mexican soldiers if he should step outside. Although I was scared to death, of course I agreed. He told me to walk like *una vieja*, an old lady, to exact sympathy. Accompanied by one of Colonel Travis's mounted soldiers carrying a white flag, I walked slowly out and handed the proposal up to *el presidente* himself. Santa Anna read it, spit, and, reaching into a side pocket for something to write with, quickly scribbled a brief reply.

Once I was back inside, Colonel Travis anxiously read Santa Anna's response and sighed heavily. He turned and told Juan Seguín that Santa Anna wouldn't guarantee anything, but he would accept their surrender. This sounded like a realistic conclusion to me, but Mr. Seguín received this message with a look of concern and sadness written on his face. He pursed his lips, shook his head no, looked down, removed his hat, and placed it over his heart.

"No, he plans to kill us all no matter what. We may as well go down fighting," Colonel Travis mumbled. "Seguín, I need to send you out with an urgent message to Colonel Houston. We need some god-damned reinforcements *now*!"

Colonel Travis looked skyward, then sobered up. He thanked me for my work and I turned to exit the Alamo for the evening.

When I arrived home, Nieves reported that our brother Justo had stopped by to say he'd seen Santa Anna's military council gathering at the Yturri house on Main Plaza shortly after noon. Mexican generals Ramírez y Sesma, Castrillón, and Cós, along with Colonels Almonte, Duque, Amat, Uruñela, José María Romero, Mariano de Salas, and a few others were in attendance. Justo knew all their names, of course. He reported that battle time was upon us, but his biggest worry, Nieves said, was for me.

Nieves continued, "He strongly insisted that you not report for Bowie duty tomorrow morning, María Andrea. I have to second that. The Mexican band's music sounds even louder now and especially eerie. I'm very worried I'll be bringing up little Francisca on my own without her mother. Possibly without her stepfather, as well. You need to stay here tomorrow, please, *hermana*. Sister, I'm begging you."

"Colonel Bowie is not going to last, Nieves. Just let me finish this job and I'll be home as soon as it's over. I promise!"

"Over how, María Andrea?" Nieves demanded. "With you on the ground and the Mexican army dancing over your body? I don't like what Justo just said. He insists that the rebels inside the Alamo don't stand a chance, sister! They're completely outnumbered. I hesitate to tell you this, but our brother Justo will be on the outside pushing in on behalf of the Mexican military."

I stood there stunned at this revelation as tears formed and found their way down my face.

Nieves ran over to hug me, weeping silently. I stood shielded by her arms with her head against my chest. I reached around to hug her back because I realized how fortunate I was to have a sister. A sister who cared and stood by me in times like this, times when Candelario's unit was off somewhere, and Edgar, our family's protector, was nowhere in sight. I had few people who cared about me besides my husband, my sisters, brothers maybe, and some of the people inside the Alamo. To hear that Justo would be fighting with the Mexican army was a revelation that made total sense in Mexican territory and yet that reality hadn't dawned on me.

Sitting down on the pallet and staring straight ahead, I didn't dare mention the exchange of messages between Colonel Travis and Santa Anna to Nieves, nor that upon leaving work that very evening, I'd heard talk of a group of Mexican soldiers advancing in a line along the *acequia*, or irrigation ditch, to the north of the Alamo. My mind was set on finishing my work. I knew Colonel Bowie would take his last breath soon.

"Wait, Señora, you knew soldiers were approaching the Alamo in formation that very night and yet you felt determined to go back the next morning? I don't think I could've done that!"

I sit back with a look of complete bewilderment on my face, waiting for Señora to answer and wondering what could have possibly possessed her!

"Those people inside the Alamo were like family to me, Miss Rizzo," she persisted. "I couldn't just not show up. That wasn't my way. Crazy, probably, but there was never any question in my mind that I needed to finish the job I was asked to do by two men I considered to be my commanding officers: Colonel William Barret Travis and General Sam Houston."

"Wow! Okay, I get it now . . . I . . . think . . ." I stammered, not sure if I really did understand how Señora could voluntarily take such an incredible risk. I watched as she paused, took a swig of water, wiped her eyes, and continued.

Late that same evening, Edgar stopped by. He mainly wanted to show off his tall, beautiful new horse, Fuego, or "Fire." As we gathered tightly outside, admiring Fuego's mane, Edgar mentioned that he'd heard that Francisca Musquíz, Ramón's wife, left her house that morning and stomped a few houses down to call upon President Santa Anna in person. She evidently asked that Mrs. Dickinson and her daughter, Angelina, who were inside the Alamo, be spared. The two were somewhere within the Alamo walls with Almeron, the husband and father. Edgar said Santa Anna supposedly agreed, saying he'd try to make sure they weren't killed, at least on purpose, anyway.

Nieves's response amused me.

"Well, that was big of him," Nieves sneered as she fed Francisca some banana fruit. "I'm trying to convince María Andrea to stay out of there tomorrow, but she won't listen. Mrs. Musquíz didn't happen to say anything about sparing *her*, did she?"

Edgar looked confused. "Why would *you* go in there, María Andrea?"

"I have a job to do, that's why, Edgar," I answered. "If you'd stick around here more, you'd know more!"

"For Christ's sake, María Andrea, you *do* need to stay away from there. Can't you tell what's happening here? Any day, quite possibly tomorrow, things will erupt." Edgar stopped hand grooming his horse, leaning in long enough to confront me on that issue.

"I'm nursing Colonel Bowie, Edgar, not loading cannons!" I assured him, walking back inside the *jacál*. But he followed hot on my heels, removing and holding his hat in his right hand after he crossed the threshold.

"María Andrea, for the love of God, you need to stay home with your sister and baby Francisca. This isn't going to be a pretty fight. What don't you get? That red flag flying over San Fernando that we talked about? Its message is clear and it's *no* joke!"

"You act like you know something, Edgar," I said, looking him straight in the eyes. "When is all of this going to come to a head? Tell me when. I know you know. You always know! Which side are you gunning for anyway?"

"Ladies, come on!" Edgar said, throwing his left arm out to his side. "You don't have to be a genius to see that it's coming any day—tonight, tomorrow maybe! The troops are lining up, "El Degüello" is playing—that beautiful song whose title suggests cutting throats, and the generals are putting their heads together, creating a final battle plan."

Edgar turned suddenly and headed for the door, shaking his head, grabbing a fistful of hair in his left hand, and exiting as if he'd said too much already.

"Thanks, Edgar. For stopping by and for the news," I said snidely, standing in the doorway as he briskly mounted his horse. He looked me sadly in the eyes, turned, and galloped off. He left me in a cloud of dust that felt uncharacteristic of him, yet quite intentional.

Nieves looked at me pleadingly, but I closed and locked the door and walked over to check on Francisca. She'd fallen into a deep slumber it seemed, so I began packing a few dried herbs for Saturday.

"Let me guess, Señora, it sounds like you went back anyway," I said. *"I'm guessing your head did feel at least a little clogged with doubts, maybe some guilt, after Edgar's visit."*

"I tried to put his visit out of my mind, Miss Rizzo. Saturday morning, once I'd climbed inside the Alamo, the first thing I heard was Bettie lamenting to Graciela that the supply of beef was gone; the kitchen was running out of food. We all had important matters to contend with, but not being able to feed the Alamo defenders was disheartening."

I looked at Señora and shook my head in disbelief. I knew she couldn't stay away. I was anxious to find out how the next twenty-four hours had played out.

Señor Pérez had donated several cattle back in February, but in order to feed over two hundred people two meals a day, the ladies went through a fair amount of food very fast! And now there would be no chance to bring in any more beeves for beef. The kitchen help would have to use what little provisions were left and everyone would receive smaller portions. Graciela stated all of this very matter-of-factly to Colonel Travis, marching back toward the kitchen shaking her head, as if it were a personal failing. As a former Chili Queen, she'd been very good at managing that kitchen, and I'm sure she took the shortages personally.

Dr. Pollard stopped by James's room to ask if we had any extra bandages or medicines. I shook my head and let him know that James didn't require bandages, and the only medicines I had were plants and honey. He was welcome to either, but he thanked me and turned to continue his search.

Besides the hospital area upstairs, another small room had been set up below to separate more seriously ill soldiers. I asked Bettie later that day why so many men were falling sick. She said it was most likely on account of the poor facilities for washing and cleaning. She said the kitchen struggled to keep towels and utensils clean and tidy since soap had run out over a week ago. In the courtyard near the cattle, she said, men, women, and children were relieving themselves in shallow holes dug for that purpose. She didn't believe the latrines should be placed so close to the animals being used to feed everyone, but Colonel Travis apparently would not concern himself with this issue. At this point, there was only one sickly cow left, and Graciela insisted it didn't look well enough to cut up for provisions. She refused to serve it.

When Dr. Pollard again passed by later that day, I shared some of my natural remedies to combat diarrhea with him. We both knew the sick ones needed water to replace the fluids being lost in their watery stools. Luckily, the well in the courtyard provided plenty of that in spite of the fact that the Mexican army had strategically blocked the water coming into the Alamo via the main *acequia*, or irrigation ditch. Rice, if the kitchen had any and could spare it, along with bread, bananas, and mashed apples would help bind things up in the body. I gave the doctor a small bit of dark chocolate and some spearmint leaves that I'd been using for James. Whether the sick ones suffered from dysentery, cholera, or typhoid was impossible to say, but whatever the diagnosis, their diarrhea had to be controlled. Dr. Pollard thanked me, turned and bounded up the stairs with the things I had shared with him.

Saturday afternoon, Colonel Travis stopped in to check on Colonel Bowie and asked if he could join his emergency call for all defenders to gather in the courtyard.

"I sure as hell will join ya, Travis!" James croaked, then coughed. "But I'll need some muscles to lift me out there, unless Señora can cast me a magic walking spell!"

Four men I didn't recognize entered to lift and tilt James's bed out and into the courtyard so he could be a part of the meeting.

I stood in the doorway, listening as Colonel Travis stood with a gravely serious look upon his face and cleared his throat. He looked around proudly, yet wistfully, at each of the defenders. Raising his shoulders up straight, he started laying out the situation clearly, with no embellishment. He praised the thirty-two men from Gonzales who'd answered his call for help so quickly, he'd hardly had time to figure out their positions. "Lieutenant George C. Kimbell's men answered our call in the name of liberty, patriotism, and everything dear to the American character. Before them, many local citizens joined us here along with Davy Crockett and some Tennessee and Kentucky sharpshooters." Travis's commentary on those within the walls resulted in rousing cheers from everyone in the courtyard. He explained that, although reinforcements had been promised, the truth was that no military relief was in sight as far as his scouts could tell.

"This, men, is our reality," Colonel Travis shouted over the music of "El Degüello" that'd started playing outside. Inside, standing under the smoke and dust of earlier weapon discharges, he faced a completely silent, but solid and determined-looking, group of anxious defenders.

"That must have been a dispiriting moment, Señora. The men obviously knew they were outnumbered at this point and that the outcome would not be good. Santa Anna's message that he'd be happy to accept their surrender but couldn't guarantee their lives surely left Colonel Travis with no favorable options."

Colonel Travis, as their commander, stood before them as a true leader: strong, courageous, and determined, in spite of the situation. From the doorway, I glanced quickly around at the faces of these fighters. I witnessed such great hope, faith, and optimism in their eyes. These defenders called upon their warrior ancestors with such fearlessness. In spite of being outnumbered, they truly believed they could defeat the Mexican forces. Their faces demonstrated a firm commitment to the cause of Texas's independence. These men looked as if they'd been made for this moment. I cannot describe the feeling adequately, I'm afraid. It was as if all the atoms of their spirits spiraled into a vitality that filled the courtyard, mingling and somehow overtaking the dust and smoke and throwing it down. Listening to them cheer the heartfelt, though bleak, revelations of their commander, I felt quite optimistic myself.

"Señora, were the wives and children present to hear any of this?"

"No, they were tucked safely within the sacristy of the church. I never saw them, but this is where Bettie and Graciela told me the others were during this time."

Mrs. Dickinson was the only one who scampered across the smoky courtyard to poke her head in James's room for a minute. She most likely wanted to check to see if he was still alive, but, not finding him in there, she sped off without uttering a word.

Before the courtyard meeting ended, Colonel Travis removed his sword and drew a long line in the dirt. He asked every man willing to stay and fight to step across his line. All but one, a Louis "Moses" Rose, stepped proudly across. Señor Rose, a Frenchman, hastily apologized to the group. Hollering out that he wasn't ready to die just yet, he literally turned and bolted as fast as his legs could carry him out of the Alamo. He had a right to make that choice.

I quickly slipped out to the courtyard to wipe Colonel Bowie's forehead and brush his hair back just before he motioned to be carried across Travis's line. The same four men picked him up, bed and all, to carry him, coughing and gagging from the dust, across the line. As I ducked back into his room, tears began streaming down my face.

This was the moment it hit me. The red flag of no quarter, cannons, knives, pistols, conversations we'd heard at Shorty's, and warnings to stay put—all of it came crashing through my head in the haze of the line drawn in that courtyard. Why hadn't I listened to Nieves? To Edgar's warning last night? I turned quickly, desperate to cover myself with my shawl and get out. I fumbled for my satchel, leaving dried herbs on the table next to Colonel Bowie's cup. I felt a sudden desperation to hold Francisca, to be with family inside our *jacál*. Maybe I had been a fool."

"So, is that what you did? Did you leave James in the courtyard at the Alamo, Señora?"

Señora Candelaria exhaled, looked down, and paused for several minutes, kneading the kerchief she held in her hands. She flattened her kerchief on one knee, picked it up, and wiped her watering eyes as she gathered the strength to continue. I debated calling it a day, but how could I in the middle of this? I felt like, one day or another, she'd have to work her way through this pain one more time.

I hastily draped my black rose-covered shawl over my head and shoulders, collected my belongings, and searched for Señor Reyes. I couldn't find him anywhere in the midst of all the rowdy men backslapping in the courtyard. All of a sudden, Colonel Travis, seeing me dash about to and fro, approached.

"Señora Candelaria, local residents may be released from the Alamo grounds at this time. You know how much we've appreciated your service. I want to let you know it's your choice whether to stay or go. If you stay, I'd ask only that you remain with Colonel Bowie tonight, sleeping on the pallet that we keep tucked under his bed. Usually Bettie sleeps there, but tonight I could let her know she should join the other women and children in the sacristy if you wish to remain with Colonel Bowie. All of this is your choice."

My mind shifted and I cried out loud. "Oh, no pressure, but good lord, Señora..."

"You've got it, Miss Rizzo. In what appeared to be his final hours, how could I leave James Bowie?"

I felt in my heart that he would not last the night, though I'd never given up trying to restore his health. The fluid in his lungs and his weakened state led me to believe he might not know or care if I stayed or left. That loneliness that had eaten him alive for as long as I'd known him was pulling him under with a fever and rattle now.

I don't know what could have possessed me, but I decided I would stay to hold his hand so he wouldn't depart this Earth without a friend at his side. I think I was his closest friend at the time. No one should have to die alone.

I turned around slowly, walked back into his room, and prayed Nieves would forgive me for not returning home that night. Tomorrow, I decided, I would simply walk off the job and steer clear of this place from that day forward.

I watched as Señora Candelaria's chin dropped to her chest. She appeared to have fallen asleep! I knew this retelling would take its toll, but now I needed to suggest that we continue another day. Caramela appeared, tail wagging wildly, and turned a few circles to settle on Señora's feet, awakening her.

"Ah, Miss Rizzo, you're still here!" *she chuckled.*

"I am, Señora!"

"Might I suggest we continue this tomorrow morning, dear?"

"I was just thinking the same thing. You must be completely exhausted. Tomorrow will be even more difficult for you, I believe."

We hugged one another, then gathered and packed our belongings. We began walking slowly in opposite directions as the sun shone lower, but still brightly, between canopies of green, leafy branches of very large oaks lining our divergent paths.

CHAPTER 29:
BATTLE OF THE ALAMO, PART III

MARCH 5 AND 6, 1836

I arrived the next morning, two hot chocolates in hand and a dog biscuit for Caramela in my pocket. There on the cloth, I spotted a rather sharp-looking nine-inch knife, two silver Mexican pesos dated 1836, and a small silver wedding band.

"Good morning, Miss Rizzo. I see you've brought me some elixir from the gods this morning, you angel, you!"

"I have indeed, Señora, plus a treat to keep Caramela from disowning you for neglect as you finish sharing the hardest part of your story with me."

"Oh, she'd never disown me—I give her such cold, strong feet to lie upon," she cackles. "And doggie biscuits, too, if I can find any!"

"Well, do you feel ready to go further into this today?"

"I do. I must tell it to you, Miss Rizzo. You've become a good friend, and I know you'll believe that what I tell you is true! It's not been colored by time, I assure you. I've been over this a thousand times."

"I am believing what you tell me, though the story is incredible and somewhat hard to digest. I'm sure you know that!"

"Don't be like some others at that time, now, and think I'm inventing this, making up a story to get compensation or draw attention to myself."

"I could never think such things after hearing all you've shared, Señora! I must admit, however, that your perspective is one that I've not heard before, even after reading so much about Texas's fight for independence. Details provided by many of those accounts are beginning to make sense now. Those accounts don't often mention what some of the local Tejano and indigenous families were contending with during this time. That history hasn't been much of the narrative. That's why your story, as someone whose family headed north on the Camino Real, is so fascinating. You are far from typical in my mind!"

"Thank you, Miss Rizzo. I shall begin by telling you about the evening of Saturday, March 5."

Strangely, an aura of incredible peace settled around the Alamo that evening. The Mexican band outside the walls stopped its awful racket. Cannon fire against the Alamo ceased. Soldiers on both sides were exhausted and in need of rest.

I stepped outside the doorway of James's little room and saw a great light in the sky—the moon! It was full, and I'd not paid much attention to it in the chaos of days prior. Maybe I'd missed it on account of the smoke from cannon fire. Muffled conversations could be heard here and there, and I saw dark silhouettes of men partially visible moving along the upper reaches where the cannons pointed east and west. Many defenders sat down to rest, weary and spent, guns cradled in their arms.

Colonel Travis hastened by, asking for James Allen, one of the couriers. Apparently, he'd decided to make one final desperate attempt to reach Colonel Fannin. His message said: "Hasten to the aid of your countrymen!" I'm sure he was thinking, "For God's sake, man, get your ass and your men over here!"

Señora scoffed at the thought, shaking her head.

Crockett reminded us that although the defenders had completely lost faith in Colonel Fannin, perhaps Colonel Travis figured one last effort must be attempted. Truth is, no one had any idea what Colonel Fannin was contending with wherever he was.

Señora shook her head, looking skeptical at what she'd just shared.

Bettie, James's cook, stopped in to check on James. She told me that Juana Alsbury had handed her valuables over to her, hoping Bettie could find a way to sew them into her hem. She asked if I might have a needle and thread. I did, a very sharp needle made from an agave point and thread made of pulled fibers from the long leaves of the same plant. I retrieved them from my satchel for her. She placed these in her apron pocket, thanked me, and reached over to touch James's arm.

"Did Colonel Travis mention that I'll be spending the night here on the pallet next to Colonel Bowie?" I asked Bettie.

"He did, darlin'. Thank you. I can barely hear his breathin' now," she said, leaning over to listen. "I'm afraid he will go to meet his maker soon. I'm so very grateful that you will be here by his side tonight."

"Thank you, Bettie," I replied, and watched as she turned and scuttled back toward the kitchen.

Later that evening, Bettie returned with the needle and thread, her skirt hem bulging and sagging quite low.

I looked up from my ammunition box, trying hard not to stare at the crude, hasty stitches in her hem. She leaned over and whispered in my ear.

"Colonel Travis stopped by the sacristy this evenin' and borrowed some of your thread. He strung it through a gold cat-eye ring and placed it around little Angelina Dickinson's neck for safekeeping. I fear we are nearing the final battle, Señora Candelaria. Do you suppose we're all going to die tonight?"

Without revealing the depth of my fears, I calmly replied, "That is what the red flag of no quarter stands for, Miss Bettie. We must say our personal prayers and be prepared. Where will you go, Bettie, if you are somehow spared?"

"This north wind is callin' me, María Andrea. If these men in here lose this battle, I'm a free woman. I will run north just as far and fast as these old shoes will take me. I got family in New Orleans, so maybe Ben or Joe, Travis's assistant, will travel with me if they make it out of here alive."

She made the sign of the cross, turned, and dashed awkwardly across the courtyard toward the sacristy, her hem chink chinking as she went.

Shortly after she left, I gazed out into the courtyard from my seat on the ammunition box. There, under the light of that full moon blinking on and off on account of cloud cover, I saw José María Esparza, Gregorio, as we all called him, and his wife, Ana Salazar, seated against the wall, resting sweetly in each other's arms. Snuggled on the other side of his father, their young son, Enrique, clung tightly to his father's right arm. Everything about that evening seemed mystical, surreal. If there's a way of knowing that death is approaching, I could feel it.

I caressed James's face, wiping it with cool water, and then combed his hair again. I finally drifted into a peaceful, if accidental, sleep upon Bettie's pallet, which I'd pulled out onto the floor next to James's bed. Someone whisked in and threw an extra blanket over me, for which I was most grateful, but I couldn't see who it was.

In the crisp twilight of early morning, I heard some rustling and glanced into the courtyard to see Señor Esparza and his son running off toward the ramp to their cannon station on the east wall. At the same time, Ana Esparza stood up and ran toward the church sacristy.

Someone who sounded like Crockett, yelled, "Near the cottonwoods on the Alameda, cavalry is saddling up!"

"The Alameda line of cottonwoods was located southeast of the Alamo, Miss Rizzo. Right over there." Señora pointed in a direction east of where we were seated.

About half an hour later, after I'd folded the blankets and pushed my pallet back under the bed, I swabbed James's head as I heard more scuffling in the dark. Someone shouted, "Two figures pulling back cannons near the north wall!"

Why Mexican soldiers would be pulling cannons back, I couldn't imagine. So, I closed and locked the door, waiting and wandering around the room in tiny circles. I finally settled upon the same artillery box I'd used as my seat since I started there and reached over for James's now-cold hand to say a prayer.

James was barely breathing that morning. I heard shots off in the distance, though I couldn't tell from which direction. Someone shouted, "Our pickets have been shot in their trenches!"

At this point, all the defenders in the Alamo ran to and fro, getting in position. From the tiny window in the door to our room, I watched the shadowy figures of Davy Crockett and his Tennessee riflemen prepare to mount the south wall just above where James and I were. Later, upon hearing scuffling, I peeked out to see them run past our doorway, now heading toward the north wall. They were sharpshooters, so I knew their positions would be critical and perhaps ever changing.

Suddenly, a bugle sounded in the darkness of the dawn. This was it, the battle for San Antonio was beginning. The terrible fight everyone knew was imminent came thundering down upon us. I knew I'd be right in the middle of it and I truly feared for my own life now. My grandiose thoughts of fighting for a better San

Antonio flew out the window in those moments. I should have gone home earlier. Why didn't I go home earlier?

Outside the Alamo walls, I heard the stomping of thousands of feet, marching together, approaching the Alamo. And ugh! That awful Mexican band started up once again.

"Have you ever heard 'El Degüello,' Miss Rizzo? It's a depressing tune that Mexico inherited from the Spanish, who evidently borrowed it from their enemies in Africa years before. It literally means 'to cut one's throat.' Who writes music for such an 'occasion?'"

"No, I've never heard that song. I'm not sure I want to. That must have given everyone the creeps!"

"Yes, if the weather didn't give us the chills, Miss Rizzo, that ominous, eerie music most certainly did!"

Señora and I took a moment to look at one another. We paused, knowing the worst was yet to come. I kept checking Señora's face to assure myself that she was strong enough to tell this. After a few minutes, I posed a question.

"What was James doing throughout this build up to the crescendo?"

"James could barely turn his head from one side to the other at this point. He looked exhausted, pale, and weak. When that bugle sounded, his head turned toward me and his fingers began to twitch. I knew he wished he could jump to action, but he was not capable of doing so."

"James," I said quietly, getting up from the ammunition box, "I want you to know that I brought Ursula's knife here with me and I will use it if I need to!" I brandished the shiny blade before his eyes.

I put my left hand over his bony, freezing fingers and set the knife down, out of his reach. I then lifted his head to give him a drink of cold elderberry tea.

He blinked and smiled ever so slightly, then turned his head back to center, closing his eyes. I held his hands, but I wasn't about to give Crockett's pistol back to him just yet.

Suddenly, a tremendous cannonade began; awful shooting and screaming commenced. I slid the knife under James's mattress and unloaded the pistol. After placing the bullets along the cracks in the outside wall, I quickly hid the empty gun under towels on the small table.

The next thing I heard brought me to my knees to pray. Someone shouted, "Colonel Travis is shot! He's down up on the north wall!"

How could these men lose their commander so soon into this battle? I couldn't imagine it. Tears fell as I pictured him in that courtyard addressing his soldiers. That man had his enemies, but from my perspective, he never faltered in the face of this very grim assignment. He'd sent notice "to all of Texas and the world" that he planned to die like a soldier, never forgetting the commitment he'd made: victory or death. He would die in these trenches. "Victory or death!" Those were his words.

Señora paused, glancing briefly at her hot chocolate, then continued.

Later, I learned what happened. Colonel Travis was trying to assist artillerymen on the north wall. Unfortunately, loading the cannons along the upper narrow walls exposed the silhouettes of our soldiers quite clearly to the Mexican army.

I kept looking over at James. If he'd heard this death announcement, he showed no sign of it. I decided to check the bolt on the door and, as I was doing so, I thought I saw Joe, Travis's assistant, run into a lower room across the courtyard where he entered and slammed the door behind him.

Almost immediately following that, I heard a soft knock at our door. Peeking out, I saw that it was Bettie, looking harried and frightened, with some kind of white powder in her dark hair.

"Tell me it isn't so!" she cried. "Colonel Travis, he isn't . . ."

"Bettie, I'm afraid it's true. You must stay back in the sacristy with the other women and children. What's it like over there now? What are you doing out here?" I asked.

"Everyone is terrified, Miss Andrea. The women are huddled in corners, praying the rosary and holding and rockin' their children. All the while, we're feeling the room shake, plaster fallin' all around us! We're hearin' the shrieks and cries of warfare, just like you are over here. We're half deaf from the roar of rifles and the constant release of Alamo artillery right above us. Those three cannons and constant musket fire are scarin' the children to death! They're wailing and need constant soothing by their mothers. We have no food for them. I can't take it, María Andrea, may I please stay here with you and James?"

I explained that I thought she might make better use of her time and talents holding and helping with the children in the sacristy. Honestly, I didn't want to keep another person so breathy and frantic in our tiny room; it might further upset James. I handed her an apple from my satchel. She understood, curtsied, ducked, and with her hemmed booty clinking and clanging, scurried back across the courtyard to the sacristy with the noise of artillery fire and the screams of dying men all around her.

No sooner had she exited than the music outside stopped again. We waited, keenly alert for any sound in the darkish quiet of that Sunday morning, March 6, 1836. Then, there it was, another bugle call. I wasn't sure what this one meant, but I wrapped Colonel Bowie in the blanket from my pallet and swabbed his forehead and cheeks again. He didn't open his eyes this time, but I could still discern very faint breaths.

All of a sudden, I heard terrible sounds of feet scurrying, followed by cries, screams, swords clanging, swearing, and shouting from the courtyard. One peek out the tiny window of our room confirmed my worst fears: the Mexican soldiers had entered the courtyard and were now swarming inside the Alamo, battering doors, rotating cannons, and firing into the courtyard itself. Mexican soldiers fired two cannons before being cut down by defender gunfire. I'd never seen such savage fighting, nor have I since. My heart raced as it shattered into a million tiny pieces.

I saw Mexican soldiers battering the bodies and faces of our Texan *soldados* with knives and swords and using rifles and muskets as clubs to beat and disfigure our men. There was no mercy, none! The fury of a thousand years came unleashed in that courtyard. Our defenders fought just as viciously. Though they were overwhelmed and didn't stand a chance, I saw our Alamo soldiers standing their ground, buying time for their fellow defenders to run to safety within the church or sacristy. Unfortunately, many escapees were caught, cut down, and bludgeoned to death by Santa Anna's soldiers.

Apparently, someone opened the small wooden gate at the east end of the palisade, and several Texan defenders shoved through while others continued shooting. I found out later that the Dolores regiment of Mexico, four hundred strong, was outside just waiting for something to do. When they at last saw a line of our Alamo defenders leaving the fort through an opening in the *abatis* right where I entered every day, Mexican General Ramírez y Sesma unleashed his company of lancers, who stabbed our men to death within moments of their attempts to fight or flee on the outside.

I heard more commotion just outside our wall, where apparently another group of defenders shoved one another through the *abatis*, trying to make a break for it. I learned that Mexican General Ramírez y Sesma waved a second company forward to intercept this group of escapees. Several *norteamericano* defenders ran to take refuge in the *acequia*. They put up a good fight, but the general ordered thirty or so more Mexican soldiers into the fray, according to Edgar's account later. Within minutes, dozens of defender corpses lay scattered on the fields east of the Alamo.

Someone, I learned later it was Mexican General Amador, entered the fort and ordered a small cannon dragged down the ramp and swung around to face the rooms across the courtyard plaza. I prayed so hard because I knew there were defenders hiding in those rooms, including Travis's assistant, Joe, who kept peeking out.

Mexican soldiers loaded that cannon and began blasting into the doors one by one. Their General Ampudia, I believe it was, followed suit by shooting a gun. *Soldados* from the Matamoros and Jiménez battalions, commanded by Colonel Romero, stormed each room, firing through the doorways, entering bayonet first, and killing any and every single person they came across.

Some defenders poked their bayonets through a hole or opened their door a crack to wave a white cloth or sock to signal surrender. I watched through our tiny window as enraged Mexicans dragged them out and killed them all anyway. So, this, then, was the reality of no quarter.

I saw one Tejano, Brigido Guerrero, begging for his life on his knees in the open courtyard. Somehow, he convinced his captors that he'd been held prisoner against his will and the Mexican soldiers let him run out. He must have told a good story!

"Señora, at this point, you couldn't leave your room and you'd been watching incredibly brutal killings going on just outside your door. What was going through your mind?"

"Miss Rizzo, I didn't take to thinking clearly about anything. There was so much action still going on. I wondered when it would be our turn, mine and James's. I wondered what part my brother Justo was playing in all of this. I prayed to every god and goddess I could think of. I prayed to the ancestors like I'd never prayed before to put an end to this massacre. And finally, I prepared mentally to journey to Xibalba to see my mother and Ábu again."

I watched Mexican *soldados* run up the stone stairwell of the convent into the hospital and heard gunfire as they dispatched, or killed, all of the sick, bedridden defenders in there. No quarter. I heard gunfire coming from the darkened hospital room on the lower floor when the door opened. Unbelievably, some of our sick and dying had weapons in hand! To retaliate, the Mexicans hauled a cannon close to that open door and fired twice, killing what turned out to be fifteen men at once. Aye, *qué barbaridad*! SUCH barbarity!"

Señora Candelaria exhaled slowly, shaking her head and wiping tears as they rolled from her eyes. In a matter of seconds, she was sobbing, her back softly heaving up and down with the memories of what had to be the trauma of a thousand sights, cries, and sorrows. I got up and put my arms around her for quite some time, squatting and rubbing her back, simply remaining silent. She eventually wiped her eyes and mouth with her kerchief and took a shaky sip of chocolate. I settled back on the curb and waited, setting my pen and writing pad down until she was ready to resume.

It's hard to describe the animalistic tendencies that overtook otherwise decent men at the time of this battle. At some point, the Mexican *soldados* were so stoked with rage, they not only took delight in killing their enemies, but a few began firing upon each other, laughing almost like they were in some deranged, hypnotic state. The fear of death and the tethers of right and wrong no longer held them in check. I learned later that Mexican General Cós ordered a bugle call in an attempt to halt the crazed bloodletting of and by his own men! I heard his bugle, but from what I could see, not one of his soldiers heeded the order.

At last, the only things left unstained by the blood of a million soldiers and their ancestral war cries were the church and the rooms along the west wall where James and I awaited. A cannon was wheeled around in the courtyard and a solid shell blasted into the façade of the church, obliterating its large oak front doors. A swarm of Mexican soldiers rushed through. I watched as men got hit above and below the artillery platform near the church. One Tejano, whose name I never knew, escaped into a side room off the nave before a Mexican soldier followed him in and chased him out, only to have a bayonet end the poor man's life from behind.

People said this battle was over within the span of about an hour and a half. Those ninety minutes felt like an eternity. Every single male Texan defender had been shot, bludgeoned, or stabbed to death. I was told that the floor of the Alamo church trickled with a shallow river of blood. I saw that trickle slowly snake its way to join other bloody streams in the courtyard just outside our door.

When at last I saw Don Manuel Pérez, a neutral neighbor, talking with Bettie in the courtyard, I wanted to throw open the door and run out, but I could still hear moaning, crying, screaming, and shouting. I feared that Mexican soldiers might be standing just outside our door, so I remained frozen, barely breathing, just to the side of the small window to our room.

Bettie proceeded to walk down the courtyard toward the north, where she was joined by a disheveled Juana Alsbury, her baby, and her distraught sister, Gertrudis Navarro. The four of them turned and walked out of the Alamo together. Oh, how I wanted to run out there and leave with them!

Just then a voice shouted, "Are there any negroes here?"

I peeked out. Joe opened his door and slowly presented himself. As I stared out at Joe, a soldier's bloody face appeared in my tiny window, looking directly at me! Oh, how many times I've seen that rabid dog face since then. It took my breath away!

Our turn had come. I could do nothing to prevent it. Soldiers at the door pounded and battered the wood. I quickly jumped up on the bed at the head, sitting with my knees folded under me. I gently placed Colonel Bowie's head in my lap. I planned to beg for mercy for the both of us. But I knew it would be useless. No sooner had the door flung open, when two Mexican soldiers with bloodstained uniforms and grisly, feral faces raced in like a couple of wild dogs. Both approached, one on each side of Colonel Bowie's bed, bayonets at the ready.

Señora Candelaria paused and put her face down in her hands. It seemed she was overcome by the overwhelming grief and trauma of that morning. I stood up, squatted by her side, and hugged her. Again, she started weeping softly. I reached down to pick up her kerchief and gently placed it in her hands. When she was ready, she wiped her eyes, stared straight ahead, and continued.

I pleaded, I cried, I begged. I shamed them, declaring that this man was no threat; he was already dying and didn't deserve to be killed like an animal.

"*Es pirata*! He's a pirate! All pirates are traitors and must die!' one of them replied, spearing Colonel Bowie in the chest. I gasped. James didn't respond and I hoped that he'd already stopped breathing; he'd never take a blow like that without reacting. Then the other . . . "

Again, a long pause, as Señora looked down at her skirt and kneaded her kerchief.

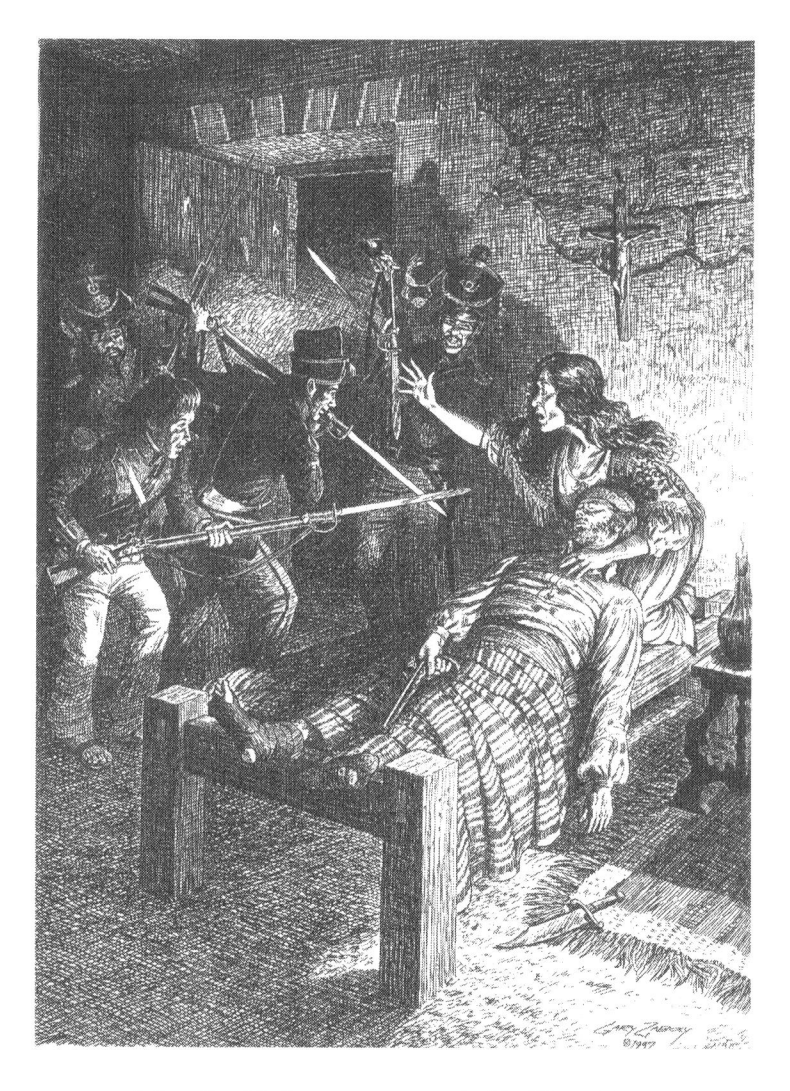

*Señora Candelaria attempts to save the life of James Bowie.
Illustration by Gary Zaboly (1997)*

Then the other soldier speared him from the other side. Together, they lifted his body up like a puppet and, laughing, threw it back down, bloody and crumpled on the bed. I felt horrified. Stunned. I don't think I moved. I prayed the Hail Mary, figuring I'd be next. I bent my head down, crying in such mental anguish. I realized my cheek was bleeding when I noticed a stain was left on James's shirt. I don't know how long I remained in that hunched over position. I honestly couldn't move. It was as if a thousand whirling windmills gathered me into the air between their blades and then time suddenly stopped all movement and sound. I may have passed out momentarily, I'm not sure.

The next thing I remember was being ordered to leave by a Mexican military man I couldn't identify. In a trance, I crawled off the bed, hastily gathered my things, and kissed James's bloody cheek goodbye. As I was doing this, I stealthily grabbed the knife from under his mattress as I covered myself with my black shawl. I walked left to leave and, without Señor Reyes's assistance this time, kicked open the small door I'd used every other day. This time, I fell down into the familiar trench in a daze.

When I could stand and brush myself off, I noticed the sun just beginning to rise. By the time I emerged from the trench over on the west side, I happened to see a carriage parked in the street. I watched as Mexican Colonel Almonte led Mrs. Dickinson and her baby Angelina from Santa Anna's headquarters to help them up into it. I walked off to the north and situated myself to the side of a large oak tree, where, slumping against it in shock, I watched the aftermath as if awakening from a terrible nightmare. I could barely breathe. The air felt thick with spirits. Spirits mingling with gun smoke.

Dreamlike, I watched as Mrs. Musquíz ran out of her house to assist Mrs. Dickinson and her baby inside the house. Hers was a house that Mrs. Dickinson had lived in for a time with the Musquíz family. Shortly after they went in, Colonel Travis's assistant, Joe, and General Santa Anna left the house, walking briskly toward the broken north wall of the Alamo. I saw Bettie, led by a soldier who left her at the front of a line of women and children being taken to the same house. Stepping aside to let the others enter first, Bettie suddenly turned around and ran, heading in my direction.

I sensed a dark rustling, a fluttering back and forth in front of me like some frantic bird. As soon as my eyes could focus, I saw that it was Bettie, stopping by the large oak where I stood. We were both shivering and quivering from shock. All about us, clouds and dust, like shrouds, hung like angry spirits in the air. That morning there were no breezes to move them off, only a wintry chill that held everything in place.

I spotted a few Mexican *soldados* wiping tears from their faces as they turned to look at the smoldering limestone structure behind them. Deflated and perhaps broken, they too were haunted by the faces and cries of those they'd just put to death. It had to be a reality that hit them hard and would haunt their dreams forever.

"Psst . . . Bettie! What's happening now?" I asked dreamily, noticing that her hair was tussled, the hem of her skirt torn to shreds.

"Women and children free," she puffed. "I'm getting out of here, Señora Candelaria. Joe, Travis's man, is identifying each of the dead captains. Santa Anna is going to burn them!"

Another horror. I choked, "Burn them? What? No proper burials? Aye, *qué barbaridad*! I'm just devastated that everything has come to this, Bettie. I pray that someday we can cleanse our minds of the horrible sights and sounds that we've witnessed here. If we cannot, I'm afraid we are destined for madness."

"Madness? I'll tell you what madness is," Bettie panted. "Those soldiers are in there right now stripping clothes, shoes, and any valuables they can find off of our dead soldiers. They got what I had," she said, lifting her skirt hem to show me its ragged edges.

"Oh Bettie, I was afraid that might happen." I replied, gasping for air at the thought of whatever assault she'd had to endure.

"Two hundred men!" I cried, swiping my nose and eyes with my shawl. Perhaps I expected Bettie to join me a moment to mourn the death of her master James, but instead, as if desperate to fly away, her large, loose figure swayed back and forth more quickly now.

"I'm destined for Louisiana, Señora. That's where some of my kinsfolk are and whatever I gotta do to get me there, I'm going to do it! Those soldiers may have taken what was in my hem, but I've got a few things in other places."

"I'm a free woman, Señora, and I've got family to find; I just accompanied Juana Alsbury and her baby Alejo to Don Navarro's house in La Villita, and that Santy Anna'll keep comin' up with things for me to do if I don't get out of here fast."

She smiled, enveloping me in a quick, bosomy hug before turning to run northward. I felt a rush of air as she left me in the early morning haze and disappeared. It was quite a while after that when I realized what was truly at stake for her in that battle. Could I really have expected her to mourn James's death? After that, I never saw Bettie again. Somehow, I imagined that she made it to Louisiana, happily reunited with family and maybe starting a family of her own.

Once Bettie was out of sight, I stumbled back toward the blur of the Alamo. I must have been in shock, because I peeked through the damaged north wall just after sunrise. I couldn't believe the carnage! There, in the center courtyard, where Colonel Travis had addressed his brave defenders only a few hours before, Santa Anna stood before his wild-eyed, crumpled, and bloody soldiers like a proud peacock. With the thrill of victory behind him, Santa Anna commended his men, thanking them for their courage and finishing with a raised fist in the air. "Viva México!" he cried.

I'm not making this up; his speech was met with silence. There was no rousing echo of "Viva!" as was customary. Maybe one or two soldiers answered in muffled voices, "viva!" But I didn't hear them. I wondered how many could muster great pride at such a moment. They were exhausted, in shock, wavering there in the misty vagueness of a gaping wound where some had quite possibly gone up against their own family members. Body parts and corpses were strewn all around, still pulsing with the fitful souls of the men who'd lost them—men whose faces and cries these soldiers would likely never forget. Brothers actually, whose only crime was in believing that future generations in Texas would be better off without one type of government or another.

Our alcalde at the time, Mayor Francisco Ruíz, walked briskly into the courtyard, accompanied by one of Santa Anna's men. Señor Ruíz had been placed under house arrest during the thirteen days of Mexican military occupation. Though a Mexican official, he came under constant suspicion of siding with the defenders. He certainly knew and liked many of these men; they were his neighbors and friends.

I believe he may well have had sympathies on both sides. Many people did. That's how senseless this bloodshed seemed.

General Antonio López de Santa Anna sent Mayor Ruíz away to do something. Soon I saw he'd fetched townspeople to bring over carts so that the dead Mexican soldiers could be loaded and taken to the cemetery just outside of town. He ordered others to fetch wood in order to burn the bodies of the Alamo defenders over near the Alameda, away from the Alamo compound.

I was still standing under that oak as a few other *vecinos* quietly approached, watching Mexican *soldados* and a reluctant Mayor Ruíz stepping over bodies and turning them over gently to identify them as commanded by Santa Anna. Mayor Ruíz was then ordered to have the townspeople lift the bloody corpses of the Alamo defenders and haul and stack them between layers of wood for burning. Señor Ruíz, holding a kerchief to his mouth, looked pale and ill. He retrieved a second handkerchief from his back pocket, covered his mouth again, and appeared to be weeping as he continued his assignment.

I watched as Milagro Espinosa, a young Tejana, ran in to search out her dead sweetheart. When she found him, she told others she wiped the grime from his face, crossed his hands on his chest, and placed a small cross there. When ordered to leave, she dipped her kerchief in his blood, placed it in her praying hands, and left, tears streaming down her face.

The bells of San Fernando rang three times. By three o'clock in the afternoon, Señor Ruíz and other *vecinos* had finished gathering and delivering wood. They placed tree limbs and wood planks in two large piles near the Alameda. The corpses of the Alamo defenders were then deposited in alternating layers—a layer of wood, topped by a layer of bodies, then another of wood, then bodies, until the grisly chore was complete.

Edgar later told me that a special audience was requested of General Cós by Francisco Esparza. The elderly Señor Esparza, who hadn't participated in the battle, came with his two brothers to make a request. Would the three of them please be allowed to search for their brother, Gregorio, inside the Alamo so they could provide a Christian burial for him? Their request, amazingly, was granted. After much searching, they found Gregorio in a small room inside the church with a musket ball to the chest and a stab wound to his side. These men lovingly carried their brother Gregorio across their backs all the way to Campo Santo, making him the only rebel defender that I know of to receive a Christian burial.

I saw an officer bring a few women he had gathered from town to tend to Mexican soldiers still moaning and crying but not yet dead inside the Alamo. With great courage, they did what they could, tending to wounds, bandaging, and comforting those who didn't have long to live. I had neither the strength nor the desire to join in this effort. I truly believe I may have been half dead, watching all of this as if it were some sort of hazy, grisly nightmare.

I continued standing numbly by, joined by several Béxareños—citizens of Béxar, now San Antonio—who gathered and watched with profound sadness at the preparations for bonfires. Even a few Mexican officers stood stoically by, no signs of exuberance visible on their faces.

By eight o'clock pm the next day, two funeral pyres, one on each side of the Alameda, burned the bodies of American, Mexican, Tejano, European, and other defenders. I imagined that the large pillars of smoke could be seen for many miles from this place. Never had a sunrise had to compete with such a fiery kiln as it did for several mornings following the bloody battle of Sunday, March 6, 1836.

I'm telling you, I'll never forget the smell of charred flesh—a stench that permeated every street of our city for months and months afterward. I heard that Mrs. Dickinson wanted to return inside the Alamo but Francisca Musquíz told her it would not be permitted because bodies were being collected for burning. None of us was thinking straight after such brutal carnage.

Fear and loathing settled in the air. Birds refused to sing, no insects buzzed, and not even the wind blew as we stood in the gray, putrid silence. None of us watching was sure what would happen next. I remember looking up into the sky to find a day shrouded as if in the bleakness of night. I wondered where the angels were. All that talk of the realities of war between my father and Justo came to mind.

Santa Anna used a New Orleans Greys banner captured at the Alamo as proof that American pirates out of Louisiana were aiding the American Texans inside the Alamo. The "rebel constitutionalist" flag—the Mexican green, white, and red, with its two stars representing Coahuila y Texas—was thrown atop the burning bodies as well. Santa Anna claimed he wanted no reminder that the devil pirates had ever considered themselves faithful citizens of Mexico.

On Monday, March 7, the morning after the battle, Nieves, Francisca, and I joined other Béxareños getting on our knees to pray all along the avenue. We watched in horror as Mrs. Dickinson and the other women and children were escorted across Main Plaza to the Musquíz home. Sweet Francisca Musquíz was now providing food for these survivors along with, perhaps, some measure of hope. Someone whispered that the final fate of these women and children prisoners was being decided that morning.

One at a time, each woman entered the Musquíz home as others waited outside in a hushed line of crying, fearful faces. Santa Anna interviewed them all, handing each widow two silver pesos and a Mexican blanket after they swore allegiance to him. Eliel Melton's widow, Juana, petrified that she would be punished for her recent marriage to one of the *norteamericanos*, begged Ana Esparza not to mention it, which of course Mrs. Esparza promised not to do. The only four who escaped the humiliating interview with the general were the two daughters of Santa Anna's old friend Angel Navarro, Bettie, and me.

Colonel Almonte translated when it was Mrs. Dickinson's turn. Santa Anna seemed quite interested when he saw her pretty baby Angelina, I heard. He kept lifting her chin and looking straight into her eyes. Finally, he offered to take both Susanna and the baby to Mexico with him. Mrs. Dickinson was aghast! As another option, Santa Anna offered to adopt little Angelina and take care of her as one of his own, offering every advantage money could provide in bringing her up in Mexico. Santa Anna, wolf that he was, reminded Mrs. Dickinson that she was now without a husband, money, and any means to provide for herself, let alone a child. It was an offer, he said, not to be taken lightly.

According to Francisca Musquíz, Mrs. Dickinson spat at his feet and replied that she'd never relinquish a child to the master of such horrors as we'd just witnessed. Santa Anna sat back in his high-backed chair, huffed, anger rising as he considered what to do with what he considered to be a very ungrateful Americana. Officer Almonte soothed matters by steering a grief-stricken, feisty Mrs. Dickinson back outside after reminding *el presidente* that Mrs. Dickinson was still in shock, though her wishes should be honored. Almonte persuaded Santa Anna to allow Mrs. Dickinson to leave and, as soon as the dictator's blood pressure went down, both mother and child were placed on a small horse, gifted with an accompanying mule loaded with food and blankets, and started down the road toward Gonzales. Colonel Almonte's assistant, Benjamin Harris, rode with Mrs. Dickinson for safety's sake.

Just beyond the Salado River, these three ran across Joe, Colonel Travis's assistant, hiding in some tall grasses. I thought he'd been blasted by a cannon during the battle, so I was thrilled when I heard this news. Happily, he joined that group on their journey. They then ran into a Mexican force at Cibolo Creek that handed Mr. Benjamin Harris a proclamation written in English by Colonel Almonte. It said something like, "To the inhabitants of Texas. . . . The supreme Mexican government has taken you under its protection and will seek for your good. The good have nothing to fear." When Edgar told me this part, I shook my head . . . many of our good had been killed by their so-called good. Interesting how barbarians paint history, isn't it? How do we ever determine which side is "good" and which side is not? It's all a matter of perspective, isn't it? Ábu had figured this out long ago.

Two days later, near Santa Anna's quarters on Main Plaza, people began gathering. Outside, various goods, jewelry, and other supplies seized from our defenders or their wives were set out, available for sale. This sale netted the Mexican military about $2,500—but let's not forget, the best items surely had already been taken by Santa Anna and his favorite officers the day before the sale. So, this magnanimous yard sale of his was, in truth, a façade. I'm telling you, the man was a devil.

The townspeople heard that John Smith had headed west with a group of well-armed and provisioned volunteers with the goal of reinforcing the Alamo on Monday, March 7. They arrived to find only the smoking remains of our beloved defenders, broken bayonets, and lovely jewelry for sale stretched across limestone half walls near the Musquíz house. Mr. Smith's soldiers were completely shocked and grief stricken.

That same Monday, we found out Colonel Houston had been hard at work on a Declaration of Independence for Texas in a small building in a town called Washington-on-the-Brazos. He assembled men in that town to read the finished draft of this declaration. Their plan was to begin organizing an army the next day, Tuesday, March 8. But just at sunset on Monday, March 7, two men rode into town to deliver the unthinkable news to them: all within the Alamo had already perished. Houston slumped to the ground and didn't move or speak for hours, we heard.

In those days, spreading information was much more complicated than it is today. Travis told John Smith that he would fire the eighteen-pound cannon morning, noon, and night as a signal that his garrison still held the Alamo. Once in Gonzales, Smith was aware that he'd heard no cannon since early Sunday. To prevent panic at this recent news from the couriers regarding the fall of the Alamo, Houston revived himself long enough to publicly pronounce that the two Tejano couriers must be spies spreading lies and took them into custody. Their news might possibly be a ruse, he concluded to the men gathered around him. If their information were true, he needed time to prepare the women of Gonzales, many of whom had just become widows.

However, Colonel Houston could not prevent the spread of the news of the Alamo catastrophe to the people of Gonzales forever. The Gonzales pronouncement had to be made. When it was finally delivered to the townspeople, nature itself fled their town as well. Silence. Nothing pierced the air except the mournful shrieks of women and the heartrending cries of now-fatherless children.

Still skeptical of this news, Houston asked Captain Juan Seguín to send two men to Casa Blanca, Seguín's ranch, to ascertain the truth of the story. Another express rider had already been sent from Béxar to Goliad with the news of the Alamo's fall, so to err on the side of caution, Houston sent orders to Fannin to blow up the presidio at Goliad and get back to Victoria, thirty or so miles north, on the Guadalupe River's east bank. But, as you know, ordering Fannin to do anything seemed like a fool's game.

Since Seguín's two Tejanos had yet to return, scouts Deaf Smith, Henry Karnes, and Robert Handy offered to set out together to get within sight of Béxar and assess the truth of the matter. They left later that morning. At eight o'clock that evening, redheaded Karnes rode back into Gonzales with news of Mrs. Dickinson's approach. Her eyewitness account served as the final confirmation for everyone in town: the Alamo battle had been lost.

Word got around that Houston spent all day Sunday the 13th organizing men and electing officers. We wondered what was to come next.

Next thing, Candelario reported to Edgar that the whole town of Gonzales was ordered to be burned. After that, officers, soldiers, and settlers quickly left, heading northeast toward the Sabine River. Deserters and couriers spread the word of the fall of the Alamo and, at the same time, sounded the alarm about a possible advance of the Mexican army. Women and children ran on foot to escape possible capture by Santa Anna and his army. This was the beginning of something people called the "Runaway Scrape."

Señora straightened her back, sighed, and shook her head. I could see Caramela a way off, munching on what looked like a corn cob, possibly a gift from a nearby street corn vendor.

"Señora, speaking of running away, you've recounted a very tough story today. I'm guessing you're tired and would welcome a rest."

"Yes, I suppose I should rest, Miss Rizzo. Just telling it again drains every ounce of energy I have. Such profound sadness and grief dwells within my bones even now; it's never left me, though it lessens with each retelling."

"Well then, why don't we take a break for a couple of days? I'll meet you here on Saturday, so you can finalize any bits of information. And I can give you my contact information. I'd appreciate it if you'd share yours with me. I'd love to stay in contact while I write the amazing history that you've shared!"

"That sounds like a good plan, Miss Rizzo. Can you see what Caramela has gotten a hold of?" *Señora shakily arose from the wooden crate after picking up her artifacts and the light-blue cloth.*

"Looks like a corn cob!" *I announced, spying her prancing toward us, weaving in and out of pedestrian feet.* "May I escort you two back home?"

"Oh, that won't be necessary, Miss Rizzo. Perhaps after our final meeting. Let me give you a hug for bearing with me for so long today."

Señora Candelaria hugged me for longer than usual and shakily reached up to touch my cheek. "I'm so grateful that I've had the good fortune to meet you, Miss Rizzo. You are the flame bearer now. You may carry this story forward in time, even as the past becomes a distant shadow. Even if the new light of the future creates more shadows, I want you to know some truths as I lived them."

"It's my pleasure, Señora. You've become an important part of my life too!" *With that, I placed all of my writing materials in my satchel and turned to walk slowly back to my hotel. I realized that Señora's account of the battle had taken an emotional toll on me as well.*

A profound sadness settled within me. Not just for all that transpired in this woman's incredible life, but also from the realization that our time together was drawing to a close. I wasn't entirely ready to say goodbye.

CHAPTER 30:
IT'S NEVER THE SAME RIVER

AND YOU'RE NEVER THE SAME PERSON

Two days later, we met up for the final time. Señora brought a beautiful bouquet of wildflowers for me and I carried a small book on herbal remedies for her. For Caramela, I brought a small bag of chicken skins, or chicharrones, for which she danced around and around my feet with such glee, I had to give her more than one.

"How are you feeling this morning, Señora? Did you sleep with the angels last night?" I handed her the small book on herbal remedies as she extended her hand with the small batch of flowers.

"I did, as a matter of fact!" she cackled. "Thank you so much for this book!"

"Of course! I thank you for these colorful flowers too! I'll take them back to Austin with me. I figured you could have written that book on herbs yourself, but it might be fun to browse through and remember some of the remedies you and Ábu used years ago."

"Oh yes, I'll enjoy looking at the pictures and trying to name all of them, Miss Rizzo. Caramela thanks you for her treats, which she's already chomping on apparently!"

"I'll give her another," I said, reopening the small bag. "She can wander with a happy belly this morning!"

Señora settled upon her wooden crate as I pulled writing utensils and a new steno pad out of my satchel. I sat on the curb for a moment, admiring the beauty of her soft, shallow cheeks and wrinkled lines.

"Señora, I know from my studies that the Battle of the Alamo was not the final battle for Texas's independence, because if it were, Spanish might be the official language here and we'd be meeting in San Antonio, Texas, a state of Mexico instead of a state within the United States."

"That's true, Miss Rizzo. A month later, in April 1836, the very important Battle of San Jacinto took place. Texans, absolutely furious over the savagery of the Alamo defeat, exacted a decisive victory, some call it revenge, over the Mexican army in the town of San Jacinto."

"Santa Anna was captured," I added, "and Texas declared its independence from Mexico. This state became a republic for nearly ten years as a result. Is there more you'd like to say about the years of the Republic of Texas?"

"Well, there were more notable tragedies during the time of the Republic, Miss Rizzo. Military defense of San Antonio became very difficult because Texas was now without Spanish, Mexican, or official American support. Texas struggled being a republic on its own. Peace talks offered one way to control some of the violence with the indigenous people that continued. Few seemed to consider that territories all across this land had been indigenous settlements long before others came to settle. But keeping the peace was another matter.

Comanche brought, or should I say "returned," young Matilda Lockhart to trade for peace agreements. This young woman had been kidnapped from Green DeWitt's colony years prior and had been brutally tortured by her captors. Her nose had been burned completely off. I honestly considered taking my daughter and finding a more peaceful place to live after I heard about what'd been done to Matilda.

More violence followed. But I was a different woman now. I found out that the Mexican land contract for Shorty's was voided when Texas became a republic. I wasn't sure what I should do or *could* do about it. True, I'd missed a couple of the final payments, but I never thought I'd lose my business. In 1838, I applied for a labor and league of land, figuring I would surely be eligible on account of my service at the Alamo. Somehow, in all the confusion, a land award in Victoria County never came through. The clerk scribbled "not recommended" on my application. I felt helpless since I'd lost my strongest advocates and business associates at the Alamo.

I'm not one to sit around moping about things for too long though. Candelario and I began working the fandangos and cantinas around town. Soon, we were blessed with three boys: Santiago, Candelario, and Amado. These three eased right in as Francisca's younger brothers. San Antonio was full of orphans without fathers or mothers at this time. Candelario and I adopted several, including a couple of Irish brothers named Henry W. Newton, age nine, and his brother George W. Newton, age seven, in the late 1850s. In that case, the judge sent for me and when I arrived, their father, Henry Senior, was already behind bars. The judge asked if Candelario and I would please take the young boys in to provide some stability for them. We did, and we never regretted it. Those two grew to become the most appreciative and loving young men. They even made their homes on either side of mine after Candelario passed away. Their real father eventually straightened up and made a life for himself.

We insisted on enrollment in school for all our children, including Francisca. No one knew better than I how important reading, writing, and mathematics would turn out to be in their lives. I owe that realization to my time with Doña Gertrudis and Colonel Cordero.

As the river of time would have it, my children married and had children of their own. I continue to watch over, guide, and protect my grandchildren, and great-grandchildren now, as they make their contributions to society in their own ways.

Señora stood slowly and shakily, brushing her skirt down flat. Reaching up to pin back a few flyaway hairs, she looked at me and asked, "Would you like to accompany me back to my home now, my dear Miss Rizzo?"

"Oh, certainly, Señora. I'll pack up my things right now!" I stammered, throwing my pen and pad into the satchel while standing to go, surprised by the abrupt wrap up. She'd held me spellbound with her final words. Caramela must have spotted Señora Candelaria standing, because once again she came bounding over to join us.

Stepping carefully, arms linked, we strolled slowly down a somewhat busy street with cars honking and buses passing. People gave us a wide berth 'til we found the sidewalk. Eventually, we crossed the San Antonio River and turned to wind our way around the magnificent limestone cathedral of San Fernando. Señora Candelaria left her wooden crate behind some bushes as we passed the church. She turned, looked up, and shakily took my face in her hands. Through her sweet, milky eyes, she said, "I love you, Miss. Rizzo. I love the reporting you're doing and I appreciate the time you took to listen to me! I'm sure you realize that there are always going to be some things people can never say. My brother Justo told me that a man named Shakespeare once said, 'The good that people do goes before them, but the evil is forever interred with their bones.' Here, the deeds of people's lives shift into prayers and the prayers float like eternal whispers around this holy ground. It's the good that we like to remember."

I looked straight ahead to hide the tears forming in my eyes as we slowly continued on our way past a pair of simple wooden gates that stood open, as if in invitation. I spied a small painted sign that read "Campo Santo."

"What did you say 'Campo Santo' means, Señora?"

"Holy ground or cemetery," she replied, taking a small piece of chicharrón from her pocket to keep Caramela with us. She proceeded to zig zag happily ahead of us, tail wagging excitedly. "It's where most of the people of my time rest now," she said, turning to pause and smile up at me before continuing down the road. "My home is in the next neighborhood, San Fernando."

Strangely, after passing under a large arch into San Fernando Cemetery, I don't remember much. I found myself seated on a grassy stump next to a small mound. There, sticking upright in the mound to my right was a simple Spanish hair comb, the same one I'd seen lying on the blue cloth when Señora told of her time at the Governor's Palace. I brushed off the headstone nearby. It read:

María Andrea Castañon de Villanueva
December 1, 1803-February 10, 1899
Alamo Heroine

I gently lifted the comb out to examine it more closely and, there on the back, stamped in tiny silver lettering, I saw:

To Ma. Andrea XO Ma. G.

Photo courtesy of Ricardo Rodriguez, San Antonio, Texas.

I sat for hours watching people come to pay their respects as I reflected on Señora Candelaria's astonishing life. Finally, dusk made its celestial approach, so I stood, brushed off my jeans, and slid the tall Spanish hair comb into a sturdy side pocket of my satchel. Checking to be sure I still carried all of my writing materials inside, I slowly made my way back toward the cemetery entrance. Tears formed, and I turned around one final time, thinking I might see Señora standing there, but she wasn't. I felt like I'd just left a very good friend, someone who had brought me to a window and let me peer out into her past and then ever so gently walked me back to the present. It was time for her to resume her personal soul's journey.

The next morning, I packed up everything from my hotel room, checked out, and, as I drove back to Austin, I thought about something one of my professors shared one day.

She said, as writers and historians, we must remember not to dwell too much on the past, nor spend all our days wondering about the future. What we truly have is the present. The present moment is ours for contemplation and action. Soon, poof, it too will become but a memory.

The memory of a strong woman such as María Andrea Castañon, later Señora Candelaria, is something I will always treasure, even in my present moments.

Portrait of Madam Candelaria by William Henry Huddle, 1891

Photo courtesy of Vee Gomez, San Antonio, Texas

The Alamo, San Antonio, Texas

ABOUT THE AUTHOR

Shawn LaTorre's appreciation of the Spanish language began while picking blueberries with her siblings alongside migrant field workers each summer in Michigan. She enjoyed being immersed in their music, joy, and conversations. Her love of Mexico grew as she continued her studies at la Universidad Ibero Americana in Mexico City, where she lived with her "Mexican mother" and visited the pyramids of Teotihuacan, the coastal areas of Cozumel, and Acapulco. She felt a true affinity to the unnamed people who came to these areas long before she did.

Shawn worked with many migrant students over the course of her twenty-five year career as an educator, always focused on teaching students rather than subjects. She took the lead in organizing a Transitional Bilingual Education Program, served as an International Baccalaureate Middle Years Program Coordinator, and was the director for a law humanities magnet program. She also served as a teacher in the Migrant Attrition Prevention Program (MAPP) at St. Edward's University.

When not writing or reading, Shawn can be found reviewing books for Story Circle Network, researching, coaxing her patio plants along, stitching, or simply riding her bike around the neighborhood to ponder new ideas.

She has been published in *Seeing Through Their Eyes* (2022) and *Kitchen Table Stories 2022: Sharing Our Lives in Food*.

ACKNOWLEDGEMENTS

First of all, I am eternally grateful to my loving husband, Joe, and family for bearing with me on what turned out to be a very long and wonderful journey. My home team listened to various chapter versions, video recorded sections for me, and provided feedback and questions that helped me clarify important points. Olivia provided several sketches to accompany this history and although we couldn't use all of them, I'm very grateful for her effort.

I would like to thank Ginger Magers, Kathy Ramke, and Irma Gonzalez of the Texas Time Travelers for reading and listening to me read sections, and then providing detailed feedback throughout the early stages of this endeavor. Kristi Fleming and Sara Wyatt, both top-notch educators, helped polish and comment on the manuscript as well.

Numerous hours in the Bexar County Archives in San Antonio were spent as Dr. David Carlson and his then office assistant, Liliana Villanueva, searched out and provided me with book resources and maps. At the University of Texas Briscoe Center in Austin, John Wheat cheerfully retrieved files and files of requested materials to assist in my research. I am so grateful for the men and women who safeguard treasures from the past and can point people to specific resources and artifacts that bring history alive for future generations.

Olga "VEE" Gomez, the great-granddaughter of Señora Candelaria, along with Reuben Perez, a descendent of one of the orphans reared by the main character, have been great sources of encouragement for me at times when I didn't think I could pull together this story in a way that would illustrate the complications of 1800s Texas for young adults. These two descendants from San Antonio had already joined forces with Robert Thonhoff, a notable author, historian, speaker, and educator, to write a factual history of Señora Candelaria. They not only wanted to honor her memory with what was known, but VEE and Reuben also encouraged me to pursue the imaginative possibilities of María Andrea Castañon's life within Spanish Texas.

Texas State Historical Association's online articles proved to be invaluable, especially once folks were relegated to researching and reading at home during the pandemic. A Facebook group headed by Ricardo Rodriguez continued posting articles, maps, and commentary that proved extremely helpful for fact checking throughout the development of my manuscript. I found this resource especially helpful for visualizing the journey of the Castañon family and others.

I wish to thank my extended family in Michigan for their encouragement and excitement as well, especially Tanya Uganski. They've all heard about my involvement with Susan Albert's Story Circle Network for years and know that our online group of writers has provided insight and encouragement to one another over many years. The support of both groups has been invaluable to my growth and development as a writer.

Finally, I must thank my editors, Mary Hall and Emma Evans, for the incredible amount of effort spent smoothing rough edges and getting a complicated interview format to work so *Footfalls to the Alamo* could be presented in such a professional final form. Their efforts, combined with those of book designer Rich Carnahan, helped bring to fruition a story that I'd been researching and imagining for over three years. I'm so grateful to have had the opportunity to work with the Publish Pros team.

Buen camino,
Shawn

POEMS, SONGS AND RECIPES

POEM BY SEÑORA CASTAÑON'S GREAT GRANDDAUGHTER

My Señora Candelaria Legend

By María Olga "Vee" Gomez

SEÑORA CANDELARIA was my incredible great grandmother.
From tales I've either heard or read she was like no other.
She reared her four children plus 22 waifs as her own.
Doing this lovingly without uttering even a moan.
Caring for others seemed to give her much pleasure.
Her joy was described as being without measure.
Candelaria was a "curandera" in those olden days.
Administering to the rich and poor in, oh, so many ways.
Her reputation was highly regarded in the Mexican town,
Eventually even to smallpox and cholera victims she felt bound.
At her small boarding house, she prepared meals galore,
Serving people like Travis, Bowie, Crockett, Austin, and more.
In March of 1836 she was asked to nurse ailing Bowie in the Alamo
As he wished to spare his kin, Juana, demanding she go.
Fearing his illness might be contagious and so,
Candelaria rushed to the rescue without saying, "No."
One day Bowie shouted, "Enough, this battle is getting too rough.
Boys, move my cot where I can help kill this enemy that's tough."
Then Candelaria watched Travis with his sword draw a line.
"If you're willing to die for Texas, this side is mine.
And if you choose to leave, the other side is thine."
'Tis' said only Louis Moses Rose admitted he wanted to go.

He departed hurriedly, but with his head held low.
Suddenly, some Mexican soldiers rushed towards Bowie's bed.
One of their knives missed him and struck Candelaria instead.
Years later she had one scar on her chin and one on her arm.
Fortunately, God spared her from much further harm.
Poor valiant Bowie met with a very gruesome end,
But before, with pistols, two soldiers to their deaths he did send.
Candelaria had nursed Bowie through the battle horrific,
The patriots were outnumbered but their spirits terrific.
That battle was an atrocious disaster as Santa Anna's army won,
Yet some Tejanos were determined not to be outdone.
Since these brave men couldn't forget the abominable foe,
A company of them marched to San Jacinto shouting, "Remember the Alamo!"
Since Candelaria cared for so many, even sick patriots, in her gentle way,
I consider her another Florence Nightingale, I sincerely say.
And I pray fervently I will meet her in Heaven someday.

POEM WRITTEN IN 2014 by Maria Olga "Vee" Gomez, direct descendant of Andrea Castañon de Villanueva.

Poem also appeared in a book entitled Angel of the Alamo by Reuben Pérez, Robert H. Thonhoff, and Olga Marie Villanueva "Vee."

LA GOLONDRINA, 1862

SONG FROM MILITARY PLAZA: A SPANISH VERSION

Adónde irá, veloz y fatigada
la golondrina que de aquí se va por si en el viento

Se hallará extraviada, buscando abrigo Y no lo encontrará.

Junto a mi cama, le pondré su nido
En dónde pueda la estación pasar. También yo estoy en la región perdido O Cielo
Santo! Y sin poder volar.

Dejé también mi patria idolatrada, esa mansión que me miró nacer. Mi vida es
hoy errante y angustida y ya no puedo
a mi mansión volver.

Ave querida, amada peregrina,
mi corazón al tuyo acercare.
Voy recordando, tierna golondrina, Recordaré mi patria y llorare.

WRITTEN BY NARCISO SERRADELL SEVILLA, physician and composer

THE SWALLOW

SONG FROM MILITARY PLAZA:
AN ENGLISH VERSION

Where will it go,
this rushed and fatigued swallow?

Tossed by the wind,
it will find itself lost and looking for cover, with nowhere to hide.
By my bed, I'll put its nest
Until the season passes.
I too, oh heavens, am lost in this place, unable to fly.

I also left my beloved homeland,
that home that saw my birth.
My life today is wandering and anguished.

I can never go home.

My dear bird,
beloved pilgrim,
our hearts are as one.
I go about remembering,
tender swallow, and will remember my country and I will cry.

WRITTEN BY NARCISO SERRADELL SEVILLA, physician and composer

DUÉRMETE MI NIÑO: A LULLABY

UNA VERSIÓN DE UN CANCIÓN DE CUNA

Duérmete mi niño,
que tengo que haceres:
lavar los pañales, y sentarme a coser.

Duérmate mi niño
que tengo que haceres:
lavar los pañales y sentarme a coser.

Ese niño quiere

que me duermo yo;
que se duerma la madre que lo parió.

Ese niño quiere

que me duermo yo;
que se duerma la madre que lo parió.

(A version of a traditional Spanish lullaby)

SLEEP MY CHILD: A LULLABY

ENGLISH VERSION

Go to sleep, my baby,
I have duties to perform:
wash the diapers, and sit a bit to sew.

Go to sleep, my baby,
I have duties to perform:
wash the diapers, and sit a bit to sew.

This child wants me to sleep!

Wants mother to sleep,
the one who gave birth to this child.

This baby wants me to sleep!

Wants mother to sleep,
the one who gave birth to this child.

(Traditional Spanish lullaby)

ALMA ANGELINA: FANDANGO FAVORITE

POPULAR FANDANGO SONG: SPANISH LYRICS

Alma Angelina
Bello y dulce despertar

Sueño hecho realidad
Eres toda la ilusión

Que a mi vida siempre acarició
Del cielo inspiración
Tienes el nombre encantador
En tu alma puso Dios

Toda la gracia y el candor
Tu risa de ángel que alegra mi vida
Y que me olvida que existe el dolor
Como una ensoñación
A mi existir llegaste tu
Como un rayo de sol
Llegaste a mi, radiando luz
Como un amanecer
Al despertar hermosa aurora
Como un ángel de amor
Que Dios me envió en ti mujer

Del cielo inspiración
Tienes el nombre encantador
En tu alma puso Dios

Toda la gracia y el candor
Tu risa de ángel...
Como una ensoñación
A mi existir llegaste tu
Como un rayo de sol
Llegaste a mi, radiando luz
Como un amanecer
Al despertar hermosa aurora
Como un ángel
de amor
Que Dios me envió en ti mujer.

(This popular song may be attributed to Felipe Valdes Leal, 1800s)

ALMA ANGELINA: FANDANGO FAVORITE

POPULAR FANDANGO SONG: ENGLISH TRANSLATION OF LYRICS

Beautiful and sweet awakening;
Dream come true,
You are all the illusion

That my life always caressed.
From heaven's inspiration
You got the lovely name.
In your soul,
God put all grace and candor.
Your angelic laughter makes my life happy.

I forget that pain exists.

Like a daydream
My existence reaches you.
Like a ray of sun,
You reached me, radiating light
Like a new day dawning.
Upon this new dawn awakening,
Like an angel of love,
God sent me to you, woman.
By heaven's inspiration.
You have this enchanted name

In your soul
God put all grace and candor.
Your angelic laughter . . .
Like a daydream
You came into my life
Like a ray of sunshine
You came to me radiating light
Like a new dawn
Upon this new day dawning
Like an angel of love
God sent me to you, woman.

(This popular song may be attributed to Felipe Valdes Leal, 1800s)

ÁBU'S YARROW WARRIOR TEA

REMEDY TO HEAL WOUNDS
AND OTHER MALADIES

This tea comes from Achillea millefolium, the Latin name for yarrow. Ábu taught that flowers (between April and October), leaves (anytime), and roots (fall) may be harvested from the yarrow plant.

Yarrow has been used for thousands of years to heal wounds, stop bleeding, and help move blood to stimulate circulation, soothe cramps, and kill the pain of toothaches. I used this tea many times with *all* kinds of citizens of Guanajuato and San Antonio. You will recall the many battles being waged during my time in those places.

Once the flowers are fully opened and not darkened, cut and collect the flower tops and leaves, but don't rinse them. Use these blossoms and leaves in your remedy.

Here is the recipe for a yarrow tea that I served frequently.

1. Take 3 or 4 yarrow blossoms with leaves. Clear them of any spiders or bugs and place in a drinking cup.
2. Pour one cup of very hot water over the top.
3. Let it sit for fifteen minutes to extract the medicinal properties of this amazing plant.
4. Strain the blossoms and leaves out and enjoy the tea!

Note: The only way I could get James to drink this somewhat bitter tea made from yarrow was by adding honey.

ÁBU'S ELDERBERRY TEA

USED TO FIGHT INFLUENZA AND STRENGTHEN THE BODY'S DEFENSES

Ábu dried elderberries after plucking them wherever and whenever she found them. Besides yarrow, this was one of her favorite natural remedies.

I served this tea often to my whole family. I used the tea or sometimes a syrup made from the berries many times with the people in San Antonio, especially in the fall and winter, to strengthen the immune system and help ward off any number of diseases.

5. Add one cup of water for each person to a saucepan.
6. Add elderberries and bring to a boil.
7. Add cinnamon and/or dried citrus peels.
8. Lower the flames or remove the saucepan from the fire and cool for five minutes.
9. Remove the berries and any herbs or citrus remains before serving. For the syrup, add a half of cup of water to one cup of elderberries. Boil the water away and then smash the berries to a liquid consistency and use as a topping for rice, toasted bread, or corn.
10. *Salúd*! To your health!

Note: The only way I could get James Bowie to drink Ábu's elderberry tea was by adding cinnamon and a bit of honey.

RESOURCES

BIBLIOGRAPHY

The following materials were invaluable resources for the writing of *Footfalls to the Alamo*.

Acosta, Teresa Palomo and Ruthe Winegarten. *Las Tejanas*: 300 Years of History. Austin: University of Texas Press, 2003.

A Revolution Remembered: *The Memoirs and Selected Correspondence of Juan N. Sequín*. Edited by Jesús F. de la Teja. Austin: Texas State Historical Association, 2002.

Allen, Paula. "Kin of Madam Candelaria Back Alamo Story." *San Antonio Express-News* (San Antonio, TX), Sept. 4, 2011.

Almaráz, Félix D. *Tragic Cavalier: Governor Manuel Salcedo of Texas, 1808–1813*. Austin: University of Texas Press, 1971.

"Another Child of the Alamo," San Antonio Sunday Light. Nov. 10, 1901. Enrique Esparza File in Daughters of the Republic of Texas Library and available on Newspapers Archives.com

Barker, Eugene C. "The Government of Austin's Colony, 1821-1831." *Southwestern Historical Quarterly* 21, no. 3 (1918): 223–52. Accessed April 14, 2021. https://www.jstor.org/stable/30234752.

Barker, Eugene C., and Herbert E. Bolton. *With the Makers of Texas*. Corpus Christi: Copano Bay Press, 2018.

Barnes, Charles Merritt. *Combats and Conquests of Immortal Heroes*. San Antonio: Guessaz & Ferlet Company, 1910.

Barr, Alwyn. "Bexar, Siege of." In *Handbook of Texas*, Texas State Historical Association, 1952. Accessed July 8, 2020. http://www.tshaonline.org/handbook/online/articles/qeb01.

Benavides, Adán. *The Béxar Archives (1717–1836): A Name Guide*. Austin: University of Texas Press, 1989.

Bender, Katie. *Ana Esparza: A Legacy of Oral History in Texas.* "A series of introductory essays inspired by the stories told at Brush Square Museum" Indexed by austintexas.gov. https://austintexas.gov/sites/default/files/files/Ana%20%20Esparza.pdf.

Brands, H.W. "The Alamo Should Never Have Happened." Texas Monthly. March 2003.

Castañeda, Carlos. *Our Catholic Heritage in Texas, 1519-1936.* Vols. 4 and 5. Austin: Von Boeckmann-Jones Company, 1936–1958. https://babel.hathitrust.org/cgi/pt?id=uva.x001740454&view=1up&seq=129.

Crimm, Ana Carolina Castillo. DeLeón: *A Tejano Family History.* Texas. University of Texas Press. 2003.

Crockett, Davy. Journal of March 2, 1836. http://www.fortworthtexasarchives.org/digital/collection/p16084coll9/id/75/

Crook, Elizabeth. *Promised Lands: A Novel of the Texas Rebellion.* New York: New York. Doubleday. 2013. Available via Internetarchive.org.

Cuate, Melodie A. *Journey to the Alamo.* Lubbock: Texas Tech University Press, 2006.

De La Forêt, Rosalee and Han, Emily. *Wild Remedies: How to Forage Healing Foods and Craft Your Own Herbal Medicine.* California. Hay House, Inc. 2020.

De Zavala, Adina. *History and Legends of the Alamo and Other Missions in and Around San Antonio. Houston.* Arte Público Press. University of Houston. 1917.

Dobie, J. Frank. "James Bowie, Big Dealer." *Southwestern Historical Quarterly* 60, no. 3 (1957): 337–57. Accessed June 26, 2020. https://www.jstor.org/stable/30235302.

Donovan, James. *The Blood of Heroes: The 13-Day Struggle for the Alamo—and the Sacrifice That Forged a Nation.* New York: Little, Brown and Company, 2012.

FamilySearch. https://www.familysearch.org/ark:/61903/1:1:6Z9X-1P4L

Field, Dr. Joseph E. *Three Years in Texas.* Austin: The Steck Company, 1935.

Fisher, Lewis F. *Chili Queens, Hay Wagons and Fandangos: The Spanish Plazas in Frontier San Antonio.* San Antonio: Maverick Publishing Company, 2014.

Ford, John S. *Origin and Fall of the Alamo, March 6, 1836.* San Antonio: Johnson Brothers Printing Company, 1896.

Gomez, María O. "Vee," Reuben M. Perez, and Robert H. Thonhoff. *María Andrea Castañon Villanueva (Señora Candelaria): Heroine of San Antonio.* San Antonio: Private Publication, 2019.

Graham, Joe S. *El Rancho in South Texas: Continuity and Change from 1750*. Denton: John E. Conner Museum and the University of North Texas Press, 1994.

Harrigan, Stephen. *The Gates of the Alamo*. New York: Vintage Books, 2000.

Holmes, Jack D. L. "Cordero y Bustamante, Manuel Antonio (1753–1823)." In *Handbook of Texas*, Texas State Historical Association, 1976. Accessed October 16, 2010. https://www.tshaonline.org/handbook/entries/cordero-y-bustamante-manuel-antonio.

"James Bowie's Nurse Witnessed Colonist Defenders' Struggle Against Santa Anna's Blood Thirsty Mercenaries." *Fort Worth Record-Telegram*. (Fort Worth, TX), Sept. 28, 1913.

John Charles Beales's *Rio Grande Colony: Letters by Eduard Ludecus, a German Colonist, to Friends in Germany in 1833–1834, Recounting His Journey, Trials, and Observations in Early Texas*. Translated and Edited by Louis E. Brister. Austin: Texas State Historical Association, 2008.

Kemp, Louis Wiltz. *Our (Unlikely) Fathers: The Signers of the Texas Declaration of Independence*. Edited by Michelle M. Haas. Corpus Christi: Copano Bay Press, 2014.

Kirkland, Elithe Hamilton. *Love Is a Wild Assault*. Fredericksburg: Shearer Publishing, 1984.

Knaggs, John R. *The Bugles Are Silent: A Novel of the Texas Revolution From the Alamo to San Jacinto*. Austin: Sunridge Publishing, 2012.

Lemon, Mark. *The Illustrated Alamo 1836: A Photographic Journey*. Abilene: State House Press, 2008.

Matovina, Timothy M. *The Alamo Remembered: Tejano Accounts and Perspectives*. Austin: University of Texas Press, 1995.

Maverick, Mary A., and George Madison Maverick. *Memoirs of Mary A. Maverick*. Corpus Christi: Copano Bay Press, 2011.

Michener, James A. *Texas*. New York: Random House, 1985.

Miller, Howard. "Stephen F. Austin and the Anglo-Texan Response to the Religious Establishment in Mexico, 1821–1836." *Southwestern Historical Quarterly* 91, no. 3 (1988): 283–316.

Muscato, Christopher. "Historical Chichimeca Peoples: Culture & History." Study.com. https://study.com/academy/lesson/historical-chichimeca-peoples-culture-history.html.

Order of Granaderos y Damas de Gálvez. "Spanish Monarchs Visit the United States." *La Granada* Newsletter (San Antonio, TX), Oct. 2015. http://granaderos.org/images/OCT2015.pdf.

Peña, José Enrique de la. *With Santa Anna in Texas: A Personal Narrative of the Revolution.* Texas A&M University Press, 1975.

Prado, Juan Jose. *Guanajuato's Legends and Traditions.* Guanajuato: Prado Hermanos, 1956.

Ragsdale, Crystal Sasse. *Women and Children of the Alamo.* State House Press. 1994.

Ryder-Taylor, Henry. *History of the Alamo and of the Local Franciscan Missions.* San Antonio: Nic Tengg, 1908.

Scheer, Mary L. *Women and the Texas Revolution.* Denton: University of North Texas Press, 2012.

Schmal, John P. "The Rise of the Aztec Empire." History of Mexico. Houston Institute for Culture, 2004. http://www.houstonculture.org/mexico/aztecs.html

Schott, Arthur. *Military Plaza: San Antonio*, date unknown, engraving, 21 x 28 cm, *Star of the Republic Museum Objects* collection, provided by the Star of the Republic Museum to the University of North Texas Libraries, The Portal to Texas History. Accessed May 3, 2021. https://texashistory.unt.edu/ark:/67531/metapth31151/m1/1.

Siringo, Charlie. *A Texas Cowboy.* Corpus Christi: Copano Bay Press, 2012.

Starr, Frederick. *In Indian Mexico.* Gutenberg Press, 1908.

Stephens, A. Ray. Texas: A Historical Atlas. Norman, Oklahoma. University of Oklahoma Press. 2010.

Stoner O'Connor, Kathryn. *Presidio La Bahía: 1721–1846.* Victoria: Wexford Publishing, 2001.

Teja, Jesús F. de la. "Social Relations in Late Colonial San Antonio." *Southwestern Historical Quarterly* 112, no. 2 (2008): 120–46. https://doi.org/10.1353/swh.2008.0028.

Teja, Jesús F. de la. "Coahuila and Texas." In H*andbook of Texas*, Texas State Historical Association, 1952. Accessed October 1, 2020. https://www.tshaonline.org/handbook/entries/coahuila-and-texas.

Teja, Jesús F. de la, and John Wheat. "Bexar: Profile of a Tejano Community, 1820-1832." *Southwestern Historical Quarterly* 89, no. 1 (1985): 7–34. Accessed May 3, 2021. https://www.jstor.org/stable/30236992.

Texas State Historical Association. *Tejanos Through Time*. Texas State Historical Association, 2016. Accessed May 7, 2019.

Texas State Historical Association. *Southwestern Historical Quarterly*. Vol. 66, July 1962– April 1963. Austin: provided by the Texas State Historical Association to the University of North Texas Libraries, The Portal to Texas History. Accessed May 15, 2020. https://texashistory.unt.edu/ark:/67531/metapth101196/.

Thonhoff, Robert H., Rueben M. Perez, and Maria O. Gomez. "Villanueva, María Andrea Castañon (1803–1899). In *Handbook of Texas*, Texas State Historical Association, 1976. Accessed October 1, 2020. https://www.tshaonline.org/handbook/entries/villanueva-maria-andrea-castanon.

Torget, Andrew J. *Seeds of Empire: Cotton, Slavery, and the Transformation of the Texas Borderlands, 1800–1850*. Denton: University of North Texas Press, 2015.

"[Transcript of a report regarding the movements of the Mexican Army and the status of the Texas Army, [March] 1836]," report, *Moses and Stephen F. Austin Papers* collection, provided by the Dolph Briscoe Center for American History to the University of North Texas Libraries, The Portal to Texas History. Accessed June 2, 2019. https://texashistory.unt.edu/ark:/67531/metapth216986/.

Vorderbrugger, Mark. *Foraging Texas*. "Know What Your Ancestors Knew." https://www.foragingtexas.com/ Accessed April 23, 2019.

Wagner, Betsy. *Spirit of Gonzales*. Self-published, 2019.

Weddle, Robert S. *San Juan Bautista: Gateway to Spanish Texas*. Austin: University of Texas Press, 1991.

Wellman, Paul. *The Iron Mistress*. 1952.

Welsh, Allie. "San Antonio Military Plaza." *Epic Century Magazine*. June 1938.

Williams, Amelia. *The Alamo Defenders: A Critical Study of the Alamo and the Personnel of its Defenders*. Ed.by Haas, Michelle. Copano Bay Press. 2010. (Originally published as "A Critical Study of the Siege of the Alamo and the Personnel of Its Defenders" a doctoral dissertation at the University of Texas. 1931.)

Yoakum, Henderson K. *History of Texas: From Its First Settlement in 1685 to Its Annexation to the United States in 1846, Volume 1*. 1856.

The following libraries and archives were invaluable to me during my research, before, during, and after the Covid pandemic.

Bexar County Archives, San Antonio, Texas—Dr. David Carlson and Lilianna Villanueva, his office assistant.

Dolph Briscoe Center for American History, Austin, Texas—Mr. John Wheat.

LBJ Library, Austin, Texas

University of Oklahoma Press, Norman, Oklahoma—Carol Zuber-Mallison, cartographer.

Stephen F. Austin State University, Nacogdoches Census Reports of 1805, 1809.

Spanish Archives of Laredo at University of North Texas (online)

Texas State Archives: Nacogdoches census records (1783-1835)

Texas State Archives: census records 1830's

Texas State Library and Archives, Austin, Texas

Made in the USA
Columbia, SC
10 December 2023